VAMPIRE ROYALTY:

Resurrection

by
Valerie Hoffman

ISBN 9780979247620

Copyright © October 2007

Published in the United States of America
Publisher:
VG Press
595 W. Granada Blvd., Suite H
Ormond Beach, FL 32174
386-677-3995
drval@bellsouth.net

VAMPIRE ROYALTY:

Resurrection

Contents

Dedication 11

Prologue 13

Chapter 1: The Nightmare 21

Chapter 2: Stalked 25

Chapter 3: Deception 31

Chapter 4: Dana's Dilemma 35

Chapter 5: The Manifestation 39

Chapter 6: Death Blow 43

Chapter 7: Coma 47

Chapter 8: The Young Overlord 55

Chapter 9: The Consuming Flames 59

Chapter 10: The Blood Bath 65

Chapter 11: Connections 73

Chapter 12: The Battered Tenant 77

Chapter 13: The Detective's Theory 81

Chapter 14: Descending into Darkness 85

Chapter 15: The Traitor 93

Chapter 16: Part of the Plan 97

Chapter 17: The Stranger 99

Chapter 18: A New Crisis 105

Chapter 19: The Sadist and the Savior 109

Chapter 20: Negotiations 113

Chapter 21: Abomination 119

Chapter 22: Imposter 127

Chapter 23: Enigmas 135

Chapter 24: Dana's Divided Devotion 139

Chapter 25: Deception 143

Chapter 26: Prisoner 147

Chapter 27: The Memento 151

Chapter 28: Revelations 155

Chapter 29: The Experiment 159

Chapter 30: Dead End 167

Chapter 31: The Spy 171

Chapter 32: Preparations 175

Chapter 33: Philanthropist or Terrorist 179

Chapter 34: Epiphany 185

Chapter 35: Propaganda 189

Chapter 36: Misguided Loyalty 195

Chapter 37: The Attack 201

Chapter 38: Deviant Daughters........................205

Chapter 39: The Next President........................209

Chapter 40: Pieces of the Puzzle........................211

Chapter 41: The Deviant Diurnals........................217

Chapter 42: Dana's Exile 219

Chapter 43: The Foundation on Trial........................223

Chapter 44: The Damsel in Distress 227

Chapter 45: First Kill........................233

Chapter 46: Mindless Puppet........................237

Chapter 47: The Time of Reckoning........................241

Chapter 48: The Bloodthirsty Demon........................247

Chapter 49: The Liability........................251

Chapter 50: False Records 255

Chapter 51: Comply or Die........................261

Chapter 52: Deadly Embrace........................265

Chapter 53: The Hitchhiker........................269

Chapter 54: The Witness........................273

Chapter 55: Back in DC 279

Chapter 56: Aspirations of Vengeance 283

Chapter 57: Intent to Kill 287

Chapter 58: Bedside Confessions 293

Chapter 59: Recovery 299

Chapter 60: Tragic Reminders 305

Chapter 61: The Earl's Discovery 309

Chapter 62: Carnage at the Castle 313

Chapter 63: Haunted Memories 317

Chapter 64: Mortal Combat 319

Chapter 65: Over the Edge 323

Chapter 66: Legacy of a Madman 325

Chapter 67: The Sacrifice 329

Epilogue 331

About the Author 337

The Author's Notes 339

Ordering Information 340

Dedication

This book is dedicated to my mom, who has never let adversity keep her down. Way to go mom!

This book is also dedicated to my husband, Norm. Without his complete devotion and attention to detail the "Vampire Royalty" series might never have made it to the drawing board. Thanks Norm for all your support. I couldn't have done it without you.

Of course, this book is also dedicated to my brother, the real Andrew Gabriel.

A NEW BEGINNING

The crescent moon hung suspended, swathed in its blanket of midnight blue. Below, the silent residential street of the upscale Bethesda neighborhood glowed softly in the perfect stillness. The windowpanes of the dark and silent homes reflected the moonlight. Dark and silent – save for one.

The colonial mansion stood as a sentinel that was separated from its neighbors by its inner glow. Lights blazed and occupants rushed through the rooms as ear-splitting screams tore through the night.

"Push," demanded the midwife.

"I *am* pushing," Victory Parker-Gabriel insisted between clenched teeth.

"Push harder!"

She groaned and wondered how much longer she could endure the agony.

"It will all be over soon," soothed her husband, as he smoothed back a lock of sweat-dampened blonde hair.

Her eyes sought and held his. As their minds merged, she felt an infusion of strength and knew that she could endure. She would endure anything for his sake. Another spasm of pain ripped through her flesh. It was the worst one yet. Squeezing her eyes shut, she grabbed fistfuls of the sheets. She sucked in her bottom lip, and clamped her teeth on it to prevent another scream. Blood dripped down her chin. Her husband wiped it away and then dabbed at her lower lip.

"One more! Hard! Now, push!"

She bore down with all of her might. Black spots danced before her eyes, while her mind tugged to be free of its restraints. Suddenly, she felt an easing of the tension between her thighs.

"I've got her!" announced the midwife triumphantly. A slap was followed by a wail.

Weak and drenched in perspiration, Victory turned her head and slumped back in complete exhaustion. The midwife bundled the baby girl in a blanket.

Andrew leaned down to gently kiss her on the cheek. "Good job, Mommy," he said before straightening and walking over to admire his new daughter. Victory held out her arms and Andrew placed the bundle on the bed next to her. They smiled at each other over the baby's head.

"She's beautiful," whispered Victory.

"Just like her mother," he asserted, while holding her hand and staring in awe at the infant.

"What will you name her?" asked the midwife, as she packed her bag.

Andrew looked at his wife.

Gazing down at her daughter, the new mother proudly announced, "Laural. Named in honor of her grandmother and my best friend."

Laural yawned contentedly and then drifted to sleep in her mother's arms.

"You should go now," insisted Victory.

He studied her intently. "I think I should stay a while longer."

She dismissively waved a hand. "I'm fine, my love. All I'm going to do for the next several hours is sleep. Besides, you promised Jordan."

His troubled turquoise gaze studied her beloved features. Her golden hair was sweat-dampened with strands clinging to her face. Her lip bore a slight abrasion where she had bitten into it just moments ago. Even as he watched, her skin restored itself.

Lifting his gaze to her eyes, he smiled. "There are definite advantages to you being a porphyrian." Their eyes met, locked, and held.

"To think," she reflected, while gazing down at her daughter, "there was a time when I didn't believe your claim to be a different species. Maybe this is selfish, but, now that I'm a mother, I can't help being glad that our daughter will enjoy a prolonged lifespan. Laural's enhanced healing powers are a blessing, too. How long do you think it'll take for her abilities to manifest?" she asked tensely.

He thoughtfully watched his new daughter. She stretched, yawned, and then blinked at him. Smiling into his wife's eyes, he said, "There is no specific age, but it will happen sometime during adolescence. The strongest usually don't manifest until late adolescence or even early adulthood. Don't worry," he reassured, "her enhanced immune system kicks in immediately." She smiled and relaxed.

He watched her warily and announced, "I'm going to message Jordan to check the site without me."

Sighing tiredly, she said, "Andrew, please go. I would never forgive myself if, by staying here ..."

There was no need for her to complete her thought. He was well aware of the risks. He frowned. He knew she was right, but he did not like leaving her so soon after childbirth. For diurnals, it was an ordeal; for porphyrians whose immune system and healing powers always shut down during pregnancy, it could be fatal.

"I'm fine. You don't need to be concerned about me. I love you. Now go."

With lowered lids, she watched him. He stood and studied her for what seemed like an eternity. Finally, she "felt" rather than saw him leave. She grimaced and then groaned. Keeping her pain at bay and preventing Andrew from reading her agony had been too much for her. As she sank into unconsciousness, a pool of blood soaked the sheets.

BUILDING THE FOUNDATION

The haunting moon cast iridescent shadows across the city streets. Dark clouds chased the crescent and, finally capturing it, they swallowed it whole, plunging the streets into eerie darkness. Below, two figures watched the transformation and were unafraid and unabashed by the suddenly gloomy night.

Jordan Rush, Earl of Rockford, prodded the collapsed wooden beam with the toe of his shoe. He grimaced as the gesture caused a minor landslide of rubble from the former Willow Grove Crematorium to cascade loudly toward the sidewalk. A dull thump echoed when the wooden beam hit the ground. He lifted apologetic bottle-green eyes to his companion.

"Forget it," sighed Andrew Gabriel, Marquis of Penbrook. "It's obvious no one could have survived this conflagration, not even Craven."

The Earl of Rockford looked around. His jade-green eyes scanned the pile of shattered glass, broken beams, and other debris. A cold shiver coursed down his spine. "Are you sure we shouldn't keep searching?"

The Marquis of Penbrook stared off into the midnight sky as if expecting the clouds covering the moon to provide the answer. "We have been looking for several hours," he said, while raising his hand to massage his neck.

"Yes," agreed Jordan, "but didn't this place have a basement?"

The marquis looked directly at him. His penetrating blue eyes shot electric sparks through the darkness. "Yes, but remember that Craven was on the top floor when the building exploded. Besides," he added, while staring deeply into the remains of the building, "I don't feel his presence."

Firmly quelling his misgivings, Jordan turned his back on all that remained of Craven's demented plans to destroy humanity. But, no matter how hard he tried, he could not escape the idea that Andrew's evil half-brother somehow would rise from the ashes to destroy their happiness.

"Come on," said Andrew. "We both could use a drink."

"Was it that rough?"

"Victory's suffering about did me in."

The earl nodded. "Sorry to bring you out tonight, but my tipster said the demolition crew is coming first thing in the morning to clear this place out."

Andrew turned and cast a final glance at the rubble. "You did the right thing to insist I come. I'm the only one Craven wouldn't be able to block."

Thirty minutes later, they were seated in a local tavern. Jordan waited for the waiter to leave before making his point. "I believe the reason Craven was able to influence so many was due to a lack of allegiance."

One eyebrow lifted sardonically as the marquis stated, "And here I thought it was sheer domination."

As he set his drink aside, the earl flushed. "For me, that was the case. I would never have betrayed you or the ethics we believe in willingly. But," he rushed on before Andrew could interject, "many of the others were tired of wandering aimlessly and drifting in and out of the diurnal world without being part of it. They were ready to be influenced by someone with a cause they could make their own. They needed a strong leader they felt connected to and they yearned for something to believe in. Most of the porphyrians who followed Craven didn't care about dominating the country. Hell, most of them preferred not to have attention drawn to them. The majority of our people still live with a superstitious fear of being discovered and annihilated. Craven was a psychopath who played on their fears, but his premise had merit. Our people are floundering, on the fringes of a society where they don't fit in and have no vested interest. A combination like that makes us ripe for another deviant to pick up where Craven left off."

Andrew bristled at the implication. Then, he carefully considered his friend's words. "I concede what you say has merit. I have also been doing a lot of thinking about this problem."

Blue eyes stared hard into green. "Do you have a solution?"

Jordan slowly sipped his martini. "We could establish an organization designed to assist both species. I thought we could call it the Willow Grove Continuing Education Foundation or something along those lines. On the surface, the organization would do exactly what the name implies: provide resources for diurnals who want to pursue higher education. However, there would also be a component designed to assist in the assimilation of porphyrians who are having difficulty in integrating into everyday diurnal society."

The marquis threw back his head and laughed. The deep baritone sound drew attention from several neighboring tables. The earl's green eyes twinkled as Andrew chuckled. Jordan was gratified to hear the sound even if it was at his expense.

Gradually, Andrew's mirth subsided. "I'm sorry, but that sounded an awful lot like a social service agency for displaced porphyrians."

He shrugged. "That's one way of looking at it."

Andrew's golden hair glowed in the lamp light. He gave his friend an appraising stare. Finally, he spoke, "I think your idea just might work."

The earl grinned, as he motioned to the waiter to bring another round. "By the way, how is Victory?"

A shadow deepened the other man's eyes. "She came through fine," he said sighing. "I just wish recovery wasn't so tenuous after childbirth."

Jordan frowned and intently studied him. Fear and anxiety were emanating from his friend.

Andrew shook his head. "I guess I worry too much. When I left, both mother and daughter were sleeping peacefully."

Jordan understood because he had lost his own mother due to the experience. Hoping to take his friend's mind off of the troubling aspect of his mate's precarious condition, he asked, "How is your baby?"

Smiling broadly, he replied, "Fit as a fiddle and an absolute angel. Both her parents are going to dote on her."

For a moment, they both paused as they remembered the two women who comprised the baby's namesake. Both Laura Warner, Victory's friend, and Crystal Gabriel, the former Marchioness of Penbrook, had fallen prey to the ruthlessness of the Maxwell men.

Shrugging aside his dark thoughts, Jordan lifted his glass. "A toast to your new daughter. May she experience much happiness. And another to a quick and complete recovery for her mom."

"I'll drink to both," agreed the marquis.

BENEATH THE ASHES

The moon slowly crept from behind the embrace of the clouds. Cascading moonbeams danced and flickered across the debris-strewn ground. Before retreating behind the clouds, it briefly illuminated the two figures that were clad in black. One of the black-clad figures grunted as he labored to pull a thick concrete block.

"Steve, come on over here and help me move this."

A young muscular man with dark hair joined his partner. Together, they shifted the concrete slab and exposed an opening that was several feet wide. Steve flicked on his flashlight and moved the beam across the shadowed interior.

"Turn that off!" hissed Rick. Surreptitiously glancing around while elbowing his friend, he added, "We're trying not to draw attention to ourselves." He wondered about the wisdom of bringing Steve in on the deal. The last job they had been involved in had landed them both in the juvenile detention facility for six months. He still considered that to be Steve's fault and resented him for it. If it weren't for his brawn, he wouldn't have considered using him at all.

"I don't even know what we're doing here," complained Steve, as he turned off the flashlight and rubbed his ribs.

Rick ground his teeth and shook his head. "I told you I saw two high-class dudes looking around here earlier. I'll bet they were looking for something they lost, something very valuable – maybe a wallet – or else they wouldn't be searching so hard."

Steve considered what his friend had said. A lost wallet meant money and credit cards. "So, how do you know they didn't already find it before they left?"

"Because," sighed Rick with exasperation, "they didn't look like they were very happy when they left. Anyway, it won't hurt to look around. The police have had this place cordoned off for days and I've been watching. Besides those dudes, we're the first on the scene."

Rick was the first to enter the opening. Landing lightly on firm ground, he turned to his friend. "Coast's clear."

A moment later, Steve was by his side. Cautiously, they moved through the basement. When they were far enough away from the opening, Rick felt that it was safe enough to cut on his flashlight. As he paused to flip the switch, Steve ran into him from behind. "Watch where you're going," he complained, while again wondering at the wisdom of including the buffoon.

Steve stumbled and fell hard against the adjacent wall. The plaster crumbled, showering them both with dust and debris. Eyes stinging and throat burning Rick turned to berate his buddy. Something gleamed behind the broken wall. He peered into the darkness. "Gold," he whispered reverently to Steve.

Steve nodded, "Do you think it's real?"

"Of course, it's real," snapped Rick, while wondering about his friend's stupidity. "You wouldn't expect people in this area to be buried in fake containers."

Eagerly, they pulled away chunks of dry wall and plaster. A small pile of gold and silver urns was strewn inside the opening. They each lifted one and examined their finds. "How much can we get for these?" asked Steve.

"I don't know, but we're gonna find out."

Steve grinned broadly. "Maybe enough to take Sally to some of those fancy restaurants she's always talking about."

"Is that all you think about? Just what Sally wants?" asked Rick with obvious irritation in his voice.

"What's wrong with wanting to keep my girl happy?" Steve asked defensively, while pushing up the sleeves of his leather jacket. "Maybe you're just jealous 'cause you ain't got a girl."

"With as much money as we're gonna make from this," he gestured toward the urns, "I can afford a higher-class bitch than Sally."

Steve bristled. Rick laughed. He got off on razzing his friend about his girl. The truth was that he was extremely jealous. He wanted Sally for himself. With the money he got for selling these pieces of gold, he hoped he could lure her away from the idiot. First, he would have to make sure Steve did not get any of the money. He knew it would be easy to trick him. Rick decided to say that they should leave the stash at his house while they waited for the heat to die down. That should fool the dummy. By the time Steve realized the deceit, it would be too late.

"Are you going to stand there or help?" asked Rick, as he bent over and lifted one of the urns.

Opening their bags, they began greedily depositing the valuables inside. Involved in their task, they never noticed the deeper shadow as it lifted and moved away from the interior wall. Rick turned as Steve grunted from behind him. Assuming that his friend had found more stash, he quickly followed. The last things he ever saw were two glowing red orbs and a wide-toothed grimace, as a sound halfway between a snarl and a growl rose from the darkness.

Chapter 1:
The Nightmare

Washington, DC, 18 years later

The fire crackled and spit sparks as the logs shifted in the flickering flames. As the couple lay cradled in each other's arms on the rug, the light from the fireplace cast an orange glow over them. Victory nuzzled her husband's neck as she snuggled closer. Andrew's hand ran up and down her side as he inhaled the fragrant aroma of roses clinging to her ivory skin and freshly washed hair.

"I could get used to coming home for lunch," said Victory, as she languorously stretched her arms above her head.

Andrew smiled and leaned forward to kiss her lightly on the lips. "I think we should incorporate it into company policy."

"Do we have to get up?" she asked, as she gazed deeply into his eyes.

"Not if you keep looking at me like that," he said, while watching the play of the firelight turn the golden hue of her hair into shades of orange and red. No matter how long he was with her, he never got tired of admiring his beautiful bride.

"You're biased," she said, reading his thoughts as she smiled up at him.

She raked her nails across his chest. His eyes turned dark aqua as their bodies melted into each other and became one.

A long time later, Andrew glanced at the grandfather clock above the mantle. "It's getting late. I'd better get back."

Victory frowned and eyed the clock as if it were an adversary. "Someday, I'm going to rid this place of all our time pieces. I mean it," she asserted, when she noticed her husband's skeptical glance. "I'm going to banish all clocks from our domain so we will no longer be slaves to time."

He laughed. "Spoken by the head of the time-driven slave department."

Grabbing one of the sofa cushions, she playfully threw it at him.

Springing like a cat on a mouse, he was upon her. With quicksilver speed, he pinned her down. She stuck out her tongue.

"You know," he said, while admiring the rise and fall of her breasts, "I would like to take advantage of this situation, but I don't want our daughter to arrive at the foundation and discover that both her parents are playing hooky."

At the mention of her daughter's name, Victory's smile faded. It was as if a cloud had blotted out the sun.

"Another nightmare?"

She hesitated, but what was the point? She sighed and slid from under him. Reaching for her discarded clothing, she said, "Laural and I were trapped in a burning building with fire blazing all around us," she paused and stared bemusedly into the fireplace. "We couldn't get out. We called for you, but you weren't there. I actually smelled the smoke and felt the heat on my skin," she said with a catch in her voice. She glanced at him, then back at the burning logs. "I felt so alone, scared, and helpless. I was so filled with sorrow because I couldn't save our child."

"Was there anyone else with you this time?"

She hesitated. She sporadically had been plagued by these nightmares for the past several months. The theme was always the same: Either she or Laural or sometimes both were in mortal peril. Equally disturbing was the fact that Andrew was never in the dreams. It was always mother and child in danger. He was never there to share their plight or to protect them. Usually, but not always, there was an ominous and unidentified figure whom she instinctively knew was responsible for their suffering.

She shook her head. "Just before I woke up I thought I heard someone laughing – laughing as if our pain brought them pleasure."

Andrew moved to her side. She shivered as he pulled her into his arms. Rubbing her back, he soothed, "It was only a dream. Nothing is going to happen to you or our child. I won't let it."

Pulling back, she wiped her tears. "I know, but Laural is so vulnerable until her abilities manifest. Even when they do, she still must understand and learn how to control them. I can't help feeling these dreams are somehow prophetic. Otherwise, why the reoccurring theme? Do you think we made a mistake by not telling her everything she should know about her abilities until they develop?" Her worries deepened while she searched his eyes.

As he pulled the navy-blue turtleneck over his muscular torso, he thought seriously about how to respond. "You and I have discussed and reaffirmed our belief that it would be best for Laural to live for the present rather than to focus on the future."

"I know," she agreed, "but that was before the dreams."

"I've been thinking that this might be your mind's way of dealing with the fact that you almost died when Laural was born."

"That was almost 18 years ago," she scoffed.

He nodded somberly. "I know. I was there."

She looked away. She still could feel the shadow of pain that lingered inside her husband whenever he remembered that fateful night. He had come home and found that she had hemorrhaged after Laural's birth. She almost had died and Andrew still was haunted by the memory. She lifted a hand to caress his face. "If anyone should be having nightmares over that episode, it would be you."

He couldn't argue the point. In order to distract her, he said, "The purchase of Silver Lining is about to go through."

Victory willingly shifted her attention. "That's great! Laural will be so happy."

Chapter 2

Stalked

The blonde teen pushed the glass double-doors. As she slung her book bag higher on her shoulder, her hand accidentally brushed against the glass. She rolled her eyes at the thought of what her father would say if he caught a glimpse of his precious pristine glass with fingerprints marring the otherwise perfect surface. She quickly wiped them away with the sleeve of her jacket. "There. All better," Laural thought, while admiring the fancy script etching of the willow tree that temporarily had been disfigured by her prints.

The hair on the back of her neck rose. She glanced over her shoulder. A group of chatting and laughing college students passed. Halfway down the block, a middle-aged woman crossed the street and hurried to catch a bus. She frowned as she continued to study the area. Several times, she had felt that she was being watched as she returned from school. No matter how often she had checked her surroundings on the ten-minute trek, she could not find anything that was out of the ordinary. Her nervousness might be stemming from her lateness since her dad was a worrywart about her safety. He might have projected some of his feelings onto her.

If she would have allowed it, he would have had her picked up from school everyday in her family's limo. Her mind recoiled at the thought. Fortunately, despite his concerns, she had been able to prevail and had gained permission to blend in with the other students who either walked home or took the bus.

Laural realized that she owed part of her success in having her way to her mom. Becoming part of the British aristocracy only after marriage, Victory understood her daughter's distress and need to fit in. She was already on the receiving end of occasional taunts from her peers. There was even a group of girls who actually went out of their way to mock her by affecting haughty poses whenever she approached.

She was glad that her mom was on her side, but she wondered how long that would last. Recently her mom had been acting weird. She had been almost as overprotective and worried as her dad. During the past few weeks, Laural had caught her mom watching her with such a sad expression on her face that Laural had to turn away. She wondered if her dad's paranoia was starting to rub off on her mother.

As she continued her progress through the building, several of the workers called to her by name. She waved, as she hurried through the posh lobby, passed the reception area, and headed for the elevator. Checking her watch, she realized that she was an hour late. It couldn't be helped. Mr. Franklyn had insisted she stay late after class to brush up on her geometry. She had to admit that he had a valid point. Midterm was only a week away and her grades were not exactly stellar.

The doors slid apart and she exited the elevator. Crossing the thick pile carpet, she walked swiftly to the door that was marked "Administrative Offices." Quickly entering, she glanced through the glass of her dad's office. His back was to her. He stood by his desk, while firmly pressing the phone to his ear. Had he realized that she was late? Hastily, she tried to slip unnoticed past his door. She wanted to avoid any questions that would lead to admitting her problems in math class.

Inside his office, Andrew was animated. "I've got great news," he boasted, as he reached to shut the office door. Dropping into the leather chair behind his desk, he continued to beam into the receiver.

"You got Silver Lining?" his wife asked excitedly.

"Yes! Mr. Briggs drove a hard bargain, but Her Ladyship, Laural Gabriel, is now the proud owner of a thoroughbred Arabian stallion."

"I think this is the best birthday present we could have gotten for her."

"Especially since she's been pestering us for her own horse since she was old enough to talk. Who taught her to talk, anyway? Her needs were much easier when they focused on teddy bears and clean diapers."

Victory laughed. "This calls for a celebration. I'm going to cook a special dinner for the occasion."

Leaning back in his leather swivel chair, Andrew inwardly

groaned. "We'll have a better chance of survival if I take us out to dinner," he muttered to himself.

"I heard that," she said with mock severity. "This time will be different."

"That's what you said last time."

"You and Laural just make sure you're on time for dinner or you'll be responsible for ruining my latest creation."

"You're late," remarked the brunette seated in front of the computer.

Laural stared at the back of her cousin's head. It still amazed her that Dana could tell when she entered the room regardless of how quietly she approached.

Shaking her head at the monitor, Dana finally turned to face her young cousin. Skeptically, she observed the torn jeans, scuffed high-top sneakers, and oversized jacket. "I know for a fact your parents can afford to dress you better than that."

Self-consciously, the adolescent looked down at her ensemble. "This is what all the kids are wearing," she protested defensively.

"Becoming a conformist at your age?"

Laural shrugged. A haunted look came over Dana's face. After a long moment, she shook herself free from the past. "Well, sit down and let's get started."

Laural sighed, as she pulled up her chair.

"What's wrong?" Dana asked, while sharply scrutinizing her.

"Nothing. It's only that I just finished studying and now I have to come here and do this without a break. Not only that, mid-terms are next week and I don't know when I'm supposed to find time to study."

She nodded sympathetically. "We'll keep it short. But I don't need to remind you that eventually you'll be in charge of the entire Willow Grove Foundation."

"No, you don't have to remind me," she said relenting. After all, she believed strongly in the cause. "Do we have any new ones today?" she asked, as she slid her chair closer to the desk.

Dana glanced at the monitor. "Two today."

"That's a lot more than usual!" exclaimed Laural.

Dana nodded. "I think our work is finally paying off and more of our people are finding out about the foundation. The idea of disguising porphyrians as immigrants fleeing from deplorable circumstances in other countries was brilliant."

"Dad and Jordan really worked hard on all the logistics of this program."

"Actually, it was your mother and Jordan who came up with that idea."

Laural turned in her chair. "Hi, Dad," she said, as she smiled up at her father.

The Marquis of Penbrook strode purposefully into the room. He was a powerfully built man with platinum blonde hair and brilliant turquoise eyes. As he leaned over his daughter's shoulder, he projected an image of unleashed energy and virile masculinity.

"What have you got there, ma petite?"

"Dana and I were reviewing the latest entries," she explained, while pushing up her sleeves.

Andrew nodded and straightened. Muscles flexed under his sweater. "How is it going, Dana?"

She smiled self-consciously. She was never completely comfortable under the marquis' scrutiny. "Pretty well. Today, we've actually picked up two. I've already sent an email to notify our halfway houses about their arrival. They should get there tomorrow."

"Good," proclaimed Jordan Rush, Earl of Rockford, as he entered the room.

Dana looked up at her fiancé and her pulse quickened. Even though they had been together for what seemed like an eternity, her heart still raced as she admired the tall, lean, and powerfully built aristocrat with strikingly bright jade-green eyes and chestnut hair that was streaked with glints of copper.

The earl strode across the room, leaned over his fiancée, and kissed her on the cheek. Straightening, he glanced at his cousin. "Andrew, if you don't mind, I'm going to take Dana away from all this for today. We're going out to dinner."

Laural looked at the happy couple and enviously wished that she had the kind of relationship that her cousins and her parents enjoyed.

"No problem," agreed the marquis. "As a matter of fact, I was just coming to collect Laural." He glanced at his daughter. "Your mom is cooking again and wants us to sample her latest creation before it gets cold."

Laural groaned even louder than her father had done earlier. Her mom's recipes were a family joke and she quickly searched her mind for an alternative. "But I just got here," she protested.

Dana glanced at her sharply and tried to message her, but Andrew intercepted the thought.

Narrowed turquoise eyes stared hard at Dana. "Nice try, but you know Laural's abilities haven't manifested yet. Now, what don't I know?" Then turning to his daughter, "What do you mean you just got here? School ended over an hour ago."

Dana squirmed uncomfortably. Even Jordan could sense the carefully controlled power just under the surface. "God help anyone who comes between Andrew and that child," he thought nervously. He wondered how his friend would cope when Laural started dating.

Laural, however, remained undaunted. With chin raised, she answered firmly, "I stayed late after school in order to get some extra help from Mr. Franklyn. My geometry could stand some improvement and the midterm is only a couple of weeks away."

He nodded. "Your mother and I were just discussing your grades. It seems a couple of your teachers have been concerned enough to bring the issue to her attention."

"That's why I stayed after school to get extra help."

"Don't schools have telephones?"

"The office was closed."

"And that cell phone we bought you?"

"Dad," Laural complained, "you took it away from me two weeks ago. Now, if you'd like to return it then I could call when I'm running late."

Andrew smiled in spite of himself. Laural's logic had turned the punishment around so that she not only had a plausible excuse, but she also managed to become the victim, as well.

"Maybe she should be a lawyer like her mom," Jordan thought.

Andrew nodded his agreement. "I'm glad to see you taking your studies so seriously and showing the initiative to take care of the problem. Now come on. Let's head home before your mom thinks we stopped for fast food."

Laural's face lit up, but one look at her father told her that he was only kidding.

"How domestic."

Both men glanced sharply at Dana.

Confused, Laural wondered about the sudden changes in the others. Undeveloped abilities sure left her out. As usual, she would have to wait for someone to go verbal before she could figure out what was going on.

"Sorry," Dana apologized ruefully. "Sometimes, those stray thoughts just pop up."

"It would help, darling," said Jordan, while placing a protective arm around her, "if you could keep from projecting them."

Andrew stared at her, but said nothing. Relief flooded through her as he refocused his attention.

Glancing at his watch, he frowned. "Earlier today, your mom mentioned that she would like to do away with time constraints," he said, while hefting his daughter's book bag, "but I don't think that applies to her dinner schedule."

Chapter 3:
Deception

Victory Parker-Gabriel stood in front of the stove. While stirring her Alfredo sauce, she read the latest legal journal. She frowned as she concentrated on the article that she was reading. Although she retained her license to practice law, her only client was the Willow Grove Foundation for Continuing Education. The foundation, which had been formed by her husband and Jordan Rush over seventeen years ago, provided an excellent opportunity to assist the disadvantaged in this country while also allowing disenfranchised porphyrians to integrate into society. Instead of existing on the fringes of humanity, they now could become part of the world in which they lived.

Born as a human, Victory knew only too well about the plight that she had shared for almost two decades. After all of those years, she still thought about the same facts over and over. Porphyrians and humans both had developed from homo sapiens, but they each evolved into a different species. The two had co-existed throughout history. Porphyrians refer to humans as diurnals while humans thought porphyrians were vampires, a label that was given in ancient times due to prejudice and superstition.

She knew the facts by rote and understood them all too well. Porphyrians, she had found out, are different in their abilities and physiology. Also, they suffer from a biochemical deficiency that can be corrected by the ingestion of hemoglobin. For centuries, porphyrians were able to obtain all of their needed nutrients only by the consumption of human blood. While the blood of animals, such as cows and pigs, could be ingested instead, it left a deficiency that led to premature death or profound madness.

Victory inwardly shuddered each time she thought about the past that still affected all of them. She was sympathetic to the plight of the early progenitors of Andrew's race. Fortunately, Andrew's ancestors developed a scientific formula that was perfected by his father. Now porphyrians drank this supplement instead of blood. PS4, as it was named, provided the nutrients and the chemical balance that were necessary for their bodies.

As Victory's focus shifted, the printed pages of the article blurred and then faded. Her sapphire-blue eyes took on a haunted look as she relived the memories of her transition from diurnal to porphyrian. Absentmindedly, she continued to stir her sauce while she recalled Andrew's original attempts to convince her that he was a separate species. An involuntary shiver raced down her spine as she remembered her lack of faith in his assertions. A lack of faith which had almost killed her. Resolutely, she shifted her attention back to the present. All of that had been a long time ago. Craven Maxwell was dead. She was a happily married woman with a beautiful daughter. Being Andrew's wife was so wonderful that she had no regrets, not even the abandoning of her dream to become a Supreme Court Justice. She vowed as soon as her husband returned home she would remind him of that fact. Her eyes drifted to the fireplace where they had made love earlier that day. "Yes," she thought, as a slight smile curved her lips, "a reminder is definitely in order."

She returned to the article. So far, the Willow Grove Foundation was working wonders in achieving their goal of assimilation. "However," she thought, while continuing to scan the article, "if the legislation proposed by Senator Randolph is endorsed, immigrants coming into this country would need to have a six-month waiting period while an extensive background check is performed." The Senator was convinced that this part of the process was essential and should be completed before the immigrants would be allowed to apply for citizenship. She was sure Andrew would want to know about the proposed changes so they could plan for this contingency.

The ringing doorbell disrupted her concentration. Sighing, she turned down the burner, stirred her cream sauce, set the journal aside, and wiped her hands on her apron. Hopefully, who ever this was would be on their way quickly enough to avoid ruining her newest creation. As she headed to the front door, she checked her watch. There was still a couple of minutes before the chicken was due to come out of the oven.

Upon opening the door, she was confronted by a man wearing

overalls and carrying a large utility case. The logo on the left breast pocket indicated that he was from the phone company. Victory glanced past him and noticed a beige and white telephone company van in the driveway. Turning back to the man, she smiled politely. His eyes raked over her. Her smile faded as he continued to stare.

"May I help you?" she asked politely but firmly.

Smiling, he said, "Yes, ma'am, I'm from the phone company. We've been having some problems in this neighborhood and are in the process of checking all the homes in the area for damage to the lines. I've already checked the outside lines and now I need to finish up by checking a couple of things inside."

She frowned and he rushed on. "I know I've probably come at a bad time," he observed, while looking at her apron, "but this is my last stop of the day before I can go home and have my own dinner."

Victory's smile returned. The man looked so forlorn that she almost invited him to stay for dinner. Then, she thought about how he had stared at her. Just to be safe, she decided to probe him even though she hated invading people's private thoughts. She sniffed. "Oh, no, the chicken! Come in and do what you need," she yelled over her shoulder, as she sped toward the kitchen, "I have to get back to my dinner before it burns. There's a phone in the den to your right."

The man started to thank her, but she was already in the kitchen. Quickly setting down the utility box, he snapped it open and extracted a sword. He stared intently at the brightly gleaming blade as it caught the last rays of the setting sun. He slowly ran his thumb across the edge and smiled crookedly as a drop of blood formed along the shallow cut. Stealthily, he crept down the long foyer to the kitchen.

Chapter 4:
Dana's Dilemma

Distractedly, Dana watched Jordan as he instructed the waiter. Glancing around at the familiar surroundings, she relaxed in her chair and allowed the tension to drain from her body. Anthony's was her favorite restaurant in DC. No matter how often they went there, she never grew tired of it. She couldn't say that for the rest of the city. She stirred restlessly, as she absentmindedly played with the tablecloth. How long could she continue to keep her feelings from the others?

"Not long," Jordan answered her unspoken question.

Startled, she glanced up. Intense green eyes bore into her and she quickly looked away. Across the room, another couple was toasting each other and laughing. A lump formed in her throat. As she again faced her fiancé, she twisted the ring on the third finger of her left hand. "I don't know what's wrong with me," she admitted, while searching his face.

Jordan took a long sip of his wine before answering. "How long have you been feeling this way?"

"Not long," she said, as she dropped her eyes.

"Do you have any idea what's going on?"

Obviously in despair, she shook her head. "I've just been feeling restless, bored, smothered – all of those things and none of them. I really don't know what's wrong. I really do believe in what we're doing. Until recently, I was as motivated and as devoted to the cause as everyone else, but lately ..." Beset by sadness, she shook her head and continued, "I've been wondering if I'm just not cut out for domesticity. Twenty years is the longest time I can remember staying in one place. I don't know where these uncharitable thoughts are coming from. Thoughts like the one I had at the foundation. I suppose I'm just not content and it's leaking out in other ways."

Jordan stared hard at her for a moment. He probed. When she

didn't resist, he intently studied her; going over every detail of her captivating features. Her wavy cascade of rich brown hair glistened in the soft light of the restaurant. Her high cheekbones, full mouth, and straight nose were perfectly proportioned within her oval face. Finely arched brows hovered like raven's wings over her deep brown eyes. She held his gaze and stared back earnestly until he finally relaxed.

While taking her hand, he tried to reassure her. "I don't have the answers for you. I wish I did. It is one of the things Andrew and I discussed while we were out today. Based on your past history, he is concerned and I can't blame him."

Resentment rose, but she quickly quelled it. He had a valid point. "How did the meeting go?"

He looked deeply into her eyes. How much did he dare to tell her? He waited until the waiter placed their meals in front of them. He noted that Dana merely moved the food around on her plate. Something was definitely wrong with her.

"The meeting went well," Jordan began. "In his usual eloquent manner, Andrew convinced the entire board of directors to provide all the necessary funding for the new equivalency diploma program. It will enable the immigrants to come up to the same competitive specifications as the rest of the community. He had everyone convinced that the graduates would be upstanding self-supporting citizens who would be beneficial to society in only a few years."

In mock salute, Dana raised her glass. "Here's to Andrew's oratory skills. If a few porphyrians also benefit from the deal, all the better!"

Jordan nodded, but raised one eyebrow as he continued to study her.

"I'm just not comfortable relying on diurnals for our financial support."

"We're not."

"You know what I mean," she challenged. "Having to get their approval on any level rubs me the wrong way. We both know Andrew could afford to do this without anyone else's financial backing. The fact that he uses federal funds just gives the diurnal bureaucrats an excuse to scrutinize the operation."

Jordan sighed and put down his fork. "Have you forgotten one of the main reasons for the agency is to promote integration?" he asked with more than a tinge of exasperation in his voice. "We've been through this before. You know that Victory's legal advice and our own research indicates this is the best way to implement our plans. It's rare in this society for even a philanthropist to use all his own money to fund a charitable organization of this magnitude. Refusing to utilize the resources available would put the entire operation under more scrutiny. Turning Andrew and our organization into a mystery would increase attention and cause people to try to discover our secrets in some covert manner. In this way, we can control the overt knowledge."

Dana nodded. It made sense. "I'm getting antsy being around diurnals all the time. I occasionally catch a stray thought and I can tell you some of their ideas are just as deviant as my father's."

Chapter 5:
The Manifestation

"There was another reason I stayed after school."

"Oh," remarked the marquis, as he swung the silver Mercedes into rush-hour traffic.

"Yes," replied Laural, as she massaged her temples.

"What was that?"

Laural leaned back against the headrest and closed her eyes. "I was helping Melissa fill out an application to apply for financial aid from the foundation."

He glanced at her and then back at the traffic. "You know we can't give her any special consideration just because she's your friend."

"I know, but she definitely qualifies and she's really smart. I'm sure she'll get the grant based on her own merit. I just thought you should know."

He nodded. He had known Melissa Anders since she and Laural had been in grade school together. He had no doubt that the intelligent and diligent student would get the grant. Melissa also had several factors in her personal life that qualified her as a hardship case. He also was aware of how protective and loyal his daughter was of her friend. He was sure that applying to the foundation had been Laural's idea.

"You're a good friend," he said, while changing lanes, "but what's wrong?" he asked, as she continued to rub her head.

"I have a headache," Laural complained, as she opened her eyes to scan the traffic. The feeling that she was being watched had returned, but no one in the congestion seemed to have any interest in anything except getting home.

Andrew glanced at her briefly, as he maneuvered the car into the passing lane. He checked his watch. "Employers should stagger work schedules to prevent rush hours," he said jokingly. He turned on the radio and pushed the button to get a traffic report. Suddenly, his finger stabbed the off button. Startled, he stared at his daughter.

"Sorry," she said, "but I couldn't handle the noise." Then, realization struck. "Oh, my God! Did I do that?"

"You certainly did," responded Andrew, while honking at a red Camaro as it tried to pass. "I think your headache might have something to do with your telepathic and telekinetic abilities starting to emerge," he said aloud, but then thought, "Sometimes, it happens this way. Headaches, nausea, agitation, and erratic power surges often occur during the transformation. Of course, some adolescent porphyrians have no side-effects. They just awaken one day and their abilities are fully in place." It appeared, however, that his daughter would not be that lucky.

"There's some Tylenol in the glove compartment," he said, as he approached the intersection. Glancing in the rearview mirror, he wondered if he should reverse course and try an alternative route. One look at the heavily congested traffic told him that it was futile. Hopefully, Victory's dinner would not be ruined by their tardiness. He smiled wistfully, as he gave his daughter a sidelong glance. "I guess you're growing up."

She wrinkled her nose. "You didn't expect me to stay a child forever?"

He sighed. "I could hope. Your mom tried to warn me that you'd grow up, but I didn't want to believe her. I guess it's about time we had a talk about what this means."

"You mean you and mom are finally going to tell me about porphyrian history? You're going to tell me what makes us different from diurnals and about the special abilities we have?"

"Don't get too excited," he cautioned grimly. "With those abilities comes responsibility."

"I know," she said in a subdued voice.

He glanced sharply at her.

"I feel like I'm being bombarded by everything I see and hear."

"Take the Tylenol, lean back, and rest until we get home. Tonight, I'll start teaching you how to control these surges."

She leaned back and closed her eyes.

"Why don't you try letting your mom know we're running late?" Victory would be surprised and delighted. Maybe, after Laural learned how to control her burgeoning powers, he and her mom could stop worrying that she was at risk each time that she left their side.

Laural started to reach for the phone, but her dad shook his head. "With your mind."

She grinned. "I heard you, Dad," she said excitedly, while tapping her head with her finger. "For the first time, I really heard what you thought."

He smiled in spite of the gridlock. "Reach out to your mom. Send her a message. Nothing fancy. Keep it simple."

"Okay," she said, while leaning back and closing her eyes again. Her brows drew together as she focused her attention.

As Andrew watched her, he smiled. Eventually, she would learn that this kind of concentration was not necessary, but the affectation was cute. Victory would be pleased. They both had been a little concerned about the delay in the manifestation of their daughter's porphyrian mental abilities. At first, Victory thought that her own human genetics were responsible. She finally could put her fears on that score to rest. After all, the strongest and most gifted ones took longer to manifest.

Abruptly, Laural's eyes flew open and she sat bolt upright. Shaking violently, she began screaming. "Mother, no, no, no!"

Suddenly, she let out an ear-piercing shriek that Andrew was sure would shatter the windows. He swerved and narrowly missed the red Camaro that angrily blared its horn. Frowning, he finally managed to pull over to the side of the road. Laural thrashed violently in the seat next to him.

"Thank goodness for the seatbelt," he thought, as he jerked to a stop. "Otherwise, she would have been seriously injured by now." As she tried to free herself from her restraint, her screams escalated again. Andrew made a grab for her belt two moments too late. Laural threw open the car door and was about to pitch headlong into the street. Her father released his belt, threw himself across the seat, grabbed her arm, and jerked her hard against him.

Holding her tightly as she convulsed, he attempted to determine the cause of the outburst. He had never heard of any porphyrian being affected like this by their first telepathic experience. While he continued to sooth her with his words, he tried to gently probe her thoughts with his mind.

Chaotic images of blood and ripped flesh assaulted him. He

recoiled. "What the hell?" He held his daughter at arm's length. Her eyes were clamped shut and her head whipped fiercely from side to side. Her body shuddered uncontrollably and beads of perspiration covered her skin.

His mind raced back through time. He tried desperately to recall if he had ever heard or read about any of his people suffering such an adverse reaction. He drew a blank. A knock on the car window caught his attention.

"Can I help?" a middle-aged woman in a business suit asked, while glancing from the marquis to Laural.

For a moment, he just stared. "My daughter is epileptic. She's having a seizure."

"Can I call for an ambulance?" she suggested, while pulling a cell phone from her purse.

He shook his head. "I already did. Thanks," he said, as he faked a smile. "It should be here any minute."

She hesitated, glanced uncertainly at Laural, and then started back to her car. After she climbed into her vehicle, she took out a pad and pen. Despite his ordeal, Andrew was impressed when he saw her copying what he assumed to be the number of his license plate. She finished writing and rejoined the rest of the rush-hour traffic. He was glad to know that caring people still existed.

Turning his attention back to his daughter, he stared with grim determination. He would have to dampen her thoughts with his own until he could determine the problem. He hoped that she hadn't connected with her mother. Victory would be a nervous wreck if she detected Laural in such trauma.

"Andrew!" The thought hit him like a blow. Fear and anxiety burst into his mind like a bomb.

"Damn," he muttered as he thought about the best way to explain this to his wife.

"Andrew, help me!"

He jerked so hard that he almost lost his grip on Laural. "Victory," he whispered softly and then shouted, "Victory!"

Chapter 6:
Death Blow

Andrew's heart raced and he broke out in a cold sweat as he finally understood the reason for his daughter's reaction. Horror flooded his mind and numbed his senses. The image that assailed him made his blood run cold. Victory was whirling with what appeared to be a pan of chicken in her hands. A man in grey overalls with a sword was slashing at her.

Through the eyes of his beloved, he watched in impotent agony as the blade arched high and then sliced through the air. It missed Victory by only inches. Dropping the pan, she protectively threw up her arms. Blood poured from wounds as the man slashed a pattern of crisscross crimson lines on her arms. The pan hit the floor and the chicken rolled several feet as the intruder stalked her.

Stunned by the attack, Victory stared at her arms, then the fallen chicken. When she looked back at her arms, the wounds already had begun to close and heal. She had known about this aspect of her porphyrian abilities, but part of her still could not believe even while she watched the process.

Warily eyeing her assailant, she slowly backed toward the kitchen door. Suddenly, he rushed her and aimed the sword straight at her face. Her eyes widened as the blade neared. The man abruptly slipped on chicken grease. As he fell, he dropped his sword. The weapon clattered when it hit the floor and then spun out of reach.

Should she try to get it before he did? While she was considering her options, the man regained his purchase and grabbed for the hilt. She hesitated while trying to decide what to do next. Her eyes ricocheted from one kitchen counter to the next in a desperate attempt to find a weapon. Seeing nothing more threatening than her pan of Alfredo sauce, she glanced at her attacker. The glint in his eyes reflected the gleam of the blade as he again swung toward her.

"Run!" Andrew's voice reverberated in her brain. She bolted, hit the kitchen door hard, and fled toward the front of the house.

"Jordan, I need you!"

The earl jerked back in his seat. His head snapped against the booth as if he had been struck. His face paled and a wave of dizziness swept through him.

"What's wrong?" asked Dana with concern.

His head cleared as he stood. "Andrew needs us - now!"

Dana stared up at him. A frown creased her brow. Still feeling nervous and edgy, she wasn't sure that she was ready to confront Andrew's inquisition about her recent erratic thoughts. She opened her mouth to protest, but one look at her fiancé's frantic features wiped the words from her mind.

Without further explanation, Jordan threw several bills down on the table and sprinted through the restaurant. Dana frowned and then opened her mind. Her eyes widened and she gasped. Mindless of the curious stares from the other diners, she ran after Jordan.

The man grabbed Victory's hair as she ran through the living room. She wrenched free, but was thrown off balance. She landed hard on the sofa, as the blade slammed into the back of the couch. She rolled onto the floor and barely had time to stand before he was on her.

The man swung the sword again. She reflexively raised her arm. This time, he struck her across the shoulder. She stumbled from the sheer force of the blow. Confusion clouded her mind while she stared at the gash in her shoulder. The blade had cut through to the bone. "This can't be happening," she thought wildly, as rivers of blood poured down her body. She expected to pass out any second from loss of blood. She thought that her system could not sustain such a shock, but, as she watched, her shoulder instantly started to mend itself.

Mesmerized by the process, she barely caught the man's next swing out of the corner of her eye. She ducked and the hilt of the sword slammed her temple. Dizzy and disoriented, she fell against the fireplace. Logs crackled and sparks flew as the sword slashed through the screen only inches from her face.

As Andrew continued to console his daughter, he knew what to expect. He briefly considered trying to break the connection between mother and daughter, but realized that any distraction from his own connection to Victory could prove fatal. While his daughter continued to sob hysterically, he tried desperately to provide mental assistance to his wife.

He wished that Laural did not have to be a part of this, but he could not shield her and reach out to Victory at the same time. "He's going for your head," he thought. "If he hits you anywhere else, you will heal, but a blow to the head could be fatal. Stop him! Use your mental persuasion to supercede his intent. Mentally tell him to give you the sword!"

Numb with shock, Victory just gazed blankly at the man. The last blow had stunned her and, for a moment, she didn't think that she could do it. From her prone position, she watched as the blade lifted.

"Now!"

Andrew's imperative reverberated through her mind. Her head throbbed. She was unsure whether it was from her assailant's blow or the force of her husband's command. Victory did as he instructed. With pinpoint precision, she thrust her mental will at her attacker and allowed her mind to combat the thoughts of the man above her. As she slowly got to her knees and stood, she wondered why he was attacking her in the first place.

"Never mind. We'll find that out soon enough," Andrew grimly assured her. He had his own ideas of what to do with someone who threatened his wife, but he did not want Victory or Laural to know.

Slowly, the man dropped his arm. The sword tip cut a deep gash through the carpet. Victory approached warily while holding out her hand to take the weapon. She hesitated and then frowned as she became aware of distant sobbing. "Laural?" she wondered, distracted by the mental echo of her daughter's sobs.

"Andrew, Laural ..."

"Stay focused," he commanded. "Laural's with ..."

Too late she realized her mistake. Temporarily diverted by her child's distress, she had shifted her attention away from her assailant. The man suddenly sprang toward her, raised his arm, and slashed downward with all of his strength.

"Abomination!" he screamed when Victory's head hit the floor with a sickening thump. A moment later, the decapitated body collapsed onto the carpet. The man threw down his weapon and quickly pulled one of the burning logs from the fireplace. He bent over the Marchioness of Penbrook, touched the burning log to her long blonde hair, and tossed the torch onto her clothing.

Cackling gleefully, the man watched as the flames caught, spread, and blazed.

"Mommy!" Laural screamed. Her body became rigid and then she collapsed into unconsciousness in her father's arms

Chapter 7:

Coma

The hallway lights cast flickering shadows over the gloomy interior of the sterile hospital room. Andrew Gabriel leaned forward on the edge of the low-back vinyl chair, paused for several seconds, and then resettled himself. He stared into the deserted corridor as if his will could force his need to be realized. Apprehensively, his gaze shifted back to the figure in the bed. He probed quickly but thoroughly. No change. Laural lay as still as a statue. The sheets were pulled up to her chest and her arms were resting by her sides. Her long blonde hair spread across the pillow like a silk blanket as it cascaded down the sheets.

Andrew exhaled slowly as he stood, cast one more troubled look toward the bed, and stepped out into the hall. Outside the door, he halted and turned to intercept the doctor who was escorting Jordan and Dana toward the room. They spied him and hurried to his side. "We got to the mansion as quickly as possible," Jordan projected, "but we were too late. We both sensed that we must come straight to you and Laural," he finished, as sorrow darkened his jade-green eyes.

He studied the distressed look on their faces. Sensing that they were about to speak, he silently cautioned them and turned toward the doctor. The physician tried to step past him, but Andrew blocked his path.

Annoyed, the doctor turned to face him. "If you don't mind, I would like to check in on my patient."

Andrew took stock of the young dark-haired internist. Silver-gray eyes stared directly into his. As if sensing that he was being tested, the doctor unconsciously straightened his shoulders. He had the natural stance of a football player, and rather than being intimidated by the marquis, he appeared ready to plow through him to attain his goal.

Despite the events of the last hour, Andrew's lips lifted into a slight smile. He always appreciated character strength. "Excuse me, Dr. Brenner, but, if you had been through what I have, you would be rather protective of your child, too."

The doctor relaxed. Sighing, he admitted, "You're probably right. I have no children so can't even imagine your anguish. But," he added firmly, "I don't know how I can possibly treat my patient if you won't let me in the room."

Andrew glanced at Jordan. The earl nodded in response to the unspoken question.

The marquis reluctantly stepped aside, even though he knew there was really nothing that the doctor could do for Laural. She was suffering from one of the most severe traumas imaginable for a porphyrian: actually being telepathically linked with a loved one during death. He knew only too well what that was like. He was not sure if anyone would be able to bring Laural back from the deep recesses where her mind had sought refuge.

"Then, why take her to a place full of diseased diurnals?"

He stared hard at Dana for a long moment. "Where would you have me take her?"

She took an involuntary step back when she saw the raw pain darkening the turquoise eyes.

"How long?" he asked silently, shifting his attention to Jordan. He motioned for them to join him as he followed the doctor into the room.

"John was the closest. He'll be here any minute with the others close behind."

Dr. Brenner checked Laural's pulse, her heart, and respiration. As he lifted her eyelids, he shone his penlight into one pupil and then the other before allowing the lids to drop. He stepped to the foot of the bed, lifted the chart, and began making notations. After snapping the chart shut, he turned to face her father.

"Unfortunately, there's been no change. I'm going to arrange for an EEG and other tests to check for brain damage. I'll schedule them for tomorrow morning. You're sure there was no head trauma?"

He shook his head. "No, I caught her when she passed out and personally carried her from the car."

"No history of seizures?"

"No."

"Has anything like this ever happened before?"

He again shook his head. "Never."

The doctor nodded and left the room.

Exhaling, Andrew closed his eyes and raked his hand through his thick platinum hair. After a long moment, deeply shadowed turquoise eyes focused on the room's other occupants. "Stay with her until security arrives."

"Where are you going?"

He headed toward the door. "To the house."

Dana gasped and Jordan gaped at him. "Why?"

He didn't answer. They didn't understand. They couldn't understand. He had to see her. He had to try. He still might be able to save her, but every second counted. The delay already might have been too long, but he knew that Victory would have wanted her child – rather than herself – to be the top priority.

"Don't leave her alone, not even for a second. Probe everyone who enters this room, both porphyrians and diurnals. I'll be back as soon as I can."

Dana walked over to the bed and gazed down at her young cousin. Jordan searched his friend's face.

Unable to withstand the mirrored pain that he saw reflected in the earl's eyes, Andrew abruptly turned his back and walked toward the door. Pausing, he stared through the window into the deepening dusk. He swallowed hard past the lump in his throat. The shades of purple, violet, and blue echoed the bruise spreading across his heart.

Even though time was of the essence he couldn't leave without letting them know what to expect. Sardonically, he said, "Too bad you guys didn't arrive a little earlier. You could have been in on the police inquisition."

"Inquisition?" questioned Jordan, trying to stall for time as he walked to his friend's side. He desperately tried to think of a reason to keep Andrew away from the mansion. There was nothing that Andrew could do other than be forced to endure more pain.

"Yes," he responded flatly, while reaching for the door handle. "It seems a concerned citizen reported me to the police as a potential kidnapper or child abuser."

Dana whirled around. Her dark hair swirled like a velvet curtain. "That's ridiculous," she sputtered.

As he started to pull open the door, Andrew looked from one to the other. "I'm just telling you in case they return with any more questions. If they do, don't volunteer anything. Just stall them until I return."

"There's more to this than we already know," Jordan stated flatly, while pulling up a chair next to the bed. "Don't go. Laural needs you."

He stared bleakly at the bed. "I've done all I can. Right now, Victory needs me more."

Dana and Jordan exchanged concerned glances. Neither wanted to voice their fears about Andrew's mental stability.

Listening intently, Andrew ascertained that there was no one within hearing distance. Looking from Jordan to Dana and then back again, he nodded. "I had to come up with some story about what happened," he said, while waving his arm toward the bed, "and I doubt the police would have believed she was psychically linked to her mother while she was being murdered."

Jordan and Dana exchanged another look. They had been aware of Victory's death. It had reverberated through them like ripples in a pond, but neither actually had seen any imagery.

"Count your blessings," Andrew said sharply. "It wasn't a pretty sight." Fighting for composure, he paused in the doorway. "In case the authorities press you, my official statement is that Laural and I walked in on the crime scene right after it occurred. The sight of her mother's butchered body was too overwhelming for Laural and she went into severe shock. Realizing there was nothing to do for my wife, I called the police and informed them of what happened on route to the hospital. It was probably fortuitous that I came here first," he added, "because, shortly after Laural was admitted, the police showed up to make sure I was Laural's father and not her abductor."

"It's a good thing you came here at least for the sake of appearances," Jordan agreed, while holding one of the unconscious girl's hands. "Even though modern medicine can't help her, someone surely would have noticed that you hadn't brought your daughter to the hospital, especially since this case is bound to become high-profile. Besides," he added, while studying the still figure in the bed, "you certainly can't take her home."

He nodded. What Jordan said made sense, but he could not shake the feeling that he had let Victory down by not immediately trying to save her.

"I'm sure the only way you could have let Victory down would've been not to attend to her child's safety," adamantly stated Dana, while staring sadly at her young cousin.

"You need to stop blaming yourself. There's nothing you could've done," asserted Jordan. He barely could stand the look of deep sorrow and fathomless pain that he saw shadowing his friend's eyes.

Andrew glared back at him. "I should've been stronger. I should've given better directions for her to deal with that man. Most of all," he finished, while closing his eyes against the images that pursued him, haunted him, mocked him, blamed him, "I should have been able to read that man's intention. I got nothing. He was a blank wall."

Jordan and Dana exchanged confused glances. Jordan ventured hesitantly, "But the only one with telepathic abilities strong enough to block you was Craven and he's been dead for over eighteen years!"

Again, Andrew paused. He slowly turned back to face them. "Maybe, I've lost some of my abilities."

"Maybe, you have," offered Dana, as she turned away from the bed.

"Dana!" Jordan chastised sharply.

"Well, I've been wanting to say this for a long time."

"Yes, but this is not the time or place."

"No," interjected Andrew, "you're right, I don't have time for this now." He yanked open the door.

"What kind of a father would leave his daughter in this condition?"

His face reddened as he glanced back over his shoulder.

Her heated gaze seared into him. "I think the reason you've lost some of your abilities is because they've atrophied. You've tried so hard to live like a diurnal that you have virtually become one yourself. You've turned your back on who you really are and where you came from. You haven't used your own abilities for so long I'm not surprised they weren't at full strength when you needed them. If you don't give up living like a diurnal and start being true to who you really are, you will lose your daughter, too."

At the look of anguish that crossed Andrew's face, Jordan decided that he should intervene. There was some truth to what his fiancée was saying, but, if she pushed Andrew too far, they might be privy to a demonstration of how much strength he still had. Standing, he stepped to Dana's side and placed his hand on her arm.

Pulling free of his grasp, she continued to glare at the marquis. "Your child needs you," she said, while emphatically pointing at the prone figure on the bed. "She needs her father with his mental ability at full strength to go into her mind and pull her back from whatever abyss she has fallen into. No diurnal doctor or porphyrian pretending to be something he's not can do that for her. You may not have been able to save Victory, but, if you lose Laural, it'll be your own fault."

The doorknob slipped from his grasp. As he descended like a hawk diving for its prey, his eyes burned with fury. Dana shrank against the side of the bed as he advanced.

"What gives you the right to lecture me? You," he sneered, while pointing accusatorily as he stalked toward her, "who played the mindless puppet to your demented father and most likely would still be under his domination if I hadn't saved your sorry ---."

Jordan interposed himself between the two. "Stop it, Andrew! This isn't about Dana and you know it."

Andrew glared at him for several seconds. His jaw muscles flexed, while his fists clenched and unclenched at his sides. Finally, he turned and strode back to the door.

"Besides, she's right."

Andrew twirled around on one heel. His turquoise eyes narrowed to twin slits. "That is something neither one of you will have to worry about again. From this point forward," he declared in a voice as hard as steel, "neither porphyrian nor diurnal gets under my guard." Abruptly, he turned, jerked open the door, and was gone.

Jordan hesitated. "I need to go after him. Will you be all right alone until John and the others arrive?"

Still shaken from the onslaught of the raw fury that had bombarded her, she stared back blankly. Gradually, her eyes refocused on the frightened face of her fiancé. "Do you have any idea why he feels the need to go back to the mansion?"

He nodded grimly. "He tried to block it, but I caught a glimpse of the living room with Victory lying on the floor." He had been assailed by an image of the blood from the decapitated body gushing from the open neck onto the carpet. He also had glimpsed the grizzly sight of her severed head lying a few feet away. It was then that he divined Andrew's intent. "I think he believes he can bring her back if he gets to her body before too much time elapses."

Pulling her chair closer to the bed and resting one hand on Laural's arm, Dana asked, "I don't understand. Even if permanent damage wasn't done to the brain, what about the fire?"

He already was rushing through the door as he called over his shoulder, "He doesn't know."

Chpater 8:

The Young Overlord

Cornwall, England, 1613

Arthur Gabriel, fifth Marquis of Penbrook, sat proudly astride his horse as he rode next to his young son. He gave the boy a sideways glance. Today was the first time that his heir was accompanying him on his monthly trek through their territory. With approval, he noted the way Andrew appeared to be intently studying his surroundings. In fact, he seemed to be imprinting every cottage, villager, and blade of grass on his mind as they wended their way through the village streets of Camelford.

"Good morn'," called a cobbler from the doorway of his shop.

"Good day to you, Thaddeus," returned the marquis, as he tipped his cap.

"It's good to see the young lord out with you this morning. Teaching him the ropes?" queried the shop owner.

"Aye, that I am, Mr. Thaddeus," agreed Arthur, who was interrupted by the young Andrew, who added, "and a hard task master he is, too."

The cobbler laughed good-naturedly. Several of his children peered in awe from the doorway. They shyly studied their noble landlords. "You make sure and mind what your sire tells you, Master Andrew. He's a good overlord and an even better man. You'll do well to learn by his example."

As they rode on, Arthur observed the adolescent from the corner of his eye. His heart swelled with pride. Andrew sat straight as an arrow on his black stallion, Thunderbolt. The horse had been a gift from the marquis in acknowledgment of his increase in status. Arthur was secretly impressed by the insight contained in his young son's remarks about their holdings. He patiently continued to answer all of Andrew's queries as the youth enthusiastically plied him with questions about everything on the estate. He was avidly interested in his surroundings. His desire for knowledge was insatiable. He studied every aspect of the land – from the villagers tending the fields to the herds in the pastures. Nothing escaped his notice. The marquis' heart filled with joy. Crystal had born him a fine son. A son he could be proud of and place his faith in. It was unfortunate that his mother wasn't here to watch him grow into such a superb man.

As they rode further through the town, Mrs. Henley, the butcher's wife, came out to greet them. While she offered them ale to slake their thirst, Andrew inquired about the health of her mother. Mrs. Henley beamed as she reported on her mom's improvement. Then, she turned to the marquis to compliment him on having such a well-mannered and considerate son.

The marquis' ears still were ringing with her praise long after they left the shop. Again, he covertly studied his son. "Yes. Someday, he will make a fine leader," he thought.

Later that day, they rode across Slaughter Bridge, which covered the marshy bog. Andrew asked him about the origins of its name.

The marquis shot a wide grin at him. "Slaughter Bridge dates back to the time of King Arthur. It is reputed to be the site of the final conflict between Arthur and his evil son, Mordred. Both died that day, but, before Arthur succumbed to his wounds, it is said that he threw Excalibur into yonder bog."

Andrew gazed thoughtfully at the area for several moments. "Why would he discard such a valuable artifact?"

"In order to keep it from falling into the hands of those who might use it for evil," he answered more harshly than he intended.

The teen was taken aback. "Have I displeased you with my questions, father?" he asked uncertainly.

The marquis smiled reassuringly, as he met his son's brilliant turquoise eyes. "Not at all. I admire your interest in our village's history. In fact, I was just thinking how proud your mother would be if she could see you on your new black stallion. You cut a fine figure, young Andrew."

Rather than being pleased, Andrew frowned. "Am I still so young?"

Compliments from the villagers floated through his mind, as he seriously studied his son. He was tall and well-built. His platinum hair gleamed in the sunlight and his pale skin glistened with health. The turquoise eyes that were searching his were intelligent and compassionate. They also had an underlying strength. He filled out his doublet and hose well, and sat his mount with confidence. In essence, Andrew was a younger version of himself.

"Nay, not so young, after all. Now that your abilities have manifested, it's time for you to take on your responsibilities to your people," he announced, while waving his hand toward the village. "Never forget, Andrew, these people are your responsibility. Your needs and theirs are entwined. You need them for prosperity and perspective on your humanity. They depend on you for protection and justice."

Andrew was not sure that he understood.

"That's all right," said his father, reading his thoughts. He clasped him on the shoulder. "In time, you will."

His father had been right. As the years passed, Andrew had become an intricate part of the villagers' lives. He had been present for the baptizing of their children, presided over their weddings, aided with the expansion of the town, and suffered through the harsh times with them. He had learned and gained strength from his father's wisdom. His father had been adamant that they must never consider themselves superior just because of their unique abilities. He emphasized integrity, honor, and strength of character. Andrew considered those traits much more valuable than physical strength and mental manipulation. Arthur Gabriel had considered his town's people to be different, but not inferior.

Over time, Andrew had come to share his father's beliefs. Eventually, he gained the villagers' affection and respect by his own merit. The feeling was mutual. A long time after his father had died and been buried beside his mother, Andrew carried on the lessons that he had gained from his father's example. He liked to think that his father's spirit guided his choices and he brought that advantage to the leadership of his people.

Chapter 9:

The Consuming Flames

Bright orange, yellow, and red flames licked greedily at the sapphire sky. A spray of sparks flew like fireflies into the night, as another beam from the two-story mansion collapsed into what had once been a proud colonial home. Now, it withered and was shrinking in on itself, a helpless victim to the onslaught of the consuming flames.

Sirens shrieked and then died as two more fire trucks quickly joined the one already parked at the curb. The revolving light cast red glows across the firefighters. Swiftly but efficiently, they began unwinding the length of hose and dragging it like an elongated python across the street.

"You two get the one on the left," yelled the chief to his officers. "Darryl and Jerry, you get the one on the right. Darin, help me get control of that blaze before the whole neighborhood goes."

The first two teams headed to the homes on either side of the mansion. They wetted down the roofs and the surrounding shrubbery to prevent the sparks from spreading the blaze. The third team went to work on the Gabriel home. The fire chief glared grimly at the escalating pyre. "We need more help here!"

Watching and waiting for the outcome, dozens of concerned citizens stood several feet beyond the fire engines. Several of them were from the neighborhood. They realized that the result of the firefighters' battle with this blaze would be pivotal in the fight between the fire and the safety or destruction of their own homes.

The silver Mercedes sped around the corner. Tires screeched in protest as they skidded to an abrupt halt. For a moment, Andrew sat frozen in shock. He could feel the heat through the closed car. The consuming flames were destroying his home and everything inside, including Victory.

"Excuse me, sir," insisted one of the firemen, as he walked up to the car, "but you need to move."

Andrew opened the car door. The fireman took a determined step to block his path. "That's my home," the marquis announced. "I need to get in there."

The fireman lifted his helmet from his head and wiped at the sooty sweat that was pouring down his brow. A black smudge streaked across his forehead as he replaced his headgear. He looked at the burning building and then back at the marquis. His eyes softened with compassion, while he shook his head, "I understand you're upset ..."

"You don't understand anything," refuted Andrew. "Now, let me pass."

The other man stared blankly ahead for several seconds, pivoted abruptly, and went back to his task. Andrew turned his attention back to the blaze. Dodging through the onlookers and speeding past the remaining firefighters, he rushed toward the burning inferno.

Suddenly, he was tackled from behind. He exhaled sharply as he landed flat on the lawn several feet away from the front steps. Trying to catch his breath, he lay stunned for several seconds. He shook off the attacker, while wondering who among them could have superceded his will. He had put up a mental barrier against the diurnals so that they wouldn't notice his flight into the house. That meant it must be a porphyrian. But who?

The weight lifted from his back and he found himself staring at a pair of brown suede loafers as they planted themselves firmly in front of his face. Glaring up at Jordan, he stood. "You're supposed to be protecting my daughter at the hospital."

"Dana is with her and security was pulling up as I left."

"I don't know why you followed me," he declared, while pushing past him, "but either help or stay out of my way."

Jordan grabbed his arm. "You can't go in there," he insisted, as he stared fixedly at the flames.

Andrew jerked his arm free. "I have to get to Victory."

Jordan stepped in front of him; his bottle-green eyes pierced him like shards of glass. "Victory's dead. If you try to get to her, you're going to die, too." They glared at each other for several seconds. "Or is that what you want – to die with her because you can't stand going on without her?"

Andrew stiffened and then sagged as the tension drained from his body. "You're right," he agreed, while staring at the house. With flames flickering in the reflection of his eyes, he continued, "If I can't find a way to keep Victory with me in this life, then I'll just have to join her in the next. Either way," he finished, pivoting and slamming his fist into the earl's jaw, "I'm going in!"

Dazed by the blow, Jordan staggered several steps. He shook his head as he fought to remain conscious. Through a haze of pain, he watched Andrew charge through the open doorway. The determined marquis was heedless of the flaming fingers of fire trying to capture him in their deadly embrace.

Andrew coughed several times, as he squinted his eyes against the stinging smoke. Billows of gray clouds surrounded him and smoke seeped into his lungs. He blinked rapidly in an effort to clear his vision. Crucial seconds of disorientation ticked by and he momentarily panicked.

Nothing seemed familiar in the dense gray smog. His eyes searched desperately, but couldn't penetrate the haze. What if he couldn't find her? His brain screamed in protest. He had to find her! He couldn't leave her in this place, not like this, not terrified and alone just like in her nightmares.

The thought of her nightmares galvanized him. She had been prophetic, after all. He concentrated and focused on visualizing the house. He was in the foyer. He stepped forward. The attack had started in the kitchen and ended in the living room near the fireplace. The fireplace, where only that morning they had made love. The memories threatened to overwhelm him. Resolutely, he pushed them aside, as he fumbled his way forward.

Blindly, he moved ahead. Pushing past an open doorway. He paused and narrowed his eyes against the smoke. He peered into the room. "The den," he thought, as a spasm of coughing seized him. Tears squeezed out of the corners of his eyes and ran down his face. He squinted against the smoke. He grasped the desk for support while another coughing fit racked his body.

Regaining control, he continued through the room. He was abruptly confronted by a scorching wall of fire. The rear study wall that joined the living room was engulfed in flames. Paralyzed by panic, he stared in desperation at the barrier. Beyond the flames, he could see nothing but more fire. Victory lay somewhere in that inferno and he had to get to her. He considered retreating so that he could look for a safer route, but he heard a crackle and a roar behind him. Abruptly, the ceiling in the study caved in. Showers of sparks flew in every direction. Tucking his head into his jacket and hands into his pockets, he dove through the wall of flames.

Andrew rolled several times across the carpet. His scorched skin felt as if it were burned clear through to his bones. He smelled the odor of burning hair and reached up to smother the flames. Agony shot through his hand as a section of his flesh singed, turned to ash, and then fell off. He stood. Another spot on his jacket was burning. He let out a groan of torment as his hand swatted the flames.

Panic stricken, he searched the room. The entire wall surrounding the fireplace was completely engulfed. Fire covered the hardwood floor and was winding its way toward the carpet. The high vaulted ceiling crackled and sizzled as it caught fire. Desperately, he scanned the room. He had seen her fall right in front of the hearth. Could she have moved? Could her body have rolled? Had the bastard taken her with him when he left?

He was so preoccupied in looking for a body that he missed it. Frowning, he glanced back, shook his head, and then moved slowly forward. He squatted and peered closely at the carpet. He ran his hand lightly across the pile of ashes, but was unwilling to accept the inevitable. "Victory's dream," he thought, "has come true." His mind reeled. The killer had taken the trouble to burn her body before setting the mansion on fire. If the murderer went to the trouble of both decapitating and burning her, then that left only one possibility.

A hand clasped his shoulder. He lifted desolate eyes to his cousin's face. Sorrow and compassion filled the green eyes that stared back at him. The earl's chestnut hair was singed in several places. Andrew watched as a large chunk of flesh withered, turned to ash, and then fell from his friend's cheek. His eyes followed the path of the flakes as they fell to the floor and mixed with those already on the carpet. His kind was extremely susceptible to ultraviolet rays and to fire. Only another porphyrian would know that.

Several feet away, a gold shimmer caught his eye. Still in shock, he sifted through the debris until he held the necklace in his hand. The points of the tiny crucifix dug into his palm as his fist clenched. Abruptly, he stood.

"I'm sorry," quietly offered Jordan. He now understood that, until this moment, his friend had been able to avoid accepting his wife's death.

Andrew stared hard at the ash-strewn floor. Images of Victory flowed through his thoughts like a waterfall that was cascading and tumbling through his mind. Slowly, they were replaced by a vision of his daughter who was lying unconscious in her hospital bed.

"She needs you."

He looked at his friend and nodded. "I know."

"There's nothing you can do here."

He gazed longingly at all that was left of the woman he loved. His wife, who had been plagued for weeks by nightmares predicting her peril, was gone forever.

Hurriedly, he turned away. "Let's get back to the hospital."

Chapter 10:
The Blood Bath

The two men strode swiftly down the hospital corridor. Andrew probed everyone he passed. He could discern no deliberate intent to cause harm to his daughter. Suddenly, he stopped and stared at a young nurse. She was bending over her desk and checking charts. Feeling his eyes on her, she turned and smiled politely. Andrew hesitated, but then smiled back, as he realized that she had only been checking Laural's chart along with those of the other patients on her shift. He felt the tension draining from his body as he approached his daughter's room.

"You're expecting more trouble?" Jordan asked with great concern. He nodded at two of his colleagues who were standing guard on either side of Laural's door. Normally, bodyguards would never be allowed to remain there, but the hospital's administration had given their authorization because of Andrew's status and connections.

"Any problems?" queried Andrew before entering.

Tim Cooper, the taller and broader of the two, shook his head. "The only two in or out since we arrived were the nurse and Dana."

Jordan frowned. "Dana's gone?"

Tim nodded. "According to John, she left right after he arrived."

They pushed through the door. John Carpenter, a lean tall man dressed in a business suit, stood as they entered. He was about 40 with dark hair and eyes that automatically scanned everyone who crossed the threshold.

The men seated themselves by the side of the bed. Before taking his chair, Andrew moved to his daughter's side. He stood and studied her for long moments, while stroking her arm. Sighing, he turned back to the others.

John opened his briefcase. Extracting a metal flask with PS4 etched across the front, he leaned forward, picked up three plastic cups from the bedside table, and poured the reddish-brown liquid into the glasses. He handed a cup to each person, took a seat, leaned back, and slowly sipped his drink. "I think Jordan's question is a good one." His eyes flicked toward the bed and then back to the marquis. "It's pertinent to security. Are you expecting more trouble?"

Andrew cocked a brow.

"I didn't mean to eavesdrop," explained the head of security, as he placed his drink on the table. "I've been monitoring all conversations within earshot and just happened to catch yours along with the rest."

Andrew nodded. "Keep monitoring," he agreed.

Jordan shot a strange look at him, but said nothing.

Andrew stared into his glass for a long time and then confronted them. "Whoever was behind this was a porphyrian."

"How do you know?"

"The murderer screamed 'abomination' at Victory just before he killed her. Besides, the method indicates someone who had knowledge of who she was and how to cause fatal damage."

Dana pulled up the collar of her trench coat against the frigid January air. She slowed her steps, as she turned into the walkway leading to the Willow Grove Foundation for Continuing Education. After slipping her key into the lock, she pushed open the glass door. She hurried through the lobby, but tensed at the sound of approaching footsteps.

"Good evening, Miss Maxwell."

She relaxed and pressed the elevator button. "Good evening, Sam," she offered to the night watchman.

"You should ask Mr. Andrew for better working hours," he said jovially.

"And a raise," she responded, as the elevator doors closed.

After entering her office, she sat at her desk and pulled her chair close to the monitor. She began sifting through the email. She opened the message from their safe house and read Joe's confirmation that the most recent "refugees" had arrived without incident. They were being briefed and would be sent over in the morning.

"All this cloak-and-dagger," she thought vehemently. "We shouldn't be hiding from them. They should be hiding from us."

She sat back and closed her eyes, as she massaged her neck.

She really needed a break. Her thoughts were becoming more erratic and hostile. Could Victory's murder have rattled her more than she thought? She had to admit that there had been no love lost between the marchioness and herself. In the beginning, she had even considered Andrew's wife to be a rival. But, over the years, she had come to respect and accept the woman. She also had grown extremely fond of the woman's daughter.

Why should Laural's mother have died at the hands of a lesser being? She was startled out of her dark thoughts by the fax machine. She turned to face the device. Leaning over, she picked up the newly printed page. The lines seemed to jump from the paper.

"How did you like the show? Act I, Scene 1: The Blood Bath. Hold the applause. Wait until you see Act II."

Dana gasped at the insidious implication of the words.

"What's wrong?"

Startled, she whirled around and dropped the fax on the floor. Her face was as white as the paper that she had been holding. She watched transfixed as it floated like a leaf to the carpet. She stared as Andrew bent over and retrieved the sheet. He held it out to her, but she shook her head.

"Read it," she insisted. Goosebumps covered her flesh and she rubbed her arms.

Frowning, he looked from the paper to the woman standing in front of him. He turned it over and handed it back. He looked at her strangely as she took the paper, but refrained from making any comment.

Confused, she looked down and gasped. "It's gone."

"What's gone?"

"There was some writing on it a moment ago. A sinister message inferring that what happened to Victory was deliberate and implying the worse was yet to come."

His body stiffened with suppressed rage. "Where did you get it?"

She looked to the fax machine.

He followed her gaze. "Fine," he said shortly, "I'll see if the telephone company can trace the call. But first I want to talk to you."

They moved over to the large rectangular cherry wood table. The table was used for conferences and it seated a dozen board members.

The huge table with its empty chairs looked deserted and strangely bereft. Andrew closed his eyes to block the image of Victory seated next to him as she always was during their meetings.

Dana warily eyed him. Had he picked up on her most recent thoughts or was he still angry about the confrontation at the hospital? Unable to endure the tension, she voiced her concerns.

"Andrew, I'm frightened. That note spooked me and the fact that the print disappeared has me scared. It's like someone is playing some sort of cat-and-mouse game with me as the prey."

He looked away. His eyes fell on his wife's office door. As his gaze drifted across her neatly scripted name on the plaque, the pain engulfed him. Clamping down hard on his grief, he glared at Dana and then shook his head. "Isn't that just a little narcissistic? So far, the only prey has been my wife – unless you know something I don't," he added, while intently studying her.

She defiantly lifted her chin. "Is that why you followed me here instead of staying at the hospital with Laural?"

Greenish blue eyes bore into her. "You know that only Jordan and I have the ability to discern your thoughts."

They stared at each other. They both knew why Andrew instead of her fiancé was there.

"All right. Do it," she offered tensely.

After several seconds, he sat back. His troubled turquoise eyes stared into the distance. No hint of duplicity regarding Victory's death had been evident, but her mind was full of disturbing ideas about diurnals.

"Did I pass inspection?"

Her voice jolted him out of his reverie. He nodded.

She sighed. "I would never harm Victory or Laural. You're right. What I said did sound self-centered, but I've been having intrusive thoughts. I feel like someone's watching me. I've been edgy and feeling like I need to take a break before I break down."

He stared at her for several seconds. "Any ideas?"

She bristled. "Are you asking if someone is manipulating me?"

He didn't respond and her temper flared. She stood up abruptly and slammed her fist on the table. "Damn it, Andrew, you know there isn't anyone left with that kind of power – except for you," she added warily.

"And we both know what you think of my abilities."

She turned her back and walked over to the bookcase. Sliding open one of the wooden panels, she extracted a bottle of PS4 and two glasses. Setting them on the table, she poured the fluid and then handed one of the glasses to her companion. Lifting the glass, she sipped slowly, while watching him over the rim.

"I know you've been through a lot and I shouldn't have said what I did, but that's how I feel. Laural's in a coma, Victory's dead, and we're getting anonymous threats through the fax machine."

"And now is the time you want to cut and run. You really haven't changed much over the years, have you?"

She glared at him. "I'd have to be stupid not to be worried. After all, it's not like we can seek conventional aid. Whoever killed Victory knew exactly who and what she was. And you, the strongest among us, wasn't even able to do anything to prevent it."

He flinched as her words struck him like a blow.

"I'm sorry," she said, as she touched his sleeve, "but I need a break. I needed one before and this has only made it worse. I've been having violent urges toward diurnals, even ones I like and trust. What happened to Victory has made me want to take all the diurnals I can find and choke the life out of them. I'd really rather take some time off before I do something I'll regret."

"I came here to find out if you had any ideas about who could be behind my wife's murder. I'm relieved you checked out clean because, when I find them, I'll be having some violent urges of my own."

"Is that right?"

Suddenly, Dana gasped. Andrew turned to see a man dressed in a trench coat covering a navy crewneck sweater and dark blue woolen dress slacks approaching from the doorway.

"I'll call security," stated Dana, as she lifted the receiver.

"Don't bother. Your security guard was the one who let me in."

"And why would he do that?" challenged Dana, while taking a menacing step toward the intruder.

Andrew lifted his arm in front of his niece to block her advance.

The man made note of the gesture. He studied them for a long time before responding.

"Because," he said arrogantly, "I am Detective Addams from homicide."

"You don't look like a police officer," Dana shot back, as her brown eyes narrowed suspiciously.

The man removed his identification from the left breast pocket of his jacket. He flipped it open to reveal the photo, identification card, and shield of Detective Brent Addams, Homicide Division, District of Columbia Metropolitan Police Department.

Andrew spoke for the first time. "What can we do for you, detective?"

With a speculative glint in his steel-gray eyes, Addams looked back and forth between the handsome man and his beautiful companion.

Andrew recognized the flash of cynicism and haunted visage of a man who had seen too much of humanity's pain and suffering. Even before the words were spoken, he knew that he would not like what the detective had to say.

Addams smiled thinly, but the expression didn't lessen the hardness of his gaze. "I'm here to ask you to come with me to the station."

"Why can't you question Lord Gabriel here?" asked Dana.

Andrew sighed wearily and massaged his temples. "Because they consider me a suspect. Isn't that right, detective?" he asked bitterly.

"You can't possibly think Lord Gabriel killed his wife," Dana asserted, while bristling with outrage.

Again, the marquis spoke before the detective could respond. "In a case like this one, the husband is always a prime suspect," he said despondently. He was not sure if he really cared what the detective thought. "However," he continued, "I did give a statement to the officers at the hospital."

Addams shook his head, which caused a stray lock of auburn hair to slip onto his forehead.

"There are some disturbing discrepancies that require further explanation."

"Why don't you just influence his thoughts and be done with this?" thought Dana with barely controlled irritation.

"That's a direct violation of our moral code." His conscience felt a slight twinge as he remembered his use of influence on the firefighter. "Besides, it would only be a short-term solution."

"Better that than being behind bars."

Andrew slightly chuckled, but quickly hid the gesture behind a cough. The detective continued to glare at him.

"I'm sorry, Detective Addams. It's been a really rough day. As you know, my daughter is in the hospital and I'm loath to leave her for too long. Could we possibly conduct your questioning there?"

Addams thought, "These rich bastards always think that they can call the shots." But aloud he said, "No, I'm sorry, but this requires you to be at the police station."

His eyes sharpened. "Do I need an attorney?"

"That's up to you."

For a moment, Andrew considered Dana's idea. After all, going to answer these fruitless inquiries would be a waste of valuable time. Instead, he could be tracking his wife's killer and insuring the wellbeing of his child. Staring beyond the detective, he noticed two uniform officers standing in the hallway.

"Am I being charged?" he asked, while trying to reign in his anger.

"That depends on if you come in willingly and the outcome of my questioning."

Chapter 11:

Connections

Doctor James Brenner entered Laural Gabriel's hospital room for the third time that evening. After a cursory inspection of the patient's vital statistics, he returned the chart to its holder at the end of the bed. He moved to the young woman's side and gripped the guard rail as he studied her pale face.

Again, he wondered why he was so drawn to this particular patient. Appreciating her long golden hair, he acknowledged that she certainly was beautiful and had delicate features. But he had seen many beautiful female patients before. It must have been her air of tragic vulnerability that intrigued him. According to the patient history sheet and the interview with her dad, she had suffered a horrific shock. But that alone did not account for the inexplicable magnetism – at least not all of it. He spontaneously had developed an urge to protect her and a desire to alleviate her distress as if it were a physical pain.

Closely watching her, he detected rapid eye movements under her closed lids. Instinctively sensing her emotional turmoil, he unconsciously reached for her hand. "Come back to us, Laural," he whispered, while brushing back a lock of golden hair from her cheek.

Suddenly, his mind was seized and held captive by horrific mental images. He jerked back in astonishment and dropped Laural's hand. Pictures of blood, gore, severed heads, and decapitated bodies raced through his mind. As he continued to back away from the bed, the thoughts faded. He shook his head in confusion. Silver eyes questioningly probed his patient.

Had they shared some sort of brief psychic link? The woman in his mind had been an exact older version of his patient. He was aware of the details of Lady Gabriel's death and those images had been too specific to be anything except visions of her. "On the other hand," he deliberated, while trying to instill reason into what he had just experienced, "since I'm so obsessed with this case, could I have imagined the thoughts?"

As he stepped closer to the bed, he checked his watch. Three days straight with hardly any sleep was probably all that his mind could take. Better clock out and get some rest. Cautiously moving closer to his patient, he reached for her hand and paused. Instead, he quickly leaned forward and kissed her cheek. With one more glance at the sleeping teen, he swiftly left the room.

"Looks like the good doctor has a crush on the boss' daughter," noted John after the physician left the room.

"It would seem so," agreed Jordan distractedly. "It's fortunate he reads clean," he added, as his troubled gaze followed the doctor's progress down the hall. He was not sure why but James Brenner's interest in Laural made him feel uneasy.

John shook his head. "Never thought I'd see the day when the boss would have us prying into their minds. I know he's been through a lot, but it seems like a severe breech of ethics to me."

Jordan shrugged. "He just lost his wife and wants to make sure the same thing doesn't happen to his child. After we find out who did this and why, Andrew will not feel like he has to be constantly on guard in order to protect Laural."

The green eyes remained disturbed as they lingered thoughtfully at the nurses' station where Doctor Brenner had paused and was conversing with the matronly head nurse. Just then, the elevator doors opened. Jordan's focus shifted and his brows drew together as he watched Dana approach. She stopped in front of him. They just stood and stared at each other.

John cleared his throat. "I'm sure you two would like some privacy. I could use some coffee," he announced, as he glanced at his watch. "The boss said he'd be back shortly, but that was over an hour ago. Maybe," he said with a voice tinged with concern, "in light of what he told us, I should check on him."

Dana threw a brief glance at him before refocusing on Jordan. "Andrew was taken to the police station for questioning."

John was startled, but Jordan kept his gaze firmly fixed on his fiancée. "Why?"

Her eyes flashed. "Because he would rather stay true to his ethics than influence the detective to let him go."

"What's wrong with you?" Jordan asked, as his green eyes probed her.

"I think Andrew's first priority should be protecting his child, not indulging in diurnal mind games."

John stiffened and Dana turned to face him. "Sorry, John. I didn't mean to imply you weren't doing your job."

He nodded and then said to Jordan, "Let me know if you need me. Otherwise, I'll be looking for a vending machine."

After he had gone, Jordan turned on her. Fire flashed from his eyes as he demanded, "What is wrong with you? First, you attacked Andrew only minutes after his wife had been murdered and now you're bad-mouthing him in front of his staff."

She stared for several seconds and then exhaled slowly. "I need a break."

He strove to keep control of his temper. "Go home and get some rest. We've got enough people to cover here."

"I need more than a good night's sleep."

He probed her thoughts. She flinched, but didn't draw back. His jaw hardened and his eyes became glacial. Abruptly, he turned his back and strode into Laural's room.

Chapter 12:

The Battered Tenant

Cornwall, England, 1739

Jordan Rush, Earl of Rockford, stood silently, while watching his friend as he toiled in the field. Andrew furrowed into the ground, took several seeds from a pouch on his waist, dropped them into the impression, and covered the opening with topsoil. Then, he repeated the process. Jordan's gaze traveled beyond the bent figure of the marquis and other field workers to where Penbrook Castle stood sentinel over the craggy Camelford cliffs.

One of the field hands glanced up and spied the earl. He smiled and waved. Jordan shouted a greeting which finally captured Andrew's attention. Flashing a broad smile, the marquis laid his hoe aside and walked toward his friend. He doffed his cap and wiped the sweat from his brow, as he fell into step beside his cousin.

"You work so hard one would think you were the tenant instead of the lord," Jordan joked with his green eyes twinkling. "Why do you do it?"

Andrew glanced around at the other field hands who laboriously were planting seeds in the fertile soil. "I think working side-by-side with them earns their respect and it makes me more aware of who they really are."

Jordan looked up at the blazing sun and then down at his friend's sweat-soaked tunic. "Why not just read them and see for yourself if you have their respect?"

Andrew was shocked and outraged. "I would never condone such a thing."

"Why not?" asked Jordan with confusion.

The young marquis strode past him and hurried into the castle. Jordan had to rush to keep up. Inside, the Lord of the Castle swiftly climbed the stone stairs, walked purposefully down the hall, and paused beside a large oak door before entering the bedroom. Despite the thickness of the wood, the sound of a couple in the throws of passion still could be heard.

"Shall I enter?" asked Andrew.

Jordan's face reddened. He was embarrassed to be listening to the couple's private moments. "Of course not."

"Why not? After all, I am 'Lord' here."

"Being lord doesn't give you the right to invade other's privacy."

"So," said Andrew with raised brows, "you would have me stay out of their bedrooms, but it's acceptable to invade their minds?"

Just then, a serving maid ran toward them. "Lord Gabriel, come quick. It's Johnny," the girl exclaimed, while trying to catch her breath.

He rushed down the steps and out into the courtyard. A group of onlookers were surrounding a figure slumped on the ground. As he approached, the crowd parted. He stared in shocked dismay at the bleeding and battered body of one of his tenants.

"What happened?" he bellowed into the crowd.

The peasants glanced surreptitiously at each other, while uncomfortably shuffling their feet. Somewhere in the distance, a baby cried out and was quieted quickly. No one spoke as the wrath of the lord sought a target.

"My Lord?"

Andrew turned back to the prone figure. His heart ached at the sight of the teen's battered face with blood oozing from several cuts. The youth struggled to speak.

Kneeling beside the lad, Andrew spoke softly. "Quiet now, Johnny. I'll have a couple of the maids tend to your wounds. You can enjoy the company and regale them with accounts of what happened to you."

Johnny smiled weakly.

"Tell me, lad, what happened?"

Johnny's voice was so weak that he had to strain to hear. "We were headed to market to sell some of our grain. Lord Maxwell's men were upon us before we even knew they were there." He paused as a coughing spasm seized him. He winced at the pain in his ribs.

Andrew held him until the spasm subsided. "Where's your wife, Johnny? Where's Mabel and little John?"

The lad squeezed his eyes as if trying to block out a terrible vision. "They're here, my Lord. They roughed us up something fierce and stole our grain. I'm sure they meant to kill us, but guards from our keep ran them off."

Andrew gestured for several guards to move the peasant into the castle. He barked orders to several more servants who were dispatched to check on Johnny's wife and child. Finally, he ordered the stolen grain to be replaced.

Jordan laid a hand on his friend's arm. "Sooner or later, you're going to have to confront him."

Andrew nodded, as he stared at the spot on the ground where his tenant had lain.

"The longer you wait, the bolder he gets."

"Fratricide is a sin I'm not sure I'm willing to commit."

"Even though he killed your father?"

"If I only knew for sure," sighed the marquis, while staring in the direction of his brother's domain.

Chapter 13:

The Detective's Theory

Andrew surveyed his surroundings. The small room was bleak in its starkness. The fluorescent lights cast the furniture into sharp relief and highlighted the putrid chartreuse of the walls. He dropped his jacket over the straight-back wooden chair and stared steadily across the scarred oak table at his inquisitor.

Addams stared back into the penetrating gaze. Dizziness and nausea threatened. He dropped his eyes to his water glass. He sipped slowly until his equilibrium returned and then set aside the glass. Unruly auburn hair fell across his forehead and he irritably pushed it back.

"Sorry the accommodations aren't what you're accustomed to," he said sarcastically.

Andrew placed his elbows on the table and steepled his fingers. "I'm not here for a social call," he commented dryly. "Let's get to whatever is on your mind, detective, so I can get back to my daughter."

Addams took stock of the other man. Realizing that the marquis was not the type to be intimidated, he stared hard into the unwavering gaze and refused to be rushed. The nausea returned and, while reconsidering his position, he glanced toward the door. If he were ill, it would be better to speed the questioning along before it became necessary for someone else to do it. He knew several guys who were chomping at the bit to get a crack at interrogating Lord Gabriel. They were anxious to take credit for any information that would break the high-profile case. He turned his stern gaze back to the marquis. He had been working too hard on this case for him to let someone else get the credit.

His steely gaze hardened. "For someone who is so concerned about getting back to his daughter, you didn't seem to be in much of a hurry when you were with Ms. Maxwell."

The greenish blue eyes darkened. "How I conduct my private life is none of your business."

Auburn brows lifted. "That depends on how this investigation turns out. Tell me how you came to report the slaying of your wife."

Andrew sighed in exasperation. "You have that information in my earlier statement."

The detective tapped his ballpoint against the side of his notepad. "Give it to me – again."

Andrew leaned back in his chair and was silent for so long that the detective thought that he was going to plead his constitutional right to the fifth amendment.

"I drove home from work with my daughter. When we entered the house, my wife was lying on the living room floor. Someone had decapitated her. There was blood pooled around the body. Her head was a few feet away. There was more blood on the carpet near her head, but not as much. My daughter began screaming hysterically and then suddenly went rigid. Her eyes rolled up into her head and she passed out. I carried her to the car and started for the hospital. I was so shocked and upset that it took several minutes before I realized I hadn't called the police. I then did so on my cell phone. I told them what we had found and where they could reach me."

Addams looked up from his notebook. "Is that your statement?"

"You know it is."

"Then, how do you explain the fire?"

He raised his eyebrows. "I can't. Can you?"

Addams leaned back until his chair groaned in protest. Pushing up his sleeves, he said soberly, "Not yet. In the meantime, I'm working on a theory. Would you like to hear what I've come up with so far?"

Andrew briefly closed his eyes as he struggled for control. "Why don't we dispense with the word games and skip to the bottom line, detective. Your theory is I killed my wife and set my own home on fire to cover it up."

"Did you?"

Andrew abruptly stood, which sent his chair crashing to the floor. Bloodlust pounded through his veins as raw fury coursed through his body. He propped his palms on the table and leaned menacingly toward the detective.

Instinctively, Addams slid his chair back several inches.

The temptation to put his fist through the investigator's smug smirk was overwhelming. Only the realization that then they would have a valid reason to detain him allowed the detective to keep his yellow teeth.

As the marquis' six-foot-three-inch frame towered over him, Addams had to crane his neck to keep eye contact.

"I've had a really bad day, detective, and my tolerance has reached its limit. My wife is dead and my daughter's in a coma. I don't have the time or patience for mind games, so let's keep this simple. I had no motive and no opportunity and, most of all, no desire to harm my cherished wife. I'm sure you've checked into my background and determined I wasn't carrying an extensive life insurance policy on my wife. I'm also sure your investigation has deduced we were happily married with no affairs on either side."

"I haven't had time to conduct a thorough investigation, but you and Ms. Maxwell looked pretty close earlier. In fact, she seemed downright possessive and very protective of you."

"You're accusing me of having an affair with my own niece?" he demanded incredulously.

They glared at each other. "Are you?"

"I'm not even going to dignify that with an answer." He leaned away from the detective and covered his eyes with his hand for a moment. He was so weary. All he wanted was to get back to Laural. "Look, detective, I appreciate your diligence, but you know I was in a car with my daughter several miles away when the crime occurred."

"A daughter who is conveniently in a coma and can't support your story."

He straightened and then dispassionately studied the man, as he considered snapping the man's neck like a twig. Deliberately, he lifted his jacket and pulled it on. His icy eyes raked over the other man. "The next time you and I speak, it will be in the presence of my attorney."

Addams stood and nodded curtly. A knock sounded at the door.

"Is everything okay?" asked a uniformed police officer who poked his head around the door. With speculation, he eyed the fallen chair and the marquis before glancing at his colleague for confirmation.

"Lord Gabriel was just leaving. Escort him out of the building - for now," he mumbled under his breath as the door closed.

Chapter 14:

Descending into Darkness

The door slowly swung inward. A sliver of light stretched across the floor. It widened as the door continued to move. A dark silhouette was framed in the doorway, but temporarily was overshadowed by the light from the hall.

Instantly alert, Jordan tensed, probed, and then relaxed. "You're back."

Andrew nodded, as he softly closed the door behind him. He moved to the side of the bed and stared at his daughter. He took her hand in his and looked toward his friend.

"Any problems?"

"Not unless you consider having to persuade every nurse that comes in here that it's all right for me to stay."

Relieved, he nodded. "I've had to do some persuading of my own in order to be allowed back in." He leaned forward to kiss Laural's cheek. "John and the others?" he asked, as he straightened.

"They returned to the agency to start the investigation. Speaking of investigations, how did it go at the police station? Do they have anything useful?"

His face hardened. "Yes, as a matter of fact, they've already solved the case," he responded sarcastically.

"What's the catch?"

"I am."

Jordan raised his brows.

Andrew raked his hand through his hair and winced at the unexpected pain. As he stared down at the seared flesh on his palm, he continued. "Detective Addams has decided that I murdered Victory, burned the house down to cover my tracks, and somehow managed to put my daughter in a coma so she can't tell anyone."

Jordan studied his friend. His platinum hair had grown back, but the flesh on his hand was still raw, although new skin was starting to cover the wound.

"I hope you used your persuasion. Because with Addams' suspicions, it would have been hell to explain that burn," he said, while gesturing toward Andrew's hand.

The marquis nodded in agreement. "By the way, I didn't get a chance to thank you for going in after me." His eyes examined his friend's cheek where the new skin was starting to cover the ugly raw flesh. "If it hadn't been for you, I'm not sure I would have come back out."

They remained silent for several minutes. Andrew studied his daughter's pale face and flaccid features. He braced himself for what he had to do. It was going to be a supreme test of his mental fortitude. He hoped that he would not fail. He must not fail. She was all that he had left.

"She's gone, isn't she?"

Startled out of his reverie, Andrew stared blankly at his friend for a few seconds. "Yes."

"I caught a brief glimpse of her packing. I don't think she meant for me to know but it slipped."

Andrew's temper flared. "Up to her old tricks. Leaving without facing her responsibilities. Well, you know Dana was never good at confrontation."

"Think you can do it?" Jordan asked, while nodding toward the bed in order to avoid discussing his fiancée's desertion.

He defiantly glared back. "You mean convince my daughter to come back into a world that no longer has her mother in it? How can I when I'm not even sure I want to be here myself."

The earl stood to face his friend. "Well, I suggest you decide and fix that decision firmly in your mind before you try to bring her back."

After the earl left the room, Andrew stood and stared at the closed door for a long time. He knew his friend would be standing guard in the hallway so that father and daughter could have as much time as they needed. Tomorrow, the staff would not even remember that they had been here. He turned to his daughter. Picking up her limp hand, he firmly held it in his grasp. As he studied her face, he caught his breath. She reminded him so much of her mother. The golden hair, smooth skin, and firm but gentle features tore at his heart. He moaned as he closed his eyes against the pain.

Instantly, memories flooded his mind. Images of Victory, Laural, and him at the beach in Cape Cod during the summer. The three of them chasing each other through the surf, collecting sea shells, and watching glorious sunsets. Together as a family riding across fields filled with heather at their Cornwall estate. The castle at Camelford had been the favorite home of his wife and daughter. Victory loved it because of the uniqueness of the castle and Laural due to its sheer barbaric beauty.

He opened his eyes and, as he studied his daughter, realized that they could never again do any of those things as a family. "I swear I'll find whoever did this and make them pay." Remembering Jordan's words, he pulled himself together. Did he really believe that life was worth living without Victory?

The last time he had lost a loved one, he had not thought that he could bear the loneliness. He had removed himself from the world of the living because there had not been any worthwhile reason to stay. But this time, he had someone who needed him.

He almost could hear his wife's admonishing voice for even considering abandoning their daughter. In Victory's nightmares, he had not been able to protect them. In reality, he had not been able to save his wife either, but Dana was right. If he lost his daughter, it would be his own fault.

He carefully studied Laural. Her eyes moved restlessly under closed lids. He watched her chest as it rose and fell with each breath. She lay defenseless and vulnerable. She had become a psychic prisoner of her own pain. He gently brushed her hair and let his fingers trail across her cheek. Moisture dampened his hand. Drawing back, he stared at the glistening teardrop as it slowly ran down his finger.

He closed his eyes and took several deep breaths to clear his thoughts. Focusing on his goal, he pushed outward with his mind. Slowly, he approached his daughter's psyche while he gently checked resistance. Finding none, he allowed himself to enter the foreground of her thoughts.

Gray mist like a gossamer veil parted as he penetrated the surface level. A kaleidoscope of chaotic images assaulted him as he probed deeper. Blood dripping, coalescing, coagulating; distorted faces; blood running from eyes, noses, and mouths. Blood growing thicker, viscous, deep red into black. Blackness, utter and complete, cold and flat. An emotional void descending deeper into darkness. A deep pit full of fear, loneliness, and pain.

Something slimy and cold slithered across his awareness. Repulsed, he drew back. He hardened his resolve and pushed further inside the deepest regions of his daughter's mind. The slimy thing tried to coil itself around his consciousness. Its tendrils grasped, bound, and pulled him down. He pushed past the point of no return, past the point where there was any semblance of sanity, past the bounds of safety, down into the deep dark pit.

Abruptly, he was bathed in a golden light. The glow was subdued and flickered weakly like a candle glow dimmed by an ever-present breeze. A familiar consciousness surrounded him, engulfed him, and diffused through him. The presence grew stronger, vibrant, and curious. He felt his daughter's life force, but he felt as if he were sensing it from a distance. Only this remnant of Laural's consciousness remained. It was objectively observing, but not actually involved.

"Laural?" he questioned warily. Briefly, there was an intensification of the sensation of consciousness along with a lifting of awareness. "I've come to bring you back." The sensation began receding like tendrils of mist drifting through the rain. Desperately, he projected his own essence into the mist. The two seemed to merge. He was unable to distinguish where his ended and her's began.

He floated for what seemed to be an eternity. He remained giving and nurturing while allowing himself to be used as a conduit for her pain. In order to save her, he instinctively sensed that he must be willing to take her deepest psychic trauma and add it to his own emotional burden even if it meant sacrificing his own spiritual cohesion.

He felt pressure. Pressure from beyond. Disoriented and groggy, he needed several seconds to register the sensation. Another pressure came, but, this time, he was able to identify it as a hand on his shoulder.

"Andrew," whispered Jordan, "it's morning. I can't hold the staff off forever."

The marquis uncrossed his arms and lifted his head from his daughter's bed. "I must have dozed off."

Jordan studied him. "You look like hell."

Too drained to respond, he just nodded.

"I hope it worked."

"So do I," said Andrew, while looking at his child and lifting her hand to his lips. "So do I."

After replacing her hand on the sheet, he quietly followed the earl from the room.

He gave his friend a long look. "I hope I don't look as bad as you."

The earl shook his head. "You look worse."

"Why don't you head home and get some rest?"

"And you?"

The turquoise eyes darkened ominously. "Whoever murdered my wife is not going to get a chance with my daughter. I'm not leaving her unguarded. I'll wait until security arrives."

"Speaking of security," said the earl, nodding toward the hallway, "the good doctor made so many visits last night I was thinking of adding him to the security team."

Andrew scowled, as he glanced over his shoulder to find Dr. Brenner almost upon them.

"Good morning, gentlemen," he offered; nodding as he entered the room.

Andrew inclined his head, then turned back to Jordan. "He wants to take her to get an EEG."

"Since you could be tied up for a while, why don't I go to work?"

"Good idea," replied the marquis. He walked back into his daughter's room, but stopped short. Jordan peered around his shoulder. They both stared in astonishment while viewing the spectacle before them. Laural sat upright in bed. She was awake, alert, and conversing animatedly with the doctor, while he checked her vital signs.

Jordan smiled broadly and slapped Andrew on the back. "Congratulations, old man. Looks like you did it! I can't wait to share the good news. Everyone will be so relieved. Do you still want me to send security over?"

Andrew nodded, but he was lost in thought. He continued to stare at his daughter. For the first time since the tragedy, he felt a slight lifting of the pain that had clamped a vise grip on his heart. The doctor looked up when he entered the room. A look of confused consternation covered his face. Following the direction of the doctor's glance, Laural noticed her father. She smiled tremulously. Andrew thought his heart would break as he read the pain in her eyes.

He approached the bed slowly as if afraid that his daughter's recovery was an illusion that would shatter if he got too close. He looked from the doctor to his daughter and back again.

Dr. Brenner shrugged. "I don't have any explanation," he said. His eyes softened as they rested on Laural. "Sometimes, it happens that way with coma patients. They just spontaneously recover. However, just to make sure, I would still like to run some tests."

"Tests?" queried Laural.

Both men looked at her. "Don't worry, ma petite," he said, while ruffling her hair. "They won't hurt."

Laural appeared momentarily annoyed and embarrassed.

Bemused by her reaction, Andrew turned to the doctor. "When will she be ready to go home?"

Laural tensed.

"Don't worry. I'm not taking you back there," he projected silently.

Laural's eyes widened for a moment and he realized that she had forgotten about the manifestation of her porphyrian abilities.

Not sure about what he had missed, Dr. Brenner looked from one to the other. "I'd like to keep her overnight for observation."

After the physician left, Andrew reached into his pocket and extracted the crucifix. He watched as it shimmered in the light. A sharp intake of breath drew his attention. Laural was staring at the necklace with a mixture of sorrow and desire etched on her young face. Slowly, Andrew reached behind her neck and clasped the chain with the tiny cross.

"I'm sure your mom would want you to have it."

Their eyes met and held. Tears flowed copiously down her cheeks. As her slight frame shook with sobs, he gathered her into his arms. He held her for a long time, crooning and rocking gently while his own tears flowed.

Later, the bedside phone rang. Glancing toward his daughter,

Andrew quickly snatched up the receiver. Laural still slept. Her rhythmic breathing gave evidence that she had not been disturbed.

"Hello?"

"Andrew," said Jordan. "You need to get over here as soon as possible."

"What's wrong?"

"I received a tip that we are going to have a surprise audit tomorrow."

"So?" he asked with great annoyance. Jordan could handle a routine audit.

"So, I've been looking over the records. It appears we have several unaccountable expenditures – personal expenditures made with federal grant money."

Chapter 15:

The Traitor

Dana lifted her head from the pillow and groaned. She checked her bedside clock. Nearly three hours had passed this time. As the lethargy lifted, she calculated. This was the fourth episode in the past three months. Slowly, she sat up. She still felt slightly dizzy. She sighed and leaned back against the headboard. Each blackout was accompanied by dizziness, nausea, and headaches. The reality hit her like a splash of ice water.

She was pregnant. She didn't want to accept it, but the evidence was clear. She closed her eyes. No, she couldn't do it. Having a child was always a risk, one that she was determined to avoid at all costs. Let the Victorys and the Crystals of the world make that kind of sacrifice. She had no desire to put her life on the line in order to reproduce.

As she gathered her strength, she glanced around the bedroom of the townhouse that she and Jordan had shared for the past two decades. Pictures of them were scattered around the apartment. Dana smiled as she remembered the places and events portrayed in the photos. Souvenirs and mementos from various trips were placed decoratively throughout the room. Her eyes softened as they rested on the alpaca carpet in front of the fireplace. They had spent many cozy winter nights making love on that carpet. Then her eyes hardened. Lovemaking was what had brought her to her present predicament.

She refused to go through with the pregnancy. She knew that her thoughts were traitorous, but she did not care. Another wave of nausea struck. Groaning, she rolled off of the bed and raced to the bathroom.

After the onslaught of morning sickness had subsided, she stood over the sink and splashed cold water on her face. As she reached for a towel, she tried to think. She stared at her reflection in the mirror while wiping the cloth across her mouth. Gradually, the image of fear and confusion was replaced by resolve and determination. Moments later, she reached for her luggage in the closet. She hastily grabbed items, haphazardly threw them in her suitcase, and raced down the hallway toward the front door.

Dana knew she had to go before anyone discovered her condition. If Jordan or Andrew found out, she would be forced to continue the unwanted pregnancy. She was sure that she was making the right choice. She had considered confiding in her fiancé or her prince, but was certain that they would care more about the unborn child than her safety. There was no getting around the fact that only fifty percent of porphyrian women who gave birth survived the ordeal. However, since only ten percent of females ever became pregnant, most considered the risk worth taking in order to perpetuate the species.

Even though she wanted to tell Jordan about her dilemma, she knew that he would not keep such a secret from Andrew. If Andrew knew, any considerations other than childbirth would be terminated. "Along with my life," she thought bitterly, as she hefted the suitcase into the trunk. She had to go somewhere that was more private where she could be alone and think.

"Still," she thought wistfully, while sliding behind the wheel of the red BMW, "it would have been nice to share the news." She wanted to seek comfort and solace while obtaining support and guidance. She even had entertained the idea that they might understand her fear. However, something inside kept her quiet. Sometimes, it was almost as if her thoughts were not her own. Frowning, she slipped the key into the ignition. That was not quite right. She felt like she was operating on some basic instinctual level – driven like a salmon upstream. Unfortunately, unlike the salmon, she had no idea about what awaited at the end of her journey.

Driving north, she intuitively headed to Pennsylvania. She eventually pulled off of the highway and followed the signs to Willow Grove. Heading into the small suburb, she finally pulled up in front of a small one-story brick building. "This is where it all began." The Willow Grove Crematorium was the first in what had been a chain of funeral structures. These were the focal points of her father's plan to destroy humanity. "He would have succeeded," she reflected, "if Andrew and Jordan hadn't intervened."

Dana shuddered as she remembered how close her father, Craven Maxwell, had come to realizing his goal. She got out and walked up the steps. She stared at the door for a long time. As she straightened her shoulders, she decided that a serious reminder of the past was what she needed. The exorcism of her abhorrent thoughts should start in the place where the horror began. Afterwards, she might be able to clear her mind of her discordant thoughts and start anew.

Fitting the key into the lock, she opened the door and slowly stepped inside. The interior was dark and gloomy. As she moved forward, a shiver ran down her spine. She advanced hesitantly. Gooseflesh rose on her arms. She stepped behind the counter with its glass case of urns. Even more slowly, she approached the door leading to the basement. Licking suddenly dry lips, she opened the door.

She frowned as uneasy thoughts struck her. "Why is the place in such good repair? Why is it so clean and orderly?" Lying abandoned for almost two decades, it should have had some natural decay, dust, mold, and cobwebs. Andrew had not maintained it for the foundation's purposes because she would have known about it. "What kind of personal reason could he have for keeping the place operational?" Then, it occurred to her. "What if Andrew doesn't know?" The implication of that raised more questions.

Abruptly, she felt dizzy. "Oh, no," she thought, "not here." Dana spun around and tried to retrace her steps before the blackness overcame her. To her horror, she realized that she was not going to make it. Even more terrifying was the realization that she was not alone.

Chapter 16:

Part of the Plan

London, England, 1766

Dana Maxwell raked her long nails down her partner's back as she arched her hips. She ardently shook her head back and forth. As she screamed out her ecstasy, her long dark hair billowed like a curtain. The man rammed hard into her several more times, then finally proclaimed his pleasure as he released inside of her.

Completely spent, he rolled to the side and collapsed on top of the tangled sheets. His fingers lightly traced circles around her erect nipples. He murmured, "Mistress Maxwell, you certainly have a way with men."

"Only with you, my lord," she replied huskily. Her sultry gaze seared into his.

He chuckled. "You know when you look at me like that, I am putty in your hands and ready to do your every bidding."

"That's what I'm counting on," she replied, as her hand stroked its way down his body.

His eyes darkened and a throaty chuckle escaped his lips as he again climbed on top of her.

After the nobleman had gone, a knock sounded at the door. Frowning slightly, Dana shrugged into her robe. She thought that her influence had been strong enough. Had he returned for another round? "That man is insatiable," she thought, while heading toward the heavy oak portal.

She threw open the door and then stepped back startled. "How did you find me?"

Fury preceded the Earl of Rockford as he angrily strode into the room. He grabbed Dana by the arms, shook her several times, then roughly tossed her onto the bed. Towering above her, he raked his eyes coldly over her body and the rumpled sheets. "Still playing your father's whore to the lords of London?"

She swept her hair out of her eyes and glared back defiantly. "What right do you have to judge me? What I do is none of your concern."

He exhaled and his eyes softened. "It would be if you'd let it."

She stood and stepped past him. "You're not part of the plan."

He grabbed her arm. "What plan is that?"

She tried to jerk free, but he held fast.

"I know all about the plot to use the Prime Minister to get you and your father to the colonies," he said tersely.

Her eyes widened.

He dropped her arm. His fury evaporated and was replaced by disillusionment and disappointment. "So, it's true. You'd leave without so much as a word."

She realized too late that he had been fishing. "You don't own me," she responded defensively.

"But your father does?"

"You know the bond between parent and child is unbreakable. You don't know what it's like because both of your parents are dead and you've never had your will dominated."

"My parents wouldn't do that even if they were alive," he insisted indignantly.

"Well, mine does. So, until he has no further use for me, I would suggest you stay away or he'll dominate your will, too."

"Not if I kill him first," he threatened, as he strode out of the door.

Chapter 17:
The Stranger

Doctor James Brenner pushed the wheelchair through the open door of Laural's hospital room. He grinned broadly at the look of surprised delight on his patient's face. "Your chariot awaits, my lady."

Laural wrinkled her nose and laughed self-deprecatingly. "You know, I really am a 'Lady'," she reported, emphasizing the title. "At least in England where they care about those things."

"That's right," agreed the doctor, while lowering the side rail. "Your dad is a marquis, right?" he asked, as his silver eyes twinkled back at her. "Well, your ladyship, allow me to be your humble escort."

She searched his eyes earnestly trying to seek out any sign of mockery.

He sobered. "Did I say something wrong?"

She studied his open features, tousled ebony hair, strong brows, straight nose, sensual lips, and sparkling silver eyes. He appeared vital and strong. As he lowered the bed rail, his white lab coat parted and revealed a broad expanse of chest with muscles that strained against the thin material of his shirt. Her skin tingled as he took her hand to help her to the chair.

As she settled herself, she ventured hesitantly, "No, it's just at school ..." Biting her lip, she broke off. She was not sure how to explain that the kids picked on her because her father was so rich. Convincing her dad to let her go to school on a bus or by foot instead of in the limo had been hard. She hated being the kids' target.

"At school," he interjected smoothly, while wheeling her into the hallway, "the other kids were jealous and didn't understand so they teased you," he finished. Protectiveness surged through him as he sensed her pain.

"How did you guess?" she asked, while waving to one of the nurses as they passed. The surprised expression on the nurse's face made Laural realize how unique it was to have a doctor giving such personal attention to one of his patients. The thought brought a warm glow to her cheeks as she met the curious stares of other patients and staff.

"I had to put up with a lot of teasing in high school, too," he responded, while waiting for a patient to move aside.

"Really?" she asked, while glancing at him in surprise. She took a few moments to think about what he had said. It was hard to imagine that anyone who was as handsome and personable as her doctor could have suffered at the hands of his peers.

"Really," he confirmed, as they continued down the hall. His eyes traveled the length of her golden hair as it trailed behind the top of the chair. More than anything he wanted to run his hands through the tresses. "I was on the football team in high school."

She craned her head to look up at him. "Sounds like prime teasing material to me."

He laughed down at her. Her blue eyes sparkled like gems. She smiled back at him. His gaze fastened on her lips and lingered there for several long moments. Time seemed to stand still as he realized that he wanted to kiss her. Resisting temptation, he replied, "I'll agree that it was not much of a hardship, but, even then, I was serious about getting into med school. That meant intense studying. Eventually, I had to choose. I chose studying. My jock buddies decided I was a traitor to the team and ostracized me the rest of the year." That was putting it mildly, he reflected. Determined to punish their star quarterback for his desertion, his "friends" had harassed and made him the butt of their jokes for the rest of the year. He had been relieved to graduate and leave high school behind.

"How awful," she commiserated.

His introspection snapped from the past and he refocused on the present. He approached the elevator, pushed the down button, and then revolved the wheelchair.

"Where are we going?" she asked more out of curiosity than interest. As long as she was able to spend time with Jim, she didn't care where they went. "Am I developing a crush on my doctor?" she wondered, while staring into his sparkling silver eyes. Yes, she decided when his hand brushed against her arm and set off sparks of pleasure.

"It's a surprise," he offered, as he placed a hand on her shoulder.

Her breath caught in her throat as the look that he gave her sent shivers of anticipation cascading down her spine. She felt dizzy and lightheaded. She tore her gaze away while she tried to decide if what she was feeling stemmed from Jim's proximity, being out of bed, or the manifestation of her abilities.

Glancing up, she became aware of her pursuers. "Can't I have any privacy?" she thought.

"Sorry," Tim answered her silent question, "Your dad's orders."

"Well, at least be discreet."

"We would never dream of intruding," teased John with a glint gleaming in his dark eyes.

Laural rolled her eyes at the telepathic banter. "It's really kind of cool," she thought, "to be able to communicate without speaking." Then, she reconsidered. "How much of my thoughts are they actually able to read?"

"Only as much as you allow," John reassured.

She glanced sharply at him.

"Okay," he amended, "more than that, but we respect each other's privacy."

"That's right," projected Tim. "No porphyrian would ever intrude on another's intimate thoughts."

"Good!" she exclaimed, as Jim backed her into the elevator. Defiantly, she pressed the button and grinned triumphantly when the doors closed and separated her from her guards.

A few moments later, the elevator doors reopened to reveal the hustle and bustle of the hospital's cafeteria. Laural's eyes widened as she surveyed the amount and variety of food displayed behind the glass cases. Several types of meats, fish, and pasta dishes were accompanied by a plethora of vegetables and potatoes. Fruits were followed by familiar desserts and other culinary confections that were completely unknown to her.

"So, this is where they keep all the good stuff," she stated, while sniffing appreciatively.

"If you consider this the good stuff," her doctor responded with laughter, while wheeling her to the end of the line, "you've been here too long."

Laural balanced the overstuffed tray as Jim guided them toward a table. He halted the wheelchair, lifted the tray, and set it on the table in front of her. Removing a cheeseburger and Coke, he pulled out a seat adjacent to her.

"Can you really eat all that?" he asked, while eyeing the numerous plates arrayed in front of her.

"Watch me," laughed Laural, as she started to rise.

"Uh-uh," reprimanded the doctor shaking his finger. "Hospital rules. You must stay in the wheelchair. You wouldn't want to get me into trouble."

"No," she agreed, while grappling with her cheeseburger, "but I feel so silly sitting in this thing when I know I'm perfectly fine."

"Humor me," he requested. Their eyes met and held. His gaze grew sober, thoughtful, and then softened. A slight tingling like a low-grade electrical pulse vibrated through him. Slowly, he lifted his napkin and dabbed at her chin.

She held her breath. She was mesmerized when his strong but gentle fingers came into contact with her skin.

"Your ketchup was dripping." She was so young and vulnerable. Sighing, he realized that she was too young even though her chart stated she would be eighteen in a few days. The difference in their ages seemed like a yawning chasm that was too wide to bridge.

Laural sensed the passing of the intimacy. She was confused and disappointed by the sudden change. Hoping that a distraction would cover her dismay, she laid down her burger and allowed her eyes to drift around the cafeteria. She observed John and Tim sipping coffee at a nearby table. She had known that it wouldn't take them long to catch up. They were being as discreet as possible. They were talking and not even glancing in her direction. She smiled slightly as she realized now that her own mental abilities were manifesting, the need for direct eye contact was not necessary for their surveillance.

"Don't you like your food or have you lost your appetite?"

Even though his tone was lightly teasing, she recognized the underlying concern. On the verge of reassuring her companion, she froze. The hairs on the back of her neck rose as an uncomfortable paranoia engulfed her. She felt as though she were suffocating and frantically cast about for the cause. It was the same feeling of being watched that she had been having for the past couple of weeks, but this one was even more intense due to her awakened porphyrian powers.

Suddenly, she spied him. A dark figure alone at a corner table. Black hair, black eyes, dressed in black, sipping black coffee. With a start, she realized for an instant that she had been inside the stranger's mind. He realized it, too. As she watched, he slowly lifted his Styrofoam coffee cup in a mock salute.

"Is something wrong?" queried Jim. His teasing note was replaced by worried tension.

His voice seemed to be coming from a great distance because she was absorbed, transfixed, and impaled by piercing onyx orbs.

"Laural, what's wrong?" her bodyguards asked silently as they pushed back their chairs in unison.

Jim covered her hand and squeezed lightly while he waved his other hand in front of her face. She snapped back to awareness. Looking past him, she saw her protectors heading determinedly toward the table.

"That man at the corner table. He's a porphyrian and he's been watching me." Both men stopped to turn toward the table that she indicated. They were puzzled by her statement because they had not picked up on any other porphyrians.

She refocused on Jim and smiled. "I'm fine. I was thinking about my mom."

He nodded understandingly. "Would you like to go back to your room?"

Surreptitiously, she glanced at the corner table. Her observer was gone. She scanned the room. So were Tim and John. Laural suddenly felt frightened and abandoned.

"I think that would be a good idea," she responded faintly.

Chapter 18:
A New Crisis

Andrew leaned back against the headrest of his armchair and massaged the back of his neck. He pushed further away from the mahogany desk as he stared in disgust at the pile of papers scattered in front of him. Drawing a long breath, he leaned his head back again and closed his eyes. "What am I going to do about this new crisis? Under the circumstances, do I even care?"

His entire existence had been devoted to assimilating his people into diurnal society. The Willow Grove Foundation was the culmination of his dream and a chance for his people to interact as a part of humanity instead of hiding from it. The mission was important and the need great, but, every time his eyes closed, all he saw was his lost love and again realized how empty his life was without her.

A knock at his door brought him up straight. His eyes collided with the portrait of Abraham Lincoln that was hanging on the opposite wall. Lincoln had grown up in poverty. Despite his humble beginnings, he had been able to use his impressive oratory skills to compel the nation to elect him as President in 1860. He had presided over the country during its most turbulent time, maintained his beliefs in spite of extreme opposition, and started the country on a path which eventually led to equality for enslaved citizens.

He looked to this historical role model as the progenitor of his own philosophy. In fact, it had been the Emancipation Proclamation issued in 1863 by this progressive individual that had sparked his own ideas of integration. Now, Lincoln appeared to be staring sorrowfully with disappointment etched into his solemn visage. Andrew felt his resolve return as renewed strength seemed to pour into him from the portrait. He silently saluted his mentor.

"Come in."

John Carpenter entered wearing a navy suit. His penetrating dark eyes scanned Andrew's face and then the piles of papers. Noting the concerned expression on his boss' face, he said softly, "She's fine. I left three of our best people with her."

His brows lifted. "I didn't know you could read me."

"I don't have to read you to know that your first concern is for your daughter."

He nodded and exhaled. "I've been plagued for Laural's whole life that someday something terrible would happen to her. I had the misguided notion that if I was diligent enough that somehow I could protect her."

"So far, you have."

"Have I?" he wondered. "What about the mysterious stranger she insists was watching her?"

"Tim and I searched the entire building and surrounding area. We couldn't find any other porphyrians besides the backup we requested. Believe me, we left her well-guarded, but I suspect her paranoia is a result of fluctuations in her heightened senses."

Andrew sighed with relief. "I suspect you're right. Just the same, I'm going to move her out of the hospital."

The other man frowned. "I'm not sure that is such a good idea."

"Why not?"

"First, because it's close by and centrally located, which makes it ideal for surveillance. Second, on the off-chance she's right and someone is watching her, it would be much harder for him to come or go unnoticed in a public hospital. Besides, where would you send her?"

The marquis briefly closed his eyes. Opening them, he exhaled slowly. "I don't have anywhere that is safer than where she is and still close enough for my comfort while I'm stuck here dealing with all this," he relented, as he waved his hand at the pile of papers on the desk.

John's eyes shifted to the stacks of documents. "How bad?"

"Bad," replied Andrew flatly, while scowling at the sheets scattered across his desk. After throwing his pen disgustedly on top of the heap, he turned to the cabinet next to his desk. Withdrawing a bottle of PS4 and two glasses, he filled both and offered one to the other man. As John leaned forward to take the drink, a glint of gold caught the light.

For several moments, Andrew stared fixedly at the tie clip. Memories flooded his mind and threatened to drown him in a tidal wave of emotion. Vividly, he remembered the day that Victory proudly had displayed her gift for John's ten years of service to the agency. He had teasingly offered to purchase the standard gold watch, but his wife had promptly pointed out that John was more in need of the clip. She had provided the persuasive argument that the head of security had always been on time for every meeting, but usually arrived with his tie in disarray. This gift would remedy that situation.

So, the tie clip had become their head of security's anniversary gift. Andrew went along good naturedly even though he was secretly sure that John would never wear it. He had been proven wrong. The security chief had been so touched that he had worn it every day. Now, realizing his boss' discomfort, he reached to undo the fastening.

Andrew held up his hand. "Don't take it off. You honor my wife's memory by wearing it, John," he continued, while moving his mind away from melancholy memories. "I don't mind telling you I am concerned. It would appear we have a mole and I haven't got time to figure out who could have betrayed us. I have to unravel this mess by tomorrow and somehow manage to convince the auditors that we are not misappropriating funds."

John blinked rapidly several times, pulled out a notepad, and began taking notes. "So far I've done well in performing two tasks at once. Do you have more instructions?"

John was among the first porphyrians who were successfully integrated into the program many years ago. He had hired him as a private investigator to safeguard his daughter and to discover who was behind Victory's death. "I don't want my wife's murder investigation to take a back seat."

John looked up sharply. Unshed tears glistened in his dark eyes, as he shook his head. "No chance of that. I know how much she meant to you and I thought highly of her, too. Don't worry. Whoever is behind this will come to justice. I don't believe the diurnal posing as a telephone repair man was acting alone. I'm also suspicious that the two events," he continued, while nodding at the papers, "may be related."

The marquis' eyes narrowed. "What do you mean?"

The investigator shifted uncomfortably under the intense scrutiny.

He took a sip from his drink before continuing. "More instinct and hunch right now. I don't have enough hard facts, but I think this is a personal vendetta against you. I'm almost positive it's one of our own. I'm doing a background check on everyone you've integrated in the past fifteen years. Anyone who dropped out of the program, a dissatisfied customer, so to speak. Also, anyone who finished but then became dissatisfied with the results. In addition I wouldn't rule out any diurnals for sabotage of this facility. There may be toes you've stepped on politically. If you happen to keep a list of known enemies, it would be helpful."

Andrew's fist crashed down hard on the desk. John was startled as papers flew onto the floor and glassware clattered. "Damn it, John. I figured out for myself it was personal the moment my wife was killed. I want answers, not suppositions."

John cleared his throat. "The diurnal is proving difficult to trace. The phone company has been hedging, but I have a meeting scheduled with the head of their personnel department later this afternoon. I'm running a check and should have news soon."

Steepling his fingers, Andrew leaned back in his chair. "I'm sorry for that outburst, John. It's just that it's been so taxing and I ..."

"Say no more. I understand."

The marquis glanced back at the portrait of Lincoln, took a deep breath, and calmly said, "All my known enemies died eighteen years ago in the explosion that demolished this very building."

"Are you sure?"

"What are you getting at?"

He shrugged. "Since we're in agreement about the personal vendetta, I think it's unwise to rule out any possibilities."

Andrew rotated his chair to face the full-length window. Staring into the cloudless azure sky, he said softly but emphatically, "They're all dead."

Chapter 19:

The Sadist and The Savior

Cornwall, England, 1769

The whip hissed as it sliced through the air and cracked hard against the peasant's naked back. As the figure fell groaning to the ground, a crimson line dripped blood onto the dirt.

"Get up, you useless piece of trash. Get up or I'll be taking your young sister Katherine home with me this eventide," snarled an enraged Craven Maxwell.

Painfully, the figure rose, stumbled, and then stood to present the master with a back already crisscrossed with bright red streaks of blood. Katherine ran forward, threw herself against her older sibling, and tried to block the next blow.

Eyes dulled by pain and resignation stared down at the weeping child. Katherine looked up. The horror and fear reflected in her eyes was too much to bear. The peasant slumped dejectedly against the wooden post.

Again, the whip hissed. The figure flinched and knew what to expect even before the blow struck. However, this time, the leather found its mark on Katherine's arm. The girl cried out in pain. Her sibling's face went white with shock and then red with rage. Stepping between the child and danger, the peasant glared and then spat in the dirt at the master's feet.

Craven grinned malevolently. "So, you still have some fight left? I thought that would have been beaten out of you by now. No matter. That will happen soon enough." He glanced at the sobbing child. "Such a pretty girl. How do you think she'll look with the scars of a whipping marring her face?"

The peasant stared beseechingly into the crowd. Someone stepped forward and quickly pulled the protesting child back into the throng. The figure straightened. Resolve and Katherine's potential peril lent fortitude to the ordeal.

Craven's eyes narrowed ominously as he drew back his arm. The other peasants stood close. They were angered by the abuse of one of their own, but were powerless to do anything about it. He was pleased by their fear and impotent rage. He preferred domination and intimidation as the means of ruling his servants. Maybe, after this display, they would think twice before defying him in the future.

"All you've done is buy Katherine a few extra hours. The day is young. I can still see to her after I finish with you."

Drawing his hand over his head in a wide arc, he decided to make a decisive example by whipping this particular peasant to death. The lesson would teach the others what to expect if they chose to flaunt his edicts. This one was useless now. His eyes roamed dispassionately over the bloody and battered body. His revulsion for all that the peasant represented grew and he almost smiled in anticipation. Despite his implied promise, he would take the young sister home before using the whip on her. She would provide good sport for his post-carnage passion.

The whip hissed. The peasant stiffened and braced for the blow. A child's scream tore through the air, but quickly was stifled. Several onlookers cried copiously as they watched, but no one dared to intervene.

Abruptly, the whip was jerked out of Craven's hand. Rage ripped through him as he turned to see who dared defy him. Could it be the spineless mate? His eyes widened in shock. His half-brother, Andrew Gabriel, Marquis of Penbrook, slammed the whip hard against his leg. He splintered the handle and rendered the tool useless.

Seconds of stunned silence hung suspended as the two brothers glared at each other. Finally, Craven asked in a softly menacing tone, "What do you think you're doing?"

The marquis' eyes raked over him. "I will not allow you to torture these people," he asserted, as he leaned over the figure slumped on the ground. Gently lifting the peasant, he removed the leather ties that bound the victim to the wooden post. The figure collapsed into his arms. Andrew's eyes dilated from shock.

"This is a woman!" he said incredulously, as his eyes roamed over the torn and bleeding flesh. He realized that he may have arrived too late to save this one. Fury toward his brother sliced through him like a knife. He checked for a pulse. It was faint and erratic but still there.

"I'm aware of that," Craven responded contemptuously.

Looking from his brother to the lass, he asked furiously, "I suppose you're also aware she's pregnant?"

"Aye, my lord, she and the babe be mine."

Andrew tore his gaze away from his brother to see a young man of about twenty with red hair and frightened brown eyes staring at the pregnant woman.

"What is your name, lad?" asked Andrew with compassion.

The young man nervously bit his lip. His eyes strayed back to his master. "Luke," he timidly announced.

"Well, Luke, go and get your belongings. You and your wife are coming home with me."

Quickly, the peasant scampered off before his master could say anything to him.

"What do you think you're doing?" asked Craven in an icy tone.

Andrew looked up from the unconscious woman. Their eyes clashed.

"It's my policy to have only hardworking hands. I don't care for peasants who can't earn their own keep. My people are well aware of the consequences for getting with child. In that state, they know their usefulness is over."

"So, you kill them," he challenged with turquoise eyes blazing.

"Katherine," groaned the figure.

Andrew leaned closer. "Don't worry, lass, you're safe now," he comforted, while pushing the matted sweat-soaked blond hair from her eyes. His gesture revealed dark blue eyes that now stared back steadily. His heart filled with compassion and respect as he read the courage and resolve in the sapphire depths. "Easy, lass, your Luke has gone to get your things. You're coming with me."

Instead of being reassured, the woman grasped his arm. Looking frantically from her master to her savior, she tried desperately to sit up, but she coughed spasmodically and then collapsed again. "Katherine," she gasped before fainting.

Andrew understood. Casting his gaze through the throng of onlookers, he located a child of about ten. She stood at the edge of the crowd, while nervously biting her lip. Fidgeting, Katherine looked at the woman, the marquis, then the master. Andrew smiled reassuringly and beckoned. As she hesitantly approached, he could see that the girl was the spitting image of her relative.

"Are you Katherine?" he asked gently.

The girl nodded and then looked longingly at her sister.

His rage escalated as he noticed the red stripe on the child's arm. Being careful not to display his feelings lest he alarm her, he continued to smile. "Yes, you can stay with her. In fact, you're coming with us, too."

Now, it was Craven's turn to rage with impotent fury.

"Yes," he confirmed, "I'm taking them with me and I'll take anyone else who wishes to leave."

"I think," Craven stated menacingly "from now on, you better stay in Camelford and leave Camborne to me. I may not have the ability to supercede you yet, but a time of reckoning will come."

Chapter 20:
Negotiations

Senator Randolph shifted in his high-back leather chair. His formidable brows knitted together as he seriously studied the visitor who was seated on the other side of his desk. Pulling off his bifocals, he nervously wiped them with his handkerchief while considering his response. Finally, he replaced his glasses and peered over the top of the lenses at the woman sitting across from him.

"I was a firm supporter of your father, but that was almost two decades ago," he replied cautiously.

"Are you still loyal to the same ideals?"

"That depends on the ideals to which you are referring."

"You in the White House, leading a strong unified country."

"What's the catch?"

She handed a sheet of paper to him. "This is a list of proposed cabinet members and other strategic appointments."

He glanced down at the list and then back at his guest. Licking his lips nervously, he said, "The idea has appeal, but I must have time to consider your proposal."

"What's to consider? I have told you what is at stake and your risk will be minimal. In fact, you would be seen as a hero by the people. Imagine the outrage of the masses when this scandal breaks." She waved her hand. "It will make the scandals of our last political leaders seem paltry by comparison."

Resting his elbows on the massive cherry wood desk, he leaned forward. His own aspirations of being in the White House had died long ago, but could they be resurrected? "Miss Maxwell, you still haven't enlightened me as to the identity of my benefactor."

She stared intently at him. "Your benefactor wishes to remain anonymous. Believe me. It's in the best interest of your campaign."

He frowned. He wasn't sure why, but he completely believed

her claims. His eyes again dropped to the paper in front of him and his frown deepened. "In order for me to receive your support, I must appoint Bill Sawyer as my Secretary of Defense?"

She nodded.

He skeptically eyed her. "And Dorothy Whitfield as Secretary of State?"

"They are the most suitable choices."

"For what?" he thought, while looking at the paper. Even by his standards, most of the people on the list were extremists. From behind the bifocals, his faded blue eyes speculatively regarded her as he tried to fathom her real purpose. Just then, he again realized how truly beautiful she was. He admired her long dark wavy hair and velvety brown eyes. His eyes strayed down to her breasts and then back up to her face. Her proposal was definitely enticing – as was she. He cleared his throat. "You say you have proof that your uncle has been using government funds to fund his own pet project. You're positive that he has been smuggling illegal aliens into the country, providing them with false identities, and passing them off as U.S. citizens?"

Dana lifted her briefcase onto the desk. Snapping open the locks, she lifted the lid, sifted through the papers, and handed several sheets to him.

Senator Randolph scanned the documents and then lowered them to the desk. Lifting his brows, he asked, "Are these authentic?"

Dana pushed her long dark hair behind her shoulder and straightened the collar of her suit. "I've already tipped off the Senate 501C(3) Finance Committee. Even now, they are scheduling their audit for tomorrow morning. I'm sure my uncle will never be able to eradicate the records in time."

He frowned. "So, this is all a set up."

She gazed steadily at him, but remained silent.

"Why wasn't I informed?"

She shrugged. "You will be informed on a need to know basis. Don't worry, Senator," she asserted, while tapping a bright red nail against the papers. "As long as you're part of the plan, you won't be left out of the loop."

He bristled. "And, if I'm not part of the plan, what then? What makes you think I need your benefactor? I could run for President without his aid or his list of preferred appointments."

Her eyes grew cold and distant as she dispassionately watched him. "You could," she agreed, "but there would be consequences if you used this information for personal gain or went public with it on your own."

He sat stunned. Had she just threatened him? He peered at her above his bifocals and cleared his throat. Tugging the handkerchief from his pocket, he nervously wiped his glasses as he considered Dana Maxwell. Her predatory stare sent shivers of apprehension and excitement racing down his spine. He had no doubt about her implication: Either go along or be permanently silenced. Anger surged through him as he realized that his fate had been sealed as soon as he had agreed to the meeting. They were playing him for a fool and using him as a puppet. But who were they and what did they really want? Thoughtfully, he contemplated his next move in this carefully contrived game of cat and mouse. Could he maneuver from the position of prey to predator?

She refastened her briefcase and then stood. "Senator, I am offering you a unique opportunity. If you are not interested, I'm sure I can find someone who is."

As she stepped away from the desk, the senator's eyes lingered on her legs. He liked his women petite and curvaceous and this one fit the bill.

Dana observed the senator as his gaze traveled from her legs, past her tweed skirt, up her torso, and to her breasts. His eyes fastened hungrily on her cleavage before moving to her face. Their eyes met.

The senator smiled smugly as he read the reciprocation in her expression. Lifting his brows, he held up a placating hand. "Not so fast, Miss Maxwell. I didn't say I wasn't interested," he stated, while allowing his eyes to slide back down her body. "I never quite trusted foreigners. Even though your uncle applied for and received citizenship, I still consider him a foreigner. I can see where a foreigner might be sabotaging our economy by infiltrating our country with other foreigners and taking jobs away from honest citizens. If that's the case, then it's my duty to rectify the situation."

She smiled, while allowing her skirt to slide suggestively up her legs as she reseated herself in the leather armchair.

Turquoise eyes flashed as Andrew glared at the young doctor

standing on the other side of his daughter's hospital bed. "I told you," he repeated firmly, "I'm taking her now."

"And I told you," insisted the doctor, "it's against medical advice to remove someone from the hospital who's just come out of a coma without at least 24 hours of observation."

Laural sat on her bed between the two men and glanced nervously from one to the other. "Dad," she said, as she placed a hand on his arm, "does it matter so much if I stay?"

He searched her eyes. "There are circumstances at work that you don't understand and I need you with me – not just for your protection, but to help me with a serious situation." He projected this thought to her as he glared back at the doctor.

Laural's eyes widened. "What else?" she asked silently.

"We can discuss it after we leave. Right now, we need to stay focused on getting you out of here. By the way, you need to practice controlling your expressions so that everything we communicate telepathically is not written all over your face. Even now, this diurnal is thinking he's missing something."

She glanced at her dad in confusion. It wasn't like him to come across as so condescending. Then, she remembered his advice. She turned pleading eyes to the doctor. "Sorry, Jim. I mean Dr. Brenner. I need to go with my dad."

She glanced swiftly at her father to see if he had noticed the use of the doctor's first name. The look that he bestowed on her confirmed that they would be discussing it later. She looked back at the doctor and smiled reassuringly. He smiled back, but she could read the concern and doubt lingering behind his silver-gray eyes.

"I'm sure I'll be fine," she asserted, while gazing steadily at him.

He shook his head. "I don't like it, especially since we haven't had a chance to conduct all the tests. And," he emphasized, "the results of the blood tests we did run are back from the lab and they have me concerned."

Andrew bristled. "I don't remember giving consent for blood to be drawn," he said sharply.

"It's a routine procedure, part of the standard work up. In your daughter's case, the lab results indicate low red blood cell count. Probably just a mild case of anemia," he squeezed Laural's arm reassuringly before continuing. "Normally, that's a minor issue and is easily managed, but, added to the fact that she's been unconscious for almost three days," he stared at the marquis, "I just don't want to run the risk of missing a potential problem."

"What's up with that?" she thought to her father.

"Don't worry, ma petite, it's just a natural deficiency corrected by the PS4 supplement."

"Ugh!" she inwardly groaned. "Now, I have to drink that nasty-tasting stuff."

Andrew smiled at her and then at the doctor. "I can assure you, Dr. Brenner, my daughter is in excellent health. The anemia is a trait that is common throughout our family."

The physician looked back and forth between father and daughter. He was certain that he had missed something. His silver-gray eyes earnestly scanned his patient's face to seek any signs of distress. Realizing that he didn't have just cause, he relented.

"Promise to take it easy for the next few days and call me immediately if there are any problems."

Laurel nodded. She wished they had found an opportunity to talk privately. She knew that he did not understand her dad's adamant position and, frankly, she was confused by his sudden change, too. If she could just talk to Jim alone, she was sure that she could set his mind at ease.

Her father said impatiently, "My daughter's wellbeing is always my primary concern."

Dr. Brenner shot him a doubtful glance, but remained silent.

Andrew's anger began to swell, but Laural intervened. "Dad, he doesn't understand." Her dad was definitely on edge, but it was understandable with the strain that he had been under for the past several days. To Dr. Brenner, she said, "I'll be fine."

The doctor hurriedly scribbled on his notepad. Handing the paper to his patient, he insisted, "Take this. It's my direct line telephone number. If your condition changes, I want to know."

Her heart warmed at the display of interest. Before she could thank him, her father spoke up.

"Is it customary to provide patients with your private number?" he demanded harshly.

The silver-gray eyes stared resolutely. "No," he admitted, while flushing slightly. "But it will alleviate some of my concerns about you insisting she be discharged against medical advice."

Chapter 21:
Abomination

Andrew watched John Carpenter approach. While walking across the room, the investigator nervously straightened his tie. The marquis frowned as he noted the absence of his tie clip. John strode further into the director's office and smiled wanly, as he seated himself across from his boss.

Studying the man's tired expression, Andrew wondered if he had pushed the investigator beyond his endurance by insisting that he take on both assignments at the same time. He was a good man who was devoted and completely loyal. Andrew knew that he would collapse before conceding.

"I've been making the rounds as you suggested and I can't determine any duplicity by any of our employees, whether diurnals or porphyrians."

He nodded. He already had surmised as much, but was glad to have confirmation. "I've got all of our available staff working on the books to straighten out the problem. Someone has leaked the story to the media and I have a press conference in an hour. John, can you give me anything I can use?"

"Yes," he affirmed, while shuffling his notes, "but I don't think you're going to want this to go to the media. Since I've ruled out everyone all the way down to the custodial staff, only two possibilities are left." He paused to clear his throat. "Jordan and Dana." John inconspicuously flinched as he anticipated his boss' reaction.

Andrew eyed him speculatively and then slowly blew out a breath. "Why do I have a feeling that was the good news?"

John grimaced and stared back bleakly. "I just met with the director of personnel at the phone company."

The marquis stiffened. "And?"

"And the reason he was so hesitant to talk is because his company has pending litigation. A lawsuit being brought by the family of Robert Brooks, the repair engineer who made the call to your home last Monday."

"You mean the man who murdered my wife."

John stared somberly at his boss for a moment, stood, and walked to the bar. He poured a glass of scotch, hesitated, and then poured a second glass. Walking back to the desk, he handed one glass to Andrew. After seating himself, he took a long pull on his drink.

Andrew followed the other man's example and then set his glass aside. "Why are they suing the phone company?"

The investigator upended his glass and drained half of the contents before answering. "Because Robert Brooks is dead. The case is still under investigation, but it seems Mr. Brooks lost control of his vehicle after returning from his final stop that day. That trip was the one to your home. On the way back to the office, he plummeted straight off the bridge and into the Potomac."

"Damn!" Andrew exclaimed, while grabbing his drink and throwing it hard against the wall. Shards of glass and scotch slowly slid down the benign face of Abraham Lincoln.

John looked at the ruined portrait. "It seems someone didn't want us to have a chance to question Mr. Brooks."

"By 'us', you mean me."

"You are one of the few among us who could have retrieved any blocked memories."

The blue eyes narrowed. "What else?"

John shifted uneasily. "I've been doing extensive research since we spoke at the hospital. You said you knew a porphyrian was behind your wife's murder due to the method chosen and because of the killer's use of the word 'abomination'." He searched through his notes. "The word bothered me because I've never heard it used in connection with a porphyrian death, so I checked into it." He made a face. "What I found doesn't make sense, but I decided to run it by you." He lifted his eyes from his notes to Andrew's face in order to determine how he was taking the news.

The marquis nodded for him to proceed.

"First, I tried linking the word with any ritual deaths or sacrifices. Then, I tried linking it with porphyrians. The search led me to ancient legends that connected the word to vampires."

He glanced up because he was certain that his boss was going to eject him from the room, but Andrew just continued to stare at him. Slightly uneasy, he continued. "According to these ancient myths, vampires would occasionally commit a blood exchange with a human by drinking the blood of the person, then allowing the victim to drink from their body. This resulted in an atrocity that was considered neither completely vampire nor human. These creatures were referred to as the 'undead' and considered an abomination by both species. The preferred methods for terminating such abominations were decapitation and complete incineration of the body."

He looked up at Andrew and added, "This matches the method used by the killer but I don't see the connection."

"I do." Andrew stood, walked to the bar, poured himself another drink, and moved toward the window. Sipping slowly, he stared into the sunset. His mind traveled back twenty years to the day when he and Victory had dined at the outdoor café in Georgetown. During lunch, she had spoken animatedly about her life, hopes, and dreams. The setting sun had surrounded her and turned her hair into a golden halo around her exquisite facial features. Her eyes had sparkled like jewels, as she described her desire to reinforce the rights of the disadvantaged. Her face shone with excitement, as she discussed her plans to become a Supreme Court judge in order to insure that justice prevailed. Listening to her share her hopes for the future touched an answering chord in his soul. He knew that he had found a kindred spirit and determined then and there that he would be with her at any cost.

Remorse filled him. Had his selfish desire to have Victory with him been worth her life? Would she have been better off if he had never intruded into her world? By now, she probably would be living her dream of being a Supreme Court justice instead of ending up as a pile of ashen remains inside an incinerated mansion.

"If there's more to this than you originally told me, I should know – not only to help with the investigation, but to protect Laural."

John's voice snapped Andrew back to the present. The mention of his daughter brought him up short. Regardless of anything else, he knew that Victory would never regret the choices that she had made which had brought them their child.

He returned to his desk, sat down, and explained to his friend.

"Twenty years ago, I was courting Victory Parker. At that time, she was a diurnal."

John started to speak, but the marquis held up his hand to forestall his questions.

"My half-brother, Craven Maxwell, discovered my interest in Victory and abducted her. He held her captive for several days while he mentally and physically tortured her." His voice trailed off. It was several seconds before he could continue. "After he had left her battered and bruised body for dead, I found out where she was. When I arrived, I found her unconscious, barely breathing, and holding on to life by a thread. After examining her numerous wounds, I discovered the main problem was that most of the blood had been drained from her body. Craven had left his equipment behind, probably just to be sure I understood what he had done." His eyes reflected the agony that he had felt. "I knew there was no way she would survive long enough for me to get her to a hospital, so I gave her a transfusion with my own blood."

John leaned back in his chair and tried to absorb everything that he had just heard. Finally, he spoke. "So, whoever killed your wife had to have known about this. Who else have you told about the transfusion?"

"No one except Dana. Only Jordan and I were there with Victory and I don't think Dana or Jordan told anyone. Victory certainly didn't. Besides, Craven and all of his followers were killed when the building exploded. Only Jordan, Dana, and I made it out alive – unless there was another survivor."

A knock sounded at the door. Andrew and John exchanged glances as Dana poked her head into the room.

"I heard about the problems and changed my mind about leaving. I'd feel like a rat abandoning a sinking ship."

Andrew grimaced, "I'm not sure I like the analogy, however, I could use the support and Jordan will be glad you're back. But," he continued with narrowing eyes, "how do you expect us to trust you when you disappear every time things get rough?"

She crossed the room. Her gaze never wavered. She knew that he was not referring just to the present situation.

"You're right. My track record speaks for itself. But," she stated firmly, as she stood before him, "my disappearances have always stemmed from a desire to protect Jordan."

He skeptically eyed her. "Is that what you were doing this time?"

"Well," she began, as her dark eyes shifted nervously toward John and she pulled up a chair, "I've been wondering about the note I found."

John frowned, but Andrew said, "Go on."

She stared down at her hands. Waves of long sable hair fell like a curtain across her face. Finally, she confronted her uncle. "I'm afraid this may be an inside job."

Staring intently, he nodded for her to continue.

She took a deep breath. "That's the reason I decided to leave. I've been suspicious for a long time about Jordan's loyalty."

John leaned forward to place his empty glass on the desk. "Anything you can tell us would be greatly appreciated because, quite honestly, I'm all out of leads. I was just telling the boss," he said, while glancing at Andrew, "that Jordan was about the only possibility left. I know that is a bitter pill for you to swallow," he continued, while turning to his employer, "but, despite how you feel about the earl, I think you should listen with an open mind."

Andrew glared hard at the investigator. Then, he stood, walked to the bar, and poured another drink. Returning to his seat, he gestured for Dana to continue while he sipped his scotch.

John lifted his empty glass and looked questioningly at Dana. She shook her head.

"I know it sounds incredible and I didn't want to face it myself. That's why I left. I feel like I'm betraying him just by talking to you, even though I know it's the right thing to do." She looked away, chewed her bottom lip, and sighed. "For months, I've been bombarded by dark thoughts from him. He's no longer committed to the cause. He's been having doubts and I've been doing double-duty by trying to cover his thoughts so no one," she looked beseechingly at Andrew, "would pick them up."

Andrew's face hardened. "These are serious allegations," he said, while putting aside his drink.

Dana looked down at her clasped hands. Tears slipped down her cheeks. "I know. I also know you don't believe me. But why else do you think my thoughts have been so erratic and hostile lately?"

He studied her for a long moment and then nodded. "I can think of several reasons, but, as far as Jordan is concerned, you're right. I don't believe you. Jordan and I have a very long history of loyal friendship. Why should I believe he's suddenly turned traitor?"

Her eyes flashed with indignation. "I may not have been completely committed to the cause in the beginning, but you know full well I've become a loyal supporter. I've been working beside the rest of you for years and I'm as devoted to the cause as everyone else."

"Everyone except the traitor," he interjected icily.

She glared at him. "It would make it all so much easier for you if it was me. You've got your mind so made up it's blinded you to any other possibility."

John held up his hand. "We're considering all possibilities."

Turquoise sparks flew from Andrew's eyes as he glared first at his niece and then at the investigator. He stood up so abruptly that his chair crashed against the wall. He stormed to the bar, refilled his glass, and stalked to the window. If he kept drinking at this rate, he knew that he would not be in any shape to conduct his upcoming press conference and meeting, but, at the moment, he didn't care. He leaned against the window frame with his back to the room and stared blindly into the deepening dusk.

Without turning, he demanded flatly, "Tell me why I should take your accusations seriously."

"Because, other than us, he's the only one left with the power to pull it off. He's been jealous of you and has become tired of being second string. He feels frustrated and, at the same time, trapped by his loyalty to you. He can't express how he feels because even that would be disloyal. The bitterness and resentment is leaking and I've been his buffer."

He pivoted to face her. Dana recoiled against the back of her chair at the tightly controlled fury emanating from the marquis. With measured steps, he advanced. Dana felt frozen in place. John stood and interposed himself between his enraged prince and the woman. Andrew locked eyes with him for several heartbeats and then moved to pick up the chair.

He leaned forward and splayed his hands on the desk. "I'm not in the mood for mind games," he said scathingly. "Even if all you say is true, I'm supposed to believe that Jordan was so bitter and resentful it drove him into a conspiracy to murder my wife?"

Silently, she challenged him.

He probed hard and deep. He searched and penetrated beyond any barriers, past decency and further. She sat rigid with eyes never faltering, never flinching. She refused to deny him access to her innermost thoughts. Eventually, he slumped back in his seat as he silently thought about her for several seconds.

"Blocking him was easier than I thought," Dana smugly bragged to herself.

The tension drained from Dana's body and she continued her onslaught. "Jordan's lost control. I think he's having blackouts. That's why he's able to block out what's really going on," she said as if in earnest.

"He's at the halfway house. He's assisting with relocation. I want you and John to go over and confine him," he commanded harshly. "If he gives you any trouble, use whatever means necessary to hold him. I don't want him tipped off, so make him think this is just routine."

"Won't he get suspicious if we go together?"

"Not if you give him the impression you are extending your search to include inhabitants of the shelter. I'd go with you," he said, while checking his watch, "but I have a conference in ten minutes and then a meeting with the Senate Finance Committee. I'll rendezvous with you at the Raven's Nest about five."

Sighing wearily, he straightened his tie and lifted his suit jacket from the back of his chair. The toll was worsening. He tried to fight off emotional exhaustion. First came Victory's death, then Laural's trauma began, and now this. He glanced from one to the other. John caught his eye and nodded imperceptibly. All of them stood and headed toward the door.

He opened it just in time to see a UPS man delivering a package to the receptionist. He probed. Ever since Victory's murder, he mentally had checked any stranger who came within striking distance. Diurnals were easy; some porphyrians were more of a challenge. The man passed inspection.

He turned back to Dana and John. "Understand that when I find whoever is responsible, I will have my pound of flesh – no matter who the traitor is."

A piercing scream echoed through the outer office. Andrew's face paled. He pushed past the others.

The receptionist sat frozen in horror at her desk. As he approached, Andrew could see that she was staring fixedly at her desk. Moving rapidly, he checked the room. No sign of danger. When he reached the frightened woman, he observed the torn brown wrapping paper and bunched up newspapers that were strewn across the desktop. He gazed past her into the packaging. A golden-haired doll lay inside. Her head was separated from her body and a miniature dagger was stuck in her chest.

Chapter 22:

Imposter

After a grueling hour of questioning by the Senate 501C(3) Finance Committee, Andrew Gabriel slid back his chair from the conference table. "Gentlemen," he finished, "as you can see, our records are in complete order. I'll leave you in the capable hands of our executive accountant, Mr. Small. I'm sure he can handle any additional questions."

While collecting his papers and shuffling them back into his file folder, he scanned the faces of the finance committee members. Several of the men looked stern, while others appeared impassive. Andrew couldn't gage how the meeting had gone by their granite expressions. Senator Randolph's aide, however, was an exception. The man glared back at him with drawn brows and compressed lips.

"Just a moment, Lord Gabriel," said one of the more silent senators. "I believe there are still some expenditures yet to be explained."

Lord Gabriel glanced around the table. "If you wish an itemized accounting of our expenditures, we have those records available. I can assure you, however, they make for tedious and quite boring reading. They're great if you suffer from insomnia."

Several chuckles followed the remark. Senator Randolph's aide still looked doubtful.

Andrew raised his hand to forestall more questions. "If you would like an itemized report of each expense, that can be arranged. Simply make Mr. Small aware of those who are requesting such documentation and it will be provided. We have receipts for everything we've spent – down to the last paper clip. Otherwise," he finished, while indicating the file folders that each member had before them, "there is a summary of our intake, expenses, and remaining revenue provided in your packets."

"I'm sure additional documentation won't be necessary," stated a distinguished iron-haired man at the far end of the table. "The reports you've provided seem to be quite thorough and easy to comprehend. Your staff is to be commended."

Andrew gave a slight nod. "Thank you, Senator Daily. Coming from you, that is high praise."

The chair of the committee inclined his head. "Let me also express our condolences for your loss. We certainly appreciate your personal attention to this issue during what must be a very trying time for you." The others nodded in agreement as he continued, "We've already taken enough of your time and, since everything seems to be in order, I think we can safely leave any remaining items for the next scheduled review."

Andrew respectfully inclined his head. "Thank you, Senator. If you need any additional information, I am at your disposal."

Senator Daily smiled. Lord Gabriel was always so gracious. Some of his colleagues would do well to emulate his example.

Andrew and his account executive passed into the hallway. After closing the conference room door, Andrew turned to the other man. "You really did a great job in there. I know it must have been nerve racking but you held up well under the pressure.

Mr. Small started to respond but the marquis held up his hand. "We'll discuss it back at the office."

Fifteen minutes later Andrew sank back in his chair behind his desk at the Willow Grove Foundation. He smiled at his longtime business associate. "Good job," he complimented again.

"Thank you," replied the wiry man leaning back in his own chair. Pulling off his glasses, he wiped them, as he regarded the man opposite him. "Any ideas?"

Andrew frowned.

"It doesn't take a genius to figure out the books were deliberately tampered with," asserted Mr. Small, replacing his glasses. "You couldn't get those kinds of mistakes in the records without purposeful intent. It would make my job easier if I knew whether I was protecting future records from honest mistakes or guarding against a mole."

"I think it would be prudent to do both."

Mr. Small jotted some notes in his file and then nodded.

A knock sounded at the office door. Andrew called out and Jordan stepped into the room.

"Sorry I'm late, but getting our newest arrivals acclimated took longer than I thought." He surveyed the remnants of the meeting. Raising his brows, he speculatively pondered the room's only occupants. "I went to the Capitol Building first but I was informed that I had missed all the fun."

Andrew frowned ominously. Jordan gazed back perplexed. Both men were startled out of their reverie by the voice at the end of the table.

"If you gentlemen will excuse me," said Mr. Small, who was shaken by the sudden tension in the room, "I'll get back to my office."

Both men remained silent until the door had closed firmly. Jordan pulled up a chair and sat across from his friend. "What message?"

Andrew narrowed his eyes. "The message I sent with John."

Jordan shifted uncomfortably, but held his gaze. "I haven't seen John."

"He and Dana left here several hours ago to meet you at the Raven's Nest."

Jordan's face hardened. "You mean Dana had the nerve to come back?"

"Yes and she had the audacity to blame you for the sabotage."

"Then, she doesn't know."

"That we're aware of her duplicity? No, she doesn't and I wanted to keep it that way until I could get there to interrogate her personally." He exhaled, while raking his hand through his hair. "I allowed Dana to think I believed her story about you. So, I sent her with John to keep you at the safe house until I could arrive. I sent John allegedly to keep you from giving Dana too much trouble."

Jordan lifted his brows. "I can't believe she would say all those things about me and even imply I had anything to do with Victory's death. I thought she loved me," he finished bitterly.

Andrew looked at him sadly, then continued, "I didn't entertain any of her outlandish accusations even for a moment. However, since you and Dana are pretty well-matched, I thought John might tip the scale in our favor. I also telepathically told him to let you know my real intentions."

The earl stared through the full-length window into the twilight. The lowering clouds portended a storm. "Not as bad as the one about to break in here," he thought, as his gaze shifted back to his cousin. "I was at the Raven's Nest all afternoon. John and Dana never showed."

Andrew sat still as a statue while assimilating the implication.

"So, what do you think happened?"

"Right before they left, I received a rather gruesome present from UPS. Someone sent a decapitated doll with a dagger in her chest." He closed his eyes. "It looked just like Victory." When his eyes opened, blazing fury shot from their depths. "I don't like being toyed with, Jordan. I hope, for Dana's sake, she's not involved. But I told John to keep a careful watch. If she tried to leave, he's to let her go. He knows to follow her and inform me of her movements."

A staccato beat tapped against the office door. Andrew frowned. Before he could forestall the intruder, the door was thrown wide. His frown deepened as he observed Tim Cooper standing in the opening.

"Sorry for the intrusion, but I was just checking to see if you wanted us to continue to stay on Laural patrol." Grinning broadly, he glanced around the room to see what impact his teasing would have on his charge. Discovering only the marquis and earl, he raised his brows in confusion. "Sorry. When I didn't see her up front, I assumed she was back here with you."

Now, it was Andrew's turn to be confused. Before he could question Tim further, the intercom buzzed. He pressed the button. "Yes?"

While apprehensively glancing from the marquis to the earl, Tim stepped further into the room. As he pulled up a chair next to Jordan, he sensed the nervous tension in both men.

"Mr. Carpenter is on line one," the secretary announced.

He pushed the button on the speakerphone. "Yes, John?"

"Dana and I started out together, but she suggested we take separate cars so her's wouldn't be left behind. Since you wanted me to remain low-key, I didn't insist. Just as expected, she tried to ditch me. When we began driving, she raced ahead of me, weaved in and out of traffic, and finally wound up several car lengths ahead in front of a tractor trailer."

Andrew glanced at Jordan's stricken face and then back to the phone. "Why did you wait so long to call?"

"I've been trying your cell phone every half-hour since we left, but I kept getting your voicemail. So, this time, I called the foundation."

Andrew reached down and turned his phone back on.

"Are you still tailing?"

"No, I turned around as soon as it became clear she was leaving the state. The way she was moving, I would have had to speed the whole time just to keep up. Also, I got a call from the lab. The preliminary results are not very enlightening. There were no prints on the wrapping or the doll. They haven't been able to trace its origin, although they're still trying. The doll itself is generic and could have been purchased anywhere."

Andrew swore under his breath. "All right. Come back in."

As he replaced the receiver, Tim started to speak, but the intercom buzzed again.

"Dr. Brenner on line two."

Andrew braced himself before lifting the receiver. As he brought the phone to his ear, he stared hard at Tim. A feeling of dread swept over him as he registered the deepening confusion on the bodyguard's face. "Why is the doctor calling? Have my men botched the mission? Did they lose track of Laural when she went for tests? Should I have allowed the tests?" he wondered to himself. He had thought that no harm could be done. Now, he worried that the doctor might have found an inexplicable discrepancy in Laural's brainwave patterns. The need to be sure that she had not suffered any lingering damage had outweighed the risks. "Could it be something else? Could Laural have had a relapse?" The questions bombarded him like a plague.

"You'll never know until you answer his call."

He stared at his lifelong companion and then opened the connection. "Yes, Doctor?"

Jordan carefully watched his friend. If something else was wrong with Laural, Andrew might buckle under the strain. Focusing on the phone conversation kept him from thinking about Dana.

"What do you mean you called to check on your patient? I'm not your patient," Andrew replied, while watching Tim as the bodyguard tensed and gripped the arms of his chair.

Jordan straightened. Then, he leaned forward to alternate his gaze between Andrew and Tim.

Andrew scowled at the bodyguard. "What's going on?" Tim opened his mouth to respond, but his employer motioned for him to be silent. The marquis frowned at the phone. "Doctor, I appreciate your concern, but it's been a long day. Would you mind making some sense?" He paused. "I see. Unfortunately, she's not available right now. She's resting." Another pause. "Yes, I will be sure to tell her you inquired. You're welcome, Doctor."

Andrew slowly hung up the phone. He closely studied Tim. The abject look of relief that swept across his face would have been comical if the situation had not been so serious, but the open and frank expression convinced Andrew of the bodyguard's sincerity.

Jordan lifted his brows. "I thought you decided to let Laural stay overnight?"

"I did."

Tim's relief shattered and was replaced by misery.

"I don't understand."

"Apparently, someone posing as me went to the hospital this afternoon and insisted that Laural be discharged."

"Then why lie to the doctor?"

"Did you expect me to tell him the truth? That would bring up more questions than I'm prepared to deal with right now, especially since I don't know the answers myself."

"You're right," he returned, while shaking his head, "I wasn't thinking."

Both men focused on Tim. He shifted uncomfortably. Perspiration broke out on his brow, but his gaze never wavered. "Did I pass inspection?"

Andrew nodded curtly. "But you failed your assignment. What happened?"

Although concerned and confused, Jordan felt a twinge of sympathy for Tim as the big man slumped dejectedly in his chair. He certainly would not want to be in his place.

"You, or at least someone who looked exactly like you, came to Laural's room and insisted she be discharged right away. Dr. Brenner protested due to the uncompleted tests and because he thought Laural needed to stay for longer observation, but you were adamant. Sorry," he amended, "the imposter was adamant."

"Didn't you question this sudden change?"

"Yes, but the imposter insisted there was a serious problem that required a change of plans. He claimed Laural was in grave jeopardy and wanted her kept close to him so he could keep a personal watch on her. Then, he told us to meet back here at about 5:30 for a security briefing on the changes to be implemented."

Andrew's fist crashed against the desk. "I specifically instructed you to probe everyone who came into contact with my daughter."

"I did," he insisted, "but I had no idea that included you."

Tim was right. There had been no way to plan for that contingency because it should have been impossible. For a moment, he was paralyzed by panic. The image of the doll on the receptionist's desk sprang into his mind. The arms of his chair snapped. Wooden splinters dropped to the floor. He shot out of the chair and bolted toward the door. "It's pretty obvious that Dana doubled back to the hospital and abducted my daughter."

Jordan could barely keep pace as Andrew raced out of the office. "I don't understand what she is up to, but does she have the ability to pull off a stunt like that?"

"Can you think of anyone else?" he threw over his shoulder, as he raced down the stairs.

Jordan drew a blank. "I can't believe she would harm Laural," he protested, while following his friend through the doorway.

Andrew paused on the pavement to confront him. "Need I remind you that Victory was murdered. Until I find out who's responsible, everyone is suspect."

Andrew strode quickly toward his car, but Jordan grabbed his arm. They halted next to the Mercedes and glared at each other. The frigid winter wind whipped sleet into their faces. "But Dana was with me that night. Remember?"

"That's the only reason she's still alive," he said tersely, as he jerked open the car door.

"Where are you going?" yelled Jordan above the gale.

Slamming the door hard, he scowled at his cousin.

Jordan stepped back from the piercing glare.

"I'm going to track them. Dana doesn't have the strength to keep me from telepathically locating Laural."

Pinpricks of pain pelted against Jordan's skin as the sleet continued to fall. "Don't you think she knows that? Andrew, this doesn't make any sense."

"Well," Andrew projected, as he gunned the engine, "during my last probe of her, she believed that she had developed the ability to block me. She's about to find out how wrong she is."

A pit settled in Jordan's stomach. "And when you find them?"

"I'm going to get answers."

Jordan flinched. "You might kill her," he whispered, but the Mercedes had already roared into the night.

Chapter 23:

Enigmas

As Jordan continued to watch the receding tail lights, he shook his head. He rushed to his dark blue Jaguar. With each step, he became more convinced that someone continued to carry the torch of Craven Maxwell.

"There are always going to be a few dissenters."

He blinked. He hadn't realized that Andrew was reading him. "You mean there's an organized group?"

"Yes, and they are determined to not only ruin me, but to exact revenge for the destruction of their leader."

"And you think Dana is connected?"

"Yes."

"Police?"

"Police and publicity. I've had enough to last me for a while. Jordan, what do you think you're doing?"

He grimaced. He had hoped that the mental dialogue would keep Andrew distracted. He should have known better. "I'm following you, of course."

"This is not your affair."

"I beg to differ since it's my fiancée you're hell-bent on destroying."

"She kidnapped my child and may be responsible for Victory's death."

"You don't know everything about the situation," he insisted, as he turned the key in the Jag's ignition. "Things just don't add up and there may be extenuating circumstances."

With his hand on the gear shift, the earl paused as a tapping sounded at the car window. Startled, he glanced over and lowered the pane.

"I want to help," said Tim. His earnest features were creased with concern.

"We need someone to stay here and cover in case any news comes through. You're in charge until John returns."

Tires peeled as Jordan pulled away from the curb. He reached out toward his friend. The force of Andrew's anger hit him like a blow. The Jag swerved as he fought to keep control. He gunned his sports car faster than the Mercedes could travel. As he rounded the next corner, his mouth set in a grim line. He passed Andrew, hit his brakes, slid, and positioned his Jag horizontally across the street. As anticipated, the Mercedes screeched to a halt only inches from his door. In a flash, he was pulling open his cousin's car door. Andrew glared and threw the car into hard reverse. Jordan flung himself into the passenger's seat and slammed the door just as the Mercedes shot forward.

He did not want Dana to be the recipient of the marquis' wrath. No matter what she had done, he still loved her. But what explanation was there for her actions? Things just didn't add up. Despite that, he didn't think he could rely on Andrew to keep himself in check. Whoever was behind this had succeeded in pushing him over the edge by taking Laural.

Andrew's features seemed carved out of granite. He swung the car around the corner, drove down two blocks, and then hung a hard left. "Don't delude yourself," he said. His voice was ice. "Laural is my priority. I'll do whatever it takes to protect her even if it means killing anyone who gets in my way."

Jordan searched his friend's profile. He didn't answer, but there was no need to respond.

They rode in silence for several minutes. Then, Jordan asked, "So, what could be Dana's motivation for the sabotage and abduction?"

The marquis was silent for several seconds before he finally answered, "I don't know why she took Laural, but she must have political aspirations to follow in her father's footsteps."

Jordan gaped. "How long have you had her under surveillance?"

"Ever since her thoughts started becoming erratic."

Jordan was outraged. "And you didn't tell me?"

Andrew said evenly, "You and I have been considering this problem for a while."

"But we never decided on a definite course of action. Why didn't you tell me you were having her watched?"

"I didn't want to put you in a position of conflicting loyalties. And, until recently, I was hoping there was another explanation."

"After all these years, you believe Dana would suddenly decide she wants to rule the country?"

"It's not called 'ruling' here. But you're right. It doesn't make sense. She's been meeting with people in high places. That still doesn't explain why she has taken my child – unless she thinks she can use her as a bargaining chip to keep me from interfering."

Jordan closed his eyes. "I'm sorry, Andrew, but I have no idea what her motivation could be. She's always had a secret part closed off even from me. My best guess," he said, as he opened his eyes, "is a nervous breakdown."

"So," Andrew asked quietly, "is Laural really safe?"

A long pause. "I don't know."

Detective Brent Addams seated himself across from the county medical examiner. Paul Edwards, a balding man in his mid-fifties, removed his glasses and wearily returned the stare. Sighing heavily, he picked up the case file in front of him and tossed it across the desk.

Addams retrieved the file and opened it. His tension mounted as he read the pages. Slowly closing the cover, he slid it on the desk. His mind whirled. First, the marchioness and now this. "Are you sure?" he asked.

The examiner pulled nervously at the lapels of his white lab coat. "Positive."

Addams pushed irritably at a stray lock of auburn hair. "But it doesn't make any sense."

"I know."

Addams frowned. "If Robert Brooks didn't have a heart attack, then what caused him to lose control of the vehicle and plummet into the Potomac?"

Edwards shrugged his rotund shoulders. "Bad brakes?"

Addams shook his head. "The truck checks out. No mechanical problems of any kind."

The examiner retrieved his glasses and peered more closely at his guest. Folding his hands, he said, "Then, detective, you have a real mystery on your hands. Robert Brooks died of asphyxiation brought on by drowning. He did not have a coronary. He was not dead or even unconscious when he hit the water."

"So, you're telling me he intentionally took a nose dive into the river?"

"I suppose suicide is always an option."

The detective's eyes flashed. "Not according to the widow."

Edwards shrugged again. "I can't speculate. I only provide the facts," he stated, while tapping the folder.

Addams scowled. "This makes as much sense as Lady Gabriel's lack of remains."

"Still nothing?"

He shook his head. "I've seen a lot of fires, even explosions, but never a crime scene where there were absolutely no dental remains or even a fragment of charred bone. It's as though she completely disintegrated."

"How sure are you she was ever really there?"

The stormy gray eyes narrowed. "I can't be sure of anything until I get some evidence or talk to the daughter. In the meantime, I've got the team sifting through the ashes and searching for any DNA evidence they can find. The further into it I get, the less sense this case makes."

"I think your best bet for answers is going to come from Lord Gabriel."

Addams stood. "I think you're right."

Chapter 24:
Dana's Divided Devotion

London, England, 1863

Logs popped and crackled in the stone hearth. The castle lay silent and dark save for the weak glow cast by the dying fire. The huge four-poster bed dominated the room. Its sheets were in disarray and its covers spilled onto the floor. The couple lay in the shadows behind the bed curtains, while contentedly basking in the afterglow of their lovemaking.

"My father sent me here to kill you," Dana confessed, as she gently ran her fingers through the hair on Jordan's chest.

Jordan leaned on one elbow, while his jade-green eyes appreciatively strayed over the beautiful brunette's curvaceous body. "Then, I must be sure to thank him. The method he chose for my demise is most pleasurable."

The canopy four-poster groaned in protest as she rolled on top of him. "I'm serious," she insisted, as she scowled down at him. "He will be furious when he discovers that my love for you has superceded his command."

He sobered and tightly clasped her. The feel of her warm firm flesh against his was arousing and he was having difficulty in concentrating. "Your father must be losing his touch by giving such an easily disregarded directive."

She stroked his cheek and let her eyes roam over his handsome face, beautiful green eyes, and the copper glints in his chestnut hair. If her father knew how much she truly loved this man, the consequences would be severe. Craven Maxwell demanded complete loyalty and tolerated nothing less. If he suspected that his daughter's devotion was divided, any competition for her allegiance would be destroyed.

As she contemplated the possibilities, she shuddered. So far, she had managed to keep her feelings private. She understood that this was due to Craven's preoccupation with his plans for revenge. She harbored no delusions. It was only a matter of time until her father discerned the truth. She had to act before that happened. She must convince Jordan about how perilous his position really was.

"He didn't make it that strong because he didn't think he needed to. If he knew about us, he would have been more adamant."

Jordan frowned. For a long moment, he stared at the hearth. The dying embers winked back at him. A shiver ran down his spine. "The castle can get mighty drafty this time of year," he thought, as he drew the coverlet over them. "I have no quarrel with your father. Why should I be of interest to him?"

"It's not you he's interested in, at least not directly. I can tell him that much," she thought, while staring into the green depths. She felt herself being pulled into the spell of warmth and security that Jordan always cast whenever she was with him. She resisted the urge to be completely honest. If she told him that Craven would be satisfied only by her complete subjugation, he would feel compelled to confront him. For both of their sakes, she couldn't let that happen.

The green eyes narrowed. What was she keeping from him? Then, he understood. "He thinks that he can get at Penbrook through me?"

Dana nodded, as she averted her face. Nestling in the crook of his arm, she stretched languorously. "He hasn't forgiven Andrew for humiliating him in front of the peasants. Besides, he wants Camelford for himself."

"He deserved the humiliation and much more," he responded hotly. "He takes Penbrook's benevolence for granted. There may come a time when Craven goes too far and their kinship will no longer protect him from Andrew's wrath."

"My father has no regard for their kinship and only disdain for Andrew's ethics."

He scoffed. "He should be grateful. Andrew's ethics are the only thing keeping him alive."

"For now."

He thoughtfully studied her. The dark eyes staring back at him were like bottomless pits. For the first time, doubts assailed him and he shifted uneasily. "But he's not strong enough to move against Penbrook."

"Not yet. In the meantime, he'll find other ways to strike."

Apprehension tinged his voice as he asked, "And what will happen to you when he discovers you've disobeyed?"

She shook her head in frustration. "Don't you care about your own safety? In case you haven't been listening, my father plans to weaken Andrew by destroying those he cares about – starting with you."

He disapprovingly gazed at her. "You're not telling me everything."

She sighed and averted her eyes. "I'm not going back."

His arms tightened. She glanced up and was immediately held captive by his compelling gaze.

He searched her eyes. "And you've decided not to stay with me."

She nodded affirmatively. "I refuse to be used as a pawn in this battle for supremacy. My father will never willingly relinquish his hold over me and, if he gets another chance, he will ensure his dominance."

"All the more reason to stay here."

Regret mixed with determination in her dark eyes. "I'm not like you. I don't have Andrew's nobility of purpose or your ethics and compassion. I may not agree with my father's methods, but I believe in his premise. I don't think our kind can live harmoniously with diurnals. I'm convinced that, if Andrew's villagers knew the truth, then the respect and affection he thrives on would turn to distrust and hatred."

He stood and began pacing agitatedly across the stone floor. "Where will you go?"

"It's better that you don't know, lest he pry it out of you."

As he spun to face her, green sparks shot from his eyes. "You don't expect me to just stand idly by and let you go?"

She sighed. What had she expected? She had known that he would feel compelled to fight. Unfortunately, he did not know how serious the situation was. If he confronted Craven, her father would realize that his hold on her was incomplete.

She watched him. His lean form was rigid with indignation and his face was drawn with worry. She knew that his concern was for her and her heart ached as she thought of losing his love. "No, I wouldn't expect you to give me up that easily."

He nodded curtly, but was too angry to speak. He moved across the room and headed toward his discarded clothing. Picking up her dress, he turned with his hand outstretched.

"Then, we're in agreement. We'll force him to relinquish his hold over you," he asserted, but she was gone.

Chapter 25:
Deception

John Carpenter pulled the BMW off the highway and into the rest area. As the windshield wipers vainly attempted to keep semi-circles of glass clear, sleet bombarded the windows and pinged off of the roof. He swept the deserted area with his perfect night vision. A lone figure that glowed pale in the darkness stepped from the shadows and slipped quietly into the car.

"Do you think he bought it?"

John nodded, as he returned to the highway. "Why not? He trusts me implicitly."

"That's because you keep feeding him information about me."

"How do you think I got him to trust me? He already knew or suspected most of the information. Keeping it from him would have made him suspicious."

She laughed hollowly. "Andrew's always been quick to judge and find me guilty."

He chuckled derisively. "You have to admit he has good reason. After all, I wouldn't call you the most loyal of his supporters."

She raised her brows. "And you are?"

He smiled cynically. "I may be a traitor, but I'm free of suspicion."

Dana pouted. Turning away, she gazed out of the window. As they headed further north, the sleet turned to flurries. "Even so, did you have to insert so much truth?"

He slid his hand up her thigh. "I did what was best for the cause."

As she spun her head to face him, her dark hair billowed like a cloak. "So, if anything goes wrong, I'm the fall guy."

He shrugged and shifted his gaze from the road to her face. "Better that than he suspect the truth."

"And what is the truth?" she asked huskily.

His arm whipped out to catch her hair. Yanking hard, he pulled her toward him. He punished her mouth for a long moment and then threw her hard. He laughed softly as her head hit the window.

She rubbed the back of her head. "You're not like my last lover."

"And don't you forget it. Jordan Rush could never be your equal."

"And you could?"

"Do you want me to pull over and prove it?"

She considered his proposal. Bright green eyes that were the color of imperial jade flashed through her mind. She struggled to control her thoughts. She had made her choice. There was no room for the Earl of Rockford in her life. Any plans they might have had for a future were dead and buried. John Carpenter was much better suited to her needs. He was ruthlessly cruel and motivated by self-interest. He understood what was at stake and who would win this battle for supremacy.

She sighed regretfully. "We don't have time. We need to make sure everything is ready for our guest's arrival. You're sure Andrew is headed in the other direction?"

"Andrew is so eager to paint you as the villain he believed every word I said. He and Jordan are halfway to Palm Beach by now."

Laural leaned her head against the seat and closed her eyes. The headache was intensifying. As she tried to combat the pain, she wondered how long the side effects from the manifestation of her mental abilities would last.

"Not much longer," responded her father to her unspoken question.

She opened her eyes and stared at her dad. "You're reading me?" she asked in surprise.

"Only deep enough to make sure you're okay."

Leaning back, she tried to doze. She felt drained. Either the emergence of her powers was using up a lot of energy or the exertion of leaving the hospital had wiped her out. She winced and opened her eyes as the car drove over several bumps.

Slightly turning her head, she peered out of the window. Her pain had been increasing steadily since her father picked her up from the hospital. She was beginning to think that staying there as Jim had suggested might have been a good idea. Thinking about her doctor brought a smile to her lips. Briefly, she wondered when she would see him again. Distracted by her thoughts, she took several seconds to register her surroundings.

Startled, she turned to look at her father. "Dad, where are we going?"

"On a trip."

"Where?" she asked.

Refusing to respond, he stared straight ahead.

"Dad?" she queried again.

Still nothing.

Hesitantly, Laural probed her father. Both of her parents had always been strict in teaching her to respect the privacy of others' thoughts, but there was something about her father's manner that she did not like. All at once, splinters of pain shot through her head. Her father's image seemed to change. He began expanding, contracting, and then morphing into someone else. Confused and frightened, she tried to speak, but another wave of pain ripped through her mind. Abruptly, she felt a slight sting in her left arm. Then, blackness.

Chapter 26:

Prisoner

Shrouds of gray mist evaporated as a bright white light penetrated Laural's consciousness. Squinting, she focused and the room went dark.

"Telekinetic powers, as well. Very impressive."

Laural heard but could not see the figure speaking from the darkness.

"I didn't know about that. Her abilities are just beginning to emerge."

"You're sure she has received no training?"

"There's been no opportunity. I checked only hours prior to Victory's death. Her abilities must have surfaced since she's been in the hospital."

"And she knows nothing?"

"Her parents were determined to keep her ignorant until her abilities emerged."

"What are they talking about?" she wondered. Her confusion deepened when she recognized that one of the voices belonged to her cousin. Still groggy, she tried to sit up. Her arms and legs were strapped with thick leather bindings to a steel examining table. She tried to move, but she was bound so tightly that she could not even squirm. Pin pricks of fear caused beads of perspiration to break out on her forehead.

"Dana, what's going on?" she asked apprehensively. Light footsteps retreated and then a door closed. "Dana?"

While she was distracted, another figure emerged from the darkness directly behind her. The figure placed electrodes on either side of her temples. She shook her head violently in an attempt to dislodge the probes, but they were stuck firmly in place. Taking a couple of deep breaths, she tried to calm herself. Focusing her energy, she mentally tried to remove the devices. Pain seared through her head. Groaning, she went limp.

"As long as you don't use your mind to resist, there will be no pain."

Laural opened her eyes. Something about the voice – a deep, sensual, and seductive quality – was hauntingly familiar. She felt as if she knew him. Awareness fluttered like gossamer wisps that were just out of reach. "Who is he? Why have I been kidnapped and taken prisoner? What part does Dana have in this? What is going to happen to me now?" Torrents of questions flooded her.

Deciding to demand answers, she tried to speak, but her mouth felt like it was filled with sawdust. Reaching out with her thoughts, she attempted to read his intent. Searing pain ripped through her head. Laughter reverberated through the room and followed her into unconsciousness.

Andrew floored the accelerator that pushed the Mercedes as fast as it could go. Jordan's knuckles turned white as he held tightly to the dashboard. "You know, we're not going to be of any use to Laural if we're dead or in jail."

The marquis' only response was the gaining of more momentum. He weaved in and out of traffic.

"Where are we going?"

Andrew gripped the steering wheel harder and eased off of the gas just long enough to career around the Toyota ahead of them. After passing the car, he again slammed his foot down on the accelerator. "John said Dana was heading south."

Jordan frowned in confusion. "I thought you were tracking."

"I'm trying, but I can't get through."

Jordan's frown deepened. "Why would Laural be deliberately blocking you?"

"She's not," he said tersely.

Jordan stiffened. "Then, that means ..." he stopped short and was unable to complete his thought.

"That means," Andrew finished grimly, "she's unconscious."

Jordan swallowed hard as he choked back his fear.

"She's not dead," Andrew insisted. "I can feel her fear and confusion. I can't read her thoughts, but she's afraid and someone who she feels is a threat is with her. In his last report, John said Dana was heading south. The Maxwells own a mansion in Miami."

Jordan's eyes briefly shifted from the highway to his friend's profile. Horns blared and other drivers cursed as the Mercedes came within inches of their vehicles. Carpenter said that Dana was heading south. For some reason, it just didn't feel right.

"So, we're going to Miami based solely on John's sketchy information and your hunch?"

"Look," Andrew replied flatly, "you insisted on coming. Besides, I couldn't just sit around and do nothing while my daughter is in danger."

"Have you been able to make contact with Dana?"

The marquis grimaced. "She's shut down and completely blocked herself off."

Jordan sighed. He also had been trying in vain to connect with his fiancée for the past several hours. "Has Laural tried to reach out?"

Andrew pounded the steering wheel in frustration. "Laural's abilities are too erratic. She doesn't know how to focus her thoughts. I get random flashes and intense feelings, but nothing I can use to find her or figure out what is happening. Then, there are long spaces of nothing. It's as though she's coming in and out of consciousness."

Jordan stared silently out of the window. He could not imagine the mental anguish of being able to feel a loved one's pain while being impotent to help.

"Victory and I made a mistake in not telling Laural long ago what she needed to know about her abilities. Because of that decision, she's now powerless to defend herself. If anything happens to her, it will be my fault."

Chapter 27:

The Memento

"So many questions! I will do my best to satisfy your curiosity."

"You can read my thoughts?" Laural asked in shock.

Abruptly, an overhead fluorescent bulb flickered and then came to life. She blinked several times. Confronting her was a dark-haired man about the same age as her father. He was dressed casually in a silk turtleneck and designer jeans. He seemed vaguely familiar. She was not certain if she knew him as an acquaintance of her parents or as an employee of the foundation. She hoped that knowing who he was might lead to understanding why he had taken her – and that knowledge might help her to escape.

As he leaned over her, his dark eyes bore hypnotically into hers. She became confused and disoriented as she was caught and held captive by his penetrating onyx orbs. She was mesmerized as he lifted several strands of her golden hair and rubbed them between his fingers. Suddenly, he yanked hard. Tears flooded the corners of her eyes.

"You look so much like your mother," he said directly into her ear, "but you have your father in you, too. For that, you will have to pay."

He moved back slightly. Laural used the opportunity to break eye contact. She scanned her surroundings. From what she could tell, she was in some kind of basement. Fluorescent lights periodically dotted the ceiling, which was made of concrete, and the walls were dull gray concrete blocks. As far as she could tell, the room was empty except for the table that she was on, several pieces of equipment that she could not identify, and a large steel furnace in the middle of the room.

The man followed her gaze. "Sorry if the accommodations are not to your liking, but it was the best I could do."

She remained silent. Obviously, she had fallen victim to a psychopath. She did not know what part Dana played in this. Could she be a victim, too? But she had been left free to come and go at will. The thought confused her and left a lump of dread that settled in the pit of her stomach.

"How do you know my dad?" she asked, while trying desperately to gain information that might give her some idea of what was going on.

"I'll be happy to explain," he agreed amiably, as he yanked her hair harder.

Tears of pain and fear flowed freely down her cheeks as he held up a thick clump of her hair and dangled it in front of her face.

"Do you think your father would like this as a memento of your birthday?"

Her mind recoiled and threatened to shut down as it had after the death of her mother. She resisted the temptation. She needed to stay alert if she was going to survive. She forced her mind to focus. She needed to know who this maniac was and how he knew so much about her. Was he able to glean all of it from her mind or did he have some other source of information?

As he carefully slipped the strands into a manila envelope, he laughed softly. "To answer your question: both."

"How is it you can read my thoughts so completely and easily while I can't detect yours at all?" she asked, while hoping to keep him distracted as she tried to connect telepathically with her dad.

"I've been around for quite some time and am quite adept. You, on the other hand, are a novice whose abilities have just begun to bloom. I've been watching and waiting because the timing of this experiment is essential. The window of opportunity only exists after your abilities manifest, but before you commence drinking the PS4 supplement."

Confused, she frowned. What was he saying? She wished fervently that her parents had shared more information. If they had, she would be able to understand and deal with this situation. Guardedly, her eyes wandered over his features. She reconsidered. She doubted that anything her parents might have told her could have prepared her for this.

Cautiously, she opened her mind and hesitantly projected her thoughts outward in search of her dad. She had no idea how to connect telepathically with her father. She did not know if she should try to send words, feelings, or images. She decided to blend them and hoped that her efforts would go undetected.

She bit her lip as she studied her captor. Her eyes roamed over his face and eventually were caught and held captive by his piercing orbs. Every nerve in her body tingled with sudden recognition.

"You're the one who has been watching me. You're the man who was in the cafeteria at the hospital!"

Vainly, she redoubled her efforts to escape. As she strained against her bonds, she lost her focus on the telepathic link with her father. Frantically, she sought her dad. He would be able to guide her like he had with her mom. Inhaling deeply, she forced herself to be calm. Slowly, she unclenched her fists and relaxed. Taking another breath to steady herself, she hesitated. She knew that she would get only one chance to reach her father.

She closed her eyes, cleared her mind, and threw all of her strength into one blast of mental energy.

"Dad, I need ... Aaagh!"

The Mercedes swerved into oncoming traffic. Jordan turned sharply to face his companion. "What the hell ..." he broke off. Andrew was chalk-white. His face was contorted with pain. Jordan wondered if Andrew was having a heart attack. "Andrew, what's wrong?"

His answer was an intense flash of extreme mental anguish. He gasped as the pain tore through his skull. It felt like his brain was on fire. He fought to remain conscious. He lifted his hands to his temple and held his head while he projected his need to his friend. Instantly, the pain receded. Jordan shook his head several times and looked at his companion.

"Laural, stay with me," Andrew gasped and then groaned. He closed his eyes briefly. "I need you to stay with me in order to find you." His eyes flew open, as he pounded the steering wheel with his fist and stomped hard on the brake. The car fishtailed and spun out of control. It ran over the median, crashed through the guard rail, and pointed into the oncoming traffic. A tractor trailer harshly blared its horn, as tires squealed in angry protest.

"We're not going to make it," Jordan thought, while staring straight into the steel grill of the oncoming truck. Suddenly, his world shattered and exploded into a million fragmented pieces.

Chapter 28:
Revelations

Laural struggled up through the darkness. Her eyelids fluttered, then closed again. Her head throbbed. For a moment, she was disoriented. Then, a voice penetrated her confusion.

"I warned you. Any use of your mental abilities results in extreme pain. You can trust me to tell you the truth, Laural. I won't lie to you. I'm not like your father."

She slowly opened her eyes. "My father has never lied to me," she said weakly but with conviction.

The man's black eyes gleamed, as he grinned smugly. "Oh, really? I'll bet he's never told you the truth about me, your mother, or our past."

"Who are you?" she asked in a hoarse whisper.

"I am the man who is finally going to have my revenge. I am the man who is going to ruin your father's plans of assimilation. I am the man who rid our kind of the abomination your father created. I am the savior of our people. I am the one who will resurrect them from the ashes of obscurity. I am your uncle, Craven Maxwell."

The Earl of Rockford slowly became aware of his surroundings. Tentatively, he checked for broken bones. None. Good. His seat belt was still in place, but he felt dizzy and nauseous. His head ached. He gingerly lifted a hand to his temple. A large lump greeted his probing fingertips. He drew back blood.

Confused, he watched as the scenery sped by the window. He was certain that the illusion of movement was due to a concussion. He closed his eyes. The vibration of the automobile belied his conclusion. The car was moving. "How can this be? The crash? The spin? The tractor trailer bearing down on us?" he questioned in vain. He blinked and turned his head toward the driver's seat. As the pain exploded, he blacked out.

Some time later, Jordan opened his eyes again. Andrew was continuing to race south. An exit sign flashed past. Still nauseous and dizzy, he had to exert a supreme effort in order to connect his thoughts and turn them into words. "How did we avoid a collision?"

As Andrew switched lanes, he explained. "We didn't. Well, at least not entirely. The semi clipped the rear bumper. I think that's when you hit your head."

"What happened to you back there?" he asked thickly. He was still slightly groggy and having difficulty in focusing.

Striking the steering wheel with his fist, Andrew snarled, "Someone has my child, is torturing her, and I can't do anything about it."

"You've lost the connection?"

Raking his hand through his hair, Andrew nodded grimly.

Jordan stared at the red streaks that forged a path through the platinum strands. Then, he glanced at his friend's hand. The gash was deep, but was starting to heal. His eyes strayed from Andrew's hand to his face. Another cut sliced its way from his right eye down across his cheek. Even as he watched, the blood slowed and then stopped.

He turned his gaze to the highway. Another exit sign flashed past. Jordan sighed. "I know where the mansion is," he offered quietly.

"So do I."

Jordan shook his head. "The Maxwells no longer own a mansion in Miami. Dana sold it years ago."

Andrew sharply glanced at him. "When were you going to tell me?"

He sighed again, while cautiously touching his head. "Right before the accident."

Andrew slammed his fist on the steering wheel. "So, we're on a wild goose chase?"

"Not exactly."

"Damn it!" he exploded. "My daughter's life is at risk. Would you mind making some sense?"

Jordan winced. "Dana sold both the Miami and Washington properties several years ago. She said they had too many bad memories. She didn't want any reminders of her father's domination." He stared earnestly at his companion. "None of this makes sense. Why would

Dana sever her ties from the past if she was still interested in her father's plans?"

Andrew shrugged. "She could've changed her mind – or," he continued angrily, "she could've been fooling us all this time. Then again, she might've been waiting for the perfect opportunity."

Jordan frowned, as he peered out the window. "An opportunity for what? To kill Victory? To kidnap Laural? To ruin the foundation? To dominate the country?" He turned to confront his friend. "I know you don't have a high opinion of Dana, but she has given every indication that she has no interest in following in her father's footsteps."

"Until recently. How do you explain her erratic thoughts and behavior? How do you explain my dead wife and my abducted daughter and your missing-in-action fiancée?"

He blew out a breath and slumped. He couldn't argue those points. She might have been duplicitous during both of the tragedies. If so, she was an incredibly good actress to have kept it up for such a long time.

"All right," he conceded. "Even if Dana is behind this, she is not acting alone."

Andrew nodded. "You're right."

Jordan glanced sharply at him and then straightened. "Get off here," he commanded as he indicated the West Palm Beach exit.

Andrew hesitated, but then flipped the turn signal. Easing the car onto the exit ramp, he looked inquiringly at his friend.

"Remember my Palm Beach home? Dana used it as a refuge once. If she's headed south, that's my best guess where she would go."

"What makes you think she would go there?"

He shrugged. "It hasn't been used in years. It's been neglected for such a long time that even I had almost forgotten about it until now. Anyway," he shrugged again, "I don't have any better ideas. Do you?"

The marquis stared at his bloody fist. Looking up, he searched his friend's features. Several crimson lines streaked Jordan's face and there was a large bruise on his forehead.

"I know it's going to get ugly, but you have my undivided loyalty. I would follow you into the pits of hell," responded the earl to the unspoken question.

Chapter 29:
The Experiment

Laural watched as Craven Maxwell paced agitatedly back and forth across the room. She was sure she was having a nervous breakdown and this was part of her mind's attempt to deal with the trauma of her mother's death. She had read in psych class that the brain, when inundated with more trauma than it can handle, develops alternative techniques for coping. She concluded that she must be in the middle of a psychotic episode. This condition apparently had brought forth an elaborate fantasy of a diabolical superhuman villain in order to make sense of her mother's death.

Maybe, instead of a break with reality, she was just dreaming, she thought desperately. A nightmare would certainly explain her present predicament. She futilely strained against the leather straps that bound her. She grimaced in pain as they cut into her skin. The pain, however, convinced her that she was not dreaming. Either she had gone completely insane or this was reality.

Laural continued to track her captor's progress, while trying to understand what he had revealed. Her brain sought to make sense of the fragments of information. "Is he really my uncle? If so, why didn't my parents tell me about him? Is he related to my mom or my dad? What is the past history he was referring to and how does it affect me? Why does he seem to hate my dad? And, above all, what part do I play in his plans for revenge?" Until she determined enough inconsistencies to think otherwise, she decided to accept her captor at face value.

Suddenly, she went rigid with shock. "You made that man kill my mother!" she blurted, while wondering at her sudden ability to decipher his thoughts. She could not be certain if she were reading him or if he were allowing access to his mind.

Apparently pleased, he grinned down at her and nodded. "A little of both. The fact that you can breech my mental barrier indicates progress. As far as your mother is concerned," he shrugged carelessly, "I rescued you from two people who should never have had you in the first place."

Laural scarcely heard what he was saying. "You bastard!" she spat venomously. "You used mental domination to impose your will on that diurnal and force him to kill my mother. Now, I'm going to kill you," she asserted vehemently. She directed a surge of her full strength against her bonds.

Craven quickly walked to the table. Grabbing her hair, he jerked her head back and slapped her face. The blow left his handprint on her cheek, but Laural did not feel the pain. She continued to struggle. Her arms and legs bulged against the leather straps, but they were too strong for her to break.

Craven watched her ineffective struggles with satisfaction. He felt a perverse pleasure course through him as he contemplated her helplessness. He had not felt this good in a long time – not since he had tortured peasants on his Camborne estate, a pleasure that had been deprived of him by this girl's father. Andrew frequently prevented many of his pleasures. Not this time. Now, it was time for his enjoyment and Andrew's turn to suffer. "Victory was only the beginning," he thought, as he maliciously stared at his niece.

Laural's eyes narrowed. Pure rage consumed common sense as she focused all of her fury and hate into a psychic blast of mental energy. A twinge of guilt penetrated her anger as Craven's eyes dulled with pain. Her parents would be disappointed in her for causing harm with her porphyrian powers. Her mother had been tenderhearted and never wanted to cause harm to any being. Even when fighting for her life, she had been hesitant about using her abilities against her attacker.

Her kind and gentle mother had been murdered by this monster. Her momentary shame was superceded by a white hot explosion of anguish. Her eyes flashed fire as she screamed her agony. Pinpointing the cause of her suffering, she projected another burst of psychic fury at her mother's murderer.

Craven gasped and quickly shielded himself.

"Not bad," he commended. "If I had it to do all over again, I would kill your mother myself. But, first, I would take the time to torture her so I could enjoy her terror and pain firsthand."

Laural tried to use her mind to hurt him again, but he was too well protected. He smugly grinned at her. "You bastard," she repeated. "I will kill you!"

Something flickered behind his eyes, but, before she could consider the implication, he slapped her again. The pain brought an insurgence of fresh fury. She took a deep breath and gathered her energy for one final burst. An ear-piercing shriek emanated from within her head and she slipped back into blackness.

Hours, perhaps days, passed before she awoke. She was so groggy that it took several minutes to determine what she was seeing. Alertness rushed to reassert itself when she discovered an intravenous needle inserted into her vein. She swallowed hard when she observed the clear liquid dripping into the plastic tubing. Flexing her hand, she tried in vain to dislodge the needle, but it was taped and wrapped several times. Her head also felt different. Looking up, she noticed that the electrodes now were attached to a machine. Paper fed through the machine and a needle spiked and dipped in a continual motion across the page.

A door opened behind her and she tensed. Craven walked into view with Dana by his side.

Fury focused her attention on her mother's murderer. It took several seconds for her to regain enough control to register what was happening. Dana pulled a girl of about her own age toward the center of the room. Craven carried a bottle of the reddish brown liquid that looked like the fluid that her parents often drank. In his other hand, he carried two glasses and a syringe.

Caught up in the drama, Laural temporarily forgot her own predicament. Transfixed, she watched in fascination as the girl walked out of her line of vision and returned a moment later with two folding chairs. Opening them, she set the chairs before the two porphyrians and then stood in front of Craven.

Ignoring the girl, Craven poured two glasses of PS4 and handed one to Dana. They touched rims and leisurely sipped the contents. "Can we count on Randolph?" he asked his daughter.

"I don't trust him, but I believe he can be manipulated."

His eyes narrowed. "I don't need to trust him. After he's served his purpose, trust will be of no relevance."

Dana's eyes strayed toward the teen on the table. Then, they quickly refocused on her father.

"Having second thoughts?" he inquired in a deceptively mild tone.

"Would it matter?"

He considered her thoughtfully. Not for the first time he wondered if he should rid himself of this albatross, but had concluded that he must wait. He wanted to experiment on her unborn fetus. Her demise had been his original intention when he had called her to him. She had walked right into the trap. However, when he had learned of her pregnancy, other options had presented themselves.

Deep in concentration, he fiddled with his drink. Randolph would serve his purpose of putting a stop to Andrew's continued integration program. "After that," he thought, while lifting his eyes to study his daughter, "I will rid myself of all my liabilities."

Draining his glass, Craven placed it aside. He stared at the girl. She slowly extended her right arm. Pulling elastic tubing from his pocket, he tied it around the girl's arm. Stabbing the needle into her vein, he drew back the plunger of the syringe. When it was full, he withdrew it. Dana unbuttoned several buttons at the bottom of her shirt.

Laural tried to assimilate what she was hearing and seeing. She continued to observe her uncle, while hoping that he would say or do something that would help her to escape. Now, she watched in amazement as Craven took the needle filled with the girl's blood and injected it into Dana's lower abdomen.

The girl continued to stand passively as Craven took hold of her other arm. He withdrew more blood and handed the needle to Dana. Withdrawing a fresh blood-filled syringe from a plastic bag in his jacket pocket, he approached the examining table. Placing the syringe next to Laural, he smirked at her.

"Don't go anywhere. I'll be right back."

He walked over to the girl, firmly took hold of her head, and sharply twisted it. Laural winced at the loud crack. Tears poured from her eyes as she watched the girl slump forward with her head hanging at an odd angle.

"Murderer!" she shot venomously. She was convinced that she was dealing with a real madman and not just a figment of her imagination. She never could have conjured anything this horrific even in an attempt to avoid accepting her mother's death.

He staggered slightly and glanced sharply at her. Recovering quickly, he studied her. "You have your father's temper, but no matter. You're still not strong enough to be a threat and, by the time you are, it won't make any difference."

His words cooled her ire as she shrank from the implication. Glancing from him to the dead girl, she asserted firmly, "I'd rather die than become a monster like you."

"Big talk from someone who already has the blood of several dead people coursing through her veins."

He nodded to Dana who moved forward, dragged the corpse across the floor to the furnace, and opened the door. The blast of heat from the flames could be felt all of the way across the room. Laural winced as she realized the girl's fate.

Unable to watch anymore, she refocused on Craven as he approached her table. "You're an animal. You should be destroyed just like a rabid dog."

Something flickered behind his eyes. She felt a small surge of satisfaction as she contemplated his discomfort.

He smiled ominously. "I wouldn't look so smug. I just sent your father a mental image of you." His eyes raked over her. "I don't think he liked it. You'd think he would at least have some appreciation. After all, I was considerate enough to let him know you're alive – for now."

He lifted the syringe and held it at eye level. Mesmerized, she watched as Craven waved the blood-filled container back and forth in front of her face. A label was attached to the front of the glass. She read the initials "VP" with a date transcribed underneath.

"My dear niece, do you have any idea of the effect diurnal blood has on the porphyrian physiology?" he asked, while tapping the needle against her arm.

Her eyes grew wide, but she didn't respond.

"No? Well, let me start by giving you a little history lesson. One of your direct ancestors was responsible for developing the original porphyrian supplement. All kinds of horrid-tasting mineral and chemical ingredients that I won't bore you with went into this concoction. It was formulated to enhance the missing nutrients and enzymes that were lacking in our own blood. Over the years, it became the mission of the House of Penbrook to improve and enhance this supplement. Finally, your grandfather perfected a liquid that not only provided the proper nutritional balance, but also improved the taste."

She stared at him.

"Am I boring you? Well, let me get to the point. I did my own research on this supplement. Although the history of the drink was always traceable, the reason behind it wasn't. A little mystery. Mysteries intrigue me. I wanted to know why it had been invented in the first place. What would happen if we didn't drink it? The information on this point is sketchy at best. From what I can gather, the drink was invented because the lack of certain enzymes and nutrients in our bodies will cause us to crave them like an addict craves drugs. The source of these ingredients can be found only in the hemoglobin of human blood."

He picked up the syringe. She watched in horrified fascination as a droplet of blood hung suspended from the needle's tip. For a moment, the drop glistened like a crimson tear. It dangled, fell, and splattered onto her skin. She felt the warm sticky liquid slide down her cheek. She grimaced. Once that blood had belonged to a living person. Her mind recoiled from the thought.

Craven lowered the syringe toward her arm. She tensed. In vain, she tried to pull away, but her restraints held fast. Carefully, he inserted the needle into her arm and depressed the plunger. She watched the blood draining from the syringe until it passed the printed label. Something stirred in the back of her mind, but slipped away. She tore her gaze away from the needle and looked up. Their eyes clashed and then locked. Drowning in the depths of the black eyes, she was seized by true terror.

"As far as I can tell," he said, while withdrawing the needle, "the only nutrient a true porphyrian needs to survive is a little sugar water," he explained, as he indicated the hypodermic needle, "and a steady diet of diurnal blood."

She looked away. He grabbed her chin and roughly jerked her to face him. "Something tells me you don't appreciate the honor I'm bestowing on you. You'll be the first porphyrian in several hundred years to regain our full powers. You, my dear niece, are the first of our kind to be bestowed with human blood before being tainted by the supplement. I and several others tried to make the transition, but our systems were already weakened by a lifetime of drinking PS4. The rejection and withdrawal symptoms proved to be horrific and eventually fatal. Do you know how I survived it?"

She only knew she wished that he hadn't.

He laughed. "Your thoughts are so transparent. I don't even need to read you. Your father actually did me a favor by leaving me for dead after he tried to kill me. I was so weak I couldn't seek human sustenance. By the time I recovered, I discovered changing the diet from PS4 to blood is lethal. I learned recently that a few porphyrians in our homeland tried it with fatal consequences. A chemical reaction occurs. I'm sure your grandfather included a reactive ingredient as a precaution against someone like me learning and acting on the truth. How ironic that his own descendent will be my triumph. Of course," he mused, "this experiment may kill you or drive you insane, but it's a risk I'm willing to take. Tell me, Laural, do you think your father will try to kill you when he realizes you've been consuming diurnal blood? Ah," he murmured silkily, as his hand stroked her cheek, "but this isn't just any diurnal blood. This is the blood from Victory Parker before he turned her into something she was never meant to be. Since Andrew's always had a soft spot for your mother, he might spare you."

Chapter 30:

Dead End

Andrew pulled the silver Mercedes into the driveway of Jordan's West Palm Beach mansion. As he extracted the key from the ignition, he studied the structure. "You're sure this is the place?" he asked doubtfully.

They both scanned the property. The two-story brick and wood structure appeared deserted. Weeds and overgrown shrubbery grew across the walkway. Mold seemed to have discovered a permanent home on the side of the house. The windows were shuttered and the doors tightly closed.

"I suppose," reasoned Jordan, while stepping out of the car, "it would make better sense to maintain the abandoned appearance since it would more likely eliminate inquisitors."

Andrew grunted. "You could be right, but I don't sense anyone here except us."

The earl nodded, as he removed his coat and left it on the car seat. The marquis followed suit. Together, they approached the front of the house.

"I'll meet you inside," said Jordan. Then, he headed toward the back of the house.

Andrew stood, while silently studying the abandoned mansion for a long moment. He listened to the lonely song of the cicadas as they sang on the waves of sultry humid night air. He boldly approached the front door. If anyone was inside, they surely would have sensed his approach. He rang the bell and then knocked. No answer. He had not expected one. He turned the knob. The door groaned in rusty protest as it swung slowly inward. He stood still for several seconds while he used his night vision to scan the empty room.

Stepping across the threshold, he closed the door and more thoroughly surveyed the room. Shadows darkened the deep recesses and corners. Furniture lay scattered around the room. Their drop cloths caused them to look like ghosts in the gloom. As he cautiously advanced, he pulled his gun from its holster.

His footsteps echoed hollowly on the hardwood floor as he passed through the living room. Entering an intersecting hallway, he glanced around. Only peeling wallpaper and dusty cobwebs confronted him. At the end of the corridor, he spied a set of stairs. He tensed. Even though he had not felt anyone's presence on the premises, his daughter's abductors could have blocked their presence and might be waiting upstairs to ambush him.

He started up the narrow staircase. He grimaced as the floorboards creaked. He certainly was not going to take anyone by surprise. He tried to project ahead, but was met by blankness. "Either there is no one up there or ..." He clamped down on the thought as he made mental contact with Jordan.

So far, the earl had found nothing out of the ordinary on the grounds. He could count on Jordan to search the remainder of the first floor while he scoured the upstairs. Even though he had tried to leave Jordan in DC, he now appreciated having someone to cover his back. If they did find Laural and he was slain in the rescue attempt, he could count on Jordan's loyalty to ensure Laural's safety.

Another floorboard groaned in protest as he continued to climb. It did not matter. If there were any porphyrians in the house, they already had been alerted to his presence. Reaching the top of the landing, he looked around. The stairs had ascended to the middle of another hallway that split in two opposite directions. Unsure about turning left or right, he decided to wait.

The wait was brief. The advancing footsteps approached warily. Andrew stepped from the shadows to intercept. Jordan nodded, while pointing down one side of the hallway with his gun. The moon offered little help to friend or foe.

"Anything of interest on the main floor?" he inquired silently.

Jordan shook his head. "Place appears to be deserted." They separated.

Several minutes later, they reunited at the head of the stairs. By mutual consent, they silently descended. After stepping through the front door, they paused on the porch.

Jordan re-holstered his weapon. "I don't understand," he mused, while scanning the surrounding area. "John said she was heading south. Since she sought refuge here before, I thought this would be the natural place for her to come."

"Just because she headed south doesn't mean she came here," stated Andrew, while replacing his own gun. "South covers a lot of area. Since she was aware of the tail and our suspicions, she could have doubled back and gone in a totally different direction." His eyes narrowed. "I think another talk with John is in order."

He started to pull the cell phone from his jacket. Before he could open it, the device began to ring. They exchanged apprehensive glances. Reluctantly, Andrew pressed the receiver to his ear.

"Hello?"

Jordan tensed as he watched his friend. He relaxed as the tension drained from Andrew's face. However, as Andrew's facial features changed from relief to confusion, then to shock, Jordan's pulse rate accelerated.

"I need to speak to John." He listened for several seconds. "I see." Several more seconds. "Yes, we're on our way back now." Andrew flipped the phone shut and stalked toward the car. "We've got more trouble," he called over his shoulder.

"What's going on?" Jordan asked, as he threw himself into his seat. The tires squealed in protest against Andrew's abuse.

The marquis remained silent. He threw the car into reverse and then drive, turned sharply, and then accelerated.

"Here we go again," Jordan thought grimly with one hand braced against the dashboard.

"According to Tim, John never made it back."

Jordan waited while his friend careened around a corner and raced through the streets of the residential neighborhood. "Thank goodness it's the middle of the night and the neighborhood's deserted," he thought, while wincing as the marquis barely missed hitting a stray dog.

"Tim's been trying to make contact with no results."

Jordan waited.

Andrew propelled the automobile to the front of a 7-Eleven. Scarcely pausing long enough to brake, he jumped from the car, threw several coins in the slot, grabbed a newspaper out of the machine, and bounded back into his seat. Streaking back onto the highway, he glanced down, scowled at the paper, and then tossed it at the earl.

Confused, Jordan stared down at the late edition of *The Washington Post* that was spread across his lap. Picking up the paper, he read. His confusion turned to shock, and then to anxiety, and finally to outrage.

Chapter 31:

The Spy

"So, would you care to learn a little family history?" questioned Craven, as he removed the syringe from Laural's arm.

She grimaced. She barely felt the sting of the needle, but whatever he was doing to her was making her sick. Her stomach ached. She had been vomiting on and off for several hours. Her head felt like it was splitting in two and she could not keep her mind focused. Several times, she had lost track of what was going on around her. She knew that she had blacked out because she had come back to awareness in the middle of a conversation on several occasions. She glared at her enemy and briefly wondered what it would feel like to tear his malevolent eyes out of their sockets.

Craven smiled as if pleased by her violent thoughts. He patted her cheek and then moved away. He was gone for an extremely long time. Her mind wandered in and out of consciousness. "Where is Dad? Why is it taking him so long to rescue me?"

When her captor finally came back into view, he smiled maliciously. "He's not going to rescue you because he doesn't care. He never did. All he ever cared about was Victory. Now that she's gone, all you are is a reminder of his loss."

Tears formed at the corners of her eyes and flowed down the sides of her face. "You're wrong about my father. Not only will he find me, but he's going to destroy you for what you've done to me and my mom."

He smiled smugly. "Oh, really? I don't see the cavalry charging in. If he does come, my guess is it will be to destroy the abomination you've become rather than save you. Now, how about that history lesson?"

On the verge of protesting the lies about her father, she hesitated. Part of her wondered if Craven was right. Another part was curious about the history that had never been told to her.

Some time later, she lay stunned and alone. She barely was able to credit the tale that her uncle had told. Part of her still wanted to deny his words, but her heightened senses had detected genuine emotions and her probing had proven that he spoke the truth. Allowing her to read him had provided validation of his claims. Connecting with Craven's mind had been an interesting experience. She had never been bombarded with such intense anger and hatred. He was a man who believed that he had been grievously wronged.

During their connection, she saw his memory of Andrew taking Craven's ancestral home and robbing him of his inheritance. She tried to process this new information in light of her own moral compass. Even if her father had taken her mom away from him and turned her from a diurnal into a porphyrian, that did not give Craven the right to kill her. Her dad's sabotage of his brother's political aspirations and his attempt to kill him did not justify what this crazed man was currently doing to her. Nevertheless, she now understood why he felt such intense loathing. With every fiber of his being, he truly believed that his quest for savage revenge was justified, but his view was just one side of the story. This overload of information and feelings left her more bewildered than ever.

In excruciating pain, she lay alone in the dark. "Think, Laural, think!" she scolded herself. She had to sift through what he had said to find something that she could use to her advantage. But trying to coordinate coherent thoughts made her head ache worse.

However, as her headache and other physical symptoms increased, her porphyrian senses were intensifying. Her eyes were able to penetrate the darkness even though Craven had not left any lights on. She was able to smell the dust and decay in the room as if they were tangible. She cocked her head and listened. She was astounded that she could hear a conversation in another part of the building.

John Carpenter rolled from atop Dana and slid across the bed. While reaching for his scattered clothing, he said over his shoulder, "What's the next step?"

Dana propped herself up on one elbow and admired the tautness of his back muscles as he leaned forward to pull on his corduroy pants. He was a handsome devil, but a devil, nonetheless.

"Isn't it convenient that the previous managers chose to live as well as work here? Otherwise," she continued stretching languorously, "we wouldn't have had the luxury of a bed. Who knows where we would have wound up," she finished, while wrinkling her nose.

He warily watched her, as he buttoned his shirt. "Is there a reason you avoided my question?"

She focused on him for a moment, but then her eyes grew distant. Another time, another place. It had not been so long ago by porphyrian's standards. A quarter of a century meant hardly anything to people who lived for centuries. Similar setting, similar question. Jordan had evidenced curiosity about her father's plans, too.

Her eyes sharpened. "I think Daddy has plans to turn Andrew's daughter against him and then set her free to kill him."

John straightened. He snatched his sweater from the back of a nearby chair. He stood gazing down at the beautiful woman leaning supinely on the bed with her body still glowing from their lovemaking. "What if Andrew winds up killing her instead?"

As she rolled toward him, her hair flowed like a curtain across the bed. She shrugged. "If I know Andrew, there's only one reason he hasn't given into his desire to withdraw from the world after Victory's death. He feels obligated to raise and provide for Laural. If both his wife and child are taken from him, he'll most likely become catatonic again."

John shook his head, as he bent to retrieve his shoes. "What about the foundation and Andrew's mission to provide for porphyrian assimilation?"

She thoughtfully regarded him before answering. Shrugging her shoulders, she explained. "Daddy has a political partner who will see to it that Andrew and his foundation are destroyed."

"And how does he plan to insure that? After all, the Willow Grove Foundation has a long-established reputation of philanthropy."

She smiled, but the expression did not reach her eyes. "By implementing so many scandals and propaganda that the foundation's reputation will be ruined. Then, the legislation will be changed on the heels of these scandals while public opinion is still outraged. Andrew and the foundation are encouraging porphyrians to enter America by legal means. These new laws will make it next to impossible for them to come here without significant scrutiny. Because of the increased difficulty, most of them will be too intimidated to try."

"So, the idea is to use Senator Randolph to destroy Andrew's mission of assimilation." He had the brief satisfaction of watching her eyes widen at the mention of the senator's name.

She narrowed her eyes. Her face hardened. "Andrew's primary mission has always been the pursuit of true love," she spat contemptuously.

He glanced at her sharply. "Nice to know where you stand on the subject," he said sarcastically. "But be careful. You almost sound like you're jealous," he surmised, while thoughtfully eyeing her. "What happens to Laural if Andrew won't kill her? She is his daughter, after all, and his last link to Victory."

"Daddy will either continue to experiment with her or kill her. He'll probably use Randolph or someone like him as a front to run the country and," she patted her stomach, "use my child to start a new race of superior porphyrians who will eventually be able to procreate much more efficiently and greatly increase our population."

He slipped the crewneck over his head. Now that he had the details, all he needed was the opportunity. He knew his boss would be angry at the risk he had taken, but he had felt compelled to try. Getting close to Dana had seemed like his best chance to find Laural and discover the rest of the plan. Andrew would be shocked for he was sure his leader had never conceived that the plot was being instigated by his dead brother.

Now, if he could just figure out how to distract Dana long enough to send Andrew a message without tipping her off. Then he considered. "Why is she so readily sharing the details of her father's plans?" he wondered. "Even though I have been accepted into the fold, could they still be testing me?"

"Yes and you failed," said Dana, answering his unspoken question. In one fluid movement, she rolled off of the bed, pulled a gun from under the mattress, and shot him between the eyes.

Chapter 32:
Preparations

Cornwall, England, 1865

The three horsemen reigned in their mounts at the crest of the hill. They stared down at the fortress and watched in grim fascination as servants and members of the household scurried around the courtyard. Jordan tugged at the Marquis of Penbrook's tunic and pointed. Andrew's gaze shifted to the spot where his friend was gesturing. His lips set in a determined line. "Thus, it is settled. We attack on the morrow," he announced firmly.

"It would appear so," agreed Sir John. He studied the troops who were readying for battle, as he drew along side his companions.

Andrew glanced shrewdly at the captain of his guard. John was a gifted strategist. With the loyalty and support of men like him, the marquis felt confident about the outcome of the upcoming battle.

"Are you sure you want to do this?" asked Jordan uncertainly.

The marquis studied the scene that was unfolding below for a long time. Troubled turquoise eyes finally lifted to meet his friend's concerned gaze. He sighed. "I don't want to do this, but it has to be done. You know as well as I do that this confrontation is long overdue. I can no longer turn a blind eye to Craven's theft of my people's livestock. I can't sit idly by while he picks off my tenants one by one. Most of all, I won't allow him to continue collecting porphyrians who are so loyal to him that they will assist in his plans to exploit the population."

Jordan turned away. "And what about Dana?"

Andrew scanned the scene below. "I don't sense her presence. Do you?"

The green eyes searched earnestly. Relief warred with regret as he replied, "No, I don't sense her. But Andrew, I don't like betraying

Dana's trust."

The marquis' eyes turned deep aqua as he continued to watch the preparations. "It's the only way. It's better to get the knowledge from her willingly than ..."

Jordan nodded. He knew the truth in what his cousin had left unsaid, but he doubted that Dana would appreciate the favor.

John drew his lord's attention. "Something isn't right."

Andrew glanced sharply at him. "What do you mean?"

As he thoughtfully studied his surroundings, John rubbed his hand across his chin. "Knowing Craven Maxwell's ego, I can't imagine he'd allow the preparations to go along without his direct supervision."

Andrew scowled.

Jordan carefully checked the courtyard and announced, "Now that you mention it, I don't see a single porphyrian."

John nodded. "It makes no sense for them to be planning a major battle against such a formidable enemy without either Craven or Thomas at the helm."

Andrew's eyes narrowed. "What do you think is going on?"

The captain of the guard shrugged. "I don't know. It just doesn't feel right."

Andrew tugged on the bridle, which caused his black stallion to prance on its hind legs. He announced, "Gather our troops. We ride for Camelford. We attack at dawn. They'll not be expecting us at first light and, regardless of the tricks my brother has planned, the surprise will gain us the advantage. Do you agree, Sir John?"

The man thought, then nodded in agreement with his lord and commander.

The marquis spared one last harsh glare below before spurring his mount. "Let us hope this will be the end of my half-brother's reign of terror."

Craven Maxwell stood at the tower window, while glaring balefully at the retreating riders as they disappeared into the night. He stiffened and then relaxed, when his captain of the guard entered.

"You saw them, Lord Craven?"

He took another sip from his goblet, then slammed the heavy silver cup down hard on the window ledge. "This is the third time in as many weeks that Andrew has come spying. I believe he is up to something." As he turned, Craven's eyes narrowed. "Care to guess what it might be, Thomas?"

Thomas grinned back. "I would guess an attack is imminent."

The black eyes thoughtfully studied him. "And the mission?"

Thomas looked disappointed. "You haven't heard?"

"News travels slowly."

"It is as you instructed. That's one diurnal who will not be causing any more problems."

"Good," rejoined Craven. "I don't want anyone interfering with how I conduct my affairs. It's bad enough that I have to leave my own land in order to escape the scrutiny of my brother. I'm certainly not interested in rebuilding my life in a country that's dominated by a misguided fool!" His eyes shifted from his companion to the window, then back. "Have everything ready for removal to the States by the morrow. The troops will be sent into Andrew's territory at sunset. While they engage the enemy, we ride hard for the coast."

"How long do you think it will take Penbrook to realize he's fighting only diurnals?" asked Thomas, while nodding toward the window.

Craven laughed hollowly and shrugged. "As long as we've set sail, what difference? My only regret is not being around to witness his suffering when he realizes he's slaughtering the same precious diurnals he vowed to save from me." He turned to confront the gathering dusk. "We'll burn down every field, barn, and cottage in our wake."

"With the peasants still in them?" Thomas asked hopefully.

"Of course."

Chapter 33:
Philanthropist or Terrorist

The silver Mercedes screeched to a halt in front of the Willow Grove Foundation for Continuing Education. The brick and concrete multi-level structure blended with the colonial buildings flanking both sides. Andrew's eyes shifted. The Capitol Building was in plain view to anyone standing on the sidewalk on East Capitol Street.

His choice for the location of the foundation had been deliberately designed. He wanted it to remind everyone who came through the program about the foundation's ideals and goals. Andrew stared at the building as he contemplated everything that it represented. Many lives and lifetimes had been spent turning the dream of integration into a reality. He would be damned if he were going to allow a few sensationalists to destroy their vision of the future.

But his vision of the future had included his wife and daughter. He felt the despair gaining ground and quickly shifted his thoughts back to the current crisis. As long as Laural needed him, he did not have the luxury of giving up. "But where is she? What's happening to her?" he agonized in his mind. Frustration and fear caused him to project his thoughts into the building in search of John. He frowned when he was confronted by a lack of response. "Why is my head of security shielding himself?" Disconcerted, he realized that he did not sense John's presence in the building.

"I still can't believe this!" Jordan raged savagely, as he shook the paper.

Andrew's attention was diverted from thoughts of his absent employee. His gaze fell from the building to the copy of the *Post*.

He scanned the article again to make sure that he had not missed any important details during his earlier haste.

"Philanthropist or Terrorist," Andrew read aloud.

"How dare they!" demanded Jordan. "Instead of focusing on almost two decades of good you have done for the underprivileged, they take one incident and blow it out of proportion."

"Good news doesn't sell papers," he replied dryly, as he continued to scan. Then, he wondered to himself, "Is there any connection between my business problems and my daughter's disappearance?" Any potential clues could not be overlooked. "I'd be a fool not to consider the possibility," he thought, while more closely studying the story.

"As if you're responsible for everyone who comes through the program for the rest of their lives."

"Aren't I?" he asked, while letting the paper drop into his lap. An idea had begun to take hold, but it was too outrageous to consider. "I should've been able to detect duplicity. The fact that I didn't makes me wonder how many more porphyrians are using our facility as a way to manipulate rather than integrate."

Affirming that he had gleaned everything that he could from the article, he tossed the paper. For a short while, he stared thoughtfully at the building. Two large vans pulled up to the curb. He tensed. About two dozen people alighted with huge well-lettered signs. They stalked toward the front of the building, but were careful to remain on the public sidewalk.

Another van sporting the logo of a local news channel pulled up. Reporters and camera crews poured forth and streamed toward the demonstrators.

Jordan sighed exasperatedly. "Oh, great!"

Andrew remained silent as he read the signs. "No More Terrorists" seemed to be the prevailing theme. "Go Home Foreigners" and "Close the Foundation" were not far behind. As they continued to watch, the picketers began chanting, "No more terrorists! No more terrorists!"

"You know, it's only a matter of time until we're noticed."

He nodded, but was not sure that he cared.

"Should we call the authorities?"

"That won't be necessary," replied Andrew, as he watched a DC Metropolitan Police patrol car and an unmarked car park behind the vans. "They're already here."

Jordan followed his friend's gaze. He frowned as he recognized Detective Brent Addams who was emerging from the second vehicle. The police had started toward the front door when they spotted the car. They consulted briefly. Then, Addams nodded to the officers. They headed purposefully toward the demonstrators while the homicide detective approached the Mercedes.

Andrew lowered the window. "Good day to you, detective."

Addams brushed back a lock of unruly auburn hair. "Not for you," he nodded toward the assembled crowd.

The marquis stared at the group. One of the protesters spotted them. Pointing at the vehicle, he drew the attention of the crowd. They descended like a swarm of angry hornets with reporters following in their wake. The police blocked their path and verbal assaults flew viciously. After casting several more angry scowls at the Mercedes, the crowd was forced back to the sidewalk by the police.

"I've had better," sighed the marquis, turning back to Addams.

Addams grew sober. "Well, I'm afraid it's about to get worse. I'm going to have to ask you to come with me."

Wearily, Andrew closed his eyes. He did not have time for this. "Not again. Look, detective, I've hardly had any sleep or food in two days. As you can see," he waved his hand toward the crowd, "my foundation is under attack and my daughter's health remains fragile."

Addams opened the car door. "Your daughter is one of the things I want to talk to you about. When I went to interview her at the hospital, I was shocked to learn that she had been removed from her physician's care."

"That's right," confirmed Andrew, while stepping out of the vehicle.

"Well," continued the detective, as he removed his notebook from his pocket, "what am I supposed to think when the one person who can provide an alibi and exonerate you from your wife's murder is unavailable?"

He opened his mouth to tell the detective that he did not care what he thought, but paused as a tug on his sleeve caught his attention. Glancing behind him, he noticed Sally Grey, his head of public relations.

"Thank goodness, you're here," she said in a voice filled

with tension, as she looked from him to Jordan. "This has been a nightmare."

"Don't worry, Sally," he reassured. "We'll take care of it."

"The only thing you're going to take care of is my questions," insisted the detective.

"She's visiting relatives."

"How can I contact her?"

"You can't."

The detective raised his eyebrows.

"I sent her away because I thought a change of scenery might help her recover. My daughter was in a coma for three days as a result of the strain from this tragedy. I don't want her upset again by you forcing her to relive the experience."

"That's understandable, but this is a murder investigation. I need her collaborating statement."

Jordan came around to their side of the car and drew Sally to one side. "Tell me what's been going on."

As Sally started to reply, a gang of noisy juveniles drove by screaming, "Terrorists!" The four of them suddenly were pelted by rocks and beer bottles. Both Andrew and Jordan moved to shield Sally. The cameras rolled and the reporters commented for the benefit of the evening news. The detective quickly jotted down the number of the license plate, walked to his car, and reported the incident to the precinct.

"Are you all right?" the marquis asked.

"Yes," responded a visibly shaken Sally. "We've been getting harassed all day."

The detective rejoined them. "I've called and requested a couple more patrol cars to ensure your staff's safety."

Andrew nodded his appreciation. "Sally, why don't you go back inside?" he suggested, while handing her over to one of the officers.

All of them watched as Sally, guarded by her police escort, re-entered the building. The protesters jeered and shouted obscenities, but no one moved to interfere. When the glass doors closed behind her, Andrew again addressed Addams.

"Detective, this is my assistant director, Jordan Rush. Jordan, it appears I must go with the detective, so please head on up and help the staff figure out how we're going to deal with this mess. As soon as I return, I want a staff meeting with proposals on how to counteract the negative PR and increase security." Then, he added silently, "Let Tim know our diurnal employees' safety is top priority. Also, find out what's going on with John. I can't reach him."

"That's the other issue I need to discuss with you," asserted the detective. Andrew's attention snapped back instantly.

"I suppose that you heard about the two men who recently held up a bank. Well, they were immigrants who were trying to gain citizenship and they received assistance from your foundation. You should be aware that, upon searching their premises, materials for the building of explosive devices were discovered."

"You can't possibly hold Lord Gabriel responsible for that! How could he know what everyone who comes through our organization does for the rest of their lives?" Jordan protested.

The hardened slate-gray eyes left no doubt that he would love to hold Andrew responsible for everything if he could. "That part is out of my jurisdiction. I'm investigating the murder of Victory Parker-Gabriel. My professional interest is in how the two cases may be related. I've been doing more investigating. I discovered your late wife was an extremely ethical attorney, who was well-known at one time for her aspirations to become a Supreme Court Justice. I wonder how a woman like that would react if she found out her husband was fronting a terrorist operation?"

Andrew stiffened. His turquoise eyes sparked as he stared in silence at the detective.

Jordan protested vehemently, "Your allegations are outrageous!"

Addams ignored the earl and glared at Andrew while continuing doggedly. "If she made her concerns known, what would the husband's reaction be? What might he do to keep her from exposing that operation?"

Jordan gasped, but Andrew's eyes never wavered. "Jordan, will you please call Tom Knox and ask him to meet me in the main homicide office in the District Building?"

Addams turned to the earl. "If that's your attorney, then tell him to clear his calendar for the day because, after my interrogation is over, Lord Gabriel will be requiring his services at the Hoover Building."

Chapter 34:

Epiphany

While he sat across from the detective, Andrew's tired eyes roamed around the room. This interrogation room was different from the previous one that he had been in. The walls, linoleum, and ceiling were a dingy beige with no decoration to distract from the monotony. Idly, he wondered what psychological impact the dull surroundings were meant to have on the criminal mind. He studied Addams from under half-closed lids. Did the detective really think that the Spartan bleakness would provoke intimidation? After the last failed attempt, he would have thought that the inspector would have developed a different strategy.

"We can wait for the arrival of your attorney," said Addams, as he leaned back in his chair and coldly regarded the marquis. "But while we wait, I'd like to get your opinion on a theory I've been working on."

The marquis raised his brows, but remained silent.

"So, we're going to play hard ball," thought Addams, dropping his chair to the floor. "I've found out some additional information I didn't mention back at the foundation."

Andrew still remained silent.

The detective's eyes hardened. "Does the name Robert Brooks mean anything to you?"

Andrew stared for several seconds. "Should it?"

He shrugged. "I don't know. He was the telephone repairman several witnesses from your neighborhood reported seeing at your home the day of the murder." He noted with smug satisfaction that he finally had the other man's attention. He continued, while closely watching the marquis, "Several of your neighbors reported seeing a telephone truck in your driveway between five and five-thirty last Monday. I contacted the phone company and found out the identity of the man working on the lines in that area. His name was Robert Brooks."

"And your theory is Robert Brooks killed my wife?" Lord Gabriel asked pointedly.

Addams shook his head, while uncomfortably noting how still the marquis had become. For a moment, he had the strangest feeling that the tables had turned and he was no longer the hunter but the prey. He cleared his throat and scowled. "I've done a background check and Mr. Brooks comes up clean. He has no record – not even a traffic ticket. From what I can gather through our investigation, it's very unlikely that he was the murderer."

He sighed. "I suppose there is a point to you telling me all this besides letting me know my phone lines are in good repair."

Addams frowned and was unsure if there was a hint of mockery in the turquoise eyes staring back at him.

"What am I doing here?" Andrew wondered. He listened to the detective drone on and on and on. He should be saving his daughter and protecting his foundation, not indulging in diurnal mind games. Dana might have had the right idea. He should influence this diurnal and be done with these pointless distractions. He straightened and refocused.

"Unfortunately," reported Addams, "this very viable witness, who is probably the last person to see your wife alive, ran his vehicle off the road and into the Potomac after leaving your home. What do you suppose would make him do that?"

Andrew exhaled in obvious exasperation. "Why don't you tell me?"

"According to the official reports, Mr. Brooks was in excellent health when, for no apparent reason, he decided to take a nosedive into the river. Do you want to know what I think?"

The blue eyes pinned him. "Not really."

"Well," drawled the detective, who now was taking pleasure in his position of power, "I find it highly suspicious that your wife was murdered and the last person to see her alive is dead. Not only that, but your only collaborating witness was in a coma and is now unable to be reached for questioning."

Andrew knew exactly where the detective was heading. He wondered again about the wisdom of using his influence. It would be so easy and beneficial. He would not even be blocking the detective's investigation. For even though the detective believed that he had a viable supposition, his conclusions were wrong. The actual facts would exonerate him, but he could not provide them nor even allow them to be exposed. Finally, he decided that the end did not justify the means. If he allowed this indulgence for personal gain, he would be starting down a path that eventually would lead to becoming just like Craven.

His brother always believed that diurnals were expendable pawns to be used for his own perverted needs. Craven would not have hesitated to influence the detective. He also would have had no compunction about using Robert Brooks to commit a heinous crime and then cause him to commit suicide. Even his demented half-brother could not have planned Andrew's present predicament any better.

"Then, there's the fire."

Andrew's attention returned to the present. "What about it?"

"Well, I find it difficult to understand how the fire started and why there are no remains of your wife to be found anywhere on the premises."

The marquis stared with overwhelming intensity. "As I understand from the fire chief, a blaze that intense would have obliterated any remains."

Addams glared. "That's one possibility. Personally, I'm working on the premise that the fire was used as a cover-up." Receiving no reaction from the other man, he continued. "My theory is that you killed your wife because she discovered your subversive activities. Then, you realized Mr. Brooks could place you at the scene an hour earlier than you claim. So, you killed him, too. Your daughter either witnessed the event or found out subsequently, so now you have disposed of her as well."

Andrew only half-heard the detective as the clues slipped slowly into place. A feeling of dread settled over him as his conviction grew. Was it even possible? Desperately, his mind searched for another alternative. No matter how hard he tried to deny it, everything else suddenly made sense with that one piece of the puzzle.

Pulling his cell phone from his jacket pocket, he flipped it open and dialed.

"Lord Gabriel, I'm sorry, but you cannot make ..."

"It's to my lawyer."

"Well, in that case," Addams conceded.

"Tom," he directed, his eyes never leaving Addams' face, "don't bother coming to homicide. Meet me at the Hoover Building."

He snapped the phone shut and gained a little satisfaction as he watched a dark flush of impotent rage stain the other man's face.

"You may call the shots at your office, but I'm in charge here."

Andrew ignored the outburst. "Your theory has no basis. You still haven't been able to come up with a motive and you have no evidence to support your conjectures. I don't require the services of an attorney to know you have no basis for detaining me. I have more pressing matters to attend to, so" he finished, as his eyes darkened, "either arrest me or release me."

They glared at each other across the scarred wooden table. Addams seriously considered throwing the rich bastard into a holding cell just to knock some of the arrogance out of him. He eyed his adversary. He would never get away with it and they both knew it. The Marquis was simply too high profile with too many friends in key positions. In fact, if he remembered correctly, the Gabriels were on good terms with Senator Daily, the police commissioner's father-in-law. "No," he thought, while grinding his teeth in vexation, "I better have a solid case before I lean too hard on this one."

Addams forced the words out between clenched teeth. "You may go – for now."

Andrew nodded curtly and rose. "Good day, detective," he said and headed to the door.

Chapter 35:
Propaganda

"Senator Randolph, Senator Randolph," exclaimed one of the throng of reporters as he pushed his microphone prominently into the senator's face. "Can you tell us more about the rumors surrounding the investigation of Lord Gabriel and the Willow Grove Foundation?"

The senator unconsciously straightened his tie. He stood in front of his large cherry wood desk. Facing the cameras, he shifted slightly to ensure that a clear shot of a copy of the Declaration of Independence that decorated his back wall shared the spotlight while he spoke.

"Yes," he said into the row of mikes lined up in front of him. "I personally will be heading the investigation into the allegations that the foundation is acting as a front to assist needy American citizens while actually infiltrating our country with foreigners whose intentions toward this country," he paused deliberately to stare hard into the camera, "pose a threat to national security."

"Excuse me, Senator," asked one of the reporters, "but isn't it true that the review committee exonerated the Willow Grove Foundation of any misappropriation of funds?"

"That was a blatant attempt by Lord Gabriel's supporters to sweep this problem under the rug. In light of recent events, I believe it is imperative to make sure a complete and thorough investigation is done."

"Excuse me, Senator," asked a veteran of the press, "the allegations you mentioned about a cover-up are serious. This agency has been around for almost twenty years with a beneficiary list of upstanding citizens a mile long."

"Yes," admitted the senator, adopting a somber pose. "That's why we are moving ahead with this investigation very slowly and allowing the Marquis of Penbrook," he said, emphasizing the title, "plenty of opportunity to respond."

"Senator, how about the rumors that you are planning to toss your hat in the ring for the next presidential election?"

The senator smiled benevolently, as his eyes shifted to a portrait of George Washington on the wall across from him. The cameras followed his gaze and briefly held the image of the first President before returning to the senator.

"That's why it is always important to examine rumors carefully," replied Randolph, while grinning broadly. "You never know when there is a grain of truth in them."

Disgusted, Andrew turned off the television. He faced his colleagues who were seated around the conference table and studied their expectant faces. Finally, his gaze rested on Jordan, his cousin and best friend, the man whom he had known since childhood. This could not be easy for him, either. After all, for all intents and purposes, he also had lost the woman that he loved and he was being investigated by the FBI, too.

Jordan frowned at him and Andrew realized that he had unconsciously projected part of his thoughts.

Andrew sorrowfully looked into his friend's green eyes. "That is only going to make the burden that much heavier for you to bear."

Jordan was perplexed.

As he addressed the rest of the group, Andrew smiled slightly. Five women and seven men gazed expectantly back at him. They were a good, loyal group who knew their business and how to get the job done. He had trained them well. Now, it was time for them to show their metal. He had invited Tim Cooper to sit in on the meeting. Even though he wasn't on the board, Andrew wanted him to hear what he had to say. Besides, he thought ruefully, it was better to have Victory's chair filled than to have it as a constant reminder of her death.

"Victory," he thought despairingly. "What would she think of me now?" He had not been able to save her and had allowed their precious child to fall into the hands of their worst enemy. For he now had no doubt that a group of porphyrians loyal to Craven had his child. "Either that or ..." he clamped down hard on the half-formed thought.

He searched the group around the table long and hard, but could discern nothing but expectant curiosity and concern. "As you all just witnessed," he began pointing toward the television, "we have our work cut out for us. It isn't going to be easy counteracting the rumors and allegations, but, since the truth is on our side, we will prevail."

The tension around the table eased slightly as they drew strength from his confidence. "I have asked you all here because I wanted to let you know about the meeting I had with the FBI. As you are aware, two of the immigrants who passed through our program last year were convicted of armed robbery. Search and seizure of their property also exposed illegally gained material appropriate for the construction of explosive devices. Although these two individuals are insisting their crimes have nothing to do with our facility, the fact that we sponsored them makes us automatically suspect in the court of public opinion."

"Possibly in the court of criminal opinion, too," someone mumbled under his breath.

Andrew carefully studied them. "If we're going to come through this, we need to rely on loyalty and integrity. I won't hold it against anyone who wishes to resign at this time." He waited. No one spoke. He smiled slightly and nodded. "I appreciate your support," he asserted, while making eye contact with each staff member. "I also appreciate the time you have spent developing our plan of action. Jordan has briefed me on the specifics and I think it will work. I'm especially impressed with the segment for the documentary on immigrant assimilation building the backbone of our country. Good work, Jeff," he congratulated a dark-haired heavyset man of about fifty.

Jeff smiled broadly. "My grandfather was an Italian immigrant. I just wish there had been an agency like this one to offer support when he arrived in the country. People have no idea of how much this agency helps the disadvantaged and I think it's about time they found out. We have several former clients who are more than grateful and ready to tell their story."

Andrew nodded, while tapping the file folder in front of him. "We have a well-developed plan that Lord Rush will help you implement."

It took several seconds for the implication to register. He nodded as he read their faces. "I'll be taking a sabbatical of an indeterminate length. During my absence, I'm going to leave Jordan in charge as acting director. I expect you to give him the same quality performance and loyalty I've come to rely on from all of you over the years."

Silence ruled the room for several seconds. He realized his announcement probably had come as a shock. Jordan stared severely at him. "I protest. This vengeance quest involves me and I think I should be with you."

Turbulent turquoise eyes studied him. "So you can keep me from exacting revenge against Dana?"

Jordan laid a hand on his friend's arm. "To be by your side when you need me and to help bring Laural home."

"If anyone has the right to time off, it would be you. But do you think that it's the best way to proceed while the agency is under attack?" queried Sally Grey, head of public relations.

"So much for righteous time off," thought Andrew.

"As you all know," he elaborated, first looking at Sally and then around the table, "my wife was slain recently and my daughter has become gravely ill. The only reason I stayed this long was to avert the funding scandal. Now, my daughter has taken a turn for the worse and my place is with her."

John Rivers, a short stocky man in his late forties, spoke. "I don't want to seem uncaring about the wellbeing of your daughter, but, as we just witnessed on the news, another scandal is upon us."

"Yes," agreed Sally. "No offense to Lord Rush, but you," she motioned toward Andrew, "are the head and heart of this agency. As far as the public is concerned, you and the Willow Grove Foundation are synonymous. It won't look very good if you're unavailable to personally negate these allegations."

"I understand your concern, but my daughter comes first. Lord Rush and I've been working around the clock to deal with any contingencies. He'll be in complete charge in my absence. I regret having to leave now, but, if I stay, other crises are sure to develop. It's impossible to keep a complex facility like this running without problems. If I delay until all the issues are resolved, I'll never leave. If anything happens to my daughter because I attended to my business instead of her health, then the saving of the business will be a hollow triumph."

Sally spoke up again. "Is there anything else we should know?"

"Such as?" he asked, while intently studying the sedate brunette. Sally was an insightful and intelligent professional who was not easily rattled. That was one of the reasons that she was in charge of dealing with the provoking position of public relations.

She shifted uncomfortably under his penetrating stare. Looking at him directly, she asked, "Does Detective Addams present any potential PR risk?"

He smiled reassuringly and belatedly realized that he had made her uncomfortable. "Detective Addams is investigating the homicide of my wife. All of you may feel free to cooperate completely."

The collective release of tension that reverberated around the room confirmed to Andrew that the detective already had been making inquiries of his staff. "I expect you all to cooperate completely with the investigation," he reasserted firmly. "Now, if there are no more questions, I'll let you get on with your assigned tasks. I have faith in your ability to maintain the integrity of our foundation."

Chapter 36

Misguided Loyalty

After the staff vacated the conference room, Andrew faced Tim and Jordan. "Well, how do you think they took it?"

Jordan exhaled. "Not well. Most of them are wondering about the sudden eruption of so many scandals. Some are even shook up enough to start looking elsewhere for employment. Most don't believe the sick daughter story. They think you are bailing out on them."

He turned to Tim. "Is that the same reading you got?"

He nodded. "Except the earl is not giving himself enough credit. There were a few dissenters, but most were content to stay under Jordan's leadership."

A fax came through. Slightly embarrassed by the praise, Jordan stood, walked over, and picked it up. As he looked at the page, his eyes widened and face paled. Andrew strode over and tore the paper from his grasp.

"Act I, Scene 2. You've lost your dear wife and soon your sweet daughter. By the time that you find her, she'll have slaughtered."

As he read, the letters began fading. He glanced at the top of the page. No return number.

"At least that part of her story was true."

"What are you talking about?"

Andrew eyed him warily because he knew that he was not going to like the answer. "I'll explain in a moment."

Turning to Tim, he held out the paper. "Just like the last one. See if the phone company can get a trace on it."

Tim took the sheet, nodded to both men, and then left the room.

Andrew reseated himself at the table. Jordan followed suit.

"The day after Victory was killed, a fax just like this one came through. It had a similar cryptic message with ink that faded after being read."

Jordan waited expectantly. Andrew sighed. "At the time, I didn't put much stock in it because Dana was the one who found it. With the way she had been acting recently …"

Jordan flushed angrily. "With the way she had been acting? You mean by telling you off?"

He leaned back. "That wasn't the only issue and you know it. Still, because of her erratic thoughts and actions lately, I wasn't sure whether or not to give credence to her story about a disappearing fax message."

Jordan started to respond, but he held up his hand.

"Wait, there's more. You're not going to like it and I'm sorry about the way I'm putting this on you, but I'm pressed for time. Every moment I delay puts Laural at more risk."

He slipped his hand into the inside pocket of his jacket and withdrew a manila envelope. Laying it on the table, he pushed it toward the earl. "When I returned from my last round of questioning by the diligent Detective Addams, this was waiting for me with the other mail."

Jordan lifted the envelope by one corner. Holding it between thumb and forefinger, he inspected both sides. Although it was as light as a feather, a ton of bricks seemed to settle in his stomach.

"No one seems to know anything about it and there's no return address."

Jordan did not like it. The plain manila envelope seemed to have taken on a malevolent presence. His hands shook as he opened the flap. For a moment, he thought that it was empty. He was unsure about whether he should be relieved or disappointed. Then, his fingers grasped hold, clutched and tugged. A bright golden clump of hair with dried blood attached to the roots dangled from his fingertips. He stared at a ribbon that was bright blue, Laural's favorite color, and a greeting card with "Happy Birthday" scrawled across the front.

Compassion and confusion clouded the jade-green eyes as he looked at his friend. "So, I assume that you know who did this," he stated, as he tapped the card. He could not bring himself to look again at the strands of golden hair.

"Yes."

"How?"

"I received a brief image."

The earl stared and then nodded.

Andrew did not elaborate about the details of the image. He did not want to speak about the sight of his daughter strapped to a metal table with a needle plunged in her arm. A shadowy figure had loomed over her and eerie laughter had echoed through his mind as the image faded.

"It was brief, but long enough for me to establish a connection. I also glimpsed enough details to determine a possible location."

The marquis' mind reeled back two decades. He remembered the day that he had found his lost love. She had been lying on an examining table and had been left for dead.

"One of our own has her?"

"Craven has her."

Stunned, Jordan fell back in his chair. His brain tried to take in what his friend had said, but he kept returning to the same conclusion. "Craven's dead. Remember? He's been dead for eighteen years!"

The marquis sighed, as he raked his fingers through his hair. At the moment, he felt every one of his three hundred and ninety years. He already had lost Victory and possibly his daughter. Would he now alienate his best friend? He straightened his shoulders. Laural was not lost yet and he would not allow his friendship with his cousin to become another casualty of his brother's warped game.

"Eighteen years ago, when the crematorium exploded, Craven survived."

The earl shook his head. His friend must be suffering from the strain. "You and I examined the remains of that site. There was nothing left but debris."

"We didn't cover all of it."

"True," replied Jordan. "We didn't search the basement only because you reminded me that Craven and the others were on the top level when the explosion occurred. We both believed that he couldn't possibly have survived the fire and such a long fall. Besides," he continued slowly, "you told me you didn't feel his presence any longer."

"That wasn't quite true."

Jordan's eyes narrowed as he asked, "What do you mean by 'That wasn't quite true?'"

Andrew would not allow himself the luxury of looking away. "I mean Craven wasn't dead."

"Why did you lie about it?" the earl demanded harshly.

Andrew closed his eyes for a moment. When he opened them, he was confronted by rage, confusion, and pain fighting for dominance on his friend's face. "I'm not sure I can explain."

Jordan slammed his fist onto the table. "You damn well better try!" he replied in a voice edged with steel. "I've been deserted by my fiancée; the organization that I cofounded is crumbling around me; my reputation is being ruined; I've lost Victory, who was like a sister to me; and my young cousin has been kidnapped. Yet, I've tried my best to be supportive to you during your grief. The least you can do is give me an explanation!"

He nodded. "Yes, I lied when I told you I didn't feel Craven's presence that day. What I felt was a life-force so faint it was like a candle's flame flickering in a strong breeze. I was certain it would extinguish itself and prevent me from having to commit fratricide. I easily could have killed Craven in self-defense or while protecting loved ones, but murdering him in cold blood when he was helpless was a different matter."

"So," Jordan responded, while trying to work his way through the shock, "out of some sense of misguided honor, Victory's dead, the business is being sabotaged, and my fiancée and your daughter are at Craven's mercy."

Andrew shook his head. "It's not that simple. A few days later, I went back to search for his body – just to be sure. By the time I returned, the demolition crew had already leveled the place. I came back again after they had left for the day, but this time I felt nothing. All of these years, I've assumed Craven had expired and had no reason to think otherwise until ..." he trailed off as his eyes rested on the clump of his daughter's hair.

Suddenly, Jordan grabbed a fist full of Andrew's shirt. He shook him so hard that the marquis was lifted several inches out of the chair. "How could you betray us? All the porphyrians who have been loyal to you, supported you, believed in you! How could you have done all this?" He gestured to the room with his other arm. "How could you have brought others of our kind here when you knew that you were putting them and everything we worked for at risk? How could you have not told anyone that there was even a possibility that Craven was still alive? Damn it, Andrew, we had a right to know!" His eyes widened. "That's why Dana's emotions have been so erratic lately!" he exclaimed, while shaking Andrew harder. "Her father's been slowly but steadily regaining influence over her. And, all this time, you let me think there was something wrong with her rather than tell me the truth!"

Andrew did not resist, but gazed steadily back at him. "I really believed he was dead."

"That's a crock of bull and you know it. You're just as aware as I am that not sensing his presence didn't necessarily mean he was dead. He could've sensed your probing and blocked you. He could've left the area. He could've done a lot of things besides dying while you've been letting us all live for the past two decades with a false sense of security. Right now, I'm not sure who's worse: you or Craven."

Andrew stared at him. "Don't you think I'm aware of the consequences?"

"Oh, no, you don't!" Jordan shoved him back into his chair, turned, and stalked to the other side of the room. "I have every right to be angry and I plan on dealing with it on my own terms. Don't you dare try to diffuse my reaction."

Andrew straightened his shirt.

Jordan expelled a long breath. "So, this is how he shows his appreciation to you for sparing his life. I guess you expect me to stay here and babysit the business while you go Craven-hunting."

"You're the only one who can do it in my absence."

Jordan scowled. "You could stay here while I track Craven. After all, I won't allow some sense of misguided loyalty to keep me from killing him."

Andrew stood. "What if he kills you first? Excuse me for being blunt, but he has more mental power than you." He shook his head. "I've learned my lesson. Victory paid with her life because of my weakness. I've lost a woman I could have loved for an eternity. I'm not making any more sacrifices on Craven's behalf!"

Jordan studied him. His anger dissolved into sorrow. "How do you know he hasn't already killed Laural?" he asked softly.

Andrew paused at the door. "He's been sending me images. Arrogance has allowed him to believe he can intrude into my thoughts and remain undetected. I have to move fast while he thinks he has the upper hand so I can retain the element of surprise. I'm allowing him to bask in his delusion of anonymity because it's my only connection with my daughter. She's still alive for now. I can't fathom what Craven's purpose is, but it may be a fate worse than death."

"What could be worse than death?" Jordan started to ask, but the marquis had already left the room.

Chapter 37:
The Attack

Cornwall, England, 1865

The dawn rose bloody red and covered the landscape with a crimson cloak as it chased away the silent shadows of darkness. Sparks of sunlight sprayed across the metal armor like ruby droplets as the troops rode down the winding slopes toward their goal. The castle was quiet. All of its occupants were still slumbering because of the previous evening's debauchery. Only a few chickens strutted around and pecked at the dirt.

In the distance, a rooster crowed and a cow bellowed. Jordan Rush, Earl of Rockford, pulled up next to his friend, cousin, and longtime companion. Glancing at Andrew, he noted the determined expression under the visor of his helmet. The early morning sun reflected off the other man's armor, dazzling his eyes. Jordan wiped a cloth across his sweating brow.

"It's hotter than Hades under this metal," he complained.

Andrew's eyes never left their target. "You'll be glad for the protection from the burning rays of the sun."

He nodded and took the remark literally. One of the most significant reasons for the early morning attack was the fact that the porphyrians would never expect it. Since extended exposure to the ultraviolet rays could be fatal, the porphyrians in the castle would assume that they were secure from attack until the evening. Jordan knew that John and Andrew were counting on that strategy to give them the element of surprise.

Stealthily, they surrounded the stone outer wall. Silent as a ghost, Sir John climbed the side of the watchtower and vaulted over the ledge. The diurnal guard's eyes widened with shock at the sudden confrontation. He opened his mouth to shout a warning, but John was too fast. Quick as a springing panther, he pounced and knocked the man unconscious with the hilt of his sword. After lowering the bridge, he beckoned for the force to advance.

Riding hard across the drawbridge, the troops pounded into the courtyard, while shrieking and screaming their war cry. Chaos reigned. Servants arose and ran from the onslaught. The attackers gave no mercy to any of their own kind for they knew that survivors would become fatal enemies.

Andrew drove his stallion further into the courtyard. Fires blazed as buildings were destroyed. He shouted orders to remind his men that nothing of his brother's holdings was to be left standing. After this day, the village of Camborne was to be added to his own. Diligently, he searched for the one whom he sought. His eyes squinted through the gray haze. A movement flickered at the corner of his eye. Rounding quickly, he turned just in time to throw up his shield and prevent a flaming arrow from burying itself in Thunderbolt's neck. His gaze sharpened. Only a porphyrian would shoot a burning arrow at him while he was fully protected by a suit of armor.

He knew that the arrow was intended to send off at least one spark that would penetrate the armor and incinerate the body inside. "It would've been a good strategy if it had worked," he thought wryly, while searching the castle wall. He would have been trapped and his protection would have become his funeral pyre.

Suddenly, Craven leaped from the wall above and landed inches in front of the stallion. A mocking smile split his face as Andrew's mount reared. Tossing aside his bow and arrows, he drew his sword.

"So, brother, you have come. I congratulate you on the morning surprise," he sneered condescendingly.

Andrew drew in his mount and jumped down to confront his foe. "Your reign of terror is over, Craven. It's best for you and yours to leave this place."

"Or what? You'll drive me off?" he scoffed, while brandishing his weapon.

"If need be," the marquis replied stonily, while drawing his sword.

Craven glanced around to surmise the situation. Noting the superior force, impressive weapons, armored protection, and havoc already being wrought, he turned and fled. Andrew raced after him.

Craven snatched a passing servant and threw the maid at the marquis.

Andrew tried to sidestep, but caught one foot in the girl's long dress. He stumbled, fell on one knee, righted himself, and then plunged ahead. Craven's lead was too great and he ground his teeth in vexation as he watched his brother gaining the top of the nearest wall.

Bracing himself at the pinnacle, Craven paused. Looking down at his brother, he yelled, "This isn't over," and then jumped.

Andrew glanced around. His people were restoring order, slaying Craven's remaining loyalists, and helping the wounded diurnals. It was over. Craven's stronghold was in ruins. His brother had been defeated and his power base destroyed.

Jordan and John approached. Their worried frowns meshed with their sweat and bloodstained faces. "Craven?" asked Jordan.

Andrew glanced toward the wall. "Gone."

"Thomas is also missing."

The marquis' eyes narrowed. "That is a dangerous combination."

"I agree," confirmed John. "Do you want me to take some of the men after them?"

He glanced around at the chaos. "No. We have more than enough to keep us busy here." Turning to Jordan, he asked, "Can you read Thomas' intent?"

He nodded. "He and Craven are heading for the coast and then will board a ship to America. Thomas is aware of my intrusion and has blocked me out, so I don't know any more details. But," he said, "before he blocked me, I saw a vision of President Lincoln being assassinated."

"By Thomas?"

"No, by a diurnal named John Wilkes Booth."

Andrew sighed sadly, deeply affected by the event. His gaze swept around the courtyard. "Unfortunately, we can't undo what's been done. I'm afraid the colonists are going to have to fend for themselves."

Chapter 38:
Deviant Daughters

Laural groaned and slowly opened her eyes. Blinking rapidly, she turned away from the bright overhead florescent. Refocusing, she scanned her surroundings until her attention was caught and held by the figures talking at the other end of the room. She raised her hands to her head. The electrodes were still in place. Irritably, she tore them off. She winced in pain as several strands of hair and some skin remained attached to the wires. She dropped them to the floor. She massaged her temples. Her head ached. She felt dizzy, lightheaded, slightly nauseous, and her muscles tingled. The bright lights hurt her eyes. Craven's voice bombarded her eardrums like screeching sirens.

She examined her restraints. Tugging against the chains binding her arms and legs to the wall, she desperately tried to pull free. After dropping the length of chain to the floor, she sighed loudly. It clattered as it struck the concrete. She angrily kicked the metal links. For a moment, she had an irresistible urge to grab the chain and tear at it until she pried it apart link by link. Struggling, she fought the violent desire. Her strength may have increased, but she was not strong enough to shred steel. At least not yet.

Again, her attention wandered to the room's other occupants. Her eyes burned with hatred as they lingered on her captor. For a moment, she felt an unfamiliar desire to attack, mangle, and tear into the flesh of her mother's murderer. As she contemplated how it would feel to have her hands wrapped around Craven's throat, she grinned, exposing extended canines. An image of her mother interposed itself in her brain. The image brought a return to sanity. She covered her face with her hands. "What is happening to me? What is that evil man doing to me? What effect is my mother's diurnal blood having on my system? Am I going to become a deviant like my uncle – or something worse?" she wondered, while she redoubled her efforts to pull free.

As she dejectedly leaned against the wall, she realized that it was no use. After the second day of injections, she had ripped through the leather straps binding her to the examining table as though they were paper. The action had been so unexpected that, before she had time to react to her freedom, Craven had inserted another needle into her arm. The syringe had been full of an anesthetic. The next time that she had opened her eyes, she was chained to the wall.

Each new surge of increased physical strength left her drained. Now, she could only sit on the cold concrete and wait. She again glanced across the room. The image of her cousin and uncle blurred until it became her parents. Her mother was weeping, her father admonishing. She tried to focus, but she could not understand what he was saying.

Tears stung her eyes as she thought of her parents. Her beautiful loving mother was dead. And if she believed Craven, her father was a treacherous insane tyrant with delusions of grandeur. That image continued to be at war with her memories of the man who used to carry her on his shoulders when she was a little girl. She could not reconcile her uncle's portrayal of the man with the father who had taught her to ride her first pony. She cried quietly as she remembered how proud both of her parents had been when she had ridden that first pony all by herself. Now, her abductor wanted her to believe that her mother was some kind of horrible atrocity and her father did not care. She shook her head. Craven's words began to haunt and affect her. "My father does care. Doesn't he? But, if he does, why isn't he here?" she asked herself.

Laural rubbed her temples. She was confused and upset by her chaotic thoughts. She could not seem to focus on any one thought long enough for it to make sense. Upstairs, a doorbell chimed. Laural screeched in agony. The sound was so loud that it ripped through her skull.

Craven nodded at his daughter and then disappeared upstairs. Dana picked up a glass full of reddish-brown liquid and hastily brought it to her cousin. Furiously, Laural grabbed the glass and hurled it across the room. Before Dana could react, she grabbed her arm and yanked. Startled, Dana fell into her cousin's grasp.

Rage and bloodlust coursed through Laural's brain as she grabbed the extra length of iron chain and wrapped it around Dana's neck. She shook her like a rag doll and laughed with glee as her cousin struggled to free herself. Abruptly, she felt the prick of a needle in her neck. Releasing her grip on Dana, she whirled around to confront her uncle. Extending her arm toward him, she strained against the steel bonds. The metal creaked and shrieked as the bolts pulled loose from the wall.

A smile curved Craven's lips as he watched the first shackle break and then the other. However, his smile faded when she showed no signs of being affected by the tranquilizer. As the last bolt tore loose from the concrete, he pushed a button on the wall.

The floor beneath Laural opened and she fell into a small square enclosure about twenty feet below. Infuriated by having been cheated of her victims, she pummeled the concrete walls. The walls were covered with small steel spikes that protruded about a quarter of an inch from the surface. Her skin ripped and blood flew as she continued to pound. Finally exhausted and in severe pain, she sprawled in the middle of the floor and then curled into a fetal position. They watched for several more seconds, but she finally appeared to have lost consciousness.

"She's progressing sooner than expected," he mused.

"What do you expect?" asked Dana, as she massaged her neck. The abrasions and bruises were already starting to heal. "She is Andrew's daughter."

He thoughtfully considered her. Then, with the swiftness of a striking snake, he grabbed her by the hair and bent her neck so far back that she thought it would snap.

Tears blurred her vision, as he said tersely, "And you're my daughter and don't you forget it. Your first allegiance is to me. I caught that little trick when you tried to switch the blood with some of the supplement. Did you really think you could fool me?"

Dana flinched. "I can't stand to see her suffer."

"Get used to it. She'll do a lot more suffering before I'm finished," he snarled, while looking down at the unconscious girl, "and your precious Andrew, too." He thoughtfully eyed her. "Better her than you, I would think – or I could try this experiment on two. Of course," he said, while patting her stomach, "I already am. Now, get upstairs and let the good doctor take a look at you. After all, I'm paying him a lot of money to take care of my future grandchild."

He shoved her toward the stairs. "By the way," he began his

question, as she quickly scrambled out of reach, "is there a particular reason I have a dead porphyrian upstairs?"

"He was a spy."

Craven nodded. "I thought as much."

She started to climb the stairs.

"It's good to know you and I have the same policy regarding traitors."

She tensed, opened the door, and quickly closed it behind her.

After she had gone, he turned back to the cell. Looking down at his niece, he murmured, "Only one phase left," and then followed his daughter up the stairs.

Chapter 39:

The Next President

Senator Randolph sat alone in his office. The weak rays of the mid-February sun permeated the austere room through the open brocade curtains. Oak paneling lined the walls and maroon carpeting covered the floor. Two of the walls were dwarfed by overflowing bookcases. He studied the replica of Monet's *Starry Nights* on the wall across from him, as he reclined behind his massive cherry wood desk. His bushy brows drew together as he considered his position. Should he continue on his current path? What choice did he have? To fade into obscurity after his term was completed? He could see the writing on the wall. He knew that his days as senator were coming to an end. His party was looking toward the future with a younger and more progressive candidate in mind. Even his sources were making no secret that he was fast losing ground with the up-and-coming voters. His constituents were leaning toward the slick good-looking, fast-talking type; a category he could not compete with.

He drummed his fingers on the desk, while his eyes lingered on the portrait of George Washington. If he could not rely on his track record and experience to keep his senatorial seat, how could he count on it to gain the presidency? He mulled over Maxwell's financing and connections. His brows drew together as his eyes shifted and landed on a photo of his late wife.

If he became President, he would owe his victory to Dana Maxwell and her mysterious benefactors. He was sure that this course of action would have Margaret turning over in her grave. He scowled at the photo of his late wife. Meg had always been self-righteous and had appointed herself as his personal conscience throughout their thirty-year marriage. It had been more of a relief then a tragedy when she had finally succumbed to breast cancer.

If he were to forge ahead with this plan, he had no doubt there would be a heavy price to pay for his benefactor's support. Would the price prove too high? How far was he willing to go to become the most powerful man in the world? He stared thoughtfully at his telephone. The call was due to come at two o'clock. He glanced at the wall clock. Two minutes to decide the fate of the rest of his life. "What would my wife advise me to do if she were alive?" he wondered, as his eyes strayed back to the photo. He grimaced. "She would adamantly oppose what I'm going to do. Yes," he thought, "Meg would definitely be against it."

A shrill ring pierced the silence. He snatched the receiver. "Hello?"

"Is everything progressing according to plan?"

"Haven't you been watching the news?"

"The news doesn't tell everything. Your backers need assurance."

He tore his eyes away from his dead wife's accusing gaze. "You can tell my 'backers' everything is going as planned."

"Have you made your decision?"

Unwillingly, his eyes shot back to the photo. Annoyed, he slammed it face down on the desk. "I'm going to be the next President of the United States."

"Good. We need to meet to discuss the specifics of your campaign. But not in DC."

He waited. She provided an address. He wrote down the directions. "You're sure this will work?" he asked.

"Getting cold feet before you even start, Senator?"

"I want to make sure I don't give up my current position for a lost cause."

"According to the news," she emphasized the last, "you're already being viewed as a hero for your hard-line approach to terrorism and being given accolades as a protector of the nation. After the scandal about the foundation blows wide open, you'll be able to ride on the wave of popular opinion right into the White House."

He glanced out the window. The roof of the White House gleamed in the mid-day sun at the other end of Pennsylvania Avenue. "Good thing it's only a short ride."

Chapter 40:

Pieces of the Puzzle

Jordan frowned as he reread the document that he was holding. Absentmindedly, he placed it on the top of the pile on his desk. He leaned back in his chair and closed his eyes, as the implications became clear. The buzzing intercom interrupted his disquieting thoughts. He pushed aside the pile of paperwork in order to reach for the phone. His swivel chair squeaked when he leaned forward. "Need to get that oiled," he thought, as he lifted the receiver. "Hello," he said distractedly, while balefully eyeing the papers that were scattered across his desk.

"Excuse the interruption," apologized the receptionist, "but there is a Miss Melissa Anders to see you."

He frowned thoughtfully. The name sounded familiar. Suddenly, his mind cleared and he groaned.

"Shall I tell her you're not available?"

"No," he sighed, while again eyeing the papers. "Send her in."

A moment later, a tall redheaded adolescent wearing a t-shirt, jeans with a matching jacket, and high-tops walked timidly into the room.

"Please sit down, Melissa," he requested. He gave the girl a welcoming smile even though he was pressed for time.

"I'm sorry to bother you with this," she replied shyly, "but the receptionist told me that both Laural and her dad are out of town."

He nodded.

"Well," she continued, while lifting her backpack onto the desk and unzipping the flap, "Mr. Franklyn asked me to deliver Laural's assignments since he knew how concerned she was about failing math class." Upon seeing his expression, she rushed on. "He didn't expect her to do them right away with everything that's happened ..." She broke off and appeared on the verge of tears. Pulling herself together, she started again. "Sorry. I really liked Laural's mom. Anyway, I think Mr. Franklyn is trying to be considerate. It's hard to know what to do when something like this happens, so I guess the best he could do was to try and keep Laural from failing math class."

Jordan took the proffered materials. He was touched by the teacher's concern.

"Lord Rush," asked Melissa, who was looking him directly in the eye, "how is Laural?"

"She's doing as well as can be expected."

She got to her feet. "I don't want to keep you. I was just wondering because she called me from the hospital, but, since she's been gone, I haven't heard from her."

"She's in Pennsylvania with relatives. I expect they're all fussing over her and keeping her so busy she just hasn't had time to call. I expect you'll hear from her any day."

"I expect you're right."

She headed toward the door. He called out, "Melissa."

She turned around.

"Your application was processed yesterday."

She flushed. "I didn't come here for that. I don't expect any special consideration because I'm Laural's friend. I'd never use my concern for my friend as an excuse to check on my application."

He smiled reassuringly. "I believe you. I just thought you would like to know. By the way, being Laural's friend had nothing to do with it. Your application was approved on its own merit."

She beamed at him and said, "Thank you," as she closed the door.

He leaned back in his chair and allowed the first warm glow that he had felt in several days to wash through him. It sure felt good to do something nice for someone and, according to her file, Melissa Anders was overdue for some niceness. The intercom buzzed again. Scowling, he checked his watch. Depressing the line, he asked, "Is it important?"

"Sorry. It's Doctor Brenner on line one and he refuses to be put off. He's called several times already and is threatening to come and camp out in the waiting room if you don't pick up."

Jordan sighed, as he lifted the receiver. "Hello."

"Lord Rush, this is Dr. Brenner."

"Yes, doctor. What can I do for you?" he asked, while tiredly massaging the back of his neck.

"Well, I'm a little concerned. I've left several messages with Lord Gabriel for Laural, but she hasn't returned them. Now, I've been told that he's not available."

Jordan closed his eyes and leaned his head against the leather headrest. He had not counted on incidentals like dealing with Laural's homework and the doctor. "That is correct."

"I see." A pause. "When will he return?"

The earl leaned forward. He raked his hand through his hair, as his eyes dropped back to the pile of papers. "I wish I knew. I'm not sure. Lord Gabriel and his daughter have gone to visit relatives." That much was true.

The doctor cleared his throat. "I'm not trying to be a nuisance. I'm just concerned about Laural. I like to follow up on my patients and she's been impossible to contact since she left the hospital. I'm not sure what to put in her chart."

Jordan wondered if he followed up this persistently on all of his patients. "As you are aware, Dr. Brenner, the Gabriels suffered a major tragedy. After Laural came out of her coma, she was understandably depressed and despondent. Her father thought it best if he sent her to stay somewhere removed from the trauma. He went to be with her as soon as he was able. I'm sure they'll return as soon as they've healed. I don't know how long that'll take."

The line was silent for several seconds. Then, the physician finally asked, "Lord Rush, can I be frank with you?"

He tensed and then straightened in his chair as he wondered what the doctor was about to impart. "Please."

"When Laural left, she didn't seem despondent. Certainly, she was saddened by the loss of her mother and horrified by the trauma. I'd classify her mood as depressed, but certainly normal under the circumstances. However, Lord Gabriel was a different matter."

His grip spasmodically tightened on the receiver. "What do you mean?"

Dr. Brenner expelled an exhausted breath as his name was paged over the hospital intercom. It was going to be another long night. In the past several days, the hospital had been besieged by an influx of wounded patients. "The crime rate must be on the rise," he thought, as he turned his attention back to the phone.

"That last day when he removed Laural from my care against my medical advice, he seemed impatient, irritable, and argumentative. It seemed almost as though he were trying to provoke an altercation. He also seemed to be having trouble with his memory. I'm concerned because he forgot about the tests, but even more because he rescinded his approval. Since Laural was a minor at that time, there was nothing I could do. Since she is now eighteen, I think she should consider having the tests."

"I'll be sure to pass on your concern."

The page sounded again. "I have to return to the ER. Is there a phone number where I can reach Laural?"

Jordan hesitated. "I wouldn't feel comfortable giving out their private unlisted number."

"An address?"

"The Gabriels guard their privacy. If you want to give a verbal or written message to me, I'll be more than happy to make sure they receive it."

"Never mind. I have to go." The doctor hung up.

Jordan was left with the feeling that James Brenner would not give up that easily. He slowly returned the receiver to its base. Dana had known about the scheduling of the tests. "So," he concluded, "it must have been Craven who abducted Laural from the hospital while Dana distracted them with her false confession and car chase. Andrew was right to suspect her. Obviously, she was in collusion with her father. But why? And how?" He closed his eyes. A piece of the puzzle was missing.

His eyes snapped open when he remembered the time. He checked his watch. He was scheduled to go in front of the inquiry board in half an hour. Gathering his papers, he left the office to walk the short distance to the Capitol Building.

As he traversed the area, he paused to admire the city's landmarks. Halting in front of the Capitol, he studied the freedom statue at the apex while reflecting on the democracy of this land that had enabled different peoples from around the world to come together and interact in one society that they could call "home."

Even another species could get a fresh start and an opportunity to integrate – as long as their true nature remained hidden. He was not naive enough to consider that any society, no matter how progressive, would accept beings whose physical and mental abilities were advanced beyond their own.

He gazed at the flag flapping gently in the breeze just beyond the marble pillars. There would be no place for them here if this society they had adopted and cultivated as their own discovered them, especially with a renegade faction inside their own group trying to exterminate rather then assimilate.

He tightened his grip on his briefcase and, with a heavy heart, trudged up the stairs. Several members of the subcommittee chaired by Senator Randolph were scheduled to make inquiries into the nature of their programs. Jordan had no concerns about his ability to field their questions. Each of their programs was perfectly legal and ethical. What concerned him was the illegal alien angle. It was a little too close for comfort. Trepidation coursed through him as he wondered how many other surprises had been planted by Dana before she left.

Chapter 41:

The Deviant Diurnals

Dana Maxwell floored the accelerator of the bright red BMW, as she headed north on the highway. No matter how fast she drove, she could not escape her churning thoughts. Her father would be pleased that the last of the counterfeit documents was in the hands of Senator Randolph. Those incriminating papers would put the final nails in the coffin of Andrew's aspirations for assimilation.

She turned up the radio, desperately trying to use the increased volume as a way to drown her own feelings. She was relieved to see an end to the foundation. She had never been completely comfortable in trying to integrate into diurnal society. Her main desire in being part of the program had been to fulfill Jordan's dreams. Now that she realized how misguided those dreams were, she no longer could continue being assaulted by the deviant thoughts of diurnals.

All of the years that she had spent in close proximity with the species had convinced her that many of them were even more demented than her father. Parents raped and killed their children; children killed their parents; children murdered other children; people took drugs in order to escape their miserable lives; while still others sold themselves and each other for money. This society that Andrew would have them join was a mess. "In fact," she thought ruefully, "if my father recruited some of the deviant diurnals, he wouldn't even need to exert his will to coerce them into annihilating each other." Some of the minds that she had probed housed more horrific thoughts than Craven had ever perpetrated.

Take Senator Randolph. His was the most diabolical mind that she had encountered since her former lover, Thomas. On the exterior, the senator seemed to be a sincere public servant who was completely concerned with the wellbeing of his country. Underneath, he craved fame and adulation to feed his ego, while he accumulated enough money and power to manipulate and control everyone around him. He was a licentious loathsome soul who desperately was trying to conceal his weaknesses from everyone – including himself.

She rubbed her mouth and was disgusted by what she had done in order to secure his cooperation. Of course, she could have influenced him to do her will, but Craven wanted it this way. She knew that the experience was intended to demonstrate her father's authority over her more than to show domination of the senator. She sighed. Her father would never forgive her for disobeying and deserting him.

She turned the BMW to the right and headed for the exit. Deep in thought, she restlessly drummed her fingers against the steering wheel. She knew that she did not agree with Andrew's idea of assimilation. What she did not know was whether she fit in with her father's plans of domination. She was not sure that a minute group of porphyrians could control the entire population – and not sure that she even cared.

She placed a hand on her stomach. In addition to ruining Andrew and debasing Laural, her baby was now part of her father's diabolical plans. She shuddered. She was being affected deeply by her cousin's mental and physical agony. Laural's powers were now so intense that she was unconsciously projecting them for miles. Dana shuddered again. Eventually, Andrew would be drawn to her like a ship to a beacon. Craven was a fool to think that he could keep father and daughter apart. He, above all, should know better. "Andrew will come and, when he does," she thought, as she parked the car in front of the crematorium, "the time of reckoning will be upon us."

She sat in the BMW, while staring fixedly at the single-story brick building. The face of the crematorium blurred and then faded, as her mind traveled through the portals of the past. Another time, another place, another choice to be made. Had it been the right one?

The brick building snapped back into focus. Dana still faced the same choices that had confronted her over a century ago. She listened intently. All was quiet. Laural might be unconscious again. If she were, that would be a blessing. Craven sensed her presence and beckoned. Reluctantly, she emerged from the car and entered the building.

Chapter 42:
Dana's Exile

Paris, France, 1889

Dana shivered against the icy grip of Paris in December. Her mood was melancholy, as she stood alone on the highest platform of the Eiffel Tower. Dark and desperate thoughts plagued her, while she stared at the sparkling lights of the city below.

"Alone. I'm always alone," she brooded, "since I left Jordan all those years ago." Had she done the right thing? At the time, she had thought so. But now? Self-imposed exile was a hardship that she could not endure much longer. Should she rejoin her father? The bond was strong, but those bottle-green eyes full of reproach kept her from the colonies.

Her hair and long billowing gown whipped behind her in the brisk breeze like a velvet curtain, while her mind circled her turbulent thoughts. Her ankle-length fur-lined cape kept her warm as she contemplated the city streets. Her night vision allowed her to see diurnals walking and driving on the streets beneath her. She let out a long breath and watched as the plume disappeared into the frigid night air. Sometimes, she almost envied the diurnals who lived their superficial and brief existence.

She stiffened as she realized that her space was about to be invaded. Her solitude was probably what caught the young diurnal's attention. She had been aware of his approach long before he had recognized her presence. She hoped that he would not be inclined to interrupt her solitary vigil. But, of course, the idea that she might prefer privacy was lost on him. Like the rest of his kind, he was so arrogant that he actually believed that he was gifting her with his presence.

He walked up casually and nonchalantly leaned on the railing next to her. For a while, he pretended to be interested in the view. "Maybe, he is," thought Dana dryly, "considering the low cut of my gown." She observed him discreetly watching her out of the corner of his eye.

Pivoting to face her, he said, "Nice view."

She spun around and started to walk away. He grabbed her sleeve. She could have broken his arm for his presumption, but she was ntrigued.

"Don't go."

Her dark eyes studied him. "Why not?"

He shrugged, dropped his hold on her sleeve, and lit a thin cigar. "I don't want to be alone."

"Why should I care what you want?"

He blew out a thin stream of smoke. "So, you've been hurt, too."

She drew her cloak more tightly around her shoulders. "What do you mean?"

He hesitated, seemed embarrassed, but then rushed on. "My fiancée broke up with me about an hour ago. Just like that," he said, snapping his fingers. "One minute, we're engaged and, the next, she's gone. Says she hopes we can still be friends."

Dana looked carefully at the diurnal for the first time. He was good-looking for his kind. He had dark hair and eyes like her own. His facial features were finely formed. His build was good, but she could tell from his protruding stomach that he would be fat in a few years. He appeared to be in his late twenties, which was relatively young for a diurnal, but he had bloodshot eyes and broken facial capillaries that advertised his drinking habits.

He took another drag on his cigar. She waved her hand in front of her face. He stamped out the butt on the railing and flicked it over the side. Why was he trying so hard to impress her? She probed. Her eyes widened and then narrowed.

Staring hard at his face, she focused all of her energy. The man hesitated, stiffened, and then relaxed. Suddenly he grinned at her conspiratorially. He climbed onto the metal railing and, with his arms spread out, he began walking the length of steel as though he were an acrobat.

She clapped delightedly.

He saluted, grabbed one of the steel beams for support, and turned to head back. He took a few steps and faltered. Several feet from safety, he suddenly froze. His face turned ashen. His eyes widened in terror as he stared down at Paris rushing up to greet him in the moonlight. An ear-piercing scream ripped through the night and was hurled back in his face by the wind.

A strong arm shot forth from the darkness to grab the man as he fell. Andrew dropped him in an undignified heap onto the steel grated floor. The man scrambled to his feet and began babbling hysterically. One glance at his audience and he decided that discretion was the better part of valor. Dana and Andrew didn't even notice his departure.

The Marquis of Penbrook glared. His eyes shot electric blue sparks of fury through the darkness. "What the hell did you think you were doing?"

She tried bravado. "Nice to see you, too."

He stared her down.

She shrugged and turned her back to him. "Can't a girl have a little fun?"

"You weren't having fun. You were going to kill him."

She spun around with eyes flashing, as she spat, "Did you read him? No, of course not. You would never violate a diurnal. Well, let me tell you that this particular diurnal you were so intent on protecting had no qualms about violating me."

His long frockcoat parted as he raised one leg to prop it on the railing. The wind plastered his platinum hair against his head, as he glanced toward the twinkling city lights laid out like jewels before him.

Impatiently, Dana protested. "That man intended to seduce me into going back to his apartment so he could rape me. Or at least try," she amended noting his skeptical gaze. "I figured I was doing this society you care so much about," she said, while waving one arm expansively toward the city, "a favor by getting rid of him before he attacked some hapless victim."

He turned to confront her. The icy winter wind bit into his face and plumes from his breath frosted the night air as he spoke. "So, you decided to save a hapless victim by making him the victim instead."

She glared back defiantly.

Troubled turquoise eyes gazed back steadily.

She looked away.

"There's going to come a time of reckoning when you're going to have to make a choice."

She turned her back so he couldn't see how much his words had affected her. "You mean your way or die?"

No answer.

She spun around to demand validation, but he was gone.

Chapter 43:

The Foundation on Trial

Jordan settled himself at the table and then adjusted the microphone. The inquiry committee sat at their assigned desk spaces on the dais across from him. Senator Randolph was in the center with two congressmen flanking him. Jordan recognized Senator Johnston and Senator Rogers. The other two men were strangers to him.

He sighed. It would have been nice to see at least one friendly face. Unfortunately, Senator Daily had received so much adverse publicity for being too soft on the foundation that he had felt obligated to resign as committee chairman. That left the position open. Senator Randolph's rising popularity and hard-line approach had made him a natural replacement.

Senator Randolph cleared his throat, as he pulled his microphone closer. "Thank you for coming, Lord Rush."

"Like I had any choice," he thought silently. He respectfully inclined his head.

"As you know, this is an inquiry rather than an indictment. Since there are no formal charges being filed, I do not believe legal representation will be necessary."

"Nevertheless," returned the earl, as he indicated a man who had just entered the room, "I'm sure you will allow our attorney to attend."

The five senators craned their necks to view the man in the navy-blue Armani suit. Boldly striding to the front of the room, he stepped to the table and set his Louis Vuitton briefcase on the table. He popped the latch and extracted a notepad, a pen, and a file folder. Finally prepared, he pulled up a chair next to his client.

"I'm sure you gentlemen are acquainted with Mr. Knox."

"Only as one of the best defense lawyers in the world," mumbled one of the congressmen.

Mr. Knox inclined his head, snapped his briefcase shut, and swung it to the floor.

"Now, if you're ready to begin," Senator Randolph continued irritably.

"Of course."

The senator held up several sheets of paper and briefly looked at them. "We have reason to believe your facility is operating as a terrorist front."

Jordan stared. "Excuse me?"

Mr. Knox's head jerked up from his notes. He started to protest, but the earl silenced him with a glance. He was curious to see where this was heading. A quick review of the other men's startled faces revealed Senator Randolph's ploy.

One of the other members scowled at his zealous colleague. "Lord Rush, I'm Senator Johnston from Virginia. We are only trying to get to the bottom of some very serious concerns. We have documentation that illustrates your facility has helped approximately 86 immigrants resettle in this country in the past year."

Jordan consulted his own paperwork. "That appears correct."

"And," continued Johnston, "there were over 5,000 immigrants petitioning for citizenship status this year."

Jordan nodded, but was not sure where this was going. He glanced at his attorney, but Mr. Knox shrugged, shook his head slightly, and leaned back in his chair.

"Well," interjected Randolph before his colleague could continue, "the committee finds it very interesting that you selected only 86 people out of 5,000."

Jordan exhaled. For this, he had missed several nights sleep? "As you are well aware from your most recent extensive investigation into our finances, the foundation can financially support only a certain number of immigrants per year."

The five consulted briefly. Senator Randolph placed his bifocals on the table. "But why these specific immigrants?"

Jordan shook his head, as he again glanced at his attorney. Mr.

Knox was leaning forward and frowning, while he gazed steadily at the committee members.

"I'm not sure what you mean."

"What criteria do you use to determine which immigrants are the recipients of your services?"

"We use several guidelines, such as financial need, lack of assistance from relatives, and deplorable circumstances that they might face if they returned to their native country."

"Is that all?"

"They also are interviewed to make sure their intentions are to be hardworking contributing members of society."

Senator Randolph stared sternly. "No inquiries about their loyalty to their new country? No psychological testing or evaluations to determine antisocial tendencies? No background checks to validate their reasons for coming to the United States?"

Jordan and Knox exchanged glances. "Excuse me gentlemen," said the earl, "but my attorney would like permission to speak."

Randolph nodded for the attorney to proceed.

"Thank you, Senator," inserted Mr. Knox. "but where is this line of questioning headed? It sounds almost as though you are implying the foundation has done something unethical?"

Senator Rogers spoke up. "The committee is concerned about the lack of appropriate reporting and guidelines that these two foreigners who head an agency that aids immigrants have followed in providing financial and other types of assistance to possible illegal aliens."

Knox's eyes glittered, as he confronted the committee. "I would respectfully remind you gentlemen that both the Earl of Rockford and the Marquis of Penbrook have been American citizens for many years. Furthermore, the foundation has an excellent reputation and offers benefits only for those citizens who have already gone through the immigration process."

"Until now," someone mumbled.

Jordan ignored the comment.

Senator Randolph balefully eyed the lawyer. Ignoring him, he confronted the earl. "I probably would get more satisfactory answers if I addressed my questions directly to the Marquis of Penbrook."

Jordan took a deep breath, recognizing that the man was bating him. "As you are aware, Lord Gabriel is out of town and unavailable to answer this inquiry."

"Which is turning into a witch hunt," he thought.

A gleam entered the senator's eyes. "How convenient. Then, we can assume you are authorized to answer all our questions?"

"Yes."

"Then, answer this," he said and then paused dramatically. "Why is it that all the names on this list of immigrants you've aided over the past year are from countries such as Iran, Iraq, and part of the former Soviet Union known to be hostile toward this country?"

"I don't believe it would be fair for my client to respond to that allegation until he has time to check into the matter more thoroughly," stated Mr. Knox.

"Then, maybe, he'll answer this," rejoined the senator. "Why is it that these same 86 people show no traceable past prior to showing up on our country's doorstep?"

Jordan was aware that the Senator knew the foundation had no responsibility for knowledge of how the immigrants conducted their lives prior to entering the country. He suspected the Senator was grandstanding for the benefit of the media and future votes. Still, for the man to be that arrogant he must have a source. "So," thought Jordan, "chalk up another one for Dana."

Chapter 44:

The Damsel in Distress

London, England, 1890

Shrill screams tore through the night. Andrew Gabriel spasmodically jerked the reigns of his midnight-black stallion. The horse's forelegs briefly pawed the air before resettling on the road. As he soothed his mount, he listened. There it was again: a woman's cry, full of fear, then quickly stifled.

Cursing, he turned Thunderbolt in the direction of the noise. He could not afford the delay, but he certainly could not ignore the possibility of someone in peril. The Whitechapel area was notorious. Since the incidents of Jack the Ripper two years ago, the section was deemed as one of the most dangerous in London.

He galloped grimly toward the commotion and was aware that every moment of delay could cost the pursuit of his quarry. The word was out that Craven had returned and was plotting revenge. It was better for him to find his brother before Craven reaped his vengeance on some innocent. As he spurred his mount, a thought occurred. "What if my brother is attacking diurnals indiscriminately? He would have to be insane to risk it, but he might do it just to increase my grief."

He rounded a corner and was brought up short by how close he was to the fray. Three menacing thugs with clubs and knives surrounded a carriage. The driver lay unconscious and his blood formed a large puddle on the ground. It was so dark in this section of town that only his perfect night vision enabled him to clearly see what was unfolding.

Two of the thugs held a struggling noblewoman, while the other roughly checked the driver. The lady's maid stood off to one side. She appeared pale and close to fainting, while she gaped at the spectacle. As the marquis rapidly covered the last few yards, he watched in fascination when the noblewoman wrenched free of her assailant, stamped hard on his foot, grabbed her maid, and started to run.

Andrew admired the noblewoman's nerve, but knew it was futile. Even as he rode into the center of the struggle, one of the villains caught her and snatched her beautiful drawstring purse from her wrist. Rage burst through him as he witnessed the woman being pummeled while she sought to regain her property.

The marquis crashed into one thug with his horse and, at the same time, slashed the other with his riding crop. The man who was examining the driver looked up and quickly jumped to his feet. Brandishing his dagger, he advanced. One lightning-quick strike and Andrew was upon him. A clean right hook laid the man on the pavement. In a flash, he rounded to confront the other two assailants, but was met by only the deserted alley.

Mildly disappointed at being deprived of the opportunity to vent some of his pent-up frustration, he strode back to his mount. As he remounted, he threw a glance at the woman. She was assisting the now conscious driver back to his feet. Her eyes met his. She smiled and started to thank him, but he cut her short.

"You shouldn't be traveling this part of town with such few attendants."

Her face flushed. "We don't journey to London often. We became separated from the rest of our party and got lost. Thank you for your kind intervention. Without you, I don't know what would have become of us."

He could guess, but decided to spare her his thoughts on the matter. His eyes roamed over her disheveled hair and clothing, but found no injuries. His gaze lifted to her face and he smiled. The soot from the alley marred her elegant features and made her look like a street urchin. "You might want to repair your appearance before you arrive at your destination," he offered helpfully.

Peering closer, he noticed a slight bruise just beginning to form along her jaw line. His smile vanished and he studied her for several seconds. Under her distress, he sensed serenity and something that he could not quite define. Their eyes locked and held. For a long moment, he was lost in the sapphire depths. He shook himself. He had a purpose

– a responsibility – and he could not afford to be distracted.

He deliberately turned his attention to the driver. "Are you well enough to drive?" he asked more harshly than he had intended.

The driver nodded.

He was aware of the confusion and emotional pain brought on by his curtness, but he still would not look at her. "Then, I would highly recommend you leave this area at once."

Needing no further encouragement, the driver climbed onto his seat and picked up the reigns. The maid scampered into the carriage. The woman watched her maid disappear into the coach and then cautiously peered around the street. Reassured that the area was free of danger, she relaxed. Despite his curtness, there was something about this man that drew her to him. However, when she turned back, all that remained of her rescuer was the sound of retreating hoof beats fading into the night.

An hour later, the Marquis of Penbrook stood under the archway that separated the foyer from the entrance to the large ballroom of his cousin's London mansion. While he waited, he patiently watched the dancers twirling and pirouetting their way around the dance floor. He nodded to several acquaintances in acknowledgment of their greetings and fended off offers from matrons who were eager to capture a dance with the elusive aristocrat for their daughters.

He pushed aside his elegant burgundy dress coat in order to pull his gold pocket watch from his brocade vest. He briefly consulted the timepiece and then snapped it closed. He accepted a glass of champagne from a passing waiter as he continued to contemplate the dancers. His eyes scanned the couples until he spotted his quarry. The Earl of Rockford was at the far end of the room. He was engaged in a waltz with a vivacious young blond.

As he continued to sip his drink, he smiled. His cousin certainly was enjoying the ladies. That was good to see, especially since Dana had deserted him. His eyes narrowed as he thoughtfully stared at his cousin's partner. She seemed familiar. The music faded and Jordan released his companion. Andrew continued to watch the woman as she left the room.

"What has you looking so serious?" asked Jordan, as he approached his friend.

Andrew glanced up sharply. He had been so lost in thought that he had not noticed the earl until he was beside him.

"I was delayed by an attempted robbery. Right before coming upon the scene, I had a premonition of Craven arbitrarily attacking diurnals as a way of lashing out at me. That would be an insane risk for him to take, but I believe his hatred would outweigh his caution."

Jordan tugged at his snowy white cravat and unbuttoned his dark-green jacket to reveal the emerald-green vest. He frowned. "Craven-hunting is dominating your life. I'm of the firm opinion your obsession with him is going to drive you insane. I invited you here to relax from the constant pressure you've been under and the first thing you do is scour the city streets for diurnals in distress."

He sighed impatiently. "I know you're disappointed that I couldn't join you for the season, but you know how much time I must devote to the estate now that I have taken over Craven's holdings."

"This isn't about that. You know as well as I that the time is coming when you'll need to absent yourself – just as we've always done and our fathers have done before us, lest the people discern the truth. The adjustment will go easier if they become accustomed to longer periods of absence."

He knew that Jordan was right. But he was caught in a trap of his own making. Now that he had banished his brother from the land, he could not leave the peasants to fend for themselves. They were now his responsibility. After their years of abuse, they needed a strong and just leader to guide them.

Andrew set down his empty glass. "I promised you one drink. I've now kept my promise." He turned to leave.

"You're not going to be any good to your villagers if you're so rundown you can't take care of them."

He glared. "You know my position. I can't afford frivolity at a time like this. As you pointed out, time is of the essence. If I weren't following up on leads to determine Craven's location, I wouldn't even be in London."

"I followed up on some leads, too." He stared into his friend's brooding gaze. "Craven's gone back to the States."

The turquoise eyes narrowed ominously. "You knew and you allowed me to stay here longer than was necessary?"

"I just found out and knew you would be here to receive the news."

Angrily, he spun around. Now that his business was complete, he could return to Cornwall.

"Lord Gabriel?"

He impatiently turned. The beautiful blond that Jordan had been dancing with earlier was gazing up at him. A bolt of lightning jolted through him as he stared at the woman. Her hair was silken sunshine, her eyes shimmering sapphires. Her deep-blue velvet gown brought out the hue of her eyes and accentuated her hourglass figure. Her heart-shaped face was that of a Greek goddess. It was like a cameo in its perfection, except for the slight bruise at her jaw line.

The feelings that he had forestalled earlier now rushed over him like a tidal wave. Although her beauty was great, it was not only that which intrigued him. She stood poised in front of him and displayed confidence with an air of vulnerability that made him want to sweep her into his arms. He felt his blood run cold and then hot, as the rest of the room seemed to disappear.

Jordan made the introduction, but the pair was oblivious to everything except each other.

"You never gave me a chance to thank you properly," she accused, while smiling up at him.

"A situation we can rectify easily enough. May I have the pleasure?" he queried, while smiling down at her. He swept Lady Elizabeth Camden, the woman destined to be the next Marchioness of Penbrook, onto the dance floor.

Chapter 45:
First Kill

The air was thick with the smell of blood. Heavy breathing vibrated through the chamber. Pain, confusion, and fear beckoned like a siren's song. Laural opened her eyes and peered expectantly into the darkness. It was time. She knew that it was time. Time for her next injection. She craved, she wanted, she needed. Part of her mind recoiled from what she had become, but instinct ruled her reactions. All that she knew was that she needed to feed and she needed to feed now!

Her stomach muscles contracted and then released, as she continued to explore her surroundings. No light penetrated the cell, but she did not need any. Her vision was so acute that she could see every crack in the floor and every spike in the wall.

She narrowed her eyes. Those spikes had been responsible for her pain. Enraged, she approached her nemesis. She drew back her fists, but hesitated. Remembering her last encounter with the wall, she tentatively stretched out one finger toward the point of the nearest spike. As her fingertip touched the edge, it sliced through the skin. She cried out in pain.

Pushing her injured finger into her mouth, she sucked the blood. Her stomach muscles contracted again, which reminded her of her need. Where was the one who brought her what she needed? She tried to focus on his name, but it eluded her. She wasn't sure it mattered. The only part that mattered was the rich and luscious liquid. She hoped that he would come soon because she was ravenous.

Why should she wait for him? Why not get what she needed herself? She looked around for a way to get to the top of the cell. Only spiked walls confronted her. No, that was not quite true. In the far corner was something. Her drink?

Cautiously, she moved toward the corner of her cell. She sniffed.

The metallic odor of blood grew stronger as she moved closer to the object. She felt dizzy and disoriented while the form swam in and out of focus. Briefly, reason tried to reassert its grip, but her stomach muscles again clenched in anticipation. She salivated as she lifted the object from the floor. The body trembled. Its breathing grew heavier and more ragged. Laural became confused. The object in her hands was not what she had been seeking. But the smell was the same. No, wait. Other odors mixed with the blood: sweat, dirt, smoke, and a pungent smell that she could not identify.

Abruptly, an ear-piercing shriek burst from the body. Laural dropped it, jumped back, and covered her ears. The noise and odor of blood were more than she could bear. Once again, she grabbed the form and dragged it – as it kicked and struggled – into the middle of the room. The need to drink was so strong that her limbs twitched and her head ached. She violently shook the object so that it would stop making that horrific noise.

As she drew the thing closer, she snarled. It wailed and sobbed while trying to break free. Laural was confused. Why did this thing that made these horrible noises smell like what she needed? It did not look like it, it did not sound like it, but it sure smelled like it. She sniffed. The odor grew stronger. Hesitantly, her tongue flicked out to lick at the spot where the odor was strongest. Fabric tore as her teeth took hold. Now, she saw it. She saw what she wanted, needed, craved.

Red liquid oozed from a gash about two inches long. Again, her tongue flicked. Good, sweet, fulfilling. She felt the gnawing in the pit of her stomach subside slightly, but not enough. Still confused, she drew back. Where was the rest?

Her lips drew back in a snarl. Blood stained teeth protruded ferociously as she tried to determine why the liquid had stopped. The thing that had been moaning softly while she was feeding began to scream again. Depravation unleashed fury. Laural smashed the figure against the nearest wall. After several seconds, the shrieking stopped. Laural released the object and it dropped to the floor.

The smell was stronger now. Starving for sustenance, she searched for the source. The wall in front of her glistened with ruby droplets. Approaching hesitantly, she flicked her tongue at one of the metal spikes. The droplets seeped into her mouth. She carefully sucked it dry and moved to the next. The third cut into her tongue. She drew back in rage. More. She needed more.

As she searched the confines of her cell, her eyes again fell on the body at her feet. Wide eyes stared up at her. Only moments ago, this had given her what she needed. Hunger gnawed at her like a ravenous lion. She desperately examined the object. The body was dotted with small open wounds that spouted thin streams of the liquid. It tried to crawl away. Annoyed, Laural straddled it. She studied the body that was struggling weakly beneath her. Only the neck, face, and one shoulder seemed to have what she wanted.

Licking and sucking each wound, she lapped up the blood like a kitten lapping cream. She finished and sat back. Still unsatisfied, she turned her attention to the original spot. The wound had started to bleed again. As her head descended, she licked her lips. The figure opened its eyes. Laural was close enough to feel the breath on her face and see the golden specks dotting the iris. She also noticed the pulse throbbing directly above the main source of the liquid. She pressed her finger against the pulse. More liquid poured out. She pressed harder. A gush of blood ran over her hand and down her arm.

Laural lifted her hand to her mouth and licked. She had figured out how to get the liquid out. Joyfully, she again pressed the vein. Again, she was rewarded by a fresh gush of liquid. This time, however, instead of bringing her hand to her mouth she lowered her head to the wound and sucked as she continued to press firmly on the vein.

"No, please, no," pleaded the figure, as the life force drained from her body.

But her pleas sounded on deaf ears as Laural, finally satiated, drew on the steady stream of blood.

Chapter 46:
Mindless Puppet

Craven watched the drama unfold as he leaned forward in his leather armchair. His pupils dilated and his face flushed as he stared mesmerized at the video display in his office. He lifted the glass of PS4 to his lips with one hand while stroking his erection with the other.

"Setting up the video camera was sheer genius if I do say so myself," he bragged to his daughter. "Not only does it provide me with entertainment, but I'm thinking of giving a copy as a present to Andrew. The original would make excellent blackmail material. Don't you agree?"

Dana didn't respond. Full of disgust, she abruptly turned away from the display. When Craven had first discussed his plans, the demise of her cousin's humanity had not been in the bargain. Originally, he had mentioned kidnapping the teen only as a way to have leverage in halting Andrew's integration process. She should have known better, but so many years had passed that she had forgotten the extent of her father's perversion and cruelty. He existed outside of the ethics and mores of society and believed that he was a law unto himself.

Moving to the other side of the room, she sat on the sofa where she would not be in the direct line of the video screen. While resting her head in her hands, she again reviewed the justification for what they were doing. Was it worth it? When she recovered from the shock of discovering that her father was still alive, she had been relieved at first to have an ally who would support her in aborting the unwanted pregnancy. Craven, however, quickly devised a more sinister plan for Jordan's progeny. He decided to use the unborn fetus as an experiment. He injected human blood into her amniotic fluid so that she would produce an infant who was blood-dependent. Craven theorized that, by drinking blood instead of the watered-down PS4, the child would prove that porphyrians could become much more powerful by feeding on human blood.

The idea of having a child who would be like Laural made her sick inside. She knew that she had to get away. Unfortunately, her father's domination over her will was complete. Andrew had been right. When it came to her dad, she was a mindless puppet and was powerless in preventing him from pulling her strings.

She glanced back at the screen. Her view was blocked by her father's head. "Just as well," she thought. She did not want to see another glimpse of Laural in that condition. Regrettably, she admitted that her father's theory had proven valid. As her cousin became more hemoglobin-tolerant, her porphyrian abilities increased exponentially.

She laid a hand on her stomach. A few short weeks ago, she had not wanted the baby. Now, she discovered a protective instinct toward the unborn infant. Could she be developing a maternal bond? Survival had prompted her to seek out this alternative in the first place. Just as she predicted, her father had been outraged to discover that she was carrying Jordan's bastard. He had agreed to assist her in the ridding of the unwanted pregnancy. Only too late did she realize his true intentions.

If she had been willing to abort, why should she care what happened to the baby? She only knew she did care about the baby, about Laural, and about herself. The problem was that she was back under her father's domination. His mental abilities were superior and, while she remained with him, her will was not her own. What could she do? She glanced at her stomach. He would never let her leave while she was carrying his dreams of the future.

She worried to herself, "Even if I could escape, where could I go? The mental bond between porphyrians is strong. Between parent and child, it's unbreakable unless ..."

"You seem very pensive," said Craven, while setting down his drink.

Dana started. Had he read her thoughts? Cautiously, she lifted her eyes to his. The black orbs probed deep. She swallowed, as her lids grew heavy and the familiar lethargy overwhelmed her.

"Come here," commanded Craven.

Dana stood and moved forward until she was beside the leather wing-back armchair.

Pulling her around in front of him, Craven again faced the screen. He watched the image of Laural sucking the blood out of her victim for several seconds and then glanced at his daughter. "Kneel," he commanded hoarsely.

Alarm superceded lethargy. She tried to resist, but, in the end, she did as she was ordered. Spreading his legs wide, his arm snaked out and curled around her head. He drew her face between his legs.

Dana's eyes opened wide with shock. Beneath the material Craven's arousal was evident. Horrified, she tried in vain to pull back, but her father's physical and mental strength overpowered her. Mentally forcing her through the motions, he compelled her to unzip his pants. Inserting her hands into the opening, she withdrew his enlarged penis.

Craven continued to watch his niece drain the life's fluid from the body. He groaned softly as his daughter stroked him. When Laural licked at the open wound, he buried his hands in his daughter's thick dark hair to press her face firmly into his lap.

Again, Dana tried to resist. Part of her mind shrieked in protest while her tongue flicked out to lightly lick the engorged tip. As Laural sucked on the wound and drew as much fluid as she could take into her mouth, Dana's mouth opened to receive the full length of her father's erection. As she sucked harder and longer with each stroke, she wondered how long this would last. Her tears of shame fell on his pants and soaked the material. She licked and sucked in the same rhythm as Laural.

She heard the sucking and swallowing build to a faster pace. Her father's strokes inside her mouth kept the tempo. As Laural's drinking increased, Dana's father pushed harder and deeper. Faster and faster. In and out. He pulsated until she thought that she would choke. She heard a long slurping sound like a soda straw sucking air from the bottom of a glass. Then, a soul-shattering dual cry of primal ecstasy split the air.

Abruptly, Dana was lifted from between Craven's legs and tossed across the room. Landing hard on the couch, her first thought was that her father had lost control in his final throws of passion. When she pushed the hair back from her face, she was confronted by electric sparks of fury shooting from familiar turquoise eyes.

Chapter 47:
The Time of Reckoning

Andrew Gabriel, Marquis of Penbrook, stood in front of his brother with his gun pointed directly at Craven's head. With deliberate slowness, Craven stood, zipped his pants, and straightened his clothing. Smoothing down his hair, he asked, "Don't you know it's polite to knock before entering a room?"

The marquis stood rigid with outrage. "Don't you know you're not supposed to have sex with your own child?"

"What happens between me and my daughter is no concern of yours. She came to me willingly."

Andrew spared Dana a glance. "The time of reckoning is here. Is this your choice?"

As she gazed deeply into his eyes, she was caught and held captive by his resolve. She knew that her choice would define her future.

He stared back. "You're pregnant."

Craven smirked. "I'm going to be a grandfather. Aren't you going to congratulate me?"

Ignoring the comment, he held his eyes on Dana's. "Is it Jordan's?"

Her face reddened with embarrassment, as she nodded and wiped her hand across her mouth.

"Then, you're coming back with me. By the way," he continued, while piercing her with his eyes, "what have you done with my daughter and John Carpenter?"

"John's dead. He tried to be a double agent and got caught."

"And Laural?" he demanded sharply.

Before she could reply, Craven intervened. "I told you," he

241

sneered menacingly, "what my daughter and I do together is none of your business."

Andrew cocked the pistol. "Before you die, would you care to tell me what you've done with my daughter?"

Craven's eyes narrowed. "How did you find us?" he countered, while glancing suspiciously at Dana.

"Your daughter didn't betray your location. You did."

He stared in disbelief and was unable to comprehend his failure.

"You definitely need work on how to project images while blocking. Now," he demanded harshly, "where is my daughter?"

Craven laughed. "She's right behind you."

Andrew turned and then blanched. Laural's image filled the screen. She stood with a bloody corpse hanging limply from her hands. She snarled and blood spewed from her lips as she shook the broken and battered body.

"I was going to send the video as a gift, but now you've ruined the surprise."

White-hot fury exploded inside his head. "You son of a bitch! I'll kill you for this," he bellowed, as he launched himself at his brother.

Craven vaulted over the sofa and narrowly escaped the marquis' grasp. "Careful, brother. That's our mother you're insulting."

A mental blast of rage struck Craven so hard that it slammed him against the wall. His face flushed and eyes narrowed as he retaliated. Andrew was hurled several feet and landed with a loud crash against the opposite side of the room. He struck the wall with a jolt that sent the gun spinning out of his hand and through the air. It landed several feet in front of Craven.

The wall trembled. An ancient sword from the Penbrook family's coat of arms clattered to the floor. Andrew recoiled as the blade narrowly missed his head. Stunned, he stared at the fallen weapon. In a flash, he was on his feet and brandishing the sword at his enemy.

"You murdering bastard. It would be poetic justice to kill you the same way you killed my wife. Don't you think?"

Craven backed away warily. He covetously eyed the gun, while wondering if he could reach it in time. Grabbing an urn from the end table, he hurled it to distract his brother long enough to retrieve the weapon.

Andrew batted the heavy receptacle out of the way, as though it were a toy.

"Do you suppose this is how Victory felt? Trapped, cornered, desperate, and afraid?" Andrew snarled, while he slashed at his brother with the sword. He smiled grimly as a crimson line appeared across Craven's upraised arm, soaked through his white dress shirt, and trickled ruby droplets onto the floor. "I plan to give you a personal close-up view of how it feels to be chopped into pieces."

Suddenly, Craven snatched one of the cushions from the couch and threw it into Andrew's face. As his opponent cleared the obstacle, Craven spun out of reach and retreated across the room.

"I know how your wife felt," he taunted. "I was as good as there. She felt alone, abandoned, terrified, and helpless. I enjoyed every minute of it. My only regret is it didn't last longer. You won't be rid of me as easily as I dispatched Victory," he gloated, while holding his injured arm. The wound already was beginning to heal.

Andrew lunged at him and shoved the sword deep into Craven's ribs before he could move out of the way. Giving no thought to the wound, Craven jerked himself free, but a clump of his flesh remained on the point of the sword.

"You must be slipping, brother. Your fear of me was obvious when you had to use a diurnal to do your dirty work. What happened to the man who used to whip his own peasants to death and rape his own servants?" he mocked, as Craven backed away. "Did you really think I would blame the diurnal?"

Craven shrugged, as he warily eyed him. "It's poetic justice. How better to kill your wife than by using those you're so hell-bent on protecting. Really, Andrew, you're the one who is slipping. I'd have thought you'd have figured it out much sooner. After all, you knew I was still alive. Certainly, you understood it would be only a matter of time before I sought revenge."

A gasp echoed through the room. Andrew glanced at Dana and was momentarily startled by the heat of accusation that was burning in her eyes. Taking advantage of his brother's distraction, Craven dove for the gun. Just as his fingers closed around the grip, it was snatched from his grasp. Shocked, he stared at his daughter. Rage flashed from his eyes. Before he could react, Andrew leapt across the few feet that was separating them and arced down with the sword. Anticipating the move, Craven ducked. The sword sliced through the air instead of his head, but the momentum drove it deep into the wall. A shot rang out. The force of the impact drove Craven back several feet before he collapsed against the wall.

Andrew quickly glanced toward Dana and then looked back at his brother. The bullet had ripped a gaping hole into the dress shirt and had torn through Craven's shoulder. The power of the impact staggered him. Sluggishly, he pushed away from the wall, streaking crimson lines in his wake. Dana again raised the gun, but Craven caught and held her gaze. Slowly, she shifted position until the gun was pointed at her uncle.

Andrew tugged on the hilt of the sword, but the force of his thrust had driven it deep into the wall. Realizing his brother's intention, he released it and snatched the gun from Dana's hand. Positioning himself between the two Maxwells, he roughly grabbed his brother and jerked him off of his feet.

Grasping him by the lapels, he lifted him with one arm, while pointing the gun at his head. "Your time is short. What did you do to Laural?"

"Do you think I'll tell you?" he sneered contemptuously.

"He gave her increasing dosages of diurnal blood. Now, she is physically and psychologically dependent on hemoglobin."

Shocked, Andrew stared at Dana. He was speechless. He could not believe what he had heard.

Craven suddenly struck with his knee. As the marquis doubled over in pain, Craven kicked his gun hand. Andrew's fingers parted and dropped the weapon into Craven's open palm. Stepping back, he directed Andrew to the couch.

"I have plans for both of our daughters. I want to see how far our abilities will extend. Laural has been providing me with a lot of data. Unfortunately, I don't think her system will tolerate much more blood without massive rejection. Her brain has already been affected and my physician reports her organs will soon swell and burst. Of course, at that point, massive internal hemorrhaging will occur. The swelling of the brain and organs is a direct result of the infusion of diurnal blood. In my enthusiasm, I may have given her too much too fast." He shrugged. "It was my first trial case. Hopefully," he continued, while eyeing Dana, "my next experiment will be more successful."

He turned back to Andrew. "But, my dear brother, I am now faced with a dilemma."

Andrew warily eyed him.

"I read your true intent to kill me in your thoughts only seconds ago." He stared hard at the marquis. "This is the first time you have ever seriously considered fratricide. Just to satisfy my curiosity, what drove you over the edge? Was it the killing of your wife? The torture of your child? Was it the demise of your dreams? Or," he continued with a malevolent gleam in his eyes, "is this a vendetta from the past? You've always blamed me for your father's death – and you were right. And, while I'm setting the record straight, I used my influence to push Elizabeth over the turret."

Andrew stiffened. His eyes closed against the pain. Elizabeth, his fiancée who was long dead and long buried, but never forgotten.

The marquis opened his eyes to confront his brother's jeering face. "Even at the end, Elizabeth still loved me. And you were so jealous of what you couldn't have that you killed her. She would have become my bride. You couldn't tolerate the fact that she loved me. We had a love you could never have or even comprehend. Both she and Victory loved me unconditionally and you killed them for it."

Craven shrugged. "It wasn't about Elizabeth. It was never about Elizabeth, just as it's not about Victory or Laural." He nodded toward the video screen. "It's always been about you, Andrew. I get pure delight from causing you pain."

Andrew's eyes narrowed into twin slits of blue ice. "I don't intend to allow anyone else to suffer or die because of your malicious sense of sibling rivalry," he asserted with a steel edge to his voice. "If it's a choice between you and my loved ones, I don't plan on making the same mistake again."

"Ah, yes," he jeered, "you mean allowing me to live after the explosion eighteen years ago. How many times have you regretted that decision? I haven't wasted my time with regrets. I've moved on. Now, here is my dilemma: My original thought was to leave you alive to suffer the loss of your wife; watch the empire you built at my expense crumble; watch your reputation among diurnals and porphyrians disintegrate; and, in the end, watch you suffer the anguish of having to hunt down and slay your own child like a rabid animal. However, now that I know you intend me harm, how can I continue as planned? No, you're much too dangerous alive. I may have to kill you, alter my plans, and then continue torturing your daughter until she dies a prolonged and tortured death filled with pain and rage. Tell me, Andrew, is that the legacy Victory would have wanted?"

Searing fury sliced through Andrew's brain. He catapulted from the sofa. A shot exploded, as the office door crashed open.

Chapter 48:

The Bloodthirsty Demon

Shot through the neck, Andrew rolled to the side. Again, Craven aimed the gun at his brother. The marquis winced while he waited for the final blow, but the shot never came. A loud ear-piercing scream reverberated through the room as a bundle of shrieking flesh hurled itself at Craven's back.

Startled, Craven dropped the gun as he tried to pry the enraged demon from his back. Andrew quickly recovered the firearm and took aim. Noting his brother's intent, Craven turned and presented Andrew with the back of his daughter, who was trying to sink her teeth into Craven's neck. He could not do it. He could not slay his own child regardless of what she had become. He slid the gun into his waistband and then joined the struggle.

Laural's elongated canines sank deep into Craven's throat. Screaming obscenities, he ripped her hair and frantically tried to loosen her grip. Laural drank deeply, but it was not enough. The taste was weak and it was not like the other. It left her unsatisfied and very angry. She dropped Craven as though he were a broken doll. He sank to his knees while blood gushed from the torn arteries in his neck.

Sparing only a glance for his brother, Andrew reached for his daughter. Spying the wound on his neck, Laural leaped onto him and fastened her teeth to the wound. As the blood was sucked from his body, Andrew began to feel dizzy and lightheaded. Using all of his remaining strength, he pried Laural from his throat. He tried to hold her in his arms. He attempted to speak and call her name, but he was too weak. The room started to spin and black spots floated in front of his eyes.

Enraged at being deprived again of what she wanted, Laural hurled the second man across the room. With a loud thump, he crumpled against the wall. She turned to look for more liquid. The other. Where was the other one? Laural looked around, but she was gone. The one at her feet still was bleeding, so she knelt down next to him. Using her finger to press on the vein, she pushed and blood flowed. She eagerly put her mouth to the wound and sucked. Spitting out the fluid, she shrieked. This was not what she wanted. Furiously, she ripped open the entire neck and then tried again. Still dissatisfied, she stood, looked around, and then sniffed. The liquid here was no good.

She sniffed the air. Her nostrils flared. Mesmerized, she tracked the scent. Retracing her steps, she approached the hallway. She could hear the ragged breathing and smell the pungent odor of fear.

Dana crouched behind the glass case. She had watched in fascinated horror as Laural quickly dispatched Craven and then Andrew. The mother-to-be was certain that the display of urns would hide her from Laural's view, but her cousin headed straight for her. It seemed as though Laural was tracking her by sense of smell. The idea had never occurred to her, but now it was too late to flee.

At first, she had been grateful for the distraction and the chance to remove herself from her father's domination. Uncertainty had caused her to hesitate. Should she wait longer to ensure that her uncle and father would survive? Her decision could mean life or death – not only for herself, but for her unborn child. Warding off an attack in her condition was not an option so she had decided to wait for Laural to leave the building. Then she would have enough time to head straight for her car and get as far away as possible. However, her plan was not going as she had expected.

Apprehensively, she looked from her cousin to her father. Craven lay motionless with a widening pool of blood surrounding him. How much blood could a porphyrian lose and still live? Would he bleed to death before the wounds could heal? Her eyes strayed further across the room to where Andrew lay in a crumpled heap. He was unconscious. No help there. Her breathing quickened as she realized her cousin's intent.

If both Andrew and Craven were no match for this bloodthirsty demon, what chance did she have? With the strength and speed born of desperation, she jumped up and pushed against the heavy glass case with all of her might. The case tilted and then rocked back. Again, she strained and used the leverage of the wall to aid her final thrust. Laural began to dive at Dana just as the heavy case toppled over. It landed with a crash on the crazed fiend.

Not waiting to check the results of the damage, Dana dashed to the front door. Hitting it hard, she half-ran and half-stumbled, as she disappeared into the darkness.

As Laural pulled herself from beneath the shattered case and metal containers, she shrieked with rage. Glass tinkled as it flew from her hair and clothing. Shards of glass and metal crunched underfoot when she pursued her prey. A primal scream tore from her throat, as she ran after the cause of her pain. Crashing through the entrance, she followed Dana into the night.

Chapter 49:

The Liability

Dawn broke and cast a misty golden, rose, and coral glow over the suburb of Alexandria. Cherry trees were just beginning to sprout new buds on their branches. Fresh spring grass hinted at warm days to come as the sprouts pushed their way to the surface. The new season welcomed the residents to a balmy mid-February morning.

Senator Randolph shed his tan camel-hair jacket as he stepped from the rented slate-gray sedan. The weather was unseasonably warm. Sweat was trickling down the inside of his long-sleeve polo shirt. Straightening, he rolled up his sleeves, as he watched the dawn breaking over the horizon. The red, orange, and violet rays cast the landscape into warm watercolors.

The lower middleclass development appeared less dingy in the first light of day. Even though the houses were neat with well-manicured lawns, there was no disguising their sad state of disrepair. In the distance, a dog barked. It brought the senator back to his purpose. He turned toward the house. The cozy two-story wood façade faced him. It was silent and waiting. No lights shone. No movement could be seen. The senator briskly walked up the flagstones and rang the bell.

Many seconds passed. Annoyed, he frowned, glanced at his watch, and then again pressed the bell. As he scanned his surroundings, he impatiently waited for several more seconds. Finally, shuffling footsteps approached. The door creaked open as far as the safety chain.

One bloodshot eye squinted through the crack. "Dad," exclaimed a surprised young man of about twenty-five. The chain rattled, as he quickly unfastened the lock and threw open the door. His large frame dwarfed the doorway. He was dressed in his pajamas; his hair was tousled; his eyes were half-closed; and his feet were bare.

"Hello, Scott," his father greeted. "May I come in?"

Disconcerted, the youth stepped aside. "This is a surprise."

The senator nodded, as he crossed the threshold. The last time that he had been here was to admonish his son about his drug habit. Scott had claimed that he did not have a problem and insisted that he could quit whenever he was ready. During the argument, it had become abundantly clear that he was not ready to do it on his father's timetable.

As he entered, his eyes swept disdainfully over the living room. Scott pushed several newspapers from a chair and his father sat. With disgust, he eyed the dishes that still contained what appeared to be the remnants of last night's dinner on the coffee table. Everything was in need of repair.

"So, this is how you squander the inheritance from your mother?"

Scott flushed, as he flopped onto a well-worn sofa across from his dad. The argument had been on going ever since his mom died six years ago and left a trust for him. Since he was already over the age of eighteen, he immediately received his inheritance instead of being required to have his father as its trustee. His mother died when he was nineteen, so he took the opportunity to move out of his father's home and into another in a community that was far away from his judgmental scrutiny – or so he thought.

Scott rolled his eyes. "It's nice to see you, too, Dad. What's shaking up there on Capitol Hill?"

"My son, the last of the bohemians," thought Randolph bitterly. "Why couldn't I have been blessed with a child who would follow in my footsteps or at least make me proud? A doctor, a lawyer, an engineer? No, my son had to be a pot-smoking, cocaine-snorting, hippie artist who cares more about his own orgies than his father's political career." Dana Maxwell was right. He was a liability.

Restlessly, Randolph jumped to his feet. "Do you have any coffee in this place? I have something important to discuss and I would like you to be sober and alert for a change."

His son yawned and stretched. He nodded toward the kitchen. "In the cupboard next to the sink. Can't remember the last time I used the coffeemaker, though. Hope it works."

He stared balefully down at his son. This child of his would never do anything except cause grief for him. He turned and moved into the kitchen. Stained counters and dirty dishes confronted him. He shook his head in revulsion. Strengthening his resolve, he pulled two mugs from the cabinet.

In a few minutes, he returned with two cups of steaming brew. He waved one cup under his son's nose like smelling salts. The strong aroma had the desired effect. Scott's eyes opened and then hazily refocused on his father. Sitting up slowly, he accepted the cup.

Senator Randolph sipped the coffee, while grimacing at the bitter taste. Regretfully, he had found no milk to take the edge off of what was surely outdated stock. "Drink up," he ordered. "I have news and I need you awake and alert so we can talk seriously."

Over the top of the mug, bloodshot eyes studied him.

Senator Randolph took another sip before speaking.

"This stuff is awful," Scott declared, while wrinkling his nose and draining his cup. "No wonder I never drink it."

"It tastes better when it's not so incredibly old."

Scott leaned back on the sofa and crossed his arms behind his head. "What brings you slumming?" he asked, as he propped his feet on the coffee table.

The senator examined him for a moment. "I'm running for President in the next election."

Astonished, his son bolted upright. "What does that have to do with me?" he asked suspiciously.

Randolph shook his head. "You're my son. What I do affects you and vice versa."

A slow light of comprehension dawned. "You want me to clean up my act and present an image more in keeping with the son of the next President?"

He nodded his head. "Yes, that's exactly what I want." He expelled a long breath. "But I realize that would be like whistling in the wind."

"Then, what do you want?" Scott asked with his face flushing slightly. He felt warm and still a little lethargic because he had not gotten home until a few hours ago. Even so, he would be damned if he was going to let his dad know about his escapades so that he could have something else to criticize.

"What I want," continued the senator, "is to be the next President.

What my country and I would like is to be proud of you, a son who could be an inspiration and role model to young people across the nation. However," he continued, while sighing regretfully, "I'll have to settle for being the grieving parent of a son who died before his time. That's not my first choice, but my bereavement will probably bring a good number of sympathy votes. Being a grieving parent will be much better for my image than being the parent of a drug addict."

His son's eyes slowly closed. Randolph was not sure that Scott had heard the entire discourse. "Par for the course," he thought ruefully. His son had never paid attention to his lectures.

He stood and approached the corpse. Feeling for a pulse, he nodded. The poison had worked just as Dana had promised. It was fast-acting with no visible signs of foul play. He just had to trust that she was right about the symptoms manifesting as a heart attack, which easily could be attributed to a drug overdose.

Gently, he turned his son so that he was lying full-length on the sofa. Picking up the coffee cups, he carefully washed and put them away. Returning everything to their original locations, he retraced his steps and quietly let himself out.

Chapter 50:

False Records

Jordan leaned forward in his chair at the head of the conference table. He stared down, re-read the glaring headline, and wished that he could make the large block letters disappear. "PHILANTHROPIC FOUNDATION FRONT FOR TERRORISTS"

He crumbled *The Washington Post* and hurled it against the far wall. Hopefully, Andrew would not see it. He had enough to worry about without the news that the foundation that he had nurtured like a second child was being torn apart.

As the other members of the board entered the room and settled into their chairs, he was pulled out of his brooding. Their faces reflected their concerns. Jordan was aware of their turbulent emotions, but elected not to probe their thoughts. The board of directors was comprised completely of diurnals. He and Andrew were in agreement regarding that issue. Although aware of the Immigrant Integration Program, none of them suspected the truth. Not even Bob Anderson, head of the program, knew that most of the immigrants were actually another species that were being assimilated into human society.

Jordan retrieved the paper, smoothed it out, and tossed it into the center of the table. Twelve pairs of eyes focused on the headline. In unison, they looked up expectantly.

"I've called this meeting to discuss the best way to handle that," he stated, while nodding toward the paper and reclaiming his seat. "Sally," he said to the head of public relations, "I would like you to set up a press conference for me. Schedule it for later this morning or early afternoon. I need some time to check on a few things so I'll have all the answers to the questions I'm sure the press will be asking. I want to give our side of the situation to the public before their opinions are formed."

She nodded and began making notes.

He looked at Bob Anderson. "Any ideas on how these false records were included after we had just finished a thorough sweep of the system?"

"Obviously," confirmed Bob, "the information was put in after the last check by someone who had access to our files."

Jordan's eyes narrowed. "That would mean one of our own employees infiltrated the records and purposely sabotaged us?"

Bob nodded and shifted nervously in his seat. "Or ..." he said, while glancing at Tim Cooper for corroboration.

"Or?" Jordan prompted, as he looked from one to the other.

"Well," offered Tim, who had been promoted to head of security by Andrew before he left, "I conducted extensive interviews with the staff and, as far as I can tell, there are no discrepancies."

At first, relief swept through the earl. Then, he frowned. "Well, I'm glad to hear our employees are loyal, but," he continued, while staring hard at Bob, "there's still a problem."

The other man slumped slightly in his chair. "I suspect one of the immigrants may have tampered with the records."

Startled glances swept around the table. The other board members shifted uncomfortably. Several pairs of eyes turned questioningly toward the head of security, while others looked at Bob Anderson for an explanation. Sally started to ask a question, but the acting director's voice cut her off.

"Mr. Anderson," queried Jordan in a steely voice, "are you telling me one of the immigrants gained access to our computer system?"

A sudden hush descended as the board members recognized the controlled tension emanating from the earl. The silence became protracted as the board members digested the information. As he looked into the hostile green eyes, Bob Anderson felt the sweat break out on his brow and a shiver run down his spine. Finally, he nodded.

Jordan turned to glare at his head of security. "How is that possible?" he demanded.

Tim started to reply, but Anderson cut him off. "It wasn't Mr. Cooper's fault," he protested.

The earl's glacier glare pivoted back to the program director. Beads of perspiration dripped down the other man's forehead and his eyes widened in shock.

"Back off," directed Tim silently, as he glanced from Jordan to

Bob. "His mind can't take it."

Jordan broke eye contact with the diurnal and redirected his attention to Tim. He stared intensely for several seconds. Tim fidgeted in his seat, but his gaze never wavered. Finally, Jordan became aware of the emotional tension in the room. He took a deep breath and slowly exhaled. They did not need immigrant breeches on top of everything else.

"Tell me," he said calmly, but firmly.

Bob looked around the conference table and then back at Jordan. "The other day when Mr. Small was putting information into the computers at the Raven's Nest, he was using the improved security system. We left him alone to do his work in peace. One of the immigrants got lost. Since he couldn't understand English, Mr. Small felt obligated to show him the way back to his room. He says he wasn't gone more than a few minutes."

Jordan directed, "Interviews of the immigrants will need to be conducted," and projected to Tim, "with special emphasis on the porphyrians." Tim nodded to show he understood.

He turned back to Bob. "Of course, I'll need you to come up with the missing backgrounds on these folks before my next meeting with the investigative committee."

He directed his next words to the entire group. "I don't need to tell you about the sensitive nature of this meeting. If you are approached by anyone asking questions, you are to offer no comments."

They soberly filed out and dispiritedly wondered how many more scandals the agency could endure. Jordan did not need to read them to know what they were thinking. He was thinking the same thing.

The intercom buzzed. "Lord Gabriel on line two."

Resolutely, he lifted the receiver. "Hello."

"What the hell is going on?" demanded Andrew.

"Can you be more specific?"

The marquis crumbled the newspaper that he had been holding into a ball and threw it across the hotel room. Draining the last of his coffee, he slammed the mug on the table. Fragments shattered and scattered across the tabletop. "The headline on *The Washington Post*."

He exhaled. "I was hoping you weren't going to see that." "H o w could I miss it?" he asked sarcastically.

"Pennsylvania is a long way from Washington."

"Not far enough. I thought that situation was under control."

"It was, but we've sprung another leak. Senator Randolph is like a dog with a bone. He's hoping the propaganda will win him the White House."

Andrew swore into the receiver.

"Leave the scandals to me. You've got more important things to take care of. Speaking of which, did you find Laural?"

Andrew drew aside the blinds on the hotel window. A blanket of snow carpeted the parking lot and covered his Mercedes. The weather had taken a cold snap after the unseasonably warm February. "Hard to believe spring will soon be here," he thought, as he dragged his mind back to Jordan's question. "Yeah," he admitted wearily, "I found her. Craven and Dana, too." He blocked the image of how he had found them so that his friend wouldn't be distressed.

"Was she okay?"

Andrew wasn't sure who he was referring to, not that it mattered, neither of them had been "okay." "No."

Jordan waited.

How much should he reveal? Since Laural probably was heading home, his friend should be prepared. "Craven caused my daughter to become addicted to human blood."

Jordan sucked in his breath.

"She's already killed at least one person and, Jordan," he paused, "she got away."

"I understand."

"No, you don't," said Andrew tersely. "I want her kept alive."

"But that's not possible," said Jordan, who was shocked at the suggestion. Andrew was aware of the danger to the diurnals, but also knew about the disaster that this might cause for their kind. Their laws were very old and very specific about this situation. If a porphyrian contracted the blood sickness, that individual was to be hunted down and destroyed – preferably quickly and quietly in order to avoid alerting the masses.

He could feel Andrew's pain and understood his friend's predicament. "Hell," he thought despairingly, "I don't want Laural dead, but, since she has turned into a blood-drinker, what is the alternative?" He knew the answer and was aware Andrew did, too.

He shuddered. Laural was too much of a liability. She needed to be disposed of before she put all of them in jeopardy.

"I plan to undo the damage Craven did."

"It's impossible. You'll wind up killing her anyway, and it'll be a very prolonged and agonizing death."

"I have to try. You can help me, if you choose. Otherwise, just don't get in my way. And Jordan," said the marquis flatly, "Craven won't get another chance to do this to anyone else."

"Laural killed him?"

"No, I did."

Jordan received the image of the office of the crematorium in disarray. He saw the overturned chairs and the blood spattered on the sofa, floor, and walls. He saw Andrew slowly picking himself up from the floor, standing, purposefully walking toward another prone figure, and leaning over as he retrieved a gun from the floor. Jordan saw the wound on Andrew's neck. The earl watched the scene as the marquis examined the gun, cocked it, and laid the muzzle against the forehead of the prone figure. Jordan recognized Craven as Andrew pulled the trigger.

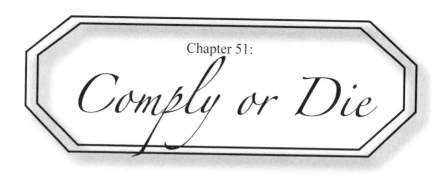

Chapter 51:

Comply or Die

London, England, 1897

Dana tumbled across the blond Adonis before allowing him to straddle her. The four-post canopy shook and creaked to the rhythm of their primal coupling. Dana thrust her hips, as she wrapped her lean legs around Thomas' waist. Her nails dug furrows down his back. Arching her neck, she groaned and then screamed as he relentlessly drove deeper inside her with every stroke.

Thomas' golden hair was soaked dark from sweat. The muscles of his upper arms and shoulders strained with his effort. He plunged, withdrew, plunged, withdrew; keeping time with his partner's screams of ecstasy. He was determined to drive the ghost of Jordan Rush from her thoughts, even if he had to tear her insides apart to do it.

The heavy oak door cracked like a shot as it was hurled against the wall. A candlestick toppled, sputtered, and then went out. A tapestry was jarred loose from the wall and fell to the floor. Before the echo of the crash died, it was supplanted by a primal scream of rage.

Thomas abruptly was torn loose from his position. Before he could protest, he felt the cold unyielding, razor-sharp edge of a sword pressed hard against his neck.

"What the hell do you think you're doing?" snarled Jordan, while pressing the blade deeper. His eyes lit with satisfaction as a thin trickle of blood slid across the steel.

Blood continued to drip from the wound as Thomas' bottle-green eyes, a mirror image of his own, bore into him. "Something you don't have the balls to do," he sneered. "Fuck Dana into submission."

"I should kill you for this." He waved his arm toward the bed where Dana reclined watching with interest.

"You haven't got the balls for that, either, brother," scornfully declared his twin.

"Try me!"

"All well and good to talk that way while you're the only one with a weapon. You know the only way you can kill me is to attack while I'm distracted and defenseless."

"He's got a point," offered Dana, while languorously leaning against the pillows.

"Whose side are you on?" protested Jordan.

She shrugged. "Whoever is victorious, of course."

Thomas chuckled. "So, this is the virtue you've been fighting so hard to protect," he said mockingly. "As you can see, she's not been forced. Dana's here of her own free will."

Jordan stared hard at his brother's mocking face for several long heartbeats and then turned his piercing gaze on Dana. Had he been wrong about their feelings for each other? "Certainly," he thought, while surveying the rumpled bed and naked woman smiling blithely at him, "this doesn't seem to be something Dana was being forced to endure." On the contrary, she gave every appearance of being completely at ease and relishing the situation.

As his doubt gave him pause, Thomas took advantage. Thrusting forward with his arm, he threw Jordan off balance. Before he could recover, Thomas lunged for his discarded clothing and pulled his own sword from its sheath. He quickly spun, swept a wide arc to counter Jordan's attack, and then dove toward his fraternal foe.

"She doesn't want you, brother."

"You don't know what she wants."

"I know it didn't take much to push you out of her mind."

"So, is that how you did it?" asked Jordan, while circling his adversary. "You had to influence her thoughts in order to have her? Was she thinking of me while you were inside her?"

Thomas lunged. Jordan sidestepped. Turning swiftly, he parried. Metal clashed against metal as the combatants struck repeatedly at each other. Thomas' green eyes filled with impotent rage. Because they were twins, he knew that they were too evenly matched for him to gain the upper hand. His eyes flicked toward the fire. If he could drive Jordan back, perhaps ...

Jordan feinted and then lunged. Thomas eyes flicked back from the fire, but it was too late. He felt the blade pierce and become buried in his groin. His eyes flew wide as shock overwhelmed him.

"I'd wager you'll think twice about using that technique again," Jordan said grimly, as he raised his sword high and arced down toward his twin's head.

Searing pain struck him from behind. He staggered. Another blow caught him across the back of the head. He turned to confront Dana. She stood with a brass candlestick firmly clasped in her hands.

"Why?" Jordan whispered, as he fought to remain conscious.

"Because," said Craven Maxwell, entering from an adjoining chamber, "I required it."

Horrified, Jordan looked from one to the other. "You betraying bitch, you trapped me. Your mental plea for help was just a trick to lure me to your father."

For a brief second, Dana appeared confused. Instantly, he understood.

Dana nodded. "Comply or die. I don't want to die and I don't want you to, either."

"You don't have the right to make that choice for me."

"From this point forward, you have no rights except those I give you," Craven intervened.

His eyes opened wide in shock. "You're talking about mental domination."

The onyx orbs bore into him. He struggled to maintain control, but he could feel the infiltration as true terror took hold.

"What you're doing is mental rape. That's forbidden."

Craven shrugged. "From now on, I'll decide what's forbidden."

"I'd rather die than be dominated by you."

Jerking his dagger from his belt, he lifted his arm high and thrust down hard toward his own forehead. Dana screamed. Did she care after all? Inches away from his forehead, his arm stopped. He pushed. He strained. Sweat stood out on his forehead and the muscles in his neck and arm bulged. Slowly, inexorably, inch by inch, his arm lowered. His fingers opened and let the knife clatter harmlessly to the floor.

"Andrew won't allow this."

Craven raised his brows. "You and I both know Andrew is not going to intervene."

The earl blanched. Craven had hit a nerve and they both knew it. He had been trying to contact his cousin for weeks with no result.

Ever since Elizabeth's death, he had not been able to detect Andrew's presence. "He'll revive eventually," he threatened hollowly.

Craven scoffed. "And, when he does, I'll be waiting. Unless I find him first. In the meantime, I think using you to help realize my plans will start to make up for all the trouble you've caused me in the past."

Chapter 52:
Deadly Embrace

Laural scrambled up the side of the ravine leading onto the highway. She covered her ears as a truck with a broken muffler sped past. Confused and frightened, she stood alone in the night. A car passed in the other direction. Glaring headlights blinded her. Blaring horns tore at her eardrums. She winced, squeezed her eyes shut, and covered her ears. A van swept her with its headlights, passed, slowed, and then stopped. Fascinated, Laural watched as the door opened and a man stepped out.

"Hey, honey, need a lift?"

Confused, she stood, while warily observing as the middle-aged man spat out the tobacco that he was chewing, hiked up his jeans over his protruding stomach, and walked toward her.

"What's the matter? Cat got your tongue?" He laughed at his own humor, as he stalked closer. His work boots made deep impressions in the snow.

Laural sniffed. Here was what she craved. She drooled slightly when her eyes fastened on his neck.

The man studied her. "You're going to catch your death out here in that," he stated, while pointing at her blouse. Looking around, he asked, "Ain't you got anything with you?" He was used to picking up hitchhikers and knew that they usually carried some possessions. They might not have much, but they usually had at least a few things in a paper bag, duffle bag, or backpack.

She continued to stare.

"Ain't you at least got a coat?" he asked nervously, as he glanced around. Could this be a set up? This good-looking girl could be luring him out to be robbed. But he didn't see anyone else and there was nowhere to hide on the abandoned stretch of highway.

Hesitantly, Laural shook her head. What was he saying? She

narrowed her eyes. The figure seemed to be contracting and then expanding. His voice seemed to be coming from a great distance even though he was only a few feet away.

"Hey, are you one of those deaf mutes or something," the man asked, as he began to become annoyed, "or are you just some wise-ass kid in need of some manners?" he continued, while stomping toward the girl. "I'll teach her some respect, too," he thought indignantly. "What the hell?" he exclaimed, as the girl collapsed to the ground. Covering the few steps to her side, he knelt next to her and felt for a pulse. Steady and strong. "Probably passed out from cold or hunger," he thought, while eyeing her pale skin and thin frame. He studied her more closely and decided that she wasn't half-bad in a skinny kind of way. Normally, he preferred his women with more meat on their bones, but any port in a storm. Glancing quickly in either direction, he hoisted the unconscious girl over his shoulder and carried her to the van.

Several minutes later, he pulled to the side of the road. He parked the vehicle behind some low-lying shrubbery and moved next to the unconscious teen. "This shouldn't take long," he thought, as he unbuckled his pants. With a little luck, the girl would not wake up until after he had finished. With a lot of luck, he would finish and then dump her on the side of the road while she was still unconscious.

He pulled his jeans past his knees and reached for the girl's pants. Awkwardly, he fumbled with the tiny pearl buttons. Suddenly, the girl's eyes snapped open and she sat up. He sighed. Now, he would have to do it the hard way.

Laural studied the man who was sitting on his haunches. Her eyes examined his exposed skin. Leaning forward, she sniffed. The odor was potent and mixed with various smells. She looked at his neck. The vein pulsed like an open invitation. Still slightly groggy, she leaned forward into the man's embrace.

Delighted by her response, he opened his arms wide and leaned back. "So, you want to be on top?" he chuckled. "That's all right with me as long as ... Hey, don't do that! My wife will see it!"

Despite his protests, the girl continued sucking on his neck. "Damned vixen is going to give me a hickie," he thought. He was aroused and dismayed at the same time. He really could not allow it, though, as much as he would like to have the trophy to show to the boys. Reaching for her face, he tugged at her mouth. He swore in pain as her teeth pierced his skin.

"Turn loose, you little she-devil!" Frantically, he tried to pull her off, but it was like trying to dislodge a pit bull. He started to feel lightheaded. He struggled harder. He flailed his arms and pushed against her with all of his might. Balling his hands into fists, he struck her head. Again and again, but to no avail. She was too strong. She was sucking the blood out of his body. The horrific thought struck him just as he slipped into unconsciousness.

The Mercedes slowed, pulled over, and stopped. Tires crunched gravel and snow slipped from beneath the car. The door opened. Andrew Gabriel stepped into the frigid night air. He cautiously approached the vehicle. He already suspected, but did not want to accept what he would find. Peering into the darkened interior, he smelled the dank odor of blood mixed with cigarettes, alcohol, and body fluids. As his eyes roamed over the disarrayed clothing, his blood boiled.

"Good thing you're already dead," he threatened the corpse. Expelling a long breath, he withdrew. Leaning against the van, he closed his eyes. The afterimage of his daughter draining the blood out of her victim lingered. Ever since she left the crematorium, Andrew had been receiving afterimages from Laural. It was unfortunate that they were not current. If they were, he might have found her by now. Trudging back to his car, he got in and rested his head on the steering wheel. He felt lonely, tired, and defeated. Another image of Laural assailed him and he jerked upright. Hardening his resolve, he slammed the door and started the engine.

Several minutes later, he parked his car near a service phone. After reaching emergency services, he anonymously reported the van. Again settling himself behind the wheel, he pulled back onto the highway. As he headed south, he cut on the windshield wipers and pointed the Mercedes towards Washington.

Dark thoughts plagued him and were periodically punctuated by chaotic mental images. Even though he had been receiving Laural's inadvertent transmissions since leaving Willow Grove, he had been unable to make sense out of them. Unfortunately, this usually reliable method of tracking was proving frustrating since his quarry was incapable of providing coherent connections. He had not understood the last image until he stumbled upon the van. He tried again. Grinding his teeth in frustration, he collected bits and pieces that were too generic to place. Long stretches of highway, cars careening past, scrub brush, and a never-ending blanket of snow were not the most revealing indicators of his daughter's location.

He pounded the steering wheel. "I have to find her before the authorities lock her up, another porphyrian tries to exterminate her, or," he thought grimly, "before she kills again."

Another image burst into his brain. He winced as he realized that Laural was in another vehicle. This time, it appeared that a well-meaning family had picked her up. Andrew grimaced and floored the accelerator. This time, it would not be a potential rapist who would fall prey to his daughter's bloodlust. As he considered what Craven had done to his child, he wished that he had not killed him so that he could have the pleasure of doing it again.

Chapter 53:

The Hitchhiker

Laural leaned against the upholstered seat, while contentedly listening to the sounds of the family. Thinking that she was asleep, the considerate hosts were whispering so that they would not disturb her slumber. The two children next to her were playing a video game. In the front seat, their parents quietly studied the road map.

Laural felt the best she had since she could remember. Finally satiated from her last liquid intake, she was feeling much calmer. Her only difficulty was the pain that she suffered whenever her eyes came into contact with the blinding glare of the sun as it reflected from the snow. She almost had circumvented the problem by sleeping during most of the day. Now that the sun was setting, she would have to keep her eyes closed only until evening. After dark, the pain would subside.

"What do you think we should do with her?"

"I think we need to take her to the authorities as soon as we reach DC."

His wife nodded in agreement. "Poor thing," she sympathized, while looking in the rearview mirror at the sleeping girl. "Can you imagine wandering along the highway without even a coat?"

"Probably a runaway," he commented dryly.

"Well, she should've run away with a coat."

Her husband grunted, as he flipped the turn signal and headed onto the off ramp marked "Washington, DC."

"The question is," he said, while glancing at the rearview mirror, "what was she running from that was so bad she couldn't even pause long enough to grab her coat?"

Laural slightly raised her lids to view the last rays of the setting sun. Sitting forward, she stretched. Now that the sun had set, her lethargy lifted and allowed her to study her surroundings.

"Hey, you're cheating!" yelled one of the children.

Laural's eyes snapped toward the noise.

"Hey, keep it down. You'll wake up our guest."

"But, Mom, she's already awake. Besides, Bobby's cheating."

"Am not!"

"Are too!"

Grimacing in pain, Laural covered her ears.

"Mom, Bobby took my Zatachi."

"Give it back."

"No, I had it first."

"You two settle down back there!"

Laural reeled from the cacophony. Each scream reverberated through her head and sent spikes of agony pounding into her skull. Suddenly, she was struck by a plastic box. Grabbing the offending toy, she crushed it between her hands and snarled as the pieces fell onto the floor.

The two boys stared in astonishment. "Dad," screamed Bobby, "she broke our Zatachi."

While shrieking incoherently, Laural bared her teeth. She grabbed the nearest of the two boys. He screamed as she slammed his face into the seat.

"She's hurting Bobby!"

Grabbing the other boy with her free hand, she squeezed his throat until the screaming stopped. Silence again.

"Oh, my God! George, pull over. She's going to kill them."

He pulled to the shoulder of the road and jumped out of the driver's seat. He ripped open the back door. Dragging the girl away from his boys was not easy. She was holding on with all of her might.

Unexpectedly, she let go. They both fell back into the snow. Frantically, he tried to get up, but she was all over him. She was ripping with her nails and tearing with her teeth. Her teeth were sinking into his throat.

A shot rang out. Laural recoiled. Releasing her hold on her victim, she slowly stood. Her back hurt and she felt odd. A river of blood turned the snow crimson. She spun around to confront her assailant.

The woman stood with her gun raised. Her hands shook as she took aim.

Confused and hurt, Laural exploded with rage. She hurled herself at the woman. Another shot rang out. The children screamed. Their father groaned and slowly staggered to his feet. Cars honked and careened to steer clear of the chaos.

Laural fell on the ground as another round tore through her skin. This time, the bullet sank deep into the flesh of her upper arm. She hit the ice-encrusted snow hard on her injured side and her arm buckled beneath her. Painfully, she lifted herself with the other arm. Staggering to her feet, she took another step toward the woman, who again raised the gun. Laural hesitated, whirled, and ran.

Chapter 54

The Witness

Jordan faced the investigative committee. He nodded to Attorney Knox, who stood, respectfully inclined his head to the senators, and then left the room. Jordan again focused his attention on the five men. They were engaged in reading the paperwork that he had provided. Finally, Senator Randolph laid his papers aside and briefly consulted with the other men.

Raising his eyebrows, Randolph stated skeptically, "It's very impressive for you to come up with all this documentation on such short notice, but how do we know this isn't the product of a desperate staff trying to keep their agency from folding?"

Jordan quelled his outrage at the ethical implications regarding his staff and replied evenly, "I offer these documents as background checks on the persons who are in question by this committee."

An overweight man who looked as if he had been poured into his business suit confronted the earl. "While we are checking into this matter, Lord Rush, you do understand that due to the serious nature of the charges we are considering options including the temporary suspension of your facility's operations."

"Excuse me, Congressman Rogers," he questioned, while adjusting his microphone, "but isn't that rather drastic?" "Not to mention illegal," he wondered silently.

Senator Randolph slammed his palm down so hard on the table that several sheets scattered and a pen rolled onto the floor. "I am outraged at your attitude, Lord Rush. Your facility is under investigation for possible terrorist activity. That is as drastic as it gets!"

Jordan glanced over their heads, nodded, and then spoke. "I would like to admit an additional piece into evidence."

"This is not a trial," stated Congressman Rogers.

"Really?" Jordan mumbled under his breath.

Mr. Knox re-entered the room. He was followed by a tall slender, balding man in his mid-thirties. The man's nervous gaze shifted from Jordan to the table. His eyes caught and held Senator Randolph's, and then skidded away.

"I would like to respectfully request that Mr. Thomas Smith be allowed to speak. Mr. Smith works in our records department and I believe you will find his input invaluable to this investigation."

Senator Randolph looked to the members of the committee, then inclined his head.

The attorney escorted Smith to Jordan's recently vacated seat. While he adjusted the mike, Smith moved restlessly for several seconds. Finally, he raised his head.

The review committee looked stern. They shuffled their papers. Senator Randolph's lips compressed into a tight line. "This is highly irregular," he stated, "but will be allowed due to the sensitive nature of this case."

Jordan angled his head toward the dais. "Thank you Senator."

The witness' eyes swung from the committee to Jordan. They finally settled on the attorney seated next to him.

"Mr. Smith," said the attorney firmly, "would you please inform the committee what you told us back at the office?"

Staring straight ahead, he said, " I am the one responsible for the sabotage of the computer systems."

"Would you kindly explain what that means?" Randolph asked.

Mr. Smith pulled a handkerchief from his inside pocket and wiped his forehead. "I erased all the documentation regarding the 86 immigrants aided by our facility this year. Then, I substituted sensitive material that I knew would cause the facility to come under scrutiny by the government."

"Why would you do such a thing?"

He searched the features of the men across from him. They stared steadily back with austere expressions that concealed their thoughts.

"I was approached on January 25th by a man in a bar. He talked to me for a little while about suspicions regarding our facility. Specifically, that our agency was suspected of harboring illegal aliens who were not refugees but terrorists. He emphasized that our own director and assistant director were foreigners and insisted they were part of the conspiracy. He also told me that it was only a matter of time before the facility was shut down; my employers exported out of the country in disgrace; and all the employees laid off. He argued that we would have a hard time getting reputable employment after such a scandal. He offered to make me a deal if I would help the cause."

"What kind of deal?"

"He offered me a large sum of money to supply him with sensitive material. Information that could be misinterpreted if taken out of context."

"If the investigation was already in progress, why did they need your assistance?"

"The man said it was in the best interest of certain parties if this matter could be resolved before the presidential primaries. He stressed the need for expediency. He insisted I would be doing my patriotic duty by helping the investigators protect the country from terrorism. He indicated I could use the money if I wanted to take time off between jobs. He made it sound like I was a civilian undercover agent. By the time I discovered I had been duped, the money had already exchanged hands and I had already used it to pay several debts. I was afraid to back out of the deal and afraid to go to my employers, so I tried to leave town."

"This is all an interesting story," said Senator Randolph, "but how do we know your employers didn't put you up to this?"

"I am testifying under oath that my employers had no knowledge of this incident." Smith paused and looked to the attorney. Knox shook his head slightly, then turned to the earl. The seconds dragged by as the committee fidgeted restlessly. Finally, Jordan finished consulting with his attorney and nodded.

The earl turned to confront the group. "Mr. Smith has already signed a sworn affidavit to what he has just told you. He is also willing to take a polygraph. Unfortunately, we don't know the identity of the man in the bar because he didn't give his real name. However we are still investigating."

Representative Johnston spoke, "Although this committee is relieved that this part of the investigation has been reviewed, there is still the matter of the two men arrested for armed robbery and illegal possession of explosive materials."

Jordan nodded to Tom Smith. Addressing the committee he said, "With your consent I would like to excuse Mr. Smith since his part of the testimony is over."

Senator Randolph nodded.

Smith left the table and quickly retreated from the room. Mr. Knox went with him. The two spoke quietly, as they strode down the center aisle.

Within moments, the attorney returned with two more men by his side.

"Gentlemen," began Jordan, waving his arm toward the two men, "these gentlemen are Mr. Kali and Mr. Radu. For the record, these two men are the alleged terrorists who were arrested for armed robbery last week."

The five committee members stared. "How did you get the Justice Department to release them?" asked Congressman Rogers.

The corners of his mouth lifted. "They're out on bond," he stated as they took their seats.

Mr. Kali adjusted the microphone, cleared his throat, and waited patiently. He was a thin dark, middle-aged man with salt-and-pepper hair. His features were plain and his eyes gentle. He was dressed in a conservative brown business suit with a cream dress shirt and pin-striped tie. He presented an image of a high-powered executive rather than a potential terrorist.

"Mr. Kali, will you please explain how you came to be in your current position?"

Kali looked from the lawyer to the earl. Then, his eyes shifted to the representatives. "I can only tell you as much as is permitted by the Federal Bureau of Investigation," he said in slightly accented English.

"Tell us what you can."

While pulling nervously at his tie, he shifted slightly. "My associate, Mr. Radu, and I went through the program at the Willow Grove Foundation two years ago. We fulfilled all the requirements and successfully gained citizenship. We were placed in good jobs and became hardworking members of society."

"What kind of requirements?" asked Senator Randolph.

"That we had no one here to support us, that the circumstances we left behind were deplorable, and that we were sincere in our interest to become hardworking loyal citizens."

"How did they determine that?"

"We were subjected to a battery of psychological tests and extensive interviews with a psychologist contracted by the agency for that purpose."

Senator Randolph continued, "Mr. Kali, from this point forward, please refrain from including Mr. Radu in your discussion. He will be interviewed separately for his side of the story."

Kali glanced at Radu and nodded.

"What happened after you left the foundation?"

"We – I mean I was employed by a small computer company. Not a fancy job, but a good one. I enjoyed it and made several good friends. One day, my friends invited me to go out to a sports bar. I wanted to fit in, so I went. While at the bar, some of my friends bet on the football game being shown on the television. Everyone seemed to be enjoying themselves and, in my eagerness to be accepted, I joined in. I won. It was not a lot of money, but I had so much fun I returned the following week. I won again. This continued for several weeks. I became addicted. Finally, one time I lost. A good amount, but I didn't worry because I was sure, based on my past successes, I would win it back. That never happened. I kept betting and losing until I was in so much debt I wasn't sure what to do."

He paused to take a sip of water.

"I had to borrow money to pay the debts and, when I could not pay back the lenders of the money, they became mean. Then, one of these men came up with the idea of robbing the bank."

His eyes skidded uncomfortably around the room, as a flush stained his cheeks. "I did not want to do it and, at first, I refused. Then, one of these men called my home and left a threatening message with my fiancée. After that, I agreed to do it." Embarrassed color flooded his face and his eyes dropped to the floor.

"Tell us about the explosives," Knox prodded gently.

Kali lifted his head. "I'm very limited in what I can say at the present time. However, I am stating for the record neither myself nor Mr. Radu knew anything about the explosive material. While we were being held for the robbery, someone broke into both our dwellings and planted that evidence."

A collective gasp sounded at the committee table. "Why would anyone want to frame you and your colleague?" demanded a flustered congressman.

"I only have my opinion."

"And that is?"

"I think it was part of a conspiracy to implicate the Willow Grove Foundation as a front for terrorists."

Mr. Kali was excused. Mr. Radu took his place. Thirty minutes later, the committee recessed. When they returned, they filed into their chairs and sifted through their paperwork. Then, the men briefly consulted. After a pause, Senator Randolph reluctantly agreed.

"In light of this new information," he said, while glaring at the earl, "we have reconsidered and decided that no further action will be taken against the Willow Grove Foundation for Continuing Education at this time. This decision will be official once validation of these witnesses' testimonies is provided. For the present, gentlemen, you are excused."

Chapter 55:
Back in DC

Laural ran haphazardly through the winding city streets. Cars honked as she darted back and forth across busy intersections. After a short distance, the feeling of being pursued faded, so she slowed to a brisk walk. Images of the blond man intruded into her thoughts. Confused, she looked around. Everywhere that she turned, pedestrians gawked as they passed. Looking down, she realized that they were staring at her clothing. Her jeans and blouse were torn and caked with crusted blood. Another image. She again looked around. Even though she turned in a complete circle, she could not locate the blonde man. As she made her way along the sidewalk, his turquoise eyes haunted her. He seemed to be trying to talk to her, but he only came across as garbled background noise. Still, focusing on his image made her feel calm and almost normal.

"Watch it!" yelled a pedestrian when Laural accidentally bumped into him. She had caused his coffee to slosh onto his sleeve because she had been so focused on the image of the blonde man that she had not been watching.

"What are you doing? Are you blind?" the man continued to shout.

Laural placed her hands over her ears. The man scowled. She snarled. Baring her teeth as she focused on his neck. Just then, another psychic flash of the blonde man bombarded her. He seemed both stern and compassionate at the same time. Something in his eyes seemed familiar. "Father?" she asked out loud. She was both confused and comforted by the sound of the word.

"I'm not your father. Are you retarded?"

"What's wrong with you? Can't you see she's hurt?"

Laural shifted her focus to encompass the woman who was approaching from behind her.

The woman gasped as she saw the bullet holes in the young girl's flesh.

"Oh, my God. She's been shot!" she exclaimed in horror, while pulling a cell phone from her purse. "No one's going to hurt you, honey. I'm going to call an ambulance to get you some help."

"She doesn't need an ambulance," scoffed the man, while brushing at his sleeve. "She needs the men with the white jackets."

The woman gaped at him. "What's wrong with you? This girl's been shot and all you can do is complain about your jacket?"

He skeptically eyed Laural. "Most likely, she got caught up in some kind of trouble. For all you know, she could be a criminal or dangerous," he offered, while backing away. "I don't want to get involved with anyone else's problems. I got enough of my own."

The woman shook her head in disbelief and then refocused on Laural. "Honey," asked the woman, as she pressed 911, "where are your parents?"

Laural gave a blank stare.

"See what I mean?" insisted the man.

She threw a disgusted look at him and he stalked off. Turning back to Laural, she smiled gently. Her smile seemed to soothe the girl and she appeared to relax.

"That's it. We'll just wait right here for the paramedics. I'll bet someone is worried about you. Is there anyone you would like me to call? Your mother or father?"

At the mention of her father, Laural tensed. Sirens sounded a few blocks away. She covered her ears as they drew closer.

"Take it easy, honey," soothed the woman, while stepping closer.

Laural bared her teeth and snarled. The woman stumbled back in shock. As the sirens drew closer, the noise level became intolerable. She shrieked, turned, and ran.

"Jordan, how did it go?" asked the marquis, while maneuvering the Mercedes around a corner.

"Very well. After Mr. Smith's confession and the testimony from Mr. Kali and Mr. Radu, I don't think even Senator Randolph will be able to resurrect that scandal." He paused. "How's the search?"

Andrew scanned the sidewalk on both sides of the street. He recognized the man that he had seen in his last connection with his daughter. The man was shaking his head in confusion and looking down an intersecting alley. Andrew turned into the alley and banged the steering wheel in frustration. The narrow street was deserted.

He watched intently as an ambulance pulled beside the curb. When the paramedic stepped from the vehicle, a middle-aged woman with a cell phone dangling limply from her hand approached him. The woman appeared agitated and frantically pointed down the alley.

Andrew cursed under his breath. "I'm really close to catching up with her. She's back in DC."

"Where are you?"

"I'm here, too," he affirmed, as he concentrated on scanning alcoves and doorways.

"I'm glad to hear it."

Andrew's attention snapped back to the conversation. "Why?" he asked, as a frown fixed itself on his face.

"Because there're quite a few who are getting nervous about having a renegade porphyrian on the loose. A few have even suggested tracking and eliminating her themselves."

His eyes narrowed to twin shards of blue ice. "You make it known that, if anyone harms my child, they'll have to answer to me."

"I've made that quite clear. But," he paused, "there're some who are quite discontent. They believe that you're implementing a different strategy for coping with this situation than you would if it had been anyone else. They're also quite concerned about exposure. If the authorities get hold of her and start doing extensive tests ..."

"You don't have to lecture me about the implications," he barked. He took a deep breath. They had a right to be concerned. "I'm going to catch her before the authorities even know what they're looking for. Just let everyone know to be on their guard. That includes you. If Laural heads to anyone, it will probably be you."

"Maybe," Jordan mused.

Chapter 56: Aspirations of Vengeance

Bethesda, Maryland, 1997

Craven sat alone at the desk in the study of his colonial mansion in Bethesda. As he continued to brood over the newspaper, he frowned. He raised his glass and took a long pull of his scotch before glancing from *The Washington Post* to the research documents. "Damn it! This explains it all," he spewed into the solitude of the room.

He laid aside the paper and continued to sip his drink, as he gazed fixedly into the fireplace. The logs crackled and flames flared. The fire helped to keep the chill of the mid-January night at bay. He now knew the answer. He vengefully swore at fate for not allowing him to find Andrew's refuge until hours after he had revived. Unfortunately, those few precious hours had made all of the difference. Instead of terminating his nemesis, he had to settle for taking his rage out on the staff of the psychiatric facility where Andrew had lain dormant for over fifty years.

The onyx orbs narrowed as he again searched through the documents scattered across the desktop. He nodded slowly as his mind catapulted back to more than a hundred years ago. There was no mistaking the likeness. The two could have been twins.

The lineage of the Camden family was straight forward and easy to follow. It had not been blessed with many descendants, so their family tree was not cluttered with many branches. According to the records, Elizabeth had an older sister and two older brothers. The sister, who was his main concern, had married and produced only one offspring, a daughter. This pattern continued with each succeeding generation giving birth to only one or two offspring, usually daughters.

His interest was in the female line. About two generations ago, one of the Camden descendants married an American merchant who was in London on business. After their marriage, she relocated and the family resided in Pennsylvania before moving to Boston. Eventually, their only daughter, Victory Parker, moved to Washington, DC.

He rubbed the glass back and forth between his palms, as he studied the photograph and read the headline of yesterday's paper: "Harvard Graduate Speaks Out against the System." He quickly scanned the story. Victory Parker, who graduated with top honors from Harvard Law School, had set the campus on its ear with her provocative speech that struck a hard blow against the country's current political situation. The outspoken and socially conscious young graduate was aspiring to become a Supreme Court Justice in order to take a direct hand in interpreting the laws of the country so they would apply more directly to the needs of the people.

He had given the article only a cursory glance, but, while flipping through the paper and searching for reports about the President's recent exploits, the story's accompanying photograph captured his attention. It held him spellbound. A beautiful young woman dressed in a black cap and gown was standing poised and confident in front of a podium, while a crowd of onlookers and her fellow graduates clapped enthusiastically. Her natural poise, intelligence, and compassion were evident even from the still shot.

Craven set down his drink and then grasped the paper so hard that his knuckles turned white. Lifting the photo section closer, he stared hard. Golden hair that was the color of liquid sunshine cascaded from under the square cap. Brilliant sapphire blue eyes promised fulfillment of her dreams. Her heart-shaped face, patrician nose, and winning smile completed the cameo-like perfection.

Craven leaned back in his chair, while steepling his fingers together. A satisfied smile curved his lips. He rejoiced as his sadistic thoughts of what he could do to this unsuspecting innocent raced through his mind. Like the director of a movie, he stopped shots, rewound, and played particularly gruesome scenes over and over. He put them in slow motion so that he could envision each atrocity in detail.

He deeply regretted how quickly he had terminated his brother's last love before fully considering the long-term opportunities. Until now, he had never contemplated the possibility that there would be another chance for a repeat performance. This time, he would ensure a final curtain call to this drama since, according to his research, Victory Parker was the last of her line.

"If I had only known," he reflected, while staring into the fire, "about the devastating effect Elizabeth's death would have on Andrew, I would have prolonged the process." He had not believed that his brother could have become so attached to a diurnal that her death would cause him to withdraw from the world. He knew that his brother cared for the lowly species, but, in his opinion, that was going a bit far even for the noble Marquis of Penbrook. Now that he knew his brother's Achilles' heel, he hardly could wait for the opportunity to use it against him.

His previous vengeful act had exceeded his expectations and had kept his brother from interfering in his plans for more than a century. He had put those years to good use by slowly but steadily manipulating his new homeland. It had taken a lot of time and planning, but it was worth it. Now, he was on the brink of ruling not just one small section of a country like he had done in Cornwall, but an entire nation.

Now Andrew had revived. The reason had remained a mystery until today. After finding the information online, everything had become clear. He had downloaded the documents so that he could study them in depth. Repeatedly, he glanced from the family tree history to the photograph.

Victory Parker was a direct descendant of Elizabeth Camden. Andrew had revived from his self-imposed hibernation because he had become aware of her presence. Now that the pieces of the puzzle were becoming clear, he wondered how he could use the information for his own advantage. Andrew had not made a move toward the woman – at least not yet. That was surprising to Craven since the revival had happened over two years ago.

He sighed in exasperation. If he could understand Andrew's motivation, then he could determine his next move. But his brother's thoughts, especially when dealing with diurnals, were always enigmatic.

He again looked down at the picture. Should he kill the girl outright? Should he use his influence to enslave her will? That would be interesting, but prudence caused him to set self-indulgence aside.

He smiled at the beaming graduate. Keeping a close eye on her until Andrew put in an appearance would be much better. When his brother came to claim her – and he had no doubt that he would – the diurnal would make an excellent bargaining chip. At that time, he could decide the best way to use her to suit his needs. "Yes," he thought maliciously, as he shredded the papers, threw them into the fire, and watched the face of Victory Parker burn into ash. "This time, my plan will be perfect." This time, he had no intention of allowing Andrew to thwart him.

Chapter 57:
Intent to Kill

Laural ran down one street and up the next. Mindless of where she was going, she operated on pure instinct.

Apprehensively, she glanced over her shoulder, as she warily approached the large brightly lit building. Was the blond man still chasing her? She scanned her surroundings. Safe. She needed to feel safe.

She paused in the driveway leading to the hospital. While gasping in pain, she studied the structure. Would she be safe here? Intuition told her that she would find what she needed behind the white walls of this building – but she hesitated. The woman had said that she had been shot. Laural tried desperately to assimilate what that meant. A flicker in her mind told her that she used to know, but she now understood only the pain. She examined the gaping hole in her shoulder and winced as the one in her back made its presence felt. The wounds had stopped bleeding hours ago, but the bullets prevented the completion of the healing process.

Staying in the shadows, she watched a rectangular vehicle with flashing lights and loudly wailing sirens speed past. Her heart raced and fear escalated as the noise threatened to overwhelm her. Covering her ears, she watched the ambulance as it stopped in front of the doors leading into the building. A body on a stretcher was moved toward the open doors. Her eyes widened when she saw the IV bottle being wheeled beside the stretcher. Its serpentine plastic tubing bit into the patient's arm. Horrid memories of her captivity by Craven surfaced and she pulled back. "Should I be in a place like this?" she wondered. An instinct deep within her insisted that she would find what she needed in this place.

No. It was not *what* but *who* she needed. The person who could make her well, make things better, and take away her pain was here.

She vaguely remembered a pair of caring silver-gray eyes and a warm smile. She felt that he had helped her before and intuitively knew that he would help again.

Suddenly, she jerked up straight. Glancing behind her, she hastily moved toward the beckoning lights of the hospital. The blond man was still following her and he was close. She was not sure what he wanted, but she was afraid. She sensed strength, power, and intent in his dogged pursuit. Although he sent messages of comfort and compassion, he vaguely reminded her of the man with the dark eyes who had held her captive. Unsure whether he was friend or foe, she moved past the busy emergency entrance and quickly continued into the brightly lit corridors.

Andrew pulled into the parking lot of the hospital just as a girl with long blond hair faded into the crowd at the entrance. Frowning, he turned off the ignition and opened the car door. "Was that Laural?" he asked himself. It had to be or he was on a wild goose chase. "But why the hospital?" he wondered. "Well, yes," he answered himself, "I guess it would be the logical place. After all, where would she go? Back to the burned-up Bethesda mansion where her mother was killed? To the foundation where her reception was uncertain? Or to a place she would associate with making her better? No, not the place," he corrected himself, "but the man."

As he headed to the entrance, he grimly picked up his pace. Dr. Brenner might not be on duty tonight, but the chances were great that he was. If he hurried, he might be able to get to the doctor before Laural did. She might not be able to find Brenner in such a large facility. Andrew knew that it was time to start considering the alternatives. He thought about the reality of an insane porphyrian driven by bloodlust who was loose in an institution for the sick and wounded. The results could be catastrophic! He finally faced the possibility that he might have to kill his own child.

Laural cautiously advanced through the hallway. The fluorescent lights hurt her eyes so she tried to stay within the darkened passages, unlit rooms, and stairwells. Unsure for whom she was searching, she allowed her intuition to guide her. Eventually, her footsteps took her to room 303. She stood in the hall near the door while vague and disconnected memories of being here replayed in her mind.

Hesitantly, she pushed the door. It slowly opened and revealed a dimly lit room with two beds. Someone was sleeping in the bed that was nearest to the door. Laural sniffed and began to salivate. The odor of what she needed was strong here. The smell had been tormenting her since she entered this place. Her stomach muscles contracted and she advanced into the room.

"Goodnight, Dr. Brenner."

"Goodnight, Sam. Your operation was successful. I'll check on you first thing in the morning."

"Thanks, Doc. The sooner you finish, the sooner I can get home."

Laural froze at the sound of the familiar voice. The memory of warm silver-gray eyes and a friendly smile caused her to return to the corridor. Squinting because of the bright lights, she spotted him as he rounded a corner at the end of the hall.

Dr. James Brenner approached the nurses' station. "I'll be in my office for a while before going home. Let me know if there is any change," he instructed.

The head nurse nodded, but he did not notice. He closed his office door and did not bother to change. Brenner threw himself into his chair and picked up the phone. He had received the urgent message from Jordan Rush while he was in surgery, but had not had time to return the call. He hoped that he could reach the earl at such a late hour. He desperately wanted news about Laural. The girl had left a serious impression on him and, even though she was too young for a romantic involvement, he still was drawn to her. Besides, it was his duty as a professional to follow up on his patient. As he dialed, he had a bad feeling about Laural and about why she was not responding to his inquiries.

He let the phone ring numerous times before replacing the receiver. He sighed in disgust. He would have to wait until morning. Standing, he prepared to head to the locker to retrieve his clothing and stand under a hot spray of water for a while. He moved around the desk and toward the door.

Unexpectedly, it was flung open. A wild and disheveled teen in torn clothing confronted him.

"Laural?" he questioned hesitantly as recognition dawned. A

powerful surge of relief swept through him. For a moment, he could do nothing but stare. As he continued to study her, his relief gave way to concern. He frowned. The girl advanced toward him. He backed up a pace. Something in the way that she was jerking her head back and forth spoke of neurological damage. Wary of making her more agitated, he assessed her torn and bloodied clothing.

"My God, Laural, what happened?" he exclaimed in shock as he spied the bullet wound.

Had she been in an accident or attacked? It was probably the latter, he realized, while shaking off his shock. "Get hold of yourself, Brenner," he sternly chastised himself. "Laural needs someone to take care of her, not to stand around gawking like a fool."

As he visually assessed her injuries, the familiar protectiveness surged through him. She was extremely pale and her face was smeared with dried blood. He wondered if she was squinting because of the pain. Although her clothing was caked with blood in several places, the only apparent injury was to her left shoulder.

He stared into her eyes. She did not manifest the slightest recognition. He sighed. Her eyes had a glassy look. She probably was suffering from a head injury or, at the very least, shock and disorientation. Cautiously, he held out his hand, while speaking slowly and softly.

"Laural, I'm here to help. Please let me take care of you," he inquired softly before frowning slightly. "Where is your father?" He was certain that Lord Gabriel would not have allowed her to be out of his sight in this condition. Had they been attacked together? Was he unconscious in the emergency room? That would explain Laural's ability to wander off unnoticed by her diligent parent.

Laural became very still and then began to shudder uncontrollably. Her eyes opened and closed several times. Her head shook. After a few moments, she quieted and weakly asked, "Father?"

"Some progress," he thought, while nodding. "Yes, father."

Suddenly, she flew at him. She was a whirl of gnashing teeth and flailing fists. He raised his arms to ward off the blows. He tried to hold her off, but she was strong. How could she be this strong? Her teeth fastened on his neck. He drew back in shock. Crashing against the desk, he and Laural toppled to the floor. She was still on top of him. Her teeth tore the flesh from his throat.

As he tried to pull her off, his fingers slipped into a second bullet hole in her back. She had been shot twice and still had enough strength to attack him. "This isn't possible," he thought incredulously, as the blood rapidly drained from his body. "She must have torn a carotid artery," he realized with surgical detachment even as he became disoriented, lightheaded, and finally unconscious.

Abruptly, Laural was lifted from the doctor's body and hurled across the room. Stunned, she lay sprawled against the far wall. After quickly closing the door, Jordan squatted down next to the prone figure of the doctor. Keeping one eye on his cousin, he checked the doctor's pulse.

"Thank goodness! He's still breathing," he thought, after examining the gash in Brenner's throat. Before calling for a nurse, he had to attend to the more immediate need.

Moving toward his cousin, he spoke softly. "I'm sorry, Laural," he explained, while pulling a gun from his waistband. "I know your dad wouldn't have the heart to do this, but it needs to be done. There is no other way," he continued, while attaching the silencer to the barrel of the pistol. "I love you," he said, as he aimed the gun at her head.

The door flew open. Andrew leapt the short distance and landed on Jordan's back. The gun shot harmlessly over Laural's head. Swinging his cousin around, Andrew threw a hard punch that landed on Jordan's jaw. The earl crashed against the wall. He again lifted his gun. Quickly, Andrew drew his own pistol and fired.

Chapter 58: Bedside Confessions

Jordan's eyes snapped open. Awareness jolted through him as he quickly scanned his surroundings. He frowned. Confusion superceded panic as he studied the unfamiliar room. He viewed wood-paneled walls, framed landscapes, Victorian furnishings, and heavy draperies that covered the windows. "This certainly is not my Georgetown brownstone," he thought, while sliding out of the four-poster bed.

A brief wave of nausea swept over him and he leaned heavily against the bedpost, while rubbing his throbbing temples. "Have I been kidnapped?" he wondered, as he scanned the room. Slowly, he straightened and then slipped into his shoes. If so, he had a very considerate and wealthy kidnapper. He noted the porcelain water pitcher and glasses on the nightstand. He helped himself to a long drink. The cold water felt good sliding down his parched throat.

Glancing around, he noticed his jacket hanging neatly in an open armoire. Across the room, a door stood ajar. He glimpsed a tiled floor and porcelain sink. He walked across the thickly carpeted floor. After putting on his jacket, he headed toward the door.

Something nagged at his memory. This place seemed familiar yet different. He shook his head in an attempt to clear the last of the cobwebs. Cautiously, he opened the bedroom door and peered into the hallway. Throwing the door open wide, he sighed in relief. Realization struck and he chuckled. He had not been in this mansion since it had been redecorated, but there was no mistaking the family estate of the Marquis of Penbrook. "So, this was Victory's idea of changing a few things around," he thought. He nodded with approval. He had to admit that he liked it better than Andrew's austere taste.

Memories from the past few weeks flooded through him and drowned his reverie. Sorrow darkened the green eyes as he relived his last conscious moments. He looked longingly at the recently vacated bed. He actually would have preferred to remain in the oblivion of unconsciousness.

Now that the dam of memories had burst, they continued to roll over him like a tidal wave. He had tried to kill Laural. Andrew had shot him. Had the episode at the hospital really happened? He longingly eyed the bed. He allowed himself to indulge in the fantasy. Had he been dreaming? Had he been visiting the Gabriels and were they now waiting downstairs for him to join them for breakfast? Should he go down and regale them with his wild tale of Craven's resurrection, Victory's death, and Laural's kidnapping?

He winced and grimaced in pain as he tentatively touched his left shoulder. The wound was still sore. So much for dreaming. If the pain was real ...

How many times had he been shot? His head still reeled. No matter what the consequences were, he did not regret his failure. His heart had not been in it, but he still believed that killing his cousin was the only way to set everyone free. He almost had succeeded. Nevertheless, he was grateful that Andrew had intervened.

"If I hadn't, you would have killed my child. I couldn't allow that."

Jordan spun around. The Marquis of Penbrook was leaning nonchalantly against the doorframe. He cautiously studied his friend, unsure of their footing. The turquoise eyes gazing back at him seemed steady and calm with no hint of malice or resentment.

He was dressed casually in a pair of khakis and a plaid flannel shirt. His sleeves were rolled up and a sweater was draped over his shoulders. As Jordan peered more closely, he noticed the dark circles under the eyes and the haggard expression. His conscience pricked as he realized how close he had come to adding to his friend's misery.

"Don't worry about that," Andrew said graciously. "It's all over."

"Is it?" he asked uncertainly.

Andrew studied him. "Do you want me to say that I forgive you for trying to kill Laural? I understand why you felt the necessity and, in your place, I probably would've done the same thing. I know you did it for the right reasons."

Ashamed, he looked away. Tears stung the back of his eyes. In a choked whisper, he asked, "Where is she?"

Andrew straightened. "Down the hall," he replied, while nodding his head. "Last door on the left. You may join us when you're ready."

He looked chagrined at his travel-worn clothing.

"I took the liberty of having some of your things sent down."

A few minutes later, Jordan, freshly cleaned and changed, walked into his cousin's room. As he studied the scene, he stopped short. Laural lay asleep or unconscious on a four-poster bed. Lacy bedspreads and blankets covered the still form, and frilly pillows propped her head. "She looks like a sleeping princess in a fairy tale," he thought, as his eyes roamed over her fair skin, delicate features, and long hair cascading down the side of the bed.

His eyes moved to study the marquis and then they opened wide. Andrew sat in a high wing-back, rose-colored chintz chair. He was pointing a gun at Jordan's head. "You already shot me once. Don't you think that was enough?"

"It depends on your intention," he replied, while the blue eyes scanned his face.

"So much for understanding my position."

"I understand yours. Now you understand mine."

"I won't try again," he promised, as he turned again to the girl on the bed. "I don't have the heart."

Jordan stood still, while allowing his thoughts to be penetrated. Slowly, the gun lowered. Andrew motioned to a chair and Jordan pulled it to the opposite side of the bed.

Staring thoughtfully at Laural, he turned to his friend and said, "I'm sorry."

"I know."

"I didn't want to do it."

"I know."

"I thought it was the only way and I knew you would never be able to do it."

No response.

After a few moments, he turned to regard his friend. Andrew was staring at him with such sadness in his eyes that Jordan shifted uncomfortably.

"I hope you never have to choose between your duty and your child."

"That's a dilemma I may not ever have to confront considering I no longer have a partner," he said bitterly.

Andrew frowned. He would never understand his friend's obsession with Dana Maxwell. Even now, he spoke as though she were the only partner that he could ever have. He knew from experience there were plenty of women, porphyrian and diurnal alike, who would jump at the chance to have a relationship with Jordan. Nevertheless, he remained devoted to Dana. Personally, he thought she was a lost cause.

"But you did have one."

Jordan glanced up. The blue eyes seemed to bore into his soul. "What are you getting at?"

"When I found Craven and Laural, Dana was with them."

"I know. You told me," he said impatiently.

Laural stirred and both men watched until she resettled.

Andrew carefully chose his words in order to avoid telling his friend more than he needed to know. "She was pregnant."

Jordan blanched. "How do you know?"

"It was obvious."

He swallowed past the lump in his throat. "Is it mine?"

"Yes."

His eyes narrowed and he frowned. "You're holding back."

Andrew stared back noncommittally. He was determined to spare his friend the details of the compromising position that Dana and Craven had been in when he discovered them.

At that moment, Laural's eyes fluttered open. Andrew stood, poured from the bedside pitcher, and lifted the glass to her lips. She swallowed a few sips and then gagged. Swiftly putting down the glass, he lifted a large porcelain bowl and held it in front of her while she emptied the contents of her stomach.

After several more dry heaves, she sank back against the pillows. The young woman was incredibly weak and exhausted. As she faded back into unconsciousness, Andrew took the bowl into the adjoining bathroom. Jordan listened to the rushing water and the clanking of the bowl as it hit the sink. Andrew finally emerged, set the bowl back on the bedside table, and sat down.

"What's in that?" asked Jordan, as he nodded toward the pitcher.

"A combination of pig and donated human blood I got from the blood bank. I'm weaning her off, but I have to do it slowly so her system won't go into shock. Yesterday, she was running a pretty high fever, but it's almost back to normal."

Startled, he asked, "How long have we been here?"

"Three days."

"This entire ordeal," Jordan said, while waving a hand toward the bed, "must break your heart. I don't think I could stand it if it were my child."

Andrew sighed. "You'd be surprised what you can do for the sake of your own child."

Jordan nodded. The knowledge that he was about to have a child already was having an impact on the way he felt. In fact, he felt that he did not want to hear the rest of what Andrew knew, so he decided to keep talking about anything else.

"How did we get here? Last I remember, we were at Washington General and I was looking down the inside of your gun barrel."

The marquis smiled slightly. "Sorry, old chap, but it was the only way I could get your attention. As you probably have realized by now, it was only a tranquilizer dart."

"Must have been pretty potent to keep me out for three days."

"I thought I would need powerful stuff if Laural was as strong as I figured she would be. Good thing I was prepared because it took several darts to bring her down."

"And Dr. Brenner?"

"The good doctor has convinced himself that he was attacked by one of the psych ward's patients."

"And how did we get from DC to Cornwall, England?"

Andrew chuckled. "I still have some influence and friends in high places in both countries."

Jordan nodded sagely.

A brief silence ensued before Andrew spoke. "Dana went to Craven of her own free will. From what I could gather in the brief time I saw her, she was petrified of dying during childbirth. She didn't think we would understand. She was afraid to confide for fear you and I would force her to go through with it. I'm not sure if she realized at first that Craven was what she was running to or if she was subconsciously drawn to him. I know he had her under his mental domination for some time and I take full responsibility for that. If she had known from the outset that he had survived, she might have been better prepared to resist."

He hesitated, looked from his friend to his daughter, and then back. Closing his eyes, he raked his hand through his hair. He did not want to do this. He was tired of the entire episode. He could feel the desire to retreat seeping through him. In an effort to counteract it, he opened his eyes and stared hard at his child.

Jordan moved to a nearby cabinet, extracted a bottle of PS4, and two glasses. Filling them, he handed one to his friend. Concerned, he watched as Andrew nodded his gratitude and quickly drained the contents. Refilling the glass, he handed it back to the marquis, who slowly sipped the second drink.

"Tell me what you're holding back," encouraged the earl with mixed emotions. "I need to know."

Shaking off his melancholy mood, Andrew squared his shoulders and confronted his friend. "Craven was using Dana's pregnancy as some kind of demented experiment. He wanted to test the theory that a porphyrian nourished by human blood would maximize porphyrian potential."

Jordan glanced toward the bed. He was confused.

"Yes, he tried it on my child, but she was already grown. He wanted to see if starting during the prenatal stage would ..."

An image assailed Jordan. He envisioned Craven injecting Dana with a syringe of blood directly into her uterus. Laural stirred and her father again repeated the earlier procedure. Deep in thought, Jordan watched as his friend washed out the bowl. As Andrew approached the bed, he stood.

"Where are you going?"

"To find my child."

When he left the room, troubled turquoise eyes followed him.

"Good luck, my friend," he projected, as Jordan descended the stairs. "You may not like what you find."

Chapter 59:

Recovery

Jordan drummed his fingers on the desk as he waited for the overseas connection. He glanced across the study to check the grandfather clock. If he hurried, he could catch the next flight and be back in DC by early tomorrow morning. The call connected. Jordan explained what he needed and Tim Cooper agreed to meet with him in the morning. As he replaced the receiver, a knock sounded at the study door.

"Come in."

The door opened. Jordan smiled broadly. "Grayson!" he exclaimed. "It's so nice to see you after all this time."

The elderly butler smiled back. "You're a sight for sore eyes, Lord Rush. I regret you'll be leaving us so soon."

The smile faded as Jordan's eyes darkened. "It couldn't be avoided. I have pressing business back in the States."

The butler nodded. "Lord Gabriel indicated you might be needing the car. Since the chauffer is on holiday, I'll be taking you to the airport. When shall I bring the car around?"

Jordan checked his watch. Remembering the time difference, he glanced again at the grandfather clock.

Inclining his head toward the butler, he said, "I should be ready in about five minutes. I want to speak with Andrew before I go."

At that moment, Andrew strode into the room. He wore a broad grin. "She's conscious and coherent for the first time."

The two men smiled back. "That's marvelous, sir," said Grayson, while heading to the door. "If you gentlemen will excuse me, I'll see to getting the car ready."

Andrew was exuberant. "She's lucid with no sign of permanent damage." He dropped into one of the overstuffed chairs. "She's speaking coherently and she recognized me. She seems to know who and where she is, and her memory is intact."

"I'm relieved. Hopefully, no permanent damage was done."

The marquis soberly nodded. "I know she still has a long way to go in regaining her strength, but, for a while, I wasn't sure she would live."

Now, it was Jordan's turn to nod soberly. "I have to go."

"You should stay a while longer and think this through."

"I've contacted Tim. He's going to start tracking."

Andrew raked his hand through his hair. "I really wish you would stay even if for just a couple of days. I could use the help with Laural and I think this plan needs further consideration."

He frowned. "What kind of consideration?"

"For one thing, what are you going to do when you find her? Who knows what effect Craven's experiments have had on her and the baby? Aiding me with Laural might give you a better idea of what to do if you find Dana in a similar condition. It will also give us a better chance to make plans." Jordan still looked skeptical, so he continued. "Besides, you don't know if she's still in the States."

The phone rang. Andrew stood and strode to the desk. After a moment, he handed the receiver to Jordan.

Jordan listened for the next few minutes in silence. Finally, he let out an exasperated breath, replied briefly, then replaced the receiver. Several seconds ticked by while he continued to stare at the phone. Eventually, he lifted his eyes to confront his friend. "Looks like you may get your wish. According to Tim, his preliminary data indicates Dana may have left the country. He recommends staying here for now while he follows up. There's no sense in going to Washington if she's headed somewhere else."

"I'll inform Grayson."

Jordan lifted the receiver. "I'll cancel my flight."

As he hung up, footsteps approached. "All settled," he announced. "I hope you have some good ideas on how to handle this." His eyes opened wide.

"Laural!" he gasped, while staring in surprise at the wan figure standing in the doorway. She was dressed in her favorite riding habit made of blue cashmere. Her hair was styled in a beautiful braid that hung down her back.

"I want to go riding, but I can't find my father. Will you take me?"

He thoughtfully studied her. Her face was pale. Her hands shook slightly as she nervously beat the riding crop against her polished equestrian boots. She seemed much too fragile to go horseback riding.

She defiantly lifted her chin. With a start, he belatedly remembered that she could read him.

"I'll go by myself," she insisted stubbornly.

He smiled at the familiar rebellious attitude. His brows raised. "Would you believe I have nothing to wear?"

Her face broke into a wide grin as she inspected his thick cable-stitched turtleneck, jeans, and loafers. "All you really need is a jacket. I wore this just to show you how serious I am. If I don't get out of here for a little while, I'll go nuts."

She was grinning, but he read the gravity behind her words. Going to her side, he reached for her hand. "Let's ride."

Jordan projected their intention to Laural's father. Andrew was shocked and apprehensive. The earl explained his daughter's determination. The marquis' laughter echoed through Jordan's mind.

"Go ahead," he finally agreed. "If she's feeling well enough to insist so strongly, that's probably a good sign. Just be careful. She's still weak."

Leading her by the hand, they headed for the stables. "When you couldn't find your dad, why didn't you try to connect with him telepathically?" he asked, as they crossed the courtyard.

"I felt like someone was watching me," admitted Laural, while shivering and glancing back at the castle.

"You're father has been watching you like a hawk ever since we got here."

"Maybe, that's it," she agreed doubtfully. "But last time I had a feeling like that was right before I was kidnapped and the time before that was when my mom was killed." She swallowed hard past the lump in her throat. "I was bonded telepathically with my mom when she died. I was trying to give her a mental message at the time. I'm still a little skittish about trying to do it again."

Jordan stopped to gaze at her. He squeezed her hand to reassure her. "Both those acts were perpetrated by Craven. You don't have to worry about him. He's dead."

Her eyes widened. Vague memories of attacking her uncle while she had been in the throws of the blood sickness flashed through her mind. Had she killed him? The uncertainty made her uneasy, but she refrained from asking Jordan. She was afraid that any sign of weakness would cause him to change his mind about their outing. Besides, she was not sure that she wanted to know the answer.

They entered the stable and Laural gasped. Her father was holding the reigns of the most beautiful stallion that she had ever seen. His coat was a glossy white with silver undertones that gleamed in the afternoon sun. He was tall and majestic with a powerful body and broad chest. His wild spirit shone through his large intelligent eyes. While the marquis gently patted him on the neck, he pranced impatiently and tugged at the end of his lead.

"Laural," he announced, while grinning broadly, "this is Silver Lining. Silver Lining, meet your new mistress."

The horse snorted and tossed his head. Laural clapped her hands in delight. Her joyful laughter echoed through the stable. Andrew and Jordan exchanged a glance. The marquis grinned; the earl grinned back.

"Is he really mine?" Laural asked. Her eyes were as large as saucers.

The marquis nodded, as he handed the bridle and paperwork to her. "He was supposed to be your birthday present. He's been waiting – rather impatiently, I might add – to make your acquaintance."

She read the registration and grinned from ear to ear before tucking the papers inside her jacket. She pressed her cheek against the velvety warm neck. Daughter and father exchanged a look. Laural understood and her heart ached.

Jordan reappeared astride a reddish-brown gelding. "Ready?"

Andrew swung his daughter into the saddle. "Enjoy the ride, ma petite, but don't tire yourself."

Laural's exhaustion transformed to exhilaration as she anticipated riding such a splendid animal.

An ominous figure stood alone on a nearby bluff and watched the happy scene unfold. In brooding silence, the figure slightly repositioned the shrubbery in order to get a better view of Laural and Jordan riding across the heather-carpeted hills.

Andrew also smiled at the sight of the happy couple. "Smile all you want now," the figure thought venomously. "You won't be smiling much longer." Unaware that he was being observed, the lord of the castle paused to talk to an elderly servant before he went inside.

"Which one should die first?" the plotter queried himself. "Laural, of course, is the weakest, but she is with the earl. Andrew is alone, but soon will be surrounded by servants." The servants were not a problem. They were less than gnats that could be swatted away. Laural should die first. Then, the earl. Then, the main event: Andrew. Saving the marquis for last would insure his prolonged suffering because he would be forced to endure the deaths of the two people who were dearest to him.

The elderly servant approached a gleaming white Rolls and climbed behind the wheel. Watching the car slowly wind its way back to the garage, the shadowy character was struck by inspiration. The devastation to the Penbrook family would be utter and complete. Everyone that Andrew had sworn to protect would be dead. The guilt and remorse would be his undoing. The lord of the manor most certainly would withdraw. However, this time, he would make sure that Andrew's forsaking of the world was permanent.

Chapter 60:
Tragic Reminders

Reigning in the powerful stallion, Laural deeply inhaled the salty tang of the sea. From the cliff, she admired the dramatic beauty of the Cornish coast that was spread out before her. Her mount snorted. She leaned forward to pat his neck. Straightening, she became lost in thought as she gazed pensively into the horizon.

Her eyes eventually drifted to the castle, her ancestral home, refuge of the Penbrooks for over a millennium. She took in a long steadying breath while absorbing the sense of connectedness that she felt to the land and its people. She knew that whatever other holdings the Gabriels might own, she always would consider this to be her home.

Its stark beauty always took her breath away. The stone fortress lay surrounded by a forest of evergreens with a backdrop of the heather hillside. Spring had come early this year and she was glad. The blossoming of flora and fauna gave her a renewed sense of vitality.

"You know," she mused, while staring at the fortress, "I was never allowed to go into that part of the castle," she remarked as she pointed. "I wonder why."

Jordan followed her direction. "I think your parents always considered it too dangerous for you to explore because it's not in good repair."

"That doesn't make any sense," she stated, as she finally turned to look at him. "The rest of the castle is kept in excellent repair and completely modernized. Why keep that part shut off?"

He stared long and hard at the projecting turret. If Andrew was not going to fix it, he should have the tragic reminder removed. "There's nothing up there but some very old and very bad memories."

She sighed ruefully. The brisk breeze blew tendrils of hair into her face. "Will you tell me what happened?"

Confused, he looked from the castle to his cousin. She had the right to know about her family history, but he was convinced that the information should come from Andrew.

"Not about the tower. Tell me what happened to me."

"You don't remember?"

She shook her head. Her eyes were haunted as they stared into his. "Not all of it, especially after Craven began injecting me with diurnal blood." She sadly reflected that it had been her mother's diurnal blood, but she determinedly pushed the thought aside. "What I do remember seems like a bad dream. I can't sort out what's real."

"Don't you think you should be asking your dad about this?"

She grimaced and turned away. "He won't tell me. He thinks I'm too weak to handle it. He just keeps avoiding my questions by insisting he's protecting me."

"He's right."

She moved away and headed Silver Lining down the hill. Jordan pulled beside her and tugged at her reigns. She stopped and glared at him.

A lump caught in his throat at the abject misery that he saw beneath the bravado. "There's something you should know," he proclaimed. Swallowing hard, he admitted, "I tried to kill you."

Her eyes widened in shock.

"When you became addicted to human blood, I realized you had to be destroyed." He read the pain and shame in her eyes, but savagely pressed his point. "I would have succeeded if your father hadn't intervened."

Her eyes brimmed. Swallowing hard, she fought back the impulse to burst into tears. She searched her cousin's face.

He stilled his chaotic thoughts so that she could read him. Finally, he said, "I'm not sure if I had to do it over again I wouldn't make the same choice. So, I think your father is a much better judge of how to protect you."

Galvanized, she jerked the reigns, spun Silver Lining in a tight circle, and galloped as fast as her steed would go. The pounding of the horse's hoofs echoed the erratic beating of her heart. He had frightened her. She was scared out of her wits, not because he had tried to destroy what she had become, but because he had not succeeded.

She had read more than he wanted her to know. She had seen

what she had become and what she had done to Jim. "How many others have I hurt?" she cried. Since her nightmares of attacking Jim were real, then what about the man in the van, the two children, and the girl? She bent low over the horse's neck and urged him on even faster. She raced toward the castle, while trying desperately to outrun her turbulent thoughts.

Chapter 61:

The Earl's Discovery

The next morning, Laural awoke to the sound of birds gaily chirping in the trees that were outside of her window. As she opened her eyes, sunshine spilled onto her face. Someone had opened the drapes and built a fire to dissipate the early morning chill. As she sat up, her eyes swept the familiar surroundings.

Her family owned many homes all over the world. In several of them, she had rooms that were much more modern and luxurious, but she loved her bedroom at Penbrook castle more than any of them. Because the ancient structure was part of her ancestral heritage and had such a long history, it was dear to her. She was especially partial to this room. As soon as she was old enough, her parents had allowed her to have free reign over its interior design. She admired the rosebud wall paper, matching bed linen, and dresser/armoire set with painted long-stemmed roses that she had helped to decorate as a child. Tears swam and then flowed down her cheeks as she recalled how her mom had personally painted each flower despite her attempts to "help."

Her dad chuckled softly. Laural's eyes sought and then found him sitting in a rose-colored wing-back chair in the far corner. He stood, approached the bed, and sat down next to her. She nestled into his arms. His warm embrace and familiar cologne soothed some of her pain. Together, they silently admired the sunrise as they gazed from her large bay window.

"Mom helped me pick out and decorate this room. I remember it like it was just yesterday."

"So do I."

"Remember when she painted the beautiful rose garden on the sides and the front of the armoire?"

"Yes."

"Then, I decided I hadn't helped enough, so I painted a matching garden on the dresser."

"I sure do."

"Only mine came out looking more like pink and red globs with green streaks for leaves and stems."

He laughed. "The dresser wasn't the only thing that came out with red and pink globs with green streaks."

"Most parents would have been mad, but you and Mom just laughed and took my picture."

"Which I am still eagerly waiting to show to perspective son-in-laws."

"Then, Mom picked up her paintbrush and patiently painted over everything until she'd made it right. She was always wanting to make things right for me."

He was silent.

"I miss her so much."

"So do I."

They sat for a long time in silence, while watching the morning change from rosy pink to bright yellow. "How do you feel, ma petite?"

"Physically stronger, but my head still feels fuzzy and I was sick several times last night."

"I know."

She glanced from her father to the armchair and then back. "How long were you there?"

He shrugged, stood, and stretched. "Long enough. I know you wanted to try getting through the night on your own, but, after the third bout of retching, I couldn't stand it. Don't look at me like that. You may be eighteen, but I'm still your father and it's my prerogative to worry."

She rolled her eyes. "You've always been overprotective."

He considered her soberly. "Under the circumstances, I don't think I've been protective enough."

"Dad, what happened wasn't your fault."

He gazed at her for a long moment and then said, "I think your electrolyte levels are returning to normal. Since you haven't gone into massive rejection or developed any organ failure, I'd like to try going back to straight PS4 today."

She grimaced. "Anything to get off the pig's blood. I never thought I'd dislike anything more than PS4."

"Why don't you wait here? I'll get our breakfast."

"I'm strong enough to go downstairs. I went riding yesterday."

He skeptically eyed her. "Jordan said you became distraught at the end and overtaxed yourself on the ride home."

"Maybe," she mumbled, not meeting his eyes. "But riding on Silver Lining was like floating on a cloud," she exclaimed, as she brightened. "He's the most wonderful present I've ever had."

He leaned over to ruffle her hair. "Indulge me. Now that you're an adult, I have a feeling I won't be able to pamper you much longer."

She leaned back against the pillows and winced.

His blue eyes immediately filled with concern. "How's your back and shoulder?"

She forced a smile. "Much better now that the bullets have been removed. There're no marks to show I was ever shot and the soreness is almost gone." Then, she abruptly changed the subject. "What about Jordan?"

"I'll ask him to join us."

"He said he tried to kill me."

Andrew gave her a long look. "He did."

"Why?"

Andrew refrained from answering.

She defiantly glared at him. "I have a right to know!"

He sighed. "I planned to tell you after you'd fully recovered. I wish Jordan had been more discrete."

"I dragged it out of him."

"How much did he tell you?"

"Only the part about trying to kill me. He feels horribly guilty. The rest I got from his thoughts."

Her father appeared disturbed.

"I didn't read him on purpose."

He nodded and then smiled reassuringly. "You just need some guidance and practice. We'll start after you recover. Now, it's time for breakfast. I'll ask Jordan to join us. After we've eaten, he and I will tell you everything."

At that moment, the bedroom door burst open. The subject of their discussion stood in the doorway. He was flushed and disheveled. Startled, they both stared. Neither knew what to make of the sudden apparition. The earl raked his hand through his chestnut hair, straightened his shirt collar, and then cleared his throat.

"Sorry," he said in a rush. "I had a bad dream. I thought Laural was in danger."

"Daddy was just on his way to get some breakfast. Would you like to sit with me while he goes to the kitchen?"

For a moment, the earl seemed torn, but then he said, "If your dad is carrying for three, I should help."

Andrew was about to protest that he could get either Lorraine, their cook, or Martha, their housekeeper, to bring up the breakfast trays, but then stopped.

"That will be great," the marquis suddenly said. "Besides, I think Lorraine may want to know Jordan's preferences since he'll be staying a few days."

Once in the hallway, Andrew turned to him. "What was all that about?"

The mask of complacency shattered. Jordan covered his face with his hands. "You need to come down and see for yourself," he cried as he strode toward the stairs, Jordan was visibly shaken. "Grayson, Lorraine, Martha, Jack, even the grooms! Andrew, your entire staff has been murdered!"

Chapter 62:

Carnage at the Castle

Andrew gasped and then flew past Jordan. The marquis took the stairs two at a time. At the bottom, he stopped short and stared in shock. Bending over the body lying at the bottom of the stairs, he put his fingers to the throat of Grayson, his family's longtime butler and friend. No pulse.

"It looks as though he was trying to warn us," Jordan assumed by observing the position of the corpse.

Dully, Andrew nodded. Grayson had been his loyal and devoted servant right up until the end. His eyes strayed up the stairs. The pattern of the blood splatter and smears on the steps told the story. Jordan was right. With his last remaining strength, the butler had tried to protect them.

The lord of the manor stood and then stumbled across the room to the hearth. Martha, their equally loyal and devoted housekeeper, lay sprawled in a pool of blood with a poker from the fireplace still clutched in her hand. He quickly moved toward the kitchen. As he passed through the door, he stopped short. In utter disbelief, he stared at the torn and mangled body of the French cook who had been in his employ for the past thirty years.

His entire household staff was dead. No, not just dead, but murdered in a carnage that surpassed the most gruesome horror movie that he had ever seen. He bolted for the back door, flew down the stairs, and sprinted across the yard. Large and foreboding, the stable loomed ahead.

Jordan caught up with him and grabbed his arm. "You may want to prepare yourself before you go in there," he warned.

Andrew's eyes blazed. "Who did this? Who is responsible for this massacre? Who would kill all these innocent people and for what reason?"

Jordan's eyes flicked back toward the castle. He briefly glanced up at the window on the second floor.

Andrew's eyes widened and then narrowed. "You think Laural did this?" he asked incredulously.

He sighed. "Who else?"

"You're insane."

"Am I?"

"She's cured."

The green eyes darkened. "Are you sure? Then, how do you explain it? The three of us are the only ones here."

"I was with her last night."

"All night?"

Andrew looked away. The memory of his daughter purging several times through the night replayed in his mind. "What if she hadn't been purging the last of the old blood?" he wondered. "What if she had been reacting to fresh kill?"

Laural sat up and swung her legs over the edge of the bed. The raised voices of Jordan and her father were coming from the courtyard below her window. She could not imagine why they had gone outside instead of bringing breakfast. They sounded agitated. Standing, on unsteady legs, she leaned against her bedpost. Yesterday's ride must have drained her more than she realized.

Struck by a horrific thought, she stiffened. Precariously, she moved toward the window. Had something happened to Silver Lining? Her heart raced as she watched the two men heading into the stable. Her father pulled open the door and then stood as if rooted to the spot. Even from this distance, she could read the shock and despair on his face.

With her worst fear confirmed, she moved toward the bedroom door. Opening it, she paused. She could hear men's voices from below. They obviously were in such a hurry that they had left the back door open. Hesitantly, she moved down the hall. Her dad had wanted her to rest and wait, but she could not sit idly by while anxiety gnawed at her nerves. A strange sense of foreboding swept through her and she shivered.

Tightening her robe, she paused. Her brow furrowed. She scanned the hallway. Nothing was wrong, but, even though she wanted to go downstairs, she felt compelled to head in the opposite direction.

Walking into one of the guest bedrooms, she paused. The room confronting her was very feminine. It had a beautiful four-poster that was similar to the one in her room. Unsure of what she was doing here, she went to the bed and sat down. She felt weak and dizzy. As she started to go back to her room to lie down, she spied a book on the bedside table. She lifted it and read the title. *Vampires: Fact or Fiction.*

Dread swept through her as her trembling fingers turned the pages. A gasp tore from her lips as she stared in horror at the large picture of her Uncle Craven. Reading the narrative, she quickly realized that it was a relative. "Could it be his father?" she questioned herself. Profoundly disturbed, she sat for several moments before laying the book aside and leaving the room.

They stepped into the stable. The scene was horrific. Andrew closed his eyes against the slaughter confronting him. All of his servants – these good people who had done nothing worse than give their service to him – were lying lifeless at his feet. Regret and remorse ripped through him. Since the Gabriel family had been lords of this land, they had treated their servants with compassion and fairness. His tenants knew they could rely on him to protect and provide for them. "Some protector I've turned out to be," he thought bitterly, as he opened his eyes to stare at the death and destruction.

Even though Jordan previously had viewed the atrocity, his bile still rose as he re-examined the bloody corpses. The three grooms lay in pools of blood. Deep gashes and stab wounds permeated their bodies. He moved to the youngest, George, and swallowed hard. The youth could not have been more than fifteen.

Andrew walked to him, bent down, and gently closed the boy's vacant eyes. Tortured turquoise eyes looked up to meet his cousin's pale face.

"This wasn't Laural."

Jordan looked at him. The earl's skepticism was apparent.

"If she were still in the throws of the blood sickness, she'd be too demented to consider strangling or stabbing her victims. This was a deliberate and well-planned attack. It was not the work of someone desperate to feed. Besides," he said as he pointed to the ground, "there's too much blood left."

"Just because there's no sign of feeding doesn't mean she couldn't have attacked them."

Andrew scanned the stable. For a moment, his eyes lingered on the only occupant left alive. Silver Lining shied and whinnied as he approached, but appeared to be unharmed.

"The rest of the horses are in the field."

He glanced toward the open door. He watched the horses grazing in the field. They had not been targets during the massacre. Was that because the killer did not have the time or did not want to kill them? He turned to his cousin. "Where's the weapon?"

Jordan stared with a blank look.

"These atrocities were committed with some sort of knife. By the look of the wounds, I guess it was a rapier. Laural wasn't hiding a sword under her pillow. So, if she did it in a frenzy, the weapon should be here somewhere."

Jordan glanced around. Something that Andrew said troubled him. His brows lowered in concentration. He replayed the scene in his mind. Grayson at the front foyer, strangled and stabbed several times in the back. Martha on the hearth, bloody and battered. She probably had been the first to feel the thrust of the blade in her chest. He tried to envision the scene. The killer had come in, strangled Grayson, and then moved to Martha. The person had used a rapier to kill the housekeeper and presumably noticed that Grayson was still alive. As he tried to get up the stairs to alert the household, he had been stabbed in the back.

The furrow between his brows deepened. "If the killer had a sword, why didn't Grayson get stabbed in the first place?" he asked himself. He let the scene unwind further. The foyer, the hearth, the fireplace, the mantle. As the last image slid into place, he gasped. "Andrew, the killer used the rapier from your coat of arms above the fireplace."

"Daddy!" The scream exploded in his head like a bomb.

"Laural!" he yelled and bolted toward the castle.

Chapter 63:
Haunted Memories

Terror gripped Andrew's heart like a vise. He tore through the rooms and raced toward the stairs. Laural was in danger. He had to get to her before Victory's tragedy became the legacy of their only child. He banished the thought before it was fully formed. Guilt kept pace with him as he hurled himself up the stairs. After everything that she had already been through he couldn't stand the thought of Laural in any more pain. As he streaked down the hall, guilt became remorse that blazed into fury. He had not been able to save his wife, but he would be damned if he would let anything else happen to Laural.

"Andrew, wait!" yelled Jordan, but to no avail. His friend was oblivious to everything except reaching his child. Jordan hesitated. If someone was threatening Laural, it probably was the same person who had killed the others. If so, that person definitely had a weapon. He looked around frantically. Andrew kept all of the weapons locked in his study. There was no time to go there to find them. As he rushed to the fireplace, he slid on Martha's congealed blood. He grimaced, but kept moving. Snatching the remaining rapier from the wall, he quickly followed his friend.

Andrew plunged into his daughter's bedroom. Empty. He glanced around frantically. Stepping back into the hallway, he looked in both directions. She had not headed down this hall or he would have passed her. With a tremendous effort, he placed panic aside and focused. Grimly, he turned in the direction of the unused tower. Light shone from an open doorway. Laural had gone in that direction and she was not alone.

He raced down the hallway and then paused. The door to one of the guest bedrooms stood open. This particular door always had been closed. He sensed that his daughter was close. Closing his eyes for a brief moment, he braced himself before entering the guest bedroom.

This was the bedroom that Victory had used when she first came to visit almost two decades ago. If he inhaled deeply, he still could smell the lingering scent of her perfume.

His eyes ripped around the room. Empty. He cursed. Where was she? Evidently, she had been here. The bed still bore an imprint where she had sat. Hopefully, his daughter had not realized where she had wandered when she entered that room. Resuming his search, he headed for the door. The book lay open. Raven Maxwell's baleful glare beckoned him from the bedside table. Walking as if in a trance, he approached the table and lifted the book.

Memories of another time haunted him when this book had caused serious problems. There had been too many questions that he had been unable to answer. He remembered the distrust, alienation, and events that were so turbulent that they almost cost Victory's life. The book dropped from his suddenly nerveless fingers as Andrew raced out of the room and down the hallway. He bolted past the frequently used portion of the castle to the closed and forbidden section that lead to the tower.

Chapter 64: Mortal Combat

Craven advanced menacingly toward the young woman, brandishing the rapier. Laural stepped back, but her legs bumped against the wrought iron railing. It gave slightly, but held. She glanced down. Flakes of rusty iron crumbled and fell into the five-hundred-foot drop. Her face paled as she fully realized her peril.

Craven grinned maliciously. His long double-breasted wool coat gave him a militant look as he threatened her with the blade. "Still haven't got the skill to send messages while blocking? No matter. This time, I want your father to find us. In fact, it's essential for him to see your demise. You see, dear niece, I'm counting on the fact that he'll blame himself for your death. The guilt will drive him into such a lethargic stupor that he'll not be able to defend himself. Then, I'll kill him."

Her eyes flashed. "You murdered my mother. I won't let you harm my dad."

"And how do you plan to stop me?" he mocked, while sliding the razor-sharp edge of the sword across her cheek.

Blood dripped down her face. The cut stung, but she refused to allow him to intimidate her. Suddenly, something within her snapped and she rushed him. She no longer cared about anything except protecting her remaining parent from this monster. He laughed and easily caught her. Her fists flailed against him. One connected with his jaw. His teeth clamped together cutting him off in mid chuckle.

"That hurt!" he glared, while pinning her arms behind her with one hand and rubbing his jaw with the other. The onyx orbs bore into her. "I almost forgot who I was dealing with. You're strong," he admitted, while slamming her hard against the railing, "but I'm stronger."

The ancient wrought iron broke. She felt the rush of air against her back. She teetered and started to slip as Craven inexorably pushed her over the edge.

"Craven," bellowed the Marquis of Penbrook, as he rushed onto the parapet, "let her go!"

Craven warily eyed him. Noting that he was unarmed, he nodded. "As you wish," he agreed with a malicious gleam sparkling in his eyes.

He released his hold. Laural wind-milled her arms as she slipped backwards. Heedless of Craven's outstretched weapon, Andrew pushed past his brother and reached for his daughter. Catching her robe, he yanked her to safety.

"Watch out!"

Andrew turned just in time to see Craven's sword swinging toward his head. The marquis ducked low and shouldered him in the ribs. Craven stumbled backwards. Jordan tossed the second rapier to his cousin.

"Get Laural out of here," ordered Andrew, while spinning around to combat his brother.

Jordan pulled the girl close. Her sapphire eyes grew huge. "Love to oblige as soon as you clear the exit."

Andrew frowned. He was baffled about how his brother had survived their last battle, but assuaging his curiosity would have to wait. Right now, his main focus was to ensure the safety of his daughter. He struck, feinted, slashed, parried, feinted, and successfully maneuvered the battle away from the entrance. He allowed his brother to drive him toward the opposite end of the walkway, thereby drawing his attention away from his daughter. He briefly glanced toward Laural and Jordan. Instead of escaping, the pair were staring at the combat. They were mesmerized. Laural's eyes widened just as Andrew felt a sharp stab of pain. Grimacing, he glanced at a streak of crimson running down his side.

"You should be dead," blurted Andrew, as he lashed out with his sword.

Craven raised his arm to counter the blow. "I would be if you hadn't been in such a hurry that you didn't bother to check. Fortunately for me," he replied, while smiling cynically, "you were too interested in catching up with Laural. In your haste, I guess you forgot that all of our body parts including the brain will heal if irrevocable damage is not sustained."

"I was so sure he couldn't live through that last injury," Andrew silently assailed himself, as he ducked and dodged and attacked. "How could I have been so stupid?" He knew perfectly well that porphyrians can heal if permanent damage is not inflicted.

His jaw set in a hard line. Once again, it was his fault that they were in peril. Craven was right. He had been so distracted by his pursuit of Laural that he had not bothered to be thorough.

"Then I'm to blame for all this."

Andrew raised his eyes. Twin pools of brilliant sapphires glittering with unshed tears stared remorsefully.

"No!" he thought back sharply.

"Watch out!" yelled Jordan.

He realized his mistake, but it was too late. Craven lunged and slammed hard against him. Andrew flew backward several feet and crashed against the wrought iron railing. Before he could rise, Craven leapt forward and kicked him. He felt the steel crack and break behind him. The railing creaked and groaned. It shifted and then pulled free of the mortar. As he fell, he heard Laural scream.

Chapter 65:
Over the Edge

Laural was rooted to the spot and stared at the gaping hole in the railing where her father had been only a moment ago. Now, he was gone. Gone, just like her mom. Craven had killed both of them – and she was all alone.

"Come on!" Jordan commanded urgently, while yanking her arm.

"We have to help him."

His mouth set in a grim line. After a five-hundred-foot drop, he doubted that there would be anything that they could do that would "help" Andrew.

"We can't help if we get killed," he protested, while eyeing Craven. "Besides, we have no weapon."

She cast one more longing look toward the broken railing and then allowed herself to be pulled forward. Jordan ran as if the devil were in pursuit. He dragged the forlorn girl in his wake. Suddenly, she felt a hard yank on her hair. For a moment, she was a rag doll in a tug of war between the two men. Viciously, Jordan turned.

"Let go of her," he hissed, as he stepped past Laural to connect his fist to Craven's jaw. The loud crack gave only momentary pleasure. Craven yanked even harder on Laural's hair. She gasped as she was jerked against her uncle's chest. The momentum swung Jordan close enough to give the advantage to Craven. He raised his arm to slash the sword through his neck.

"Noooo!" Laural screamed, as she violently kneed Craven in the groin. He doubled over in pain. Groaning, he dropped the rapier and momentarily relaxed his hold on her hair. Before she could pull away completely, he grabbed her again.

"Bitch!" he snarled with spittle spewing from his lips and daggers shooting from his eyes.

Laural struggled fiercely as her uncle lifted her and carried her to the railing. Swinging his leg back, he kicked viciously at the rusty iron several times. It screeched in protest, but finally broke. Laural glanced over her shoulder and froze in terror as she watched the waves splashing over the jagged rocks below.

"Laural!" Jordan yelled, as he launched himself at Craven's back.

The three of them reeled and spun. They briefly pirouetted across the ledge. Jordan's arms came around from behind and pinned Craven's arms flat against his sides. The position kept him from tossing Laural, but also locked her in his embrace. Craven flexed. His muscles bulged. Jordan's grip tightened. Craven launched himself at the opening.

"Is he suicidal?" the earl wondered as the other man dove straight toward the edge.

Laural realized his intent. "Jordan," she screamed, "let go. He's going to ..."

At that moment, Craven stopped short and doubled over so fast that the breath was knocked out of his prisoner. Caught off guard, the earl was hurled over Craven's shoulders and was catapulted into the night.

Chapter 66: Legacy of a Madman

Andrew Gabriel, Marquis of Penbrook, winced while he struggled to retain his hold on the face of the cliff. The wind buffeted him as it tried to dislodge and claim him for its trophy. His fingers were scraped raw and bleeding from digging into handholds that did not exist. His blood-slick hands lost their grip and he began to slide. His wounded body slammed hard into the rough outcrops, while he desperately grabbed at everything. Finally seizing a jutting rock, he clung for a few seconds and mercifully caught his breath.

After a few moments, he regained his momentum. He raised his head. The walkway was still several feet above. The wrought iron was still breaking. He ducked his head as another piece shot past. Looking down, he observed its descent and watched in fascination as the metal hit the jagged rocks below and was washed out to sea. A glint of metal lodged between the rocks caught his attention. He wished fervently for time to retrieve the rapier before confronting Craven. Laural was at the mercy of that bastard and every second could be the difference between life and death.

As if to lend credence to his fear, a loud scream pierced the air.

Grunting, he scrambled up the final few feet and heaved himself over the edge. The sight confronting him made his blood run cold. Craven was shoving a violently struggling Laural over the opposite edge of the parapet.

"Not again," he thought bleakly. For a moment, his vision blurred and he thought that she was his long-dead fiancée, Elizabeth, who was dangling precariously. His brother's laughter rang hollowly in his ears.

Another scream. Andrew's mind snapped back to the present. He catapulted himself toward his brother's back. Just then, Craven kicked Laural's legs out from under her. She seemingly floated for a moment in thin air and then fell. Andrew lunged for his daughter. He caught her nightgown, but it wasn't enough. Her weight dragged them both over the edge into darkness. As they fell, he heard triumphant maniacal laughter echoing through the air.

Jordan shook his head and stumbled to his feet. Dazed and bloody, he stared for a moment at the narrow outcrop of rock that had broken his fall. When he peered over its edge at the jagged rocks several hundred feet below, he realized how lucky he had been.

A scream tore through the night. Laural! He had to get to Laural. But without a weapon, how could he defeat Craven? Physically, they were too well-matched. Mentally, Craven had the upper hand. Despite his misgivings, he had to try. His mouth set in a grim line. His fate probably was sealed, but if he were going to die, he would take the bastard with him. Then, everyone else would be safe. He owed it to the future of his race and to his own unborn child. He had to protect them from the legacy of this madman.

With great stealth, he crept to a position that he thought would bring him behind his adversary. He prayed Craven had not retrieved his weapon. He heard a commotion above him. He gnashed his teeth in vexation. From this position, he could not tell what was happening. "To hell with caution," he decided, as he climbed onto the walkway.

Craven smiled with malicious delight as he leaned forward to watch his brother and niece plummet to their deaths. He had been waiting for more than three centuries for the demise of Andrew Gabriel and he intended to savor every moment. At long last, he was now free to dominate his kind and take advantage of the diurnals without the interference of the Penbrooks. His next steps were to locate his daughter and continue his research. If his experiment bore fruit, he would be heralded as the progenitor of a new breed of porphyrians.

As he thought about his daughter, some of the joy of his triumph was dampened. He would have liked to have had her at his side, but her loyalty was fickle. Her feelings for Jordan Rush interfered with her devotion to him and his cause. He could not abide her divided loyalty.

As he continued to watch father and daughter tumbling toward their watery graves, he contemplated a solution. A gleam entered his eyes when he thought of Jordan's crushed body on the rocks. Now that he was dead, his daughter's wayward tendencies might, at last, be under control. "And if not?" he mentally shrugged. "She will be expendable after the birth."

Craven had been so consumed by his thoughts of gore and glory that he had not sensed the man behind him. Swiftly snatching the rapier from the ground, Jordan charged. He raised the blade high. Craven started to turn. Jordan let out a primal scream of raw rage and slashed down with all of his might.

Craven's head was cut cleanly off his neck. The decapitated body fell at his feet and the head rolled several feet away. For a moment, Craven seemed to be staring malevolently at him. He kicked the head over the railing and into the night.

Rushing to the edge, he looked down. His perfect night vision enabled him to see the two figures doing a macabre downward dance through the darkness. "Please, God, not them, not both," he whispered as a quiet prayer. "Please, God! Oh, God, no!"

Chapter 67:

The Sacrifice

This time, Andrew was determined that she would live. He was not able to save Elizabeth. He was not able to save Victory. But, this time, he would not fail. Grabbing the folds of her nightgown, he dragged his daughter into his embrace. Twisting their bodies, he positioned her so that she was on top of him while he held her at arm's length from his body. As the wind whistled past, they stared deeply into each other's eyes.

"I'm sorry, my baby."

"I love you, Daddy."

She eyed the jagged rocks below. "Will it hurt much?"

Shielding her from the truth, he smiled gently. "A little."

Her eyes widened as she guessed his intent. "You're going to die trying to keep me from getting hurt."

He remained silent.

She struggled to get free of his hold, but his arms were like bands of steel. "You can't sacrifice yourself for me."

He smiled tenderly, as his eyes traveled over her features. They were so much like Victory's. "Yes, I can. I'm your father."

Laural's eyes widened in fear and she screamed as her father's body slammed into the rocks. She screamed again at the sound of bones cracking. Both of his arms broke. She was hurled away from him. She rolled and tumbled down the jagged outcrop. She felt the stones cutting her skin and ripping her gown as she smashed on the beach several feet below.

Oblivious of her own pain, she picked herself up and hastily climbed back onto the jagged outcrop. Her father lay with his eyes closed. Splintered rib bones protruded through his shirt. Blood from several wounds spilled over the rocks. Fearing the worst, she knelt next to him. Suddenly, his eyes opened.

"Promise," he insisted weakly.

She stared. "Daddy, please don't die. I need you."

"Promise," he insisted, as blood poured out of his nose and mouth.

"Please!" Laural begged desperately. "Tell me you'll heal."

Slowly, he shook his head. Every gasp was an effort.

She noticed blood and other fluids that she could not identify leaking from a large gash on the back of his head. For a moment, her mind was thrown back to the day when her mother died. In the car, her father had mentally messaged her mom: "He's going for your head. If he hits you anywhere else, you will heal, but a blow to the head could be fatal."

As he continued to block her from his pain, he smiled gently. "Promise!"

She nodded in agreement. Tears blurred her vision, as she reached for his hand. He smiled, rolled to the side, and fell into the roaring surf.

"Daddy!" she screamed, as she jumped to her feet. About to plunge in after him, she was suddenly seized from behind. She struggled frantically as her father's body was pulled out into the frothing surf. "Let go of me!" she yelled, while repeatedly kicking Jordan in the shin. He grunted, but held fast. Abruptly, she turned and buried her face in his jacket. She sobbed uncontrollably, while Jordan sorrowfully and impotently watched as the Marquis of Penbrook sank into the sea.

Epilogue

EXONERATION

Jordan Rush shook hands with the final members of the 501C(3) investigative committee as they left the conference room. Senator Randolph was the last to leave. Turning to the earl, he cleared his throat before offering, "I'm sorry about Lord Gabriel. Despite our recent differences, I respected him."

"Sure, you did," Jordan thought and then replied, "Thank you, Senator. There will be a memorial service on Friday. Would you like to attend?"

"I'll be there and I hope the foundation will be able to continue despite the loss."

The green eyes glittered. "You can count on it. That's what Andrew would have wanted."

After the door closed, Jordan turned to his two companions. "Any news, Tim?"

Tim Cooper straightened in his chair and consulted his notes. "She seems to have disappeared for the moment. We know more about where she isn't than where she is."

Jordan clenched his fists in frustration. "By the time we find them, the baby will be grown."

Tim stood. "We're working on it. The number of places we have to check is staggering! We're trying to determine where Dana might've gone to give birth since porphyrian women need special help."

"I don't care how much manpower it takes. Just do it."

He nodded and left.

Jordan turned his attention to the room's other occupant. Laural was staring out of the wall-length window. Jordan walked up behind her. "Are you going to make it?" he asked, while placing a hand on her shoulder.

She turned to face him. He flinched at the desolation reflected in her eyes.

"Yes," she said softly, "but only because I promised. I feel so alone and abandoned." Her face crumpled as she cried. "First, my mom. Then, my dad. Now, I have no one."

"You have me," he offered. He pulled her into his arms and comfortingly patted her back. "I know they were your parents and I don't mean to take anything away from that, but I also loved your mom and dad. As cousins and best friends, your father and I shared a tight bond for almost four centuries."

She brushed away her tears. "You're right. I'm being selfish by thinking only about myself when you've suffered a major loss, too."

As his eyes searched hers, he frowned. "There's nothing selfish about grieving for your parents. I lost both of mine. Although, it was a long time ago, it still hurts sometimes. I only meant that we can share our grief and be there for each other."

A firm tapping sounded at the office door. Laural collected herself, as Jordan strode over to admit the visitor. Detective Addams strode purposefully into the room. The two men greeted by nodding. Addams seated himself at one end of the conference table, opened his notebook, and waited while Laural took a seat next to her cousin.

"Thank you for agreeing to come here, Detective Addams," she said. She smiled graciously.

"It's the least I could do under the circumstances. While this is only a formality, you realize it still needs to be done."

She nodded. Taking a deep breath, she stated clearly and firmly, "My father was with me in the car for at least an hour before we reached home. He was with me the whole time and we entered the house together. My mom was already dead when we arrived."

"Thank you," he said compassionately. He asked a few more questions before he rose. "I'll keep you updated about the progress of your mother's case. If you think of anything else, please call." He extended his hand. "I'm very sorry for both of your losses." He shook hands with Laural and then with Jordan.

Laural smiled softly. "At least, they're together, which is where they both would choose to be."

RAVEN

"Push," demanded the midwife.

"I *am* pushing," Dana groaned between clenched teeth.

"Push harder!"

Dana bore down as hard as she could. Suddenly, she felt an easing of the unbearable tension between her thighs.

"One more ought to do it. Ah, there he is. I've got him."

Exhausted, Dana dropped back against the bed. A slap followed by loud wailing caught her attention. Weak and drenched in perspiration, she turned her head to the side. The midwife was bundling the baby in a blanket.

"It's a boy," the midwife confirmed, while lifting the infant to her shoulder and lightly patting his back.

Dana held out her arms. The midwife smiled. She started to move the baby away from her when her face suddenly contorted. Covering her momentary confusion, she smiled.

"This young man must be very hungry," she cooed, as she placed the infant in his mother's arms. "He's trying to get what he needs from my neck. Sorry, sweetie," she said. She used a cloth to wipe the saliva from her skin. "That's not where baby meals come from."

"That's what you think," Dana thought, as she lifted the infant to her breast.

"Have you thought of a name for him?"

"Yes. His name is Raven."

"Quite an unusual name," commented the midwife, while packing her bag.

"It's a family name that goes back to his grandfather."

The following evening descended dark and dreary. Carefully, Dana checked her trunks. Everything they needed for their voyage had been delivered to the ship on the previous evening. Taking the key from her pocket, she slipped it into the lock. Opening the lid, she double-checked the supplies. It would be disastrous to be at sea and find that certain supplies were lacking. Clothes, diapers, and the special formula for her infant. She had bypassed questions by telling the authorities that her son was anemic and needed special supplements that his doctor had supplied for the trip. Unscrewing the lid, she peered into the container. The reddish-brown liquid moved sluggishly up the side of the bottle as she tilted it.

Sensing his next meal, the baby started to wail. Dana walked over to the bassinette. Lifting her child, she cradled him in her arms and slipped the bottle into his open mouth. Greedily, he sucked the contents. After he fell asleep, she slipped out on deck. Crew members were busily preparing the ship for departure. Dana wandered over to the rail to gaze pensively at the New York skyline. The warning horn sounded as the ship slowly began to pull out of the harbor.

She knew that both her father and Andrew were dead. She had sensed it. She should be relieved since her son was now safe. But had Andrew told Jordan? She had to assume the worst. If so, Jordan would be tracking them. She could not blame him. Raven was his son. She wondered if Jordan would kill his own son in order to keep the legacy of Craven Maxwell from continuing. She was not sure so decided that she would not take a chance.

She smiled ironically. Previously, she had been willing to sacrifice the child to save herself. Now, she was willing to protect him at all costs. A wave of dizziness swept through her. She clutched the rail. It would take some time to recuperate.

Hopefully, by the time they reached London, she would be stronger. "I have to be," she thought resolutely, as she turned her back on the land of integration. "Raven's existence depends on it. There's only one more loose end." She pulled out her cell phone.

TYING UP LOOSE ENDS

"Senator Randolph, may I have a word with you?"

Randolph looked back. His brows drew together as he noticed Detective Brent Addams hurrying across the pavement. As he waited by the door of his jet-black Mercedes, he impatiently jangled his keys.

Addams moved closer in order to speak discreetly. "I just wanted to assure you we are doing everything possible to catch your son's murderer. Believe me, Senator, this crime will not go unpunished."

Randolph stared into the detective's earnest features. "Detective Addams," he said severely, "to the best of my knowledge, my son's death was caused by a heart attack."

Addams momentarily was taken aback. "I'm sorry, Senator. I thought you knew."

"Knew what?" he asked sharply.

After pushing back an unruly lock of auburn hair, Addams confided, "The medical examiner has determined that your son's death was the result of poisoning." Noting the look of incredulity, he rushed on. "He would've missed it entirely except that he is working on another case where the same chemical was used to induce a heart attack. Since the chemical is so rare, I'm working on the theory the two cases might be related. I just wanted to reassure you that I will do everything in my power to make sure the person responsible is brought to justice."

Randolph thoughtfully studied him. "I appreciate your special attention to this matter, detective. Your reputation precedes you. With you on the case, I have no doubt it's only a matter of time before it's solved."

"Yes, sir, you can count on me," he stated firmly, while pushing back the same lock of unruly hair. "It can't hurt to be on the good side of the next President," he thought with anticipation. Of course, Randolph was not yet in the White House, but, according to the polls, it was a foregone conclusion.

As he pulled away from the curb, Randolph flipped open his cell phone. He dialed and waited for the connection. He glanced in the rearview mirror and watched the Willow Grove Foundation fall farther and farther behind. Pulling up to the next stop light, he spoke into the phone.

"I want Detective Brent Addams pulled off my son's case," he commanded sternly and then flipped the phone closed.

The cell phone rang. He frowned. He was certain that he had been explicit. "Hello!" he barked with annoyance seething from his lips.

"Senator Randolph, I was sorry to hear about your son."

The Senator flipped the phone closed. Goosebumps rose on frigid skin. Opening the glove compartment, he grabbed the gleaming nine-millimeter Glock, raised it, inserted the barrel into his mouth, and pulled the trigger.

About the Author

Valerie Hoffman is a totally blind author and psychotherapist. She resides in Ormond Beach, Florida with her husband, Norman. She enjoys traveling and cooking, as well as writing, of course, and is currently at work on the fouth novel in the "Vampires Royalty" series.

The Author's Notes

In ancient times many unexplained medical problems and diseases were blamed on vampires. Porphyria, the blood disease which factors prominently in the "Vampire Royalty" series, is only one of the illnesses which uninformed and superstitious people attributed to vampirism. Rabies, which was passed on by biting of the victim, and anemia, which could cause weakness and lethargy, were often thought to be a direct result of interaction with the undead.

Vampires were also used as scapegoats in order to provide reasons for societal catastrophes, such as the plague and sudden infant death syndrome. Before the advent of modern medicine and a better understanding of disease, people were even sometimes mistakenly buried alive. These unfortunate victims would then rise from their graves only to be accosted by frightened villagers determined to keep the dead from rising.

Even the Catholic church played its part in perpetuating the vampire legend. It has been well documented that, at one time, the church held the belief that anyone who was excommunicated, born with certain birth defects, or committed suicide was a vampire.

Hopefully, our dogmatic fear and persecution of those who are different will continue to fade over time. With the advent of advanced medical knowledge, sufferers of rare blood diseases can now look forward to receiving blood transfusions instead of a stake through the heart.

In "Vampire Royalty: Resurrection" I chose to take certain liberties with the method in which the investigation of the Willow Grove Foundation was conducted. While trying to stay as close as possible to real life interpretation of the United States Constitution and the way Congress might address the issues presented in this book, it is after all a work of fiction. I took creative license when necessary in order to provide for the transitional flow of the novel. I hope readers will enjoy the book with the spirit it was intended for fun and entertainment.

-VH

For single copies or bulk purchases of
this and other books by
Valerie Hoffman:

Send your payment to:
VG Press
595 W. Granada Blvd., Suite H
Ormond Beach FL 32174

or call:
386-677-3995

or order via email:
drval@bellsouth.net

One book: $9.95
plus shipping and handling: $3.95
The total is $13.90

If you are ordering by mail within the United States, please add $11.20 for each additional book ordered at the same time. (This price already includes $1.25 for postage and handling.) For the mailing costs for non-USA deliveries, please call 386-677-3995 or send an email that includes the name of your country to: drval@bellsouth.net.

Please allow two to four weeks for delivery within the United States.

For payment by check or money order, please mail to the address above.

Please call or email to learn if the price or postage has changed.

You may order from most bookstores.